The Collected
Supernatural and Weird
Fiction of
Leonid Andreyev
Volume 1

The Collected Supernatural and Weird Fiction of Leonid Andreyev Volume 1

Fourteen Short Stories and Four Novelettes of the Strange and Unusual Including 'At the Roadside Station', 'Carelessness', 'In the Train', 'Laughter', 'The Man Who Found the Truth', 'Judas Iscariot' and 'A Dilemma'

Leonid Andreyev

LEONAUR

The Collected
Supernatural and Weird
Fiction of
Leonid Andreyev
Volume 1
Fourteen Short Stories and Four Novelettes of the Strange and Unusual Including 'At the Roadside Station', 'Carelessness', 'In the Train', 'Laughter', 'The Man Who Found the Truth', 'Judas Iscariot' and 'A Dilemma'
by Leonid Andreyev

FIRST EDITION

Leonaur is an imprint of Oakpast Ltd

ISBN: 978-1-917666-08-4 (hardcover)
ISBN: 978-1-917666-09-1 (softcover)

http://www.leonaur.com

Publisher's Notes

The views expressed in this book are not necessarily those of the publisher.

Contents

"Men May Rise on Stepping Stones of Their Dead Selves to Higher Things"

Have you ever happened to walk in a burial-ground?

Those little walled-in, quiet corners, overgrown with luscious grass, so small, and yet to ravenous, possess a peculiar dolorous poetry all their own.

Day after day thither are borne new corpses, a whole, immense, living, noisy city has been already borne thither one by one, and lo! the new city which has grown in its place is awaiting its turn—and the little corners remain ever the same, small, still, ravenous.

The peculiar air in them, the peculiar silence, and the lisping of the trees different there to anywhere else, are all mournful, pensive, tender. It is as though those white birches could not forget all those weeping eyes, which have sought the sky betwixt their green branches, and as though it were no wind, but deep sighs which keep swaying the air and the fresh leaves.

You, too, wander about the graveyard silent and pensive. Your ear is conscious of the gentle echoes of deep groans and tears, while your eyes rest on rich monuments, and modest wooden crosses; and the unmarked tombs of strangers, covering their dead, who were strangers when living, unmarked, unobserved. And you read the inscriptions on the monuments, and all these people who have disappeared from the world rise up in your imagination. You see them young, laughing, loving; you see them hale, loquacious, insolently confident in the endlessness of life.

And they are dead.

★★★★★★★★★★★★★

But is it necessary to go out of one's house to visit a burial ground?

Is it not sufficient for this purpose, that the darkness of night should envelope you, and have swallowed up all the sounds of day?

How many rich and sumptuous monuments! How many unmarked graves of strangers!

But is night needful in order to visit a graveyard? Is not daytime enough, restless, noisy day, sufficient unto which is the evil thereof?

Look into your own soul, and then, be it day or night, you will find there a burial ground. Small greedy, having devoured so much! And a gentle, sorrowful, whisper will ye hear, an echo of by-gone heavy groans, when the dead was dear, whom ye left in the tomb, and could not forget nor cease to love. And monuments ye will see, and inscriptions half blotted out with tears; and still, obscure, little tombs; small and ominous mounds, under which is hidden something which once was living, although ye knew not its life, nor remarked its death. But, maybe, it was the very best in your soul.

But why talk about it? Look for yourselves. And have you not indeed thus looked into your burial-ground every day, every single day of the long, weary year? Maybe as late as yesterday you recalled the dear departed, and wept over them. Maybe only yesterday you buried someone who had long been seriously ill, and had been forgotten even in life.

Lo! under the heavy marble surrounded by iron rails rests Love of mankind, and her sister Faith in them. How beautiful were they, and wondrous kind—these sisters. What bright light burned in their eyes, what strange power was wielded by their tender white hands!

With what a caress did those white hands bring the cold drink to lips burning with thirst, and did feed the hungry. With what gentle care did they touch the sores of the sick, and healed them!

And they are dead, these sisters. They died of cold, as is said on the monument. They could not bear the icy wind in which life enveloped them.

And there, further on, a slanting cross marks the place where a Talent, is buried in the earth. How bold it was, how noisy, how happy! It undertook anything, wished to do everything, and was confident that it could conquer the world.

And it is dead—died but lately, quietly, and unnoticed. One day it went among men, for long it was lost there, and it came back defeated, sad. Long it wept, long it strove to say something, and then without having said it—died.

And here is a long row of little sunken mounds. Who lies here?

Ah! yes. These are children. Little, keen, sportive Hopes. There were so many of them, they were so merry, and the soul was peopled with them. But one by one they died. They were so many, and they made such merriment in the soul.

It is quiet in the resting-place, and the leaves of the white birches rustle sadly.

★★★★★★★★★★★★★★★★

But let the dead arise! Ye grim tombs open wide, crumble to dust ye heavy monuments, ye iron bars give place!

Be it but for one day, for one moment, give freedom to those whom ye are smothering with your weight, and darkness!

Ye think they are dead! Oh, no! they live! They are silent, but they live.

They live!

Let them see the shining of the blue, cloudless sky, let them breathe the pure air of spring, let them be intoxicated with warmth and love.

Come to me my Talent that fell asleep. Why dost so drolly rub thine eyes. Does the sun blind thee? Does it not shine bright indeed? Thou laughest? Oh laugh, laugh on—there is so little of laughter among mankind. I too will laugh with thee. Look! There flies a swallow—let us fly after it! Has the tomb made thee too heavy? And what is that strange horror I see in thine eyes—like a reflexion of the darkness of the tomb? No, no, don't! Don't cry. Don't cry, I say!

So glorious, indeed, is life for the risen!

And ye my dear little Hopes! What charming laughing faces are yours! Who art thou, stout, funny little cherub? I know thee not. And wherefore laughest thou? Has the tomb itself been unable to afright thee? Gently, my children, gently! Why dost insult it—see'st not how little, pale and weak it is become? Live ye in the world—and do not worry me. Do ye not see that I, too, have been in the tomb, and now my head is giddy with the sun, and the air, and gladness.

Ah! how glorious is life for the risen!

Come to me ye lovely, majestic Sisters. Let me kiss your gentle white hands. What do I see? Is it bread ye are carrying? Did not the darkness of the tomb terrify you—so tender, womanly and weak; under the whelming mass did ye still think of bread for the hungry? Let me kiss your feet. I know where they will soon be going, your light, swift little feet. And I know that wherever they pass by flowers will spring up—wondrous, sweet-smelling flowers. Ye call. We will come, then.

Hither! my risen Talent—why stand gazing at the fleeting clouds. Hither! my little sportive Hopes.

Stop!

I hear music. Don't shout so, cherub. Whence these wondrous sounds? Gentle, melodious, madly joyful, and sad, they speak of life eternal——

Nay, be ye not afraid. This will soon pass away. I weep, indeed, for joy! Ah! how glorious is life for the risen!

The Man Who Found the Truth

CHAPTER 1

I was twenty-seven years old and had just maintained my thesis for the degree of Doctor of Mathematics with unusual success, when I was suddenly seized in the middle of the night and thrown into this prison. I shall not narrate to you the details of the monstrous crime of which I was accused—there are events which people should neither remember nor even know, that they may not acquire a feeling of aversion for themselves; but no doubt there are many people among the living who remember that terrible case and "the human brute," as the newspapers called me at that time. They probably remember how the entire civilised society of the land unanimously demanded that the criminal be put to death, and it is due only to the inexplicable kindness of the man at the head of the Government at the time that I am alive, and I now write these lines for the edification of the weak and the wavering.

I shall say briefly: My father, my elder brother, and my sister were murdered brutally, and I was supposed to have committed the crime for the purpose of securing a really enormous inheritance.

I am an old man now; I shall die soon, and you have not the slightest ground for doubting when I say that I was entirely innocent of the monstrous and horrible crime, for which twelve honest and conscientious judges unanimously sentenced me to death. The death sentence was finally commuted to imprisonment for life in solitary confinement.

It was merely a fatal linking of circumstances, of grave and insignificant events, of vague silence and indefinite words, which gave me the appearance and likeness of the criminal, innocent though I was. But he who would suspect me of being ill-disposed toward my strict judges would be profoundly mistaken. They were perfectly right, perfectly right. As people who can judge things and events only by their

11

appearance, and who are deprived of the ability to penetrate their own mysterious being, they could not act differently, nor should they have acted differently.

It so happened that in the game of circumstances, the truth concerning my actions, which I alone knew, assumed all the features of an insolent and shameless lie; and however strange it may seem to my kind and serious reader, I could establish the truth of my innocence only by falsehood, and not by the truth.

Later on, when I was already in prison, in going over in detail the story of the crime and the trial, and picturing myself in the place of one of my judges, I came to the inevitable conclusion each time that I was guilty. Then I produced a very interesting and instructive work; having set aside entirely the question of truth and falsehood on general principles, I subjected the facts and the words to numerous combinations, erecting structures, even as small children build various structures with their wooden blocks; and after persistent efforts I finally succeeded in finding a certain combination of facts which, though strong in principle, seemed so plausible that my actual innocence became perfectly clear, exactly and positively established.

To this day I remember the great feeling of astonishment, mingled with fear, which I experienced at my strange and unexpected discovery; by telling the truth I lead people into error and thus deceive them, while by maintaining falsehood I lead them, on the contrary, to the truth and to knowledge.

I did not yet understand at that time that, like Newton and his famous apple, I discovered unexpectedly the great law upon which the entire history of human thought rests, which seeks not the truth, but verisimilitude, the appearance of truth—that is, the harmony between that which is seen and that which is conceived, based on the strict laws of logical reasoning. And instead of rejoicing, I exclaimed in an outburst of *naïve*, juvenile despair: "Where, then, is the truth? Where is the truth in this world of phantoms and falsehood?" (See my "*Diary of a Prisoner*" of June 29, 18—.)

I know that at the present time, when I have but five or six more years to live, I could easily secure my pardon if I but asked for it. But aside from my being accustomed to the prison and for several other important reasons, of which I shall speak later, I simply have no right to ask for pardon, and thus break the force and natural course of the lawful and entirely justified verdict. Nor would I want to hear people apply to me the words, "a victim of judicial error," as some of my gentle visitors expressed themselves, to my sorrow. I repeat, there was no error, nor could there be any error in a case in which a combination of definite circumstances inevitably lead a normally constructed and developed mind to the one and only conclusion.

I was convicted justly, although I did not commit the crime—such is the simple and clear truth, and I live joyously and peacefully my last few years on earth with a sense of respect for this truth.

The only purpose by which I was guided in writing these modest notes is to show to my indulgent reader that under the most painful conditions, where it would seem that there remains no room for hope or life—a human being, a being of the highest order, possessing a mind and a will, finds both hope and life. I want to show how a human being, condemned to death, looked with free eyes upon the world, through the grated window of his prison, and discovered the great purpose, harmony, and beauty of the universe—to the disgrace of those fools who, being free, living a life of plenty and happiness, slander life disgustingly.

Some of my visitors reproach me for being "haughty"; they ask me where I secured the right to teach and to preach; cruel in their reasoning, they would like to drive away even the smile from the face of the man who has been imprisoned for life as a murderer.

No. Just as the kind and bright smile will not leave my lips, as an evidence of a clear and unstained conscience, so my soul will never be darkened, my soul, which has passed firmly through the defiles of life, which has been carried by a mighty will power across these terrible abysses and bottomless pits, where so many daring people have found their heroic, but, alas! fruitless, death.

And if the tone of my confessions may sometimes seem too positive to my indulgent reader, it is not at all due to the absence of modesty in me, but it is due to the fact that I firmly believe that I am right, and also to my firm desire to be useful to my neighbour as far as my faint powers permit.

Here I must apologise for my frequent references to my "*Diary of a Prisoner*," which is unknown to the reader; but the fact is that I consider the complete publication of my "*Diary*" too premature and perhaps even dangerous. Begun during the remote period of cruel disillusions, of the shipwreck of all my beliefs and hopes, breathing boundless despair, my note book bears evidence in places that its author was, if not in a state of complete insanity, on the brink of insanity. And if we recall how contagious that illness is, my caution in the use of my "*Diary*" will become entirely clear.

O, blooming youth! With an involuntary tear in my eye, I recall your magnificent dreams, your daring visions and outbursts, your impetuous, seething power—but I should not want your return, blooming youth! Only with the greyness of the hair comes clear wisdom, and that great aptitude for unprejudiced reflection which makes of all old men philosophers and often even sages.

CHAPTER 2

Those of my kind visitors who honour me by expressing their delight and even—may this little indiscretion be forgiven me!—even their adoration of my spiritual clearness, can hardly imagine what I was when I came to this prison. The tens of years which have passed over my head and which have whitened my hair cannot muffle the slight agitation which I experience at the recollection of the first moments when, with the creaking of the rusty hinges, the fatal prison doors opened and then closed behind me forever.

Not endowed with literary talent, which in reality is an indomitable inclination to invent and to lie, I shall attempt to introduce myself to my indulgent reader exactly as I was at that remote time.

I was a young man, twenty-seven years of age—as I had occasion to mention before—unrestrained, impetuous, given to abrupt deviations. A certain dreaminess, peculiar to my age; a self-respect which was easily offended and which revolted at the slightest insignificant provocation; a passionate impetuosity in solving world problems; fits of melancholy alternated by equally wild fits of merriment—all this gave the young mathematician a character of extreme unsteadiness, of sad and harsh discord.

I must also mention the extreme pride, a family trait, which I inherited from my mother, and which often hindered me from taking the advice of riper and more experienced people than myself; also, my extreme obstinacy in carrying out my purposes, a good quality in itself, which becomes dangerous, however, when the purpose in question is not sufficiently well founded and considered.

Thus, during the first days of my confinement, I behaved like all other fools who are thrown into prison. I shouted loudly and, of course, vainly about my innocence; I demanded violently my immediate freedom and even beat against the door and the walls with my fists. The door and the walls naturally remained mute, while I caused myself a rather sharp pain. I remember I even beat my head against the wall, and for hours I lay unconscious on the stone floor of my cell; and for some time, when I had grown desperate, I refused food, until the persistent demands of my organism defeated my obstinacy.

I cursed my judges and threatened them with merciless vengeance. At last, I commenced to regard all human life, the whole world, even Heaven, as an enormous injustice, a derision and a mockery. Forgetting that in my position I could hardly be unprejudiced, I came with the self-confidence of youth, with the sickly pain of a prisoner, gradually to the complete negation of life and its great meaning.

Those were indeed terrible days and nights, when, crushed by the walls, getting no answer to any of my questions, I paced my cell endlessly and hurled one after another into the dark abyss all the great valuables which life has bestowed upon us: friendship, love, reason and justice.

In some justification to myself I may mention the fact that during the first and most painful years of my imprisonment a series of events happened which reflected themselves rather painfully upon my psychic nature. Thus, I learned with the profoundest indignation that the girl, whose name I shall not mention and who was to become my wife, married another man. She was one of the few who believed in my innocence; at the last parting she swore to me to remain faithful to me unto death, and rather to die than betray her love for me—and within one year after that she married a man I knew, who possessed certain good qualities, but who was not at all a sensible man.

I did not want to understand at that time that such a marriage was natural on the part of a young, healthy, and beautiful girl. But, alas! we all forget our natural science when we are deceived by the woman we love—may this little jest be forgiven me! At the present time Mme. N. is a happy and respected mother, and this proves better than anything else how wise and entirely in accordance with the demands of nature and life was her marriage at that time, which vexed me so painfully.

I must confess, however, that at that time I was not at all calm. Her exceedingly amiable and kind letter in which she notified me of her marriage, expressing profound regret that changed circumstances and a suddenly awakened love compelled her to break her promise to me—that amiable, truthful letter, scented with perfume, bearing the traces of her tender fingers, seemed to me a message from the devil himself.

The letters of fire burned my exhausted brains, and in a wild ecstasy I shook the doors of my cell and called violently:

15

"Come! Let me look into your lying eyes! Let me hear your lying voice! Let me but touch with my fingers your tender throat and pour into your death rattle my last bitter laugh!"

From this quotation my indulgent reader will see how right were the judges who convicted me for murder; they had really foreseen in me a murderer.

My gloomy view of life at the time was aggravated by several other events. Two years after the marriage of my *fiancée*, consequently three years after the first day of my imprisonment, my mother died—she died, as I learned, of profound grief for me. However strange it may seem, she remained firmly convinced to the end of her days that I had committed the monstrous crime. Evidently this conviction was an inexhaustible source of grief to her, the chief cause of the gloomy melancholy which fettered her lips in silence and caused her death through paralysis of the heart.

As I was told, she never mentioned my name nor the names of those who died so tragically, and she bequeathed the entire enormous fortune, which was supposed to have served as the motive for the murder, to various charitable organisations. It is characteristic that even under such terrible conditions her motherly instinct did not forsake her altogether; in a postscript to the will, she left me a considerable sum, which secures my existence whether I am in prison or at large.

Now I understand that, however great her grief may have been, that alone was not enough to cause her death; the real cause was her advanced age and a series of illnesses which had undermined her once strong and sound organism. In the name of justice, I must say that my father, a weak-charactered man, was not at all a model husband and family man; by numerous betrayals, by falsehood and deception he had led my mother to despair, constantly offending her pride and her strict, unbribable truthfulness. But at that time, I did not understand it; the death of my mother seemed to me one of the most cruel manifestations of universal injustice, and called forth a new stream of useless and sacrilegious curses.

I do not know whether I ought to tire the attention of the reader with the story of other events of a similar nature.

I shall mention but briefly that one after another my friends, who remained my friends from the time when I was happy and free, stopped visiting me. According to their words, they believed in my innocence, and at first warmly expressed to me their sympathy. But our lives, mine in prison and theirs at liberty, were so different that gradually under the pressure of perfectly natural causes, such as forgetfulness, official and other duties, the absence of mutual interests, they visited me ever more and more rarely, and finally ceased to see me entirely. I cannot recall without a smile that even the death of my mother, even the betrayal of the girl I loved did not arouse in me such a hopelessly bitter feeling as these gentlemen, whose names I remember but vaguely now, succeeded in wresting from my soul.

What horror! What pain! My friends, you have left me alone! My friends, do you understand what you have done? You have left me alone. Can you conceive of leaving a human being alone? Even a serpent has its mate, even a spider has its comrade—and you have left a human being alone! You have given him a soul—and left him alone! You have given him a heart, a mind, a hand for a handshake, lips for a kiss—and you have left him alone! What shall he do now that you have left him alone?

Thus, I exclaimed in my "*Diary of a Prisoner*," tormented by woeful perplexities. In my juvenile blindness, in the pain of my young, senseless heart, I still did not want to understand that the solitude, of which I complained so bitterly, like the mind, was an advantage given to man over other creatures, in order to fence around the sacred mysteries of his soul from the stranger's gaze.

Let my serious reader consider what would have become of life if man were robbed of his right, of his duty to be alone. In the gathering of idle chatterers, amid the dull collection of transparent glass dolls, that kill each other with their sameness; in the wild city where all doors are open, and all windows are open—passers-by look wearily through the glass walls and observe the same evidences of the hearth and the alcove. Only the creatures that can be alone possess a face; while those that know no solitude—the great, blissful, sacred solitude of the soul—have snouts instead of faces.

And in calling my friends "perfidious traitors" I, poor youth that I was, could not understand the wise law of life, according to which neither friendship, nor love, nor even the tenderest attachment of sister and mother, is eternal. Deceived by the lies of the poets, who proclaimed eternal friendship and love, I did not want to see that which my indulgent reader observes from the windows of his dwelling—how friends, relatives, mother and wife, in apparent despair and in tears, follow their dead to the cemetery, and after a lapse of sometime return from there. No one buries himself together with the dead, no one asks the dead to make room in the coffin, and if the grief-stricken wife exclaims, in an outburst of tears, "Oh, bury me together with him!" she is merely expressing symbolically the extreme degree of her despair—one could easily convince himself of this by trying, in jest, to push her down into the grave.

And those who restrain her are merely expressing symbolically their sympathy and understanding, thus lending the necessary aspect of solemn grief to the funeral custom.

Man must subject himself to the laws of life, not of death, nor to the fiction of the poets, however beautiful it may be. But can the fictitious be beautiful? Is there no beauty in the stern truth of life, in the mighty work of its wise laws, which subjects to itself with great disinterestedness the movements of the heavenly luminaries, as well as the restless linking of the tiny creatures called human beings?

CHAPTER 3

Thus, I lived sadly in my prison for five or six years.

The first redeeming ray flashed upon me when I least expected it.

Endowed with the gift of imagination, I made my former *fiancée* the object of all my thoughts. She became my love and my dream.

Another circumstance which suddenly revealed to me the ground under my feet was, strange as it may seem, the conviction that it was impossible to make my escape from prison.

During the first period of my imprisonment, I, as a youthful and enthusiastic dreamer, made all kinds of plans for escape, and some of them seemed to me entirely possible of realisation. Cherishing deceptive hopes, this thought naturally kept me in a state of tense alarm and hindered my attention from concentrating itself on more important and substantial matters. As soon as I despaired of one plan, I created another, but of course I did not make any progress—I merely moved within a closed circle. It is hardly necessary to mention that each transition from one plan to another was accompanied by cruel sufferings, which tormented my soul, just as the eagle tortured the body of Prometheus.

One day, while staring with a weary look at the walls of my cell, I suddenly began to feel how irresistibly thick the stone was, how strong the cement which kept it together, how skilfully and mathematically this severe fortress was constructed. It is true, my first sensation was extremely painful; it was, perhaps, a horror of hopelessness.

I cannot recall what I did and how I felt during the two or three months that followed. The first note in my diary after a long period of silence does not explain very much. Briefly I state only that they made new clothes for me and that I had grown stout.

The fact is that, after all my hopes had been abandoned, the consciousness of the impossibility of my escape once for all extinguished also my painful alarm and liberated my mind, which was then already inclined to lofty contemplation and the joys of mathematics.

But the following is the day I consider as the first real day of my liberation. It was a beautiful spring morning (May 6) and the balmy, invigorating air was pouring into the open window; while walking back and forth in my cell I unconsciously glanced, at each turn, with a vague interest, at the high window, where the iron grate outlined its form sharply and distinctly against the background of the azure, cloudless sky.

"Why is the sky so beautiful through these bars?" I reflected as I walked. "Is not this the effect of the aesthetic law of contrasts, according to which azure stands out prominently beside black? Or is it not, perhaps, a manifestation of some other, higher law, according to which the infinite may be conceived by the human mind only when it is brought within certain boundaries, for instance, when it is enclosed within a square?"

When I recalled that at the sight of a wide-open window, which was not protected by bars, or of the sky, I had usually experienced a desire to fly, which was painful because of its uselessness and absurdity—I suddenly began to experience a feeling of tenderness for the bars; tender gratitude, even love. Forged by hand, by the weak human hand of some ignorant blacksmith, who did not even give himself an account of the profound meaning of his creation; placed in the wall by an equally ignorant mason, it suddenly represented in itself a model of beauty, nobility and power. Having seized the infinite within its iron squares, it became congealed in cold and proud peace, frightening the ignorant, giving food for thought to the intelligent and delighting the sage!

Chapter 4

In order to make the further narrative clearer to my indulgent reader, I am compelled to say a few words about the exclusive, quite flattering, and, I fear, not entirely deserved, position which I occupy in our prison. On one hand, my spiritual clearness, my rare and perfect view of life, and the nobility of my feelings, which impress all those who speak to me; and, on the other hand, several rather unimportant favours which I have done to the warden, have given me a series of privileges, of which I avail myself, rather moderately, of course, not desiring to upset the general plan and system of our prison.

Thus, during the weekly visiting days, my visitors are not limited to any special time for their interviews, and all those who wish to see me are admitted, sometimes forming quite a large audience. Not daring to accept altogether the assurances made somewhat ironically by the warden, to the effect that I would be "the pride of any prison," I may say, nevertheless, without any false modesty, that my words are treated with proper respect, and that among my visitors I number quite a few warm and enthusiastic admirers, both men and women. I shall mention that the warden himself and some of his assistants honour me by their visits, drawing from me strength and courage for the purpose of continuing their hard work. Of course I use the prison library freely, and even the archives of the prison; and if the warden politely refused to grant my request for an exact plan of the prison, it is not at all because of his lack of confidence in me, but because such a plan is a state secret. . . . .

Our prison is a huge five-storey building. Situated in the outskirts of the city, at the edge of a deserted field, overgrown with high grass, it attracts the attention of the wayfarer by its rigid outlines, promising him peace and rest after his endless wanderings. Not being plastered, the building has retained its natural dark red colour of old brick, and at close view, I am told, it produces a gloomy, even threatening, impression, especially on nervous people, to whom the red bricks recall blood and bloody lumps of human flesh. The small, dark, flat windows with iron bars naturally complete the impression and lend to the whole a character of gloomy harmony, or stern beauty. Even during good weather, when the sun shines upon our prison, it does not lose any of its dark and grim importance, and is constantly reminding the people that there are laws in existence and that punishment awaits those who break them.

My cell is on the fifth storey, and my grated window commands a splendid view of the distant city and a part of the deserted field to the right. On the left, beyond the boundary of my vision, are the outskirts of the city, and, as I am told, the church and the cemetery adjoining it. Of the existence of the church and even the cemetery I had known before from the mournful tolling of the bells, which custom requires during the burial of the dead.

Quite in keeping with the external style of architecture, the interior arrangement of our prison is also finished harmoniously and properly constructed. For the purpose of conveying to the reader a clearer idea of the prison, I will take the liberty of giving the example of a fool who might make up his mind to run away from our prison. Admitting that the brave fellow possessed supernatural, Herculean strength and broke the lock of his room—what would he find? The corridor, with numerous grated doors, which could withstand cannonading—and armed keepers. Let us suppose that he kills all the keepers, breaks all the doors, and comes out into the yard—perhaps he may think that he is already free. But what of the walls? The walls which encircle our prison, with three rings of stone?

I omitted the guard advisedly. The guard is indefatigable. Day and night I hear behind my doors the footsteps of the guard; day and night his eye watches me through the little window in my door, controlling my movements, reading on my face my thoughts, my intentions and my dreams. In the daytime I could deceive his attention with lies, assuming a cheerful and carefree expression on my face, but I have rarely met the man who could lie even in his sleep. No matter how much I would be on my guard during the day, at night I would betray myself by an involuntary moan, by a twitch of the face, by an expression of fatigue or grief, or by other manifestations of a guilty and uneasy conscience.

Only very few people of unusual will power are able to lie even in their sleep, skilfully managing the features of their faces, sometimes even preserving a courteous and bright smile on their lips, when their souls, given over to dreams, are quivering from the horrors of a monstrous nightmare—but, as exceptions, these cannot be taken into consideration. I am profoundly happy that I am not a criminal, that my conscience is clear and calm.

"Read, my friend, read," I say to the watchful eye as I lay myself down to sleep peacefully. "You will not be able to read anything on my face!"

And it was I who invented the window in the prison door.

I feel that my reader is astonished and smiles incredulously, mentally calling me an old liar, but there are instances in which modesty is superfluous and even dangerous. Yes, this simple and great invention belongs to me, just as Newton's system belongs to Newton, and as Kepler's laws of the revolution of the planets belong to Kepler.

21

Later on, encouraged by the success of my invention, I devised and introduced in our prison a series of little innovations, which were concerned only with details; thus, the form of chains and locks used in our prison has been changed.

The little window in the door was my invention, and, if anyone should dare deny this, I would call him a liar and a scoundrel.

I came upon this invention under the following circumstances: One day, during the roll call, a certain prisoner killed with the iron leg of his bed the inspector who entered his cell. Of course, the rascal was hanged in the yard of our prison, and the administration lightmindedly grew calm, but I was in despair—the great purpose of the prison proved to be wrong since such horrible deeds were possible. How is it that no one had noticed that the prisoner had broken off the leg of his bed? How is it that no one had noticed the state of agitation in which the prisoner must have been before committing the murder?

By taking up the question so directly I thus approached considerably the solution of the problem; and indeed, after two or three weeks had elapsed, I arrived simply and even unexpectedly at my great discovery. I confess frankly that before telling my discovery to the warden of the prison I experienced moments of a certain hesitation, which was quite natural in my position of prisoner. To the reader who may still be surprised at this hesitation, knowing me to be a man of a clear, unstained conscience, I will answer by a quotation from my "*Diary of a Prisoner*," relating to that period:

> How difficult is the position of the man who is convicted, though innocent, as I am. If he is sad, if his lips are sealed in silence, and his eyes are lowered, people say of him: 'He is repenting; he is suffering from pangs of conscience.'
>
> If in the innocence of his heart he smiles brightly and kindly, the keeper thinks: 'There, by a false and feigned smile, he wishes to hide his secret.'
>
> No matter what he does, he seems guilty—such is the force of the prejudice against which it is necessary to struggle. But I am innocent, and I shall be myself, firmly confident that my spiritual clearness will destroy the malicious magic of prejudice.

And on the following day the warden of the prison pressed my hand warmly, expressing his gratitude to me, and a month later little holes were made in all doors in every prison in the land, thus opening a field for wide and fruitful observation.

The entire system of our prison life gives me deep satisfaction. The hours for rising and going to bed, for meals and walks are arranged so rationally, in accordance with the real requirements of nature, that soon they lose the appearance of compulsion and become natural, even dear habits. Only in this way can I explain the interesting fact that when I was free, I was a nervous and weak young man, susceptible to colds and illness, whereas in prison I have grown considerably stronger and that for my sixty years I am enjoying an enviable state of health. I am not stout, but I am not thin, either; my lungs are in good condition and I have saved almost all my teeth, with the exception of two on the left side of the jaw; I am good natured, even tempered; my sleep is sound, almost without any dreams. In figure, in which an expression of calm power and self-confidence predominates, and in face, I resemble somewhat Michaelangelo's "Moses"—that is, at least what some of my friendly visitors have told me.

But even more than by the regular and healthy regime, the strengthening of my soul and body was helped by the wonderful, yet natural, peculiarity of our prison, which eliminates entirely the accidental and the unexpected from its life. Having neither a family nor friends, I am perfectly safe from the shocks, so injurious to life, which are caused by treachery, by the illness or death of relatives—let my indulgent reader recall how many people have perished before his eyes not of their own fault, but because capricious fate had linked them to people unworthy of them. Without changing my feeling of love into trivial personal attachments, I thus make it free for the broad and mighty love for all mankind; and as mankind is immortal, not subjected to illness, and as a harmonious whole it is undoubtedly progressing toward perfection, love for it becomes the surest guarantee of spiritual and physical soundness.

My day is clear. So are also my days of the future, which are coming toward me in radiant and even order. A murderer will not break into my cell for the purpose of robbing me, a mad automobile will not crush me, the illness of a child will not torture me, cruel treachery will not steal its way to me from the darkness. My mind is free, my heart is calm, my soul is clear and bright.

The clear and rigid rules of our prison define everything that I must not do, thus freeing me from those unbearable hesitations, doubts, and errors with which practical life is filled. True, sometimes there penetrates even into our prison, through its high walls, something which ignorant people call chance, or even Fate, and which is only an inevitable reflection of the general laws; but the life of the prison, agitated for a moment, quickly goes back to its habitual rut, like a river after an overflow. To this category of accidents belong the above-mentioned murder of the Inspector, the rare and always unsuccessful attempts at escape, and also the executions, which take place in one of the remotest yards of our prison.

There is still another peculiarity in the system of our prison, which I consider most beneficial, and which gives to the whole thing a character of stern and noble justice. Left to himself, and only to himself, the prisoner cannot count upon support, or upon that spurious, wretched pity which so often falls to the lot of weak people, disfiguring thereby the fundamental purposes of nature.

I confess that I think, with a certain sense of pride, that if I am now enjoying general respect and admiration, if my mind is strong, my will powerful, my view of life clear and bright, I owe it only to myself, to my power and my perseverance. How many weak people would have perished in my place as victims of madness, despair, or grief? But I have conquered everything! I have changed the world. I gave to my soul the form which my mind desired. In the desert, working alone, exhausted with fatigue, I have erected a stately structure in which I now live joyously and calmly, like a king. Destroy it—and tomorrow I shall begin to build a new structure, and in my bloody sweat I shall erect it! For I must live!

Forgive my involuntary pathos in the last lines, which is so unbecoming to my balanced and calm nature. But it is hard to restrain myself when I recall the road I have travelled. I hope, however, that in the future I shall not darken the mood of my reader with any outbursts of agitated feelings. Only he shouts who is not confident of the truth of his words; calm firmness and cold simplicity are becoming to the truth.

P.S.—I do not remember whether I told you that the criminal who murdered my father has not been found as yet.

Chapter 5

Deviating from time to time from the calm form of a historical narrative I must pause on current events. Thus, I will permit myself to acquaint my readers in a few lines with a rather interesting specimen of the human species which I have found accidentally in our prison.

One afternoon a few days ago the warden came to me for the usual chat, and among other things told me there was a very unfortunate man in prison at the time upon whom I could exert a beneficent influence. I expressed my willingness in the most cordial manner, and for several days in succession I have had long discussions with the artist K., by permission of the warden. The spirit of hostility, even of obstinacy, with which, to my regret, he met me at his first visit, has now disappeared entirely under the influence of my discussion. Listening willingly and with interest to my ever-pacifying words he gradually told me his rather unusual story after a series of persistent questions.

He is a man of about twenty-six or twenty-eight, of pleasant appearance, and rather good manners, which show that he is a well-bred man. A certain quite natural unrestraint in his speech, a passionate vehemence with which he talks about himself, occasionally a bitter, even ironical laughter, followed by painful pensiveness, from which it is difficult to arouse him even by a touch of the hand—these complete the make-up of my new acquaintance. Personally, to me he is not particularly sympathetic, and however strange it may seem I am especially annoyed by his disgusting habit of constantly moving his thin, emaciated fingers and clutching helplessly the hand of the person with whom he speaks.

K. told me very little of his past life.

"Well, what is there to tell? I was an artist, that's all," he repeated, with a sorrowful grimace, and refused to talk about the "immoral act" for which he was condemned to solitary confinement.

"I don't want to corrupt you, grandpa—live honestly," he would jest in a somewhat unbecoming familiar tone, which I tolerated simply because I wished to please the warden of the prison, having learned from the prisoner the real cause of his sufferings, which sometimes assumed an acute form of violence and threats. During one of these painful minutes, when K.'s will power was weak, as a result of insomnia, from which he was suffering, I seated myself on his bed and treated him in general with fatherly kindness, and he blurted out everything to me right there and then.

Not desiring to tire the reader with an exact reproduction of his hysterical outbursts, his laughter and his tears, I shall give only the facts of his story.

K.'s grief, at first not quite clear to me, consists of the fact that instead of paper or canvas for his drawings he was given a large slate and a slate pencil. (By the way, the art with which he mastered the material, which was new to him, is remarkable. I have seen some of his productions, and it seems to me that they could satisfy the taste of the most fastidious expert of graphic arts. Personally, I am indifferent to the art of painting, preferring live and truthful nature.) Thus, owing to the nature of the material, before commencing a new picture, K. had to destroy the previous one by wiping it off his slate, and this seemed to lead him every time to the verge of madness.

"You cannot imagine what it means," he would say, clutching my hands with his thin, clinging fingers. "While I draw, you know, I forget entirely that it is useless; I am usually very cheerful and I even whistle some tune, and once I was even incarcerated for that, as it is forbidden to whistle in this cursed prison. But that is a trifle—for I had at least a good sleep there. But when I finish my picture—no, even when I approach the end of the picture, I am seized with a sensation so terrible that I feel like tearing the brain from my head and trampling it with my feet. Do you understand me?"

"I understand you, my friend, I understand you perfectly, and I sympathise with you."

"Really? Well, then, listen, old man. I make the last strokes with so much pain, with such a sense of sorrow and hopelessness, as though I were bidding goodbye to the person, I loved best of all. But here I have finished it. Do you understand what it means? It means that it has assumed life, that it lives, that there is a certain mysterious spirit in it. And yet it is already doomed to death, it is dead already, dead like a herring. Can you understand it at all? I do not understand it. And, now, imagine, I—fool that I am—I nevertheless rejoice, I cry and rejoice. No, I think, this picture I shall not destroy; it is so good that I shall not destroy it. Let it live. And it is a fact that at such times I do not feel like drawing anything new, I have not the slightest desire for it. And yet it is dreadful. Do you understand me?"

"Perfectly, my friend. No doubt the drawing ceases to please you on the following day—"

"Oh, what nonsense you are prating, old man! (That is exactly what he said. 'Nonsense.') How can a dying child cease to please you? Of course, if he lived, he might have become a scoundrel, but when he is dying—No, old man, that isn't it. For I am killing it myself. I do not sleep all night long, I jump up, I look at it, and I love it so dearly that I feel like stealing it. Stealing it from whom? What do I know? But when morning sets in I feel that I cannot do without it, that I must take up that cursed pencil again and create anew. What a mockery! To create! What am I, a galley slave?"

"My friend, you are in a prison."

"My dear old man! When I begin to steal over to the slate with the sponge in my hand I feel like a murderer. It happens that I go around it for a day or two. Do you know, one day I bit off a finger of my right hand so as not to draw any more, but that, of course, was only a trifle, for I started to learn drawing with my left hand. What is this necessity for creating! To create by all means, create for suffering—create with the knowledge that it will all perish! Do you understand it?"

"Finish it, my friend, don't be agitated; then I will expound to you, my views."

Unfortunately, my advice hardly reached the ears of K. In one of those paroxysms of despair, which frighten the warden of our prison, K. began to throw himself about in his bed, tear his clothes, shout and sob, manifesting in general all the symptoms of extreme mortification. I looked at the sufferings of the unfortunate youth with deep emotion (compared with me he was a youth), vainly endeavouring to hold his fingers which were tearing his clothes. I knew that for this breach of discipline new incarceration awaited him.

"O, impetuous youth," I thought when he had grown somewhat calmer, and I was tenderly unfolding his fine hair which had become entangled, "how easily you fall into despair! A bit of drawing, which may in the end fall into the hands of a dealer in old rags, or a dealer in old bronze and cemented porcelain, can cause you so much suffering!" But, of course, I did not tell this to my youthful friend, striving, as anyone should under similar circumstances, not to irritate him by unnecessary contradictions.

"Thank you, old man," said K., apparently calm now. "To tell the truth you seemed very strange to me at first; your face is so venerable, but your eyes. Have you murdered anybody, old man?"

I deliberately quote the malicious and careless phrase to show how in the eyes of lightminded and shallow people the stamp of a terrible accusation is transformed into the stamp of the crime itself. Controlling my feeling of bitterness, I remarked calmly to the impertinent youth:

"You are an artist, my child; to you are known the mysteries of the human face, that flexible, mobile and deceptive masque, which, like the sea, reflects the hurrying clouds and the azure ether. Being green, the sea turns blue under the clear sky and black when the sky is black, when the heavy clouds are dark. What do you want of my face, over which hangs an accusation of the most cruel crime?"

But, occupied with his own thoughts, the artist apparently paid no particular attention to my words and continued in a broken voice:

"What am I to do? You saw my drawing. I destroyed it, and it is already a whole week since I touched my pencil. Of course," he resumed thoughtfully, rubbing his brow, "it would be better to break the slate; to punish me they would not give me another one—"

"You had better return it to the authorities."

"Very well, I may hold out another week, but what then? I know myself. Even now that devil is pushing my hand: 'Take the pencil, take the pencil.'"

At that moment, as my eyes wandered distractedly over his cell, I suddenly noticed that some of the artist's clothes hanging on the wall were unnaturally stretched, and one end was skilfully fastened by the back of the cot. Assuming an air that I was tired and that I wanted to walk about in the cell, I staggered as from a quiver of senility in my legs, and pushed the clothes aside. The entire wall was covered with drawings!

The artist had already leaped from his cot, and thus we stood facing each other in silence. I said in a tone of gentle reproach:

"How did you allow yourself to do this, my friend? You know the rules of the prison, according to which no inscriptions or drawing on the walls are permissible?"

"I know no rules," said K. morosely.

"And then," I continued, sternly this time, "you lied to me, my friend. You said that you did not take the pencil into your hands for a whole week."

"Of course, I didn't," said the artist, with a strange smile, and even a challenge. Even when caught red-handed, he did not betray any signs of repentance, and looked rather sarcastic than guilty. Having examined more closely the drawings on the wall, which represented human figures in various positions, I became interested in the strange reddish-yellow colour of an unknown pencil.

"Is this iodine? You told me that you had a pain and that you secured iodine."

"No. It is blood."

"Blood?"

"Yes."

I must say frankly that I even liked him at that moment.

"How did you get it?"

"From my hand."

"From your hand? But how did you manage to hide yourself from the eye that is watching you?"

He smiled cunningly, and even winked.

"Don't you know that you can always deceive if only you want to do it?"

My sympathies for him were immediately dispersed. I saw before me a man who was not particularly clever, but in all probability terribly spoiled already, who did not even admit the thought that there are people who simply cannot lie. Recalling, however, the promise I had made to the warden, I assumed a calm air of dignity and said to him tenderly, as only a mother could speak to her child:

"Don't be surprised and don't condemn me for being so strict, my friend. I am an old man. I have passed half of my life in this prison; I have formed certain habits, like all old people, and submitting to all rules myself, I am perhaps overdoing it somewhat in demanding the same of others. You will of course wipe off these drawings yourself—although I feel sorry for them, for I admire them sincerely—and I will not say anything to the administration. We will forget all this, as if nothing had happened. Are you satisfied?"

He answered drowsily:

"Very well."

"In our prison, where we have the sad pleasure of being confined, everything is arranged in accordance with a most purposeful plan and is most strictly subjected to laws and rules. And the very strict order, on account of which the existence of your creations is so short lived, and, I may say, ephemeral, is full of the profoundest wisdom. Allowing you to perfect yourself in your art, it wisely guards other people against the perhaps injurious influence of your productions, and in any case, it completes logically, finishes, enforces, and makes clear the meaning of your solitary confinement. What does solitary confinement in our prison mean? It means that the prisoner should be alone. But would he be alone if by his productions he would communicate in some way or other with other people outside?"

By the expression of K.'s face I noticed with a sense of profound joy that my words had produced on him the proper impression, bringing him back from the realm of poetic inventions to the land of stern but beautiful reality. And, raising my voice, I continued:

"As for the rule you have broken, which forbids any inscription or drawing on the walls of our prison, it is not less logical. Years will pass; in your place there may be another prisoner like you—and he may see that which you have drawn. Shall this be tolerated? Just think of it!

And what would become of the walls of our prison if everyone who wished it were to leave upon them his profane marks?"

"To the devil with it!"

This is exactly how K. expressed himself. He said it loudly, even with an air of calmness.

"What do you mean to say by this, my youthful friend?"

"I wish to say that you may perish here, my old friend, but I shall leave this place."

"You can't escape from our prison," I retorted, sternly.

"Have you tried?"

"Yes, I have tried."

He looked at me incredulously and smiled. He smiled!

"You are a coward, old man. You are simply a miserable coward."

I—a coward! Oh, if that self-satisfied puppy knew what a tempest of rage, he had aroused in my soul he would have squealed for fright and would have hidden himself on the bed. I—a coward! The world has crumbled upon my head, but has not crushed me, and out of its terrible fragments I have created a new world, according to my own design and plan; all the evil forces of life—solitude, imprisonment, treachery, and falsehood—all have taken up arms against me, but I have subjected them all to my will. And I who have subjected to my-self even my dreams—I am a coward?

But I shall not tire the attention of my indulgent reader with these lyrical deviations, which have no bearing on the matter. I continue.

After a pause, broken only by K.'s loud breathing, I said to him sadly:

"I—a coward! And you say this to the man who came with the sole aim of helping you? Of helping you not only in word but also in deed?"

"You wish to help me? In what way?"

"I will get you paper and pencil."

The artist was silent. And his voice was soft and timid when he asked, hesitatingly:

"And—my drawings—will remain?"

"Yes; they will remain."

It is hard to describe the vehement delight into which the ex-alted young man was thrown; *naïve* and pure-hearted youth knows no bounds either in grief or in joy. He pressed my hand warmly, shook me, disturbing my old bones; he called me friend, father, even "dear old phiz" (!) and a thousand other endearing and somewhat *naïve* names. To my regret our conversation lasted too long, and, notwithstanding the entreaties of the young man, who would not part with me, I hurried away to my cell.

I did not go to the warden of the prison, as I felt somewhat agitated. At that remote time, I paced my cell until late in the night, striving to understand what means of escaping from our prison that rather foolish young man could have discovered. Was it possible to run away from our prison? No, I could not admit and I must not admit it. And gradually conjuring up in my memory everything I knew about our prison, I understood that K. must have hit upon an old plan, which I had long discarded, and that he would convince himself of its impracticability even as I convinced myself. It is impossible to escape from our prison.

But, tormented by doubts, I measured my lonely cell for a long time, thinking of various plans that might relieve K.'s position and thus divert him from the idea of making his escape. He must not run away from our prison under any circumstances. Then I gave myself to peaceful and sound sleep, with which benevolent nature has rewarded those who have a clear conscience and a pure soul.

By the way, lest I forget, I shall mention the fact that I destroyed my "*Diary of a Prisoner*" that night. I had long wished to do it, but the natural pity and faint-hearted love which we feel for our blunders and our shortcomings restrained me; besides, there was nothing in my "*Diary*" that could have compromised me in any way. And if I have destroyed it know it is due solely to my desire to throw my past into oblivion and to save my reader from the tediousness of long complaints and moans, from the horror of sacrilegious cursings. May it rest in peace!

CHAPTER 6

Having conveyed to the warden of our prison the contents of my conversation with K., I asked him not to punish the young man for spoiling the walls, which would thus betray me, and I, to save the youth, suggested the following plan, which was accepted by the warden after a few purely formal objections.

"It is important for him," I said, "that his drawings should be preserved, but it is apparently immaterial to him in whose possession these drawings are. Let him, then, avail himself of his art, paint your portrait, Mr. warden, and after that the portraits of the entire staff of your officials. To say nothing of the honour you would show him by this condescension—an honour which he will surely know how to appreciate—the painting may be useful to you as a very original ornament in your drawing room or study. Besides, nothing will prevent us from destroying the drawings if we should not care for them, for the *naïve* and somewhat selfish young man apparently does not even admit the thought that anybody's hand would destroy his productions."

Smiling, the warden suggested, with a politeness that flattered me extremely, that the series of portraits should commence with mine. I quote word for word that which the warden said to me:

Your face actually calls for reproduction on canvas. We shall hang your portrait in the office.

The zeal of creativeness—these are the only words I can apply to the passionate, silent agitation in which K. reproduced my features. Usually talkative, he now maintained silence for hours, leaving unanswered my jests and remarks.

"Be silent, old man, be silent—you are at your best when you are silent," he repeated persistently, calling forth an involuntary smile by his zeal as a professional.

My portrait would remind you, my indulgent reader, of that mysterious peculiarity of artists, according to which they very often transmit their own feelings, even their external features, to the subject upon which they are working. Thus, reproducing with remarkable likeness, the lower part of my face, where kindness and the expression of authoritativeness and calm dignity are so harmoniously blended, K. undoubtedly introduced into my eyes his own suffering and even his horror. Their fixed, immobile gaze; madness glimmering somewhere in their depth; the painful eloquence of a deep and infinitely lonely soul—all that was not mine.

"Is this I?" I exclaimed, laughing, when from the canvas this terrible face, full of wild contradictions, stared at me. "My friend, I do not congratulate you on this portrait. I do not think it is successful."

"It is you, old man, you! It is well drawn. You criticise it wrongly. Where will you hang it?"

He grew talkative again like a magpie, that amiable young man, and all because his wretched painting was to be preserved for some time. O impetuous, O happy youth! Here I could not restrain myself from a little jest for the purpose of teaching a lesson to the self-confident youngster, so I asked him, with a smile:

"Well, Mr. Artist, what do you think? Am I murderer or not?"

The artist, closing one eye, examined me and the portrait critically. Then whistling a polka, he answered recklessly: "The devil knows you, old man!"

I smiled. K. understood my jest at last, burst out laughing and then said with sudden seriousness:

"You are speaking of the human face but do you know that there is nothing worse in the world than the human face? Even when it tells the truth, when it shouts about the truth, it lies, it lies, old man, for it speaks its own language. Do you know, old man, a terrible incident happened to me? It was in one of the picture galleries in Spain. I was examining a portrait of Christ, when suddenly—Christ, you understand, Christ—great eyes, dark, terrible suffering, sorrow, grief, love—well, in a word—Christ. Suddenly I was struck with something; suddenly it seemed to me that it was the face of the greatest wrong-doer, tormented by the greatest unheard-of woes of repentance—Old man, why do you look at me so! Old man!"

Nearing my eyes to the very face of the artist, I asked him in a cautious whisper, as the occasion required, dividing each word from the other:

"Don't you think that when the devil tempted Him in the desert, He did not renounce him, as He said later, but consented, sold Himself—that He did not renounce the devil, but sold Himself. Do you understand? Does not that passage in the Gospels seem doubtful to you?"

Extreme fright was expressed on the face of my young friend. Forcing the palms of his hands against my chest, as if to push me away, he ejaculated in a voice so low that I could hardly hear his indistinct words:

"What? You say Jesus sold Himself? What for?"

I explained softly:

"That the people, my child, that the people should believe Him."

"Well?"

I smiled. K.'s eyes became round, as if a noose was strangling him. Suddenly, with that lack of respect for old age which was one of his characteristics, he threw me down on the bed with a sharp thrust and jumped away into a corner. When I was slowly getting up from the awkward position into which the unrestraint of that young man had forced me—I fell backward, with my head between the pillow and the back of the bed—he cried to me loudly:

"Don't you dare! Don't you dare get up, you Devil."

But I did not think of rising to my feet. I simply sat down on the bed, and, thus seated, with an involuntary smile at the passionate outburst of the youth, I shook my head good naturedly and laughed.

"Oh, young man, young man! You yourself have drawn me into this theological conversation."

But he stared at me stubbornly, wide eyed, and kept repeating:

"Sit there, sit there! I did not say this. No, no!"

"You said it, you, young man—you. Do you remember Spain, the picture gallery! You said it and now you deny it, mocking my clumsy old age. Oh!"

K. suddenly lowered his hands and admitted in a low voice:

"Yes. I said it. But you, old man—"

I do not remember what he said after that—it is so hard to recall all the childish chatter of this kind, but unfortunately too light-minded young man. I remember only that we parted as friends, and he pressed my hand warmly, expressing to me his sincere gratitude, even calling me, so far as I can remember, his "saviour."

By the way, I succeeded in convincing the warden that the portrait of even such a man as I, after all a prisoner, was out of place in such a solemn official room as the office of our prison. And now the portrait hangs on the wall of my cell, pleasantly breaking the cold monotony of the pure white walls.

Leaving for a time our artist, who is now carried away by the portrait of the warden, I shall continue my story.

Chapter 7

My spiritual clearness, as I had the pleasure of informing the reader before, has built up for me a considerable circle of men and women admirers. With self-evident emotion I shall tell of the pleasant hours of our hearty conversations, which I modestly call "My talks."

It is difficult for me to explain how I deserved it, but the majority of those who come to me regard me with a feeling of the profoundest respect, even adoration, and only a few come for the purpose of arguing with me, but these arguments are usually of a moderate and proper character. I usually seat myself in the middle of the room, in a soft and deep armchair, which is furnished me for this occasion by the warden; my hearers surround me closely, and some of them, the more enthusiastic youths and maidens, seat themselves at my feet.

Having before me an audience more than half of which is composed of women, and entirely disposed in my favour, I always appeal not so much to the mind as to the sensitive and truthful heart. Fortunately, I possess a certain oratorical power, and the customary effects of the oratorical art, to which all preachers, beginning in all probability with Mohammed, have resorted, and which I can handle rather cleverly, allow me to influence my hearers in the desired direction. It is easily understood that to the dear ladies in my audience I am not so much the Sage, who has solved the mystery of the iron grate, as a great martyr of a righteous cause, which they do not quite understand. Shunning abstract discussions, they eagerly hang on every word of compassion and kindness, and respond with the same. Allowing them to love me and to believe in my immutable knowledge of life, I afford them the happy opportunity to depart at least for a time from the coldness of life, from its painful doubts and questions.

I say openly without any false modesty, which I despise even as I despise hypocrisy, there were lectures at which I myself being in a state of exaltation, called forth in my audience, especially in my nervous lady visitors, a mood of intense agitation, which turned into hysterical laughter and tears. Of course, I am not a prophet; I am merely a modest thinker, but no one would succeed in convincing my lady admirers that there is no prophetic meaning and significance in my speeches.

I remember one such lecture which took place two months ago. The night before I could not sleep as soundly as I usually slept; perhaps it was simply because of the full moon, which affects sleep, disturbing and interrupting it. I vaguely remember the strange sensation which I experienced when the pale crescent of the moon appeared in my window and the iron squares cut it with ominous black lines into small silver squares. . . .

When I started for the lecture, I felt exhausted and rather inclined to silence than to conversation; the vision of the night before disturbed me. But when I saw those dear faces, those eyes full of hope and ardent entreaty for friendly advice; when I saw before me that rich field, already ploughed, waiting only for the good seed to be sown, my heart began to burn with delight, pity and love. Avoiding the customary formalities which accompany the meetings of people, declining the hands outstretched to greet me, I turned to the audience, which was agitated at the very sight of me, and gave them my blessing with a gesture to which I know how to lend a peculiar majesty.

"Come unto me," I exclaimed; "come unto me; you who have gone away from that life. Here, in this quiet abode, under the sacred protection of the iron grate, at my heart overflowing with love, you will find rest and comfort. My beloved children, give me your sad soul, exhausted from suffering, and I shall clothe it with light. I shall carry it to those blissful lands where the sun of eternal truth and love never sets."

Many had begun to cry already, but, as it was too early for tears, I interrupted them with a gesture of fatherly impatience, and continued:

"You, dear girl, who came from the world which calls itself free— what gloomy shadows lie on your charming and beautiful face! And you, my daring youth, why are you so pale? Why do I see, instead of the ecstasy of victory, the fear of defeat in your lowered eyes? And you, honest mother, tell me, what wind has made your eyes so red? What furious rain has lashed your wizened face? What snow has whitened your hair, for it used to be dark?"

But the weeping and the sobs drowned the end of my speech, and besides, I admit it without feeling ashamed of it, I myself brushed away more than one treacherous tear from my eyes. Without allowing the agitation to subside completely, I called in a voice of stern and truthful reproach:

"Do not weep because your soul is dark, stricken with misfortunes, blinded by chaos, clipped of its wings by doubts; give it to me and I shall direct it toward the light, toward order and reason. I know the truth. I have conceived the world! I have discovered the great principle of its purpose! I have solved the sacred formula of the iron grate! I demand of you—swear to me by the cold iron of its squares that henceforth you will confess to me without shame or fear all your deeds, your errors and doubts, all the secret thoughts of your soul and the dreams and desires of your body!"

"We swear! We swear! We swear! Save us! Reveal to us the truth! Take our sins upon yourself! Save us! Save us!" numerous exclamations resounded.

I must mention the sad incident which occurred during that same lecture. At the moment when the excitement reached its height and the hearts had already opened, ready to unburden themselves, a certain youth, looking morose and embittered, exclaimed loudly, evidently addressing himself to me:

"Liar! Do not listen to him. He is lying!"

The indulgent reader will easily believe that it was only by a great effort that I succeeded in saving the incautious youth from the fury of the audience. Offended in that which is most precious to a human being, his faith in goodness and the divine purpose of life, my women admirers rushed upon the foolish youth in a mob and would have beaten him cruelly. Remembering, however, that there was more joy to the pastor in one sinner who repents than in ten righteous men, I took the young man aside where no one could hear us, and entered into a brief conversation with him.

"Did you call me a liar, my child?"

Moved by my kindness, the poor young man became confused and answered hesitatingly:

"Pardon me for my harshness, but it seems to me that you are not telling the truth."

"I understand you, my friend. You must have been agitated by the intense ecstasy of the women, and you, as a sensible man, not inclined to mysticism, suspected me of fraud, of a hideous fraud. No, no, don't excuse yourself. I understand you. But I wish you would understand me. Out of the mire of superstitions, out of the deep gulf of prejudices and unfounded beliefs, I want to lead their strayed thoughts and place them upon the solid foundation of strictly logical reasoning. The iron grate, which I mentioned, is not a mystical sign; it is only a formula, a simple, sober, honest, mathematical formula. To you, as a sensible man, I will willingly explain this formula. The grate is the scheme in which are placed all the laws guiding the universe, which do away with chaos, substituting in its place strict, iron, inviolable order, forgotten by mankind. As a bright-minded man you will easily understand—"

"Pardon me. I did not understand you, and if you will permit me I—But why do you make them swear?"

"My friend, the soul of man, believing itself free and constantly suffering from this spurious freedom, is demanding fetters for itself—to some these fetters are an oath, to others a vow, to still others simply a word of honour. You will give me your word of honour, will you not?"

"I will."

"And by this you are simply striving to enter the harmony of the world, where everything is subjected to a law. Is not the falling of a stone the fulfilment of a vow, of the vow called the law of gravitation?"

I shall not go into detail about this conversation and the others that followed. The obstinate and unrestrained youth, who had insulted me by calling me liar, became one of my warmest adherents.

I must return to the others. During the time that I talked with the young man, the desire for penitence among my charming proselytes reached its height. Not patient enough to wait for me, they commenced in a state of intense ecstasy to confess to one another, giving to the room an appearance of a garden where dozens of birds of paradise were twittering at the same time. When I returned, each of them separately unfolded her agitated soul to me. . . .

I saw how, from day to day, from hour to hour, terrible chaos was struggling in their souls with an eager inclination for harmony and order; how in the bloody struggle between eternal falsehood and immortal truth, falsehood, through inconceivable ways, passed into truth, and truth became falsehood. I found in the human soul all the forces in the world, and none of them was dormant, and in the mad whirlpool each soul became like a fountain, whose source is the abyss of the sea and whose summit the sky. And every human being, as I have learned and seen, is like the rich and powerful master who gave a masquerade ball at his castle and illuminated it with many lights; and strange masks came from everywhere and the master greeted them, bowing courteously, and vainly asking them who they were; and new, ever stranger, ever more terrible, masks were arriving, and the master bowed to them ever more courteously, staggering from fatigue and fear.

And they were laughing and whispering strange words about the eternal chaos, whence they came, obeying the call of the master. And lights were burning in the castle—and in the distance lighted windows were visible, reminding him of the festival, and the exhausted master kept bowing ever lower, ever more courteously, ever more cheerfully. My indulgent reader will easily understand that in addition to a certain sense of fear which I experienced, the greatest delight and even joyous emotion soon came upon me—for I saw that eternal chaos was defeated and the triumphant hymn of bright harmony was rising to the skies. . . .

Not without a sense of pride I shall mention the modest offerings by which my kind admirers were striving to express to me their feelings of love and adoration. I am not afraid of calling out a smile on the lips of my readers, for I feel how comical it is—I will say that among the offerings brought me at first were fruit, cakes, all kinds of sweet-meats. But I am afraid, however, that no one will believe me when I say that I have actually declined these offerings, preferring the observance of the prison regime in all its rigidness.

At the last lecture, a kind and honourable lady brought me a basketful of live flowers. To my regret, I was compelled to decline this present, too.

"Forgive me, madam, but flowers do not enter into the system of our prison. I appreciate very much your magnanimous attention—I kiss your hands, madam—" I said, "but I am compelled to decline the flowers. Travelling along the thorny road to self-renunciation, I must not caress my eyes with the ephemeral and illusionary beauty of these charming lilies and roses. All flowers perish in our prison, madam."

Yesterday another lady brought me a very valuable crucifix of ivory, a family heirloom, she said. Not afflicted with the sin of hypocrisy, I told my generous lady frankly that I do not believe in miracles.

"But at the same time," I said, "I regard with the profoundest respect Him who is justly called the Saviour of the world, and I honour greatly His services to mankind.

"If I should tell you, madam, that the Gospel has long been my favourite book, that there is not a day in my life that I do not open this great Book, drawing from it strength and courage to be able to continue my hard course—you will understand that your liberal gift could not have fallen into better hands. Henceforth, thanks to you, the sad solitude of my cell will vanish; I am not alone. I bless you, my daughter."

I cannot forego mentioning the strange thoughts brought out by the crucifix as it hung there beside my portrait. It was twilight; outside the wall the bell was tolling heavily in the invisible church, calling the believers together; in the distance, over the deserted field, overgrown with high grass, an unknown wanderer was plodding along, passing into the unknown distance, like a little black dot. It was as quiet in our prison as in a sepulchre. I looked long and attentively at the features of Jesus, which were so calm, so joyous compared with him who looked silently and dully from the wall beside Him. And with my habit, formed during the long years of solitude, of addressing inanimate things aloud, I said to the motionless crucifix:

"Good evening, Jesus. I am glad to welcome You in our prison. There are three of us here: You, I, and the one who is looking from the wall, and I hope that we three will manage to live in peace and in harmony. He is looking silently, and You are silent, and Your eyes are closed—I shall speak for the three of us, a sure sign that our peace will never be broken."

They were silent, and, continuing, I addressed my speech to the portrait:

"Where are you looking so intently and so strangely, my unknown friend and roommate? In your eyes I see mystery and reproach. Is it possible that you dare reproach Him? Answer!"

And, pretending that the portrait answered, I continued in a different voice with an expression of extreme sternness and boundless grief:

"Yes, I do reproach Him. Jesus, Jesus! Why is Your face so pure, so blissful? You have passed only over the brink of human sufferings, as over the brink of an abyss, and only the foam of the bloody and miry waves have touched You. Do You command me, a human being, to sink into the dark depth? Great is Your Golgotha, Jesus, but too reverent and joyous, and one small but interesting stroke is missing—the horror of aimlessness!"

Here I interrupted the speech of the portrait, with an expression of anger.

"How dare you," I exclaimed; "how dare you speak of aimlessness in our prison?"

They were silent; and suddenly Jesus, without opening His eyes— He even seemed to close them more tightly—answered:

"Who knows the mysteries of the heart of Jesus?"

I burst into laughter, and my esteemed reader will easily understand this laughter. It turned out that I, a cool and sober mathematician, possessed a poetic talent and could compose very interesting comedies.

I do not know how all this would have ended, for I had already prepared a thundering answer for my roommate when the appearance of the keeper, who brought me food, suddenly interrupted me. But apparently my face bore traces of excitement, for the man asked me with stern sympathy:

"Were you praying?"

I do not remember what I answered.

CHAPTER 8

Last Sunday a great misfortune occurred in our prison: The artist K., whom the reader knows already, ended his life in suicide by flinging himself from the table with his head against the stone floor. The fall and the force of the blow had been so skilfully calculated by the unfortunate young man that his skull was split in two. The grief of the warden was indescribable. Having called me to the office, the warden, without shaking hands with me, reproached me in angry and harsh terms for having deceived him, and he regained his calm, only after my hearty apologies and promises that such accidents would not happen again. I promised to prepare a project for watching the criminals which would render suicide impossible. The esteemed wife of the warden, whose portrait remained unfinished, was also grieved by the death of the artist.

Of course, I had not expected this outcome, either, although a few days before committing suicide, K. had provoked in me a feeling of uneasiness. Upon entering his cell one morning, and greeting him, I noticed with amazement that he was sitting before his slate once more drawing human figures.

"What does this mean, my friend?" I inquired cautiously. "And how about the portrait of the second assistant?"

"The devil take it!"

"But you—"

"The devil take it!"

After a pause I remarked distractedly:

"Your portrait of the warden is meeting with great success. Although some of the people who have seen it say that the right moustache is somewhat shorter than the left—"

"Shorter?"

"Yes, shorter. But in general, they find that you caught the likeness very successfully."

K. had put aside his slate pencil and, perfectly calm, said:

"Tell your warden that I am not going to paint that prison riffraff anymore."

After these words there was nothing left for me to do but leave him, which I decided to do. But the artist, who could not get along without giving vent to his effusions, seized me by the hand and said with his usual enthusiasm:

"Just think of it, old man, what a horror! Every day a new repulsive face appears before me. They sit and stare at me with their froglike eyes. What am I to do? At first, I laughed—I even liked it—but when the froglike eyes stared at me every day I was seized with horror. I was afraid they might start to quack—qua-qua!"

Indeed, there was a certain fear, even madness, in the eyes of the artist—the madness which shortly led him to his untimely grave.

"Old man, it is necessary to have something beautiful. Do you understand me?"

"And the wife of the warden? Is she not—"

I shall pass in silence the unbecoming expressions with which he spoke of the lady in his excitement. I must, however, admit that to a certain extent the artist was right in his complaints. I had been present several times at the sittings, and noticed that all who had posed for the artist behaved rather unnaturally. Sincere and *naïve*, conscious of the importance of their position, convinced that the features of their faces perpetuated upon the canvas would go down to posterity, they exaggerated somewhat the qualities which are so characteristic of their high and responsible office in our prison. A certain bombast of pose, an exaggerated expression of stern authority, an obvious consciousness of their own importance, and a noticeable contempt for those on whom their eyes were directed—all this disfigured their kind and affable faces.

But I cannot understand what horrible features the artist found where there should have been a smile. I was even indignant at the superficial attitude with which an artist, who considered himself talented and sensible, passed the people without noticing that a divine spark was glimmering in each one of them. In the quest after some fantastic beauty, he lightmindedly passed by the true beauties with which the human soul is filled. I cannot help feeling sorry for those unfortunate people who, like K., because of a peculiar construction of their brains, always turn their eyes toward the dark side, whereas there is so much joy and light in our prison!

When I said this to K. I heard, to my regret, the same stereotyped and indecent answer:

"The devil take it!"

All I could do was to shrug my shoulders. Suddenly changing his tone and bearing, the artist turned to me seriously with a question which, in my opinion, was also indecent:

"Why do you lie, old man?"

I was astonished, of course.

"I lie?"

"Well, let it be the truth, if you like, but why? I am looking and thinking. Why did you say that? Why?"

My indulgent reader, who knows well what the truth has cost me, will readily understand my profound indignation. I deliberately mention this audacious and other calumnious phrases to show in what an atmosphere of malice, distrust, and disrespect I have to plod along the hard road of suffering. He insisted rudely:

"I have had enough of your smiles. Tell me plainly, why do you speak so?"

Then, I admit, I flared up:

"You want to know why I speak the truth? Because I hate falsehood and I commit it to eternal anathema! Because fate has made me a victim of injustice, and as a victim, like Him who took upon Himself the great sin of the world and its great sufferings, I wish to point out the way to mankind. Wretched egoist, you know only yourself and your miserable art, while I love mankind."

My anger grew. I felt the veins on my forehead swelling.

"Fool, miserable dauber, unfortunate schoolboy, in love with colours! Human beings pass before you, and you see only their froglike eyes. How did your tongue turn to say such a thing? Oh, if you only looked even once into the human soul! What treasures of tenderness, love, humble faith, holy humility, you would have discovered there! And to you, bold man, it would have seemed as if you entered a temple—a bright, illuminated temple. But it is said of people like you—'*do not cast your pearls before swine.*'"

The artist was silent, crushed by my angry and unrestrained speech. Finally, he sighed and said:

"Forgive me, old man; I am talking nonsense, of course, but I am so unfortunate and so lonely. Of course, my dear old man, it is all true about the divine spark and about beauty, but a polished boot is also beautiful. I cannot, I cannot! Just think of it! How can a man have such moustaches as he has? And yet he is complaining that the left moustache is shorter!"

He laughed like a child, and, heaving a sigh, added:

"I'll make another attempt. I will paint the lady. There is really something good in her. Although she is after all—a cow."

He laughed again, and, fearing to brush away with his sleeve the drawing on the slate, he cautiously placed it in the corner.

Here I did that which my duty compelled me to do. Seizing the slate, I smashed it to pieces with a powerful blow. I thought that the artist would rush upon me furiously, but he did not. To his weak mind my act seemed so blasphemous, so supernaturally horrible, that his deathlike lips could not utter a word.

"What have you done?" he asked at last in a low voice. "You have broken it?"

And raising my hand I replied solemnly:

"Foolish youth, I have done that which I would have done to my heart if it wanted to jest and mock me! Unfortunate youth, can you not see that your art has long been mocking you, that from that slate of yours the devil himself was making hideous faces at you?"

"Yes. The devil!"

"Being far from your wonderful art, I did not understand you at first, nor your longing, your horror of aimlessness. But when I entered your cell today and noticed you at your ruinous occupation, I said to myself: It is better that he should not create at all than to create in this manner. Listen to me."

I then revealed for the first time to this youth the sacred formula of the iron grate, which, dividing the infinite into squares, thereby subjects it to itself. K. listened to my words with emotion, looking with the horror of an ignorant man at the figures which must have seemed to him to be cabalistic, but which were nothing else than the ordinary figures used in mathematics.

"I am your slave, old man," he said at last, kissing my hand with his cold lips.

"No, you will be my favourite pupil, my son. I bless you."

And it seemed to me that the artist was saved. True, he regarded me with great joy, which could easily be explained by the extreme respect with which I inspired him, and he painted the portrait of the warden's wife with such zeal and enthusiasm that the esteemed lady was sincerely moved. And, strange to say, the artist succeeded in making so strangely beautiful the features of this woman, who was stout and no longer young, that the warden, long accustomed to the face of his wife, was greatly delighted by its new expression. Thus, everything went on smoothly, when suddenly this catastrophe occurred, the entire horror of which I alone knew.

Not desiring to call forth any unnecessary disputes, I concealed from the warden the fact that on the eve of his death the artist had thrown a letter into my cell, which I noticed only in the morning. I did not preserve the note, nor do I remember all that the unfortunate youth told me in his farewell message; I think it was a letter of thanks for my effort to save him. He wrote that he regretted sincerely that his failing strength did not permit him to avail himself of my instructions. But one phrase impressed itself deeply in my memory, and you will understand the reason for it when I repeat it in all its terrifying simplicity.

"I am going away from your prison," thus read the phrase.

And he really did go away. Here are the walls, here is the little window in the door, here is our prison, but he is not there; he has gone away. Consequently I, too, could go away. Instead of having wasted dozens of years on a titanic struggle, instead of being tormented by the throes of despair, instead of growing enfeebled by horror in the face of unsolved mysteries, of striving to subject the world to my mind and my will, I could have climbed the table and—one instant of pain—I would be free; I would be triumphant over the lock and the walls, over truth and falsehood, over joys and sufferings. I will not say that I had not thought of suicide before as a means of escaping from our prison, but now for the first time it appeared before me in all its attractiveness.

In a fit of base faint-heartedness, which I shall not conceal from my reader, even as I do not conceal from him my good qualities; perhaps even in a fit of temporary insanity I momentarily forgot all I knew about our prison and its great purpose. I forgot—I am ashamed to say—even the great formula of the iron grate, which I conceived and mastered with such difficulty, and I prepared a noose made of my towel for the purpose of strangling myself. But at the last moment, when all was ready, and it was but necessary to push away the taboret, I asked myself, with my habit of reasoning which did not forsake me even at that time: But where am I going? The answer was: I am going to death. But what is death? And the answer was: I do not know.

These brief reflections were enough for me to come to myself, and with a bitter laugh at my cowardice I removed the fatal noose from my neck. Just as I had been ready to sob for grief a minute before, so now I laughed—I laughed like a madman, realising that another trap, placed before me by derisive fate, had so brilliantly been evaded by me. Oh, how many traps there are in the life of man! Like a cunning fisherman, fate catches him now with the alluring bait of some truth, now with the hairy little worm of dark falsehood, now with the phantom of life, now with the phantom of death.

My dear young man, my fascinating fool, my charming silly fellow—who told you that our prison ends here, that from one prison you did not fall into another prison, from which it will hardly be possible for you to run away? You were too hasty, my friend, you forgot to ask me something else—I would have told it to you. I would have told you that omnipotent law reigns over that which you call non-existence and death just as it reigns over that which you call life and existence. Only the fools, dying, believe that they have made an end of themselves—they have ended but one form of themselves, in order to assume another form immediately.

Thus, I reflected, laughing at the foolish suicide, the ridiculous destroyer of the fetters of eternity. And this is what I said addressing myself to my two silent roommates hanging motionlessly on the white wall of my cell:

"I believe and confess that our prison is immortal. What do you say to this, my friends?"

But they were silent. And having burst into good-natured laughter—What quiet roommates I have! I undressed slowly and gave myself to peaceful sleep. In my dream I saw another majestic prison, and wonderful jailers with white wings on their backs, and the chief warden of the prison himself. I do not remember whether there were any little windows in the doors or not, but I think there were. I recall that something like an angel's eye was fixed upon me with tender attention and love. My indulgent reader will, of course, guess that I am jesting. I did not dream at all. I am not in the habit of dreaming.

Without hoping that the warden, occupied with pressing official affairs, would understand me thoroughly and appreciate my idea concerning the impossibility of escaping from our prison, I confined myself, in my report, to an indication of several ways in which suicides could be averted. With magnanimous short-sightedness peculiar to busy and trusting people, the warden failed to notice the weak points of my project and clasped my hand warmly, expressing to me his gratitude in the name of our entire prison.

On that day I had the honour, for the first time, to drink a glass of tea at the home of the warden, in the presence of his kind wife and charming children, who called me "Grandpa." Tears of emotion which gathered in my eyes could but faintly express the feelings that came over me.

At the request of the warden's wife, who took a deep interest in me, I related in detail the story of the tragic murders which led me so unexpectedly and so terribly to the prison. I could not find expressions strong enough—there are no expressions strong enough in the human language—to brand adequately the unknown criminal, who not only murdered three helpless people, but who mocked them brutally in a fit of blind and savage rage.

As the investigation and the autopsy showed, the murderer dealt the last blows after the people had been dead. It is very possible, however—even murderers should be given their due—that the man, intoxicated by the sight of blood, ceased to be a human being and became a beast, the son of chaos, the child of dark and terrible desires. It was characteristic that the murderer, after having committed the crime, drank wine and ate biscuits—some of these were left on the table together with the marks of his bloodstained fingers. But there was something so horrible that my mind could neither understand nor explain: the murderer, after lighting a cigar himself, apparently moved by a feeling of strange kindness, put a lighted cigar between the closed teeth of my father.

I had not recalled these details in many years. They had almost been erased by the hand of time, and now while relating them to my shocked listeners, who would not believe that such horrors were possible, I felt my face turning pale and my hair quivering on my head. In an outburst of grief and anger I rose from my armchair, and straightening myself to my full height, I exclaimed:

"Justice on earth is often powerless, but I implore heavenly justice, I implore the justice of life which never forgives, I implore all the higher laws under whose authority man lives. May the guilty one not escape his deserved punishment! His punishment!"

Moved by my sobs, my listeners there and then expressed their zeal and readiness to work for my liberation, and thus at least partly redeem the injustice heaped upon me. I apologised and returned to my cell.

Evidently my old organism cannot bear such agitation any longer; besides, it is hard even for a strong man to picture in his imagination certain images without risking the loss of his reason. Only in this way can I explain the strange hallucination which appeared before my fatigued eyes in the solitude of my cell. As though benumbed, I gazed aimlessly at the tightly closed door, when suddenly it seemed to me that someone was standing behind me. I had felt this deceptive sensation before, so I did not turn around for some time. But when I turned around at last, I saw—in the distance, between the crucifix and my portrait, about a quarter of a yard above the floor—the body of my father, as though hanging in the air.

It is hard for me to give the details, for twilight had long set in, but I can say with certainty that it was the image of a corpse, and not of a living being, although a cigar was smoking in its mouth. To be more exact, there was no smoke from the cigar, but a faintly reddish light was seen. It is characteristic that I did not sense the odour of tobacco either at that time or later—I had long given up smoking. Here—I must confess my weakness, but the illusion was striking—I commenced to speak to the hallucination. Advancing as closely as possible—the body did not retreat as I approached, but remained perfectly motionless—I said to the ghost:

"I thank you, father. You know how your son is suffering, and you have come—you have come to testify to my innocence. I thank you, father. Give me your hand, and with a firm filial hand-clasp I will respond to your unexpected visit. Don't you want to? Let me have your hand. Give me your hand, or I will call you a liar!"

I stretched out my hand, but of course the hallucination did not deem it worthwhile to respond, and I was forever deprived of the opportunity of feeling the touch of a ghost. The cry which I uttered and which so upset my friend, the jailer, creating some confusion in the prison, was called forth by the sudden disappearance of the phantom—it was so sudden that the space in the place where the corpse had been seemed to me more terrible than the corpse itself.

Such is the power of human imagination when, excited, it creates phantoms and visions, peopling the bottomless and ever silent emptiness with them. It is sad to admit that there are people, however, who believe in ghosts and build upon this belief nonsensical theories about certain relations between the world of the living and the enigmatic land inhabited by the dead. I understand that the human ear and eye can be deceived—but how can the great and lucid human mind fall into such coarse and ridiculous deception?

I asked the jailer:

"I feel a strange sensation, as though there were the odour of cigar smoke in my cell. Don't you smell it?"

The jailer sniffed the air conscientiously and replied:

"No, I don't. You only imagined it."

If you need any confirmation, here is a splendid proof that all I had seen, if it existed at all, existed only in the net of my eye.

CHAPTER 9

Something altogether unexpected has happened; the efforts of my friends, the warden and his wife, were crowned with success, and for two months I have been free, out of prison.

I am happy to inform you that immediately upon my leaving the prison I occupied a very honourable position, to which I could hardly have aspired, conscious of my humble qualities. The entire press met me with unanimous enthusiasm. Numerous journalists, photographers, even caricaturists (the people of our time are so fond of laughter and clever witticisms), in hundreds of articles and drawings reproduced the story of my remarkable life. With striking unanimity, the newspapers assigned to me the name of "Master," a highly flattering name, which I accepted, after some hesitation, with deep gratitude.

I do not know whether it is worth mentioning the few hostile notices called forth by irritation and envy—a vice which so frequently stains the human soul. In one of these notices, which appeared, by the way, in a very filthy little newspaper, a certain scamp, guided by wretched gossip and baseless rumours about my chats in our prison, called me a "zealot and liar." Enraged by the insolence of the miserable scribbler, my friends wanted to prosecute him, but I persuaded them not to do it. Vice is its own proper punishment.

The fortune which my kind mother had left me and which had grown considerably during the time I was in prison has enabled me to settle down to a life of luxury in one of the most aristocratic hotels. I have a large retinue of servants at my command and an automobile—a splendid invention with which I now became acquainted for the first time—and I have skilfully arranged my financial affairs. Live flowers brought to me in abundance by my charming lady visitors give to my nook the appearance of a flower garden or even a bit of a tropical forest.

My servant, a very decent young man, is in a state of despair. He says that he had never seen such a variety of flowers and had never smelled such a variety of odours at the same time. If not for my advanced age and the strict and serious propriety with which I treat my visitors, I do not know how far they would have gone in the expression of their feelings. How many perfumed notes! How many languid sighs and humbly imploring eyes! There was even a fascinating stranger with a black veil—three times she appeared mysteriously, and when she learned that I had visitors she disappeared just as mysteriously.

I will add that at the present time I have had the honour of being elected an honorary member of numerous humanitarian organisations such as "The League of Peace," "The League for Combating Juvenile Criminality," "The Society of the Friends of Man," and others. Besides, at the request of the editor of one of the most widely read newspapers, I am to begin next month a series of public lectures, for which purpose I am going on a tour together with my kind impresario.

I have already prepared my material for the first three lectures and, in the hope that my reader may be interested, I shall give the synopsis of these lectures.

First Lecture

Chaos or order? The eternal struggle between chaos and order. The eternal revolt and the defeat of chaos, the rebel. The triumph of law and order.

Second Lecture

What is the soul of man? The eternal conflict in the soul of man between chaos, whence it came, and harmony, whither it strives irresistibly. Falsehood, as the offspring of chaos, and Truth, as the child of harmony. The triumph of truth and the downfall of falsehood.

Third Lecture the Explanation of the Sacred Formula
of the Iron Grate

As my indulgent reader will see, justice is after all not an empty sound, and I am getting a great reward for my sufferings. But not daring to reproach fate which was so merciful to me, I nevertheless do not feel that sense of contentment which, it would seem, I ought to feel. True, at first, I was positively happy, but soon my habit for strictly logical reasoning, the clearness and honesty of my views, gained by contemplating the world through a mathematically correct grate, have led me to a series of disillusions.

I am afraid to say it now with full certainty, but it seems to me that all their life of this so-called freedom is a continuous self-deception and falsehood. The life of each of these people, whom I have seen during these days, is moving in a strictly defined circle, which is just as solid as the corridors of our prison, just as closed as the dial of the watches which they, in the innocence of their mind, lift every minute to their eyes, not understanding the fatal meaning of the eternally moving hand, which is eternally returning to its place, and each of them feels this, even as the circus horse probably feels it, but in a state of strange blindness each one assures us that he is perfectly free and moving forward. Like the stupid bird which is beating itself to exhaustion against the transparent glass obstacle, without understanding what it is that obstructs its way, these people are helplessly beating against the walls of their glass prison.

I was greatly mistaken, it seems, also in the significance of the greetings which fell to my lot when I left the prison. Of course, I was convinced that in me they greeted the representative of our prison, a leader hardened by experience, a master, who came to them only for the purpose of revealing to them the great mystery of purpose. And when they congratulated me upon the freedom granted to me, I responded with thanks, not suspecting what an idiotic meaning they placed on the word. May I be forgiven this coarse expression, but I am powerless now to restrain my aversion for their stupid life, for their thoughts, for their feelings.

Foolish hypocrites, fearing to tell the truth even when it adorns them! My hardened truthfulness was cruelly taxed in the midst of these false and trivial people. Not a single person believed that I was never so happy as in prison. Why, then, are they so surprised at me, and why do they print my portraits? Are there so few idiots that are unhappy in prison? And the most remarkable thing, which only my indulgent reader will be able to appreciate, is this: Often distrusting me completely, they nevertheless sincerely go into raptures over me, bowing before me, clasping my hands and mumbling at every step, "Master! Master!"

If they only profited by their constant lying—but, no; they are perfectly disinterested, and they lie as though by some one's higher order; they lie in the fanatical conviction that falsehood is in no way different from the truth.

Wretched actors, even incapable of a decent makeup, they writhe from morning till night on the boards of the stage, and, dying the most real death, suffering the most real sufferings, they bring into their deathly convulsions the cheap art of the harlequin. Even their crooks are not real; they only play the roles of crooks, while remaining honest people; and the role of honest people is played by rogues, and played poorly, and the public sees it, but in the name of the same fatal falsehood it gives them wreaths and bouquets.

And if there is really a talented actor who can wipe away the boundary between truth and deception, so that even they begin to believe, they go into raptures, call him great, start a subscription for a monument, but do not give any money. Desperate cowards, they fear themselves most of all, and admiring delightedly the reflection of their spuriously made-up faces in the mirror, they howl with fear and rage when someone incautiously holds up the mirror to their soul.

My indulgent reader should accept all this relatively, not forgetting that certain grumblings are natural in old age. Of course, I have met quite a number of most worthy people, absolutely truthful, sincere, and courageous; I am proud to admit that I found among them also a proper estimate of my personality. With the support of these friends of mine I hope to complete successfully my struggle for truth and justice. I am sufficiently strong for my sixty years, and, it seems, there is no power that could break my iron will.

At times I am seized with fatigue owing to their absurd mode of life. I have not the proper rest even at night.

The consciousness that while going to bed I may absent-mindedly have forgotten to lock my bedroom door compels me to jump from my bed dozens of times and to feel the lock with a quiver of horror.

Not long ago it happened that I locked my door and hid the key under my pillow, perfectly confident that my room was locked, when suddenly I heard a knock, then the door opened, and my servant entered with a smile on his face. You, dear reader, will easily understand the horror I experienced at this unexpected visit—it seemed to me that someone had entered my soul. And though I have absolutely nothing to conceal, this breaking into my room seems to me indecent, to say the least.

I caught a cold a few days ago—there is a terrible draught in their windows—and I asked my servant to watch me at night. In the morning I asked him, in jest:

"Well, did I talk much in my sleep?"

"No, you didn't talk at all."

"I had a terrible dream, and I remember I even cried."

"No, you smiled all the time, and I thought—what fine dreams our Master must see!"

The dear youth must have been sincerely devoted to me, and I am deeply moved by such devotion during these painful days.

Tomorrow I shall sit down to prepare my lectures. It is high time!

CHAPTER 10

My God! What has happened to me? I do not know how I shall tell my reader about it. I was on the brink of the abyss, I almost perished. What cruel temptations fate is sending me! Fools, we smile, without suspecting anything, when some murderous hand is already lifted to attack us; we smile, and the very next instant we open our eyes wide with horror. I—I cried. I cried. Another moment and deceived, I would have hurled myself down, thinking that I was flying toward the sky.

It turned out that "the charming stranger" who wore a dark veil, and who came to me so mysteriously three times, was no one else than Mme. N., my former *fiancée*, my love, my dream and my suffering.

But order! order! May my indulgent reader forgive the involuntary incoherence of the preceding lines, but I am sixty years old, and my strength is beginning to fail me, and I am alone. My unknown reader, be my friend at this moment, for I am not of iron, and my strength is beginning to fail me. Listen, my friend; I shall endeavour to tell you exactly and in detail, as objectively as my cold and clear mind will be able to do it, all that has happened. You must understand that which my tongue may omit.

I was sitting, engaged upon the preparation of my lecture, seriously carried away by the absorbing work, when my servant announced that the strange lady in the black veil was there again, and that she wished to see me. I confess I was irritated, that I was ready to decline to see her, but my curiosity, coupled with my desire not to offend her, led me to receive the unexpected guest. Assuming the expression of majestic nobleness with which I usually greet my visitors, and softening that expression somewhat by a smile in view of the romantic character of the affair, I ordered my servant to open the door.

"Please be seated, my dear guest," I said politely to the stranger, who stood as dazed before me, still keeping the veil on her face.

She sat down.

"Although I respect all secrecy," I continued jestingly, "I would nevertheless ask you to remove this gloomy cover which disfigures you. Does the human face need a mask?"

The strange visitor declined, in a state of agitation.

"Very well, I'll take it off, but not now—later. First, I want to see you well."

The pleasant voice of the stranger did not call forth any recollections in me. Deeply interested and even flattered, I submitted to my strange visitor all the treasures of my mind, experience and talent. With enthusiasm I related to her the edifying story of my life, constantly illuminating every detail with a ray of the Great Purpose. (In this I availed myself partly of the material on which I had just been working, preparing my lectures.) The passionate attention with which the strange lady listened to my words, the frequent, deep sighs, the nervous quiver of her thin fingers in her black gloves, her agitated exclamations—inspired me.

Carried away by my own narrative, I confess, I did not pay proper attention to the queer behaviour of my strange visitor. Having lost all restraint, she now clasped my hands, now pushed them away, she cried and availing herself of each pause in my speech, she implored:

"Don't, don't, don't! Stop speaking! I can't listen to it!"

And at the moment when I least expected it she tore the veil from her face, and before my eyes—before my eyes appeared her face, the face of my love, of my dream, of my boundless and bitter sorrow. Perhaps because I lived all my life dreaming of her alone, with her alone I was young, with her I had developed and grown old, with her I was advancing to the grave—her face seemed to me neither old nor faded—it was exactly as I had pictured it in my dreams—it seemed endlessly dear to me.

What has happened to me? For the first time in tens of years I forgot that I had a face—for the first time in tens of years I looked helplessly, like a youngster, like a criminal caught red-handed, waiting for some deadly blow.

"You see! You see! It is I. It is I! My God, why are you silent? Don't you recognise me?"

Did I recognise her? It were better not to have known that face at all! It were better for me to have grown blind rather than to see her again!

"Why are you silent? How terrible you are! You have forgotten me!"

"Madam—"

Of course, I should have continued in this manner; I saw how she staggered. I saw how with trembling fingers, almost falling, she was looking for her veil; I saw that another word of courageous truth, and the terrible vision would vanish never to appear again. But some stranger within me—not I—not I—uttered the following absurd, ridiculous phrase, in which, despite its chilliness, rang so much jealousy and hopeless sorrow:

"Madam, you have deceived me. I don't know you. Perhaps you entered the wrong door. I suppose your husband and your children are waiting for you. Please, my servant will take you down to the carriage."

Could I think that these words, uttered in the same stern and cold voice, would have such a strange effect upon the woman's heart? With a cry, all the bitter passion of which I could not describe, she threw herself before me on her knees, exclaiming:

"So, you do love me!"

Forgetting that our life had already been lived, that we were old, that all had been ruined and scattered like dust by Time, and that it can never return again; forgetting that I was grey, that my shoulders were bent, that the voice of passion sounds strangely when it comes from old lips—I burst into impetuous reproaches and complaints.

"Yes, I did deceive you!" her deathly pale lips uttered. "I knew that you were innocent—"

"Be silent. Be silent."

"Everybody laughed at me—even your friends, your mother whom I despised for it—all betrayed you. Only I kept repeating: 'He is innocent!'"

Oh, if this woman knew what she was doing to me with her words! If the trumpet of the angel, announcing the day of judgment, had resounded at my very ear, I would not have been so frightened as now. What is the blaring of a trumpet calling to battle and struggle to the ear of the brave? It was as if an abyss had opened at my feet. It was as if an abyss had opened before me, and as though blinded by lightning, as though dazed by a blow, I shouted in an outburst of wild and strange ecstasy:

"Be silent! I—"

If that woman were sent by God, she would have become silent. If she were sent by the devil, she would have become silent even then. But there was neither God nor devil in her, and interrupting me, not permitting me to finish the phrase, she went on:

"No, I will not be silent. I must tell you all. I have waited for you so many years. Listen, listen!"

But suddenly she saw my face and she retreated, seized with horror.

"What is it? What is the matter with you? Why do you laugh? I am afraid of your laughter! Stop laughing! Don't! Don't!"

But I was not laughing at all, I only smiled softly. And then I said very seriously, without smiling:

"I am smiling because I am glad to see you. Tell me about yourself."

And, as in a dream, I saw her face and I heard her soft terrible whisper:

"You know that I love you. You know that all my life I loved you alone. I lived with another and was faithful to him. I have children, but you know they are all strangers to me—he and the children and I myself. Yes, I deceived you, I am a criminal, but I do not know how it happened. He was so kind to me, he made me believe that he was convinced of your innocence—later I learned that he did not tell the truth, and with this, just think of it, with this he won me."

"You lie!"

"I swear to you. For a whole year he followed me and spoke only of you. One day he even cried when I told him about you, about your sufferings, about your love."

"But he was lying!"

"Of course, he was lying. But at that time, he seemed so dear to me, so kind that I kissed him on the forehead. Then we used to bring you flowers to the prison. One day as we were returning from you—listen—he suddenly proposed that we should go out driving. The evening was so beautiful—"

"And you went! How did you dare go out with him? You had just seen my prison, you had just been near me, and yet you dared go with him. How base!"

"Be silent. Be silent. I know I am a criminal. But I was so exhaust-ed, so tired, and you were so far away. Understand me."

She began to cry, wringing her hands.

"Understand me. I was so exhausted. And he—he saw how I felt—and yet he dared kiss me."

"He kissed you! And you allowed him? On the lips?"

"No, no! Only on the cheek."

"You lie!"

"No, no. I swear to you."

I began to laugh.

"You responded? And you were driving in the forest—you, my *fiancée*, my love, my dream! And all this for my sake? Tell me! Speak!"

In my rage I wrung her arms, and wriggling like a snake, vainly trying to evade my look, she whispered:

"Forgive me; forgive me."

"How many children have you?"

"Forgive me."

But my reason forsook me, and in my growing rage I cried, stamp-ing my foot:

"How many children have you? Speak, or I will kill you!"

I actually said this. Evidently, I was losing my reason completely if I could threaten to kill a helpless woman. And she, surmising apparently that my threats were mere words, answered with feigned readiness:

"Kill me! You have a right to do it! I am a criminal. I deceived you. You are a martyr, a saint! When you told me—is it true that even in your thoughts you never deceived me—even in your thoughts!"

And again, an abyss opened before me. Everything trembled, eve-rything fell, everything became an absurd dream, and in the last effort to save my extinguishing reason I shouted:

"But you are happy! You cannot be unhappy; you have no right to be unhappy! Otherwise, I shall lose my mind."

But she did not understand. With a bitter laugh, with a senseless smile, in which her suffering mingled with bright, heavenly joy, she said:

"I am happy! I—happy! Oh, my friend, only near you I can find happiness. From the moment you left the prison I began to despise my home. I am alone there; I am a stranger to all. If you only knew how I hate that scoundrel! You are sensible; you must have felt that you were not alone in prison, that I was always with you there—"

56

"And he?"

"Be silent! Be silent! If you only heard with what delight I called him scoundrel!"

She burst into laughter, frightening me by the wild expression on her face.

"Just think of it! All his life he embraced only a lie. And when, deceived, happy, he fell asleep, I looked at him with wide-open eyes, I gnashed my teeth softly, and I felt like pinching him, like sticking him with a pin."

She burst into laughter again. It seemed to me that she was driving wedges into my brain. Clasping my head, I cried:

"You lie! You lie to me!"

Indeed, it was easier for me to speak to the ghost than to the woman. What could I say to her? My mind was growing dim. And how could I repulse her when she, full of love and passion, kissed my hands, my eyes, my face? It was she, my love, my dream, my bitter sorrow!

"I love you! I love you!"

And I believed her—I believed her love. I believed everything. And once more I felt that my locks were black, and I saw myself young again. And I knelt before her and wept for a long time, and whispered to her about my sufferings, about the pain of solitude, about a heart cruelly broken, about offended, disfigured, mutilated thoughts. And, laughing and crying, she stroked my hair. Suddenly she noticed that it was grey, and she cried strangely:

"What is it? And life? I am an old woman already."

On leaving me she demanded that I escort her to the threshold, like a young man; and I did. Before going she said to me:

"I am coming back tomorrow. I know my children will deny me—my daughter is to marry soon. You and I will go away. Do you love me?"

"I do."

"We will go far, far away, my dear. You wanted to deliver some lectures. You should not do it. I don't like what you say about that iron grate. You are exhausted, you need a rest. Shall it be so?"

"Yes."

"Oh, I forgot my veil. Keep it, keep it as a remembrance of this day. My dear!"

In the vestibule, in the presence of the sleepy porter, she kissed me. There was the odour of some new perfume, unlike the perfume with which her letter was scented. And her coquettish laugh was like a sob as she disappeared behind the glass door.

That night I aroused my servant, ordered him to pack our things, and we went away. I shall not say where I am at present, but last night and tonight trees were rustling over my head and the rain was beating against my windows. Here the windows are small, and I feel much better. I wrote her a rather long letter, the contents of which I shall not reproduce. I shall never see her again.

But what am I to do? May the reader pardon these incoherent questions. They are so natural in a man in my condition. Besides, I caught an acute rheumatism while travelling, which is most painful and even dangerous for a man of my age, and which does not permit me to reason calmly. For some reason or another I think very often about my young friend K., who went to an untimely grave. How does he feel in his new prison?

Tomorrow morning, if my strength will permit me, I intend to pay a visit to the warden of our prison and to his esteemed wife. Our prison—

CHAPTER 11

I am profoundly happy to inform my dear reader that I have completely recovered my physical as well as my spiritual powers. A long rest out in the country, amid nature's soothing beauties; the contemplation of village life, which is so simple and bright; the absence of the noise of the city, where hundreds of wind-mills are stupidly flapping their long arms before your very nose, and finally the complete solitude, undisturbed by anything—all these have restored to my unbalanced view of the world all its former steadiness and its iron, irresistible firmness. I look upon my future calmly and confidently, and although it promises me nothing but a lonely grave and the last journey to an unknown distance, I am ready to meet death just as courageously as I lived my life, drawing strength from my solitude, from the consciousness of my innocence and my uprightness.

After long hesitations, which are not quite intelligible to me now, I finally resolved to establish for myself the system of our prison in all its rigidness. For that purpose, finding a small house in the outskirts of the city, which was to be leased for a long term of years, I hired it. Then with the kind assistance of the warden of our prison, (I cannot express my gratitude to him adequately enough in words,) I invited to the new place one of the most experienced jailers, who is still a young man, but already hardened in the strict principles of our prison.

Availing myself of his instruction, and also of the suggestions of the obliging warden, I have engaged workmen who transformed one of the rooms into a cell. The measurements as well as the form and all the details of my new, and, I hope, my last dwelling are strictly in accordance with my plan.

My cell is 8 by 4 yards, 4 yards high, the walls are painted grey at the bottom, the upper part of the walls and the ceiling are white, and near the ceiling there is a square window 1½ by 1½ yards, with a massive iron grate, which has already become rusty with age. In the door, locked with a heavy and strong lock, which issues a loud creak at each turn of the key, there is a small hole for observation, and below it a little window, through which the food is brought and received. The furnishing of the cell: a table, a chair, and a cot fastened to the wall; on the wall a crucifix, my portrait, and the rules concerning the conduct of the prisoners, in a black frame; and in the corner a closet filled with books.

This last, being a violation of the strict harmony of my dwelling, I was compelled to do by extreme and sad necessity; the jailer positively refused to be my librarian and to bring the books according to my order, and to engage a special librarian seemed to me to be an act of unnecessary eccentricity. Aside from this, in elaborating my plans, I met with strong opposition not only from the local population, which simply declared me to be insane, but even from the enlightened people. Even the warden endeavoured for some time to dissuade me, but finally he clasped my hand warmly, with an expression of sincere regret at not being in a position to offer me a place in our prison.

I cannot recall the first day of my confinement without a bitter smile. A mob of impertinent and ignorant idlers yelled from morning till night at my window, with their heads lifted high (my cell is situated in the second story), and they heaped upon me senseless abuse; there were even efforts—to the disgrace of my townspeople— to storm my dwelling, and one heavy stone almost crushed my head. Only the police, which arrived in time, succeeded in averting the catastrophe. When, in the evening, I went out for a walk, hundreds of fools, adults and children, followed me, shouting and whistling, heaping abuse upon me, and even hurling mud at me. Thus, like a persecuted prophet, I wended my way without fear amidst the maddened crowd, answering their blows and curses with proud silence.

What has stirred these fools? In what way have I offended their empty heads? When I lied to them, they kissed my hands; now, when

I have re-established the sacred truth of my life in all its strictness and purity, they burst into curses, they branded me with contempt, they hurled mud at me. They were disturbed because I dared to live alone, and because I did not ask them for a place in the "common cell for rogues." How difficult it is to be truthful in this world!

True, my perseverance and firmness finally defeated them. With the *naïveté* of savages, who honour all they do not understand, they commenced, in the second year, to bow to me, and they are making ever lower bows to me, because their amazement is growing ever greater, their fear of the inexplicable is growing ever deeper. And the fact that I never respond to their greetings fills them with delight, and the fact that I never smile in response to their flattering smiles, fills them with a firm assurance that they are guilty before me for some grave wrong, and that I know their guilt.

Having lost confidence in their own and other people's words, they revere my silence, even as people revere every silence and every mystery. If I were to start to speak suddenly, I would again become human to them and would disillusion them bitterly, no matter what I would say; in my silence I am to them like their eternally silent God. For these strange people would cease believing their God as soon as their God would commence to speak. Their women are already re-garding me as a saint. And the kneeling women and sick children that I often find at the threshold of my dwelling undoubtedly expect of me a trifle—to heal them, to perform a miracle. Well, another year or two will pass, and I shall commence to perform miracles as well as those of whom they speak with such enthusiasm.

Strange people, at times I feel sorry for them, and I begin to feel really angry at the devil who so skilfully mixed the cards in their game that only the cheat knows the truth, his little cheating truth about the marked queens and the marked kings. They bow too low, however, and this hinders me from developing a sense of mercy, otherwise—smile at my jest, indulgent reader—I would not restrain myself from the temptation of performing two or three small, but effective miracles.

I must go back to the description of my prison.

Having constructed my cell completely, I offered my jailer the fol-lowing alternative: He must observe with regard to me the rules of the prison regime in all its rigidness, and in that case, he would inherit all my fortune according to my will, or he would receive nothing if he failed to do his duty. It seemed that in putting the matter before him so clearly, I would meet with no difficulties. Yet at the very first instance, when I should have been incarcerated for violating some prison regulation, this *naïve* and timid man absolutely refused to do it; and only when I threatened to get another man immediately, a more conscientious jailer, was he compelled to perform his duty. Though he always locked the door punctually, he at first neglected his duty of watching me through the peephole; and when I tried to test his firmness by suggesting a change in some rule or other to the detriment of common sense he yielded willingly and quickly. One day, on trapping him in this way, I said to him:

"My friend, you are simply foolish. If you will not watch me and guard me properly, I shall run away to another prison, taking my legacy along with me. What will you do then?"

I am happy to inform you that at the present time all these misunderstandings have been removed, and if there is anything I can complain of it is rather excessive strictness than mildness. Now that my jailer has entered into the spirit of his position this honest man treats me with extreme sternness, not for the sake of the profit but for the sake of the principle. Thus, in the beginning of this week he incarcerated me for twenty-four hours for violating some rule, of which, it seemed to me, I was not guilty; and protesting against this seeming injustice I had the unpardonable weakness to say to him:

"In the end I will drive you away from here. You must not forget that you are my servant."

"Before you drive me away, I will incarcerate you," replied this worthy man.

"But how about the money?" I asked with astonishment. "Don't you know that you will be deprived of it?"

"Do I need your money? I would give up all my own money if I could stop being what I am. But what can I do if you violate the rule and I must punish you by incarcerating you?"

I am powerless to describe the joyous emotion which came over me at the thought that the consciousness of duty had at last entered his dark mind, and that now, even if in a moment of weakness, I wanted to leave my prison, my conscientious jailer would not permit me to do it. The spark of firmness which glittered in his round eyes showed me clearly that no matter where I might run away, he would find me and bring me back; and that the revolver which he often forgot to take before, and which he now cleans every day, would do its work in the event I decided to run away.

And for the first time in all these years I fell asleep on the stone floor of my dark cell with a happy smile, realising that my plan was crowned with complete success, passing from the realm of eccentricity to the domain of stern and austere reality. And the fear which I felt while falling asleep in the presence of my jailer, my fear of his resolute look, of his revolver; my timid desire to hear a word of praise from him, or to call forth perhaps a smile on his lips, re-echoed in my soul as the harmonious clanking of my eternal and last chains.

Thus, I pass my last years. As before, my health is sound and my free spirit is clear. Let some call me a fool and laugh at me; in their pitiful blindness let others regard me as a saint and expect me to perform miracles; an upright man to some people, to others—a liar and a deceiver—I myself know who I am, and I do not ask them to understand me. And if there are people who will accuse me of deception, of baseness, even of the lack of simple honour—for there are scoundrels who are convinced to this day that I committed murder—no one will dare accuse me of cowardice, no one will dare say that I could not perform my painful duty to the end. From the beginning till the end, I remained firm and unbribable; and though a bugbear, a fanatic, a dark horror to some people, I may awaken in others a heroic dream of the infinite power of man.

I have long discontinued to receive visitors, and with the death of the warden of our prison, my only true friend, whom I visited occasionally, my last tie with this world was broken. Only I and my ferocious jailer, who watches every movement of mine with mad suspicion, and the black grate which has caught in its iron embrace and muzzled the infinite—this is my life. Silently accepting the low bows, in my cold estrangement from the people I am passing my last road.

I am thinking of death ever more frequently, but even before death I do not bend my fearless look. Whether it brings me eternal rest or a new unknown and terrible struggle, I am humbly prepared to accept it.

Farewell, my dear reader! Like a vague phantom you appeared before my eyes and passed, leaving me alone before the face of life and death. Do not be angry because at times I deceived you and lied— you, too, would have lied perhaps in my place. Nevertheless, I loved you sincerely, and sincerely longed for your love; and the thought of your sympathy for me was quite a support to me in my moments and days of hardship. I am sending you my last farewell and my sincere advice. Forget about my existence, even as I shall henceforth forget about yours forever.

★★★★★★★★★★★★★★★★

A deserted field, overgrown with high grass, devoid of an echo, extends like a deep carpet to the very fence of our prison, whose majestic outlines subdue my imagination and my mind. When the dying sun illumines it with its last rays, and our prison, all in red, stands like a queen, like a martyr, with the dark wounds of its grated windows, and the sun rises silently and proudly over the plain—with sorrow, like a lover, I send my complaints and my sighs and my tender reproach and vows to her, to my love, to my dream, to my bitter and last sorrow. I wish I could forever remain near her, but here I look back—and black against the fiery frame of the sunset stands my jailer, stands and waits.

With a sigh I go back in silence, and he moves behind me noiselessly, about two steps away, watching every move of mine.

Our prison is beautiful at sunset.

A Dilemma

A.k.a. *The Thought*

A Story of Mental Perplexity
On the 11th of December of the year 1900 Anton Ignatyeff Kerz-
hentseff, a physician by profession, perpetrated a murder. The evidence
presented in connection with the act itself, as well as certain circum-
stances which preceded the crime, gave cause to suspect the abnormality
of Kerzhentseff's mental faculties.
Placed for purposes of investigation in the Elizavetinsk Psychiatric
Hospital, Kerzhentseff was subjected to a severe and attentive surveil-
lance of several capable alienists, the recently deceased Prof. Derzhem-
bitzky being among the number. Here are the documents furnished in
connection with the case by no less a personage than Dr. Kerzhentseff
himself a month after the test had begun; together with other data they
formed the groundwork of expert judgment.

1

Till the present moment, gentlemen experts, I have concealed the
truth; but now circumstances compel me to reveal it. Realising this,
you will comprehend that this business is not at all so simple a matter
as it would seem to the ignorant; not at all a matter of the straitjacket
or the handcuffs. The thing involved here is neither the one nor the
other, but is more terrible than the two combined.

My victim, Alexis Konstantinovich Saveloff, was my companion
in the gymnasia and in the university, though in our professions our
ways were apart. I, as you know, am a physician; while he completed
a course of jurisprudence. I cannot say that I did not love the man; he
was always sympathetic toward me, and I never had a more intimate
friend than he. Notwithstanding the possession of these sympathetic
traits, he did not belong to the class of men capable of commanding
my respect. The astonishing softness and yieldingness of his nature, his

strange uncertainty in the domain of thought and feeling, the capricious extremes of his views, and the unsoundness of his constantly changing judgments impelled me to regard him as a child or a woman.

Those near to him, suffering now and then from his caprices, and at the same time, owing to an illogical human nature, loving him, found a justification for his shortcomings and their own attitude, by calling him an "artist." Indeed, this worthless word seemed to justify him completely; and that which to the normal mind would appear as silly was made to seem indifferent or even good. Such is the power of words that even I at one time succumbed to the popular misconception and eagerly overlooked the petty shortcomings of Alexis. Of grand faults, as indeed of all big things, he was incapable. His literary productions amply attest this fact; they are full of things petty and empty, notwithstanding those short-sighted critics who delight to assail newly-revealed talents. Handsome and shallow were his productions, even as their author was handsome and shallow.

When Alexis died, he was thirty-one years old, about a year younger than myself.

Alexis was married. Gazing upon his wife now, in mourning for her husband, you can have but a faint idea of her former beauty. She has grown ugly. Her cheeks are colourless and the skin of her face is flabby, aged—aged like a worn glove. And she has wrinkles. They are wrinkles now, but another year will pass and these will become deep furrows and trenches. How she did love him! And her eyes have ceased to sparkle, and they laugh no longer; formerly they were wont to laugh always, even when they ought to have wept. I have had the opportunity to see her for about a minute, having met her by accident at the district attorney's office, and was astounded at the change. She was powerless even to cast an angry look upon me. What a pitiful figure!

Only three persons—Alexis, I and Tatiana Nikolayevna—knew that five years ago, two years before the marriage of Alexis, I had proposed to Tatiana Nikolayevna and had been rejected. Of course, it is a mere conjecture about the three; more likely Tatiana Nikolayevna has another half-score of friends who had been apprised in detail of Dr. Kerzhentseff's onetime desire to marry, and of his humiliating rejection. I do not know whether she remembers that she laughed then; probably she does not remember—she laughed so often. Remind her, if you will: *on the fifth of September she laughed*. If she should deny it—and she will deny it—recall to her the circumstances. I, that strong man who never had shed a tear, stood before her and trembled.

I trembled and saw how she bit her lips, and I already had stretched out my arms to embrace her, when she lifted her eyes, and there was laughter in them. My arms remained suspended in the air. She began to laugh and she laughed for a long time—as long as it pleased her. Later, however, she apologised.

"Please forgive me," she said, but her eyes laughed.

I also smiled, and though I could forgive her laughter, I never could condone my own smile. This was on the fifth of September, six o'clock in the evening, according to St. Petersburg time. I have added the last remark because we were at that moment in a railroad station; and I see now before me clearly the big white time schedule and the rows of figures running up and down.

Alexis Konstantinovich also had been killed precisely at six o'clock—a curious coincidence which might reveal much to the perspicacious person.

One of the reasons for placing me here has been the absence of motive responsible for the crime. Do you perceive now that a motive existed? Of course, it was not jealousy. The latter presupposes an ardent temperament and a weakness of mental faculties—that is something directly antagonistic to a cool, reasoning nature like mine. Revenge? Yes, sooner that—if it is necessary to employ an old word for defining a new and unfamiliar emotion. The case is this: Tatiana Nikolayevna once more had caused me to blunder, and it irritated me. Knowing Alexis well, I was convinced that Tatiana Nikolayevna, married to him, would be unhappy and would long for me; therefore, I insisted that Alexis, who was in love with her, should marry her. Only a month preceding his tragic death he remarked to me:

"It is to you that I owe my present happiness. Isn't that so, Tanya?"

She glanced at me and said: "That's true," while her eyes smiled. I also smiled. Presently we all laughed, as, embracing Tatiana Nikolayevna—they never felt abashed before me—he added:

"Yes, brother, you missed your stroke."

This misplaced and tactless joke shortened his life a whole week, as originally, I had intended to kill him on the eighteenth of December.

Their marriage turned out to be a happy one, and especially happy was she. His love toward Tatiana Nikolayevna was not intense; and in general, he was not capable of deep love. He had his favourite occupation—literature—which carried his interests beyond the bounds of the bedchamber. She, however, loved only him, and lived only in him. He was a victim to physical indispositions, such as frequent headaches and insomnia, and these, of course, caused him much suffering. And she considered it a happiness to look after the sick man and to gratify his capricious desires. When a woman loves she becomes altogether incomprehensible.

Day after day I saw her smiling face, her happy face, young, beautiful, without care. I thought: this is my doing. I wished to give her a dissolute husband and deprive her of my company, but instead I have given her a husband whom she loves, and at the same time she manages to keep me near her. Here is an explanation of this singularity: she was more clever than her husband, and loved to chat with me, and, having had her chat, she would go to sleep with him and be happy.

I cannot recall when the thought to kill Alexis first came to me. It appeared somehow imperceptibly; but from the first minute it became old, as if I had been born with it. I know that I wished to make Tatiana Nikolayevna unhappy, and that at first, I had thought of various schemes less fatal to Alexis. I have been always an enemy of unnecessary violence. Taking advantage of my influence over Alexis, I had thought of causing him to fall in love with another woman or of making a drunkard of him (he had an inclination toward this last), but none of these plans was practical.

The obstacle consisted in the fact that Tatiana Nikolayevna would have contrived to remain happy, even in the event of her husband's taking to another woman, or in spite of having to listen to his drunken chatter and being compelled to accept his drunken caresses. It was essential to her that this man should live, and in one way or another she would have served him. Such slavish natures exist. Slave-like, they cannot understand or value the strength of others than their master. The world has seen clever women, good women and talented women, but it has yet to see a just woman.

I candidly admit that this is not for the purpose of securing your unnecessary condescension, but rather to demonstrate the straightforward and normal manner in which was born my resolution, and that it was a no slight struggle with my compassion towards the man whom I had sentenced to death. I had pity for the terror he experienced just before he died, and for those moments of suffering he endured when his head was being crushed. I had pity—I don't know whether you'll comprehend—for the head itself. There is extraordinary beauty in a harmoniously working living organism, and death, like disease, like age, is first of all deformity. I remember how, many years ago, upon graduating from the university, I had gotten hold of a young and beautiful dog having extraordinarily strong limbs. It cost me much mental effort to take its skin, as my experiment demanded. For a long time afterward, I recalled the animal with regret.

If Alexis had not been so sickly and weak—who knows, perhaps I should not have killed him. To this day, however, I am sorry for his beautiful head. Tell this to Tatiana Nikolayevna, if you please. Beautiful, beautiful was that head. Its eyes were its only weakness. They were pale, without fire and energy.

I should not have killed Alexis had the critics really been justified in attributing to him the supreme literary gift. The roads of life are dark, and great is the need of masterly men as beacon-bearers. Each of them should be guarded as a rare jewel. It is these few who justify the existence of a thousand good-for-nothings and the commonplace. *Alexis, however, was not a genius.*

This is not the place for a critical article, but if you will read the more well-known productions of the deceased, you cannot but agree with me that they are unnecessary to life. They are necessary to a lot of satiated people in want of diversion, but not to life, nor to us, engaged upon solving life's problems. At a time when the author, employing the power of his thought and genius, should have created new life, Saveloff clung in his books to the old, not making an effort to solve life's hidden significance. His solitary story which appealed to me, encroaching as it did upon the domain of the unexplored, was a story called "*A Secret*"—that was the sole exception.

Worse still, Alexis was beginning to show evidence of having "written himself out," his happy existence having deprived him of his last teeth, which are so essential to the "biting into" life and to the gnawing of it. He frequently spoke to me of his doubts, and I saw that they were fundamental. I sounded him on his plans of his future labours exactly and minutely. His lamenting admirers may rest assured there was nothing new or grand in them. From among those near to Alexis only his wife failed to see the decline of his talent; nor would she ever have seen it. Do you know why? She did not always read her husband's productions. When I once made an attempt to open her eyes even slightly, she simply considered me a wretch. Seeing that we were alone, she said:

"You cannot forgive him something else."

"What is that?"

"That he is my husband and that I love him. If Alexis were not so attached to you. . . ."

She faltered, and I anticipatingly finished her thought.

"You'd drive me out?"

Her eyes flashed laughter. And, smiling innocently, she pronounced slowly:

"No. I would let you remain."

And I, understand, never, even by a single word or gesture, let her know that I continued to love her. I thought to myself: so much the better that she has guessed.

The thought of taking a man's life did not leave me. I knew that this was a crime severely punishable by the law; but then nearly all we do is considered as criminal; only the blind do not perceive this. Those believing in God consider a crime as committed before God; others consider a crime as before the people; such as I consider a crime as before myself. It would have been a great crime if, having decided it necessary to kill Alexis, I had failed to carry out this resolution. That people classify crimes as grand and petty, and call murder a grand crime, is nothing more than a conventional and pitiful lie before oneself—an attempt to conceal oneself from the answer behind one's own spine.

I did not fear myself—that was more important than all else. The most terrible thing to the murderer, the criminal, is not the police, nor the court, but he himself, his nerves, the potent protest of his entire body trained in the familiar traditions. You will recall Raskolnikoff, that pitifully and absurdly lost man, and the benightedness of his like. I had given much time and much thought to this question, imagining myself as I should be after the murder. I will not say that I became convinced fully of my tranquillity. Such a conviction could not find existence in a thinking man capable of considering all possibilities. However, having gathered carefully all facts of my past, taking into account the strength of my will, the vigour of my unexhausted nervous system, my deep and sincere contempt of the existing morals, I could maintain a relative confidence in the successful issue of the undertaking. It would not be amiss to relate here one interesting fact out of my life.

Upon one occasion, when I was yet a student of the fifth semester, having stolen fifteen *roubles* of students' money confided to my care, I asserted that the cashier had made a mistake in his accounts, and all believed me. It was more than a simple theft. It was not a case where the needy one stole from the rich man. Here was not solely a violated confidence; it was the deprivation of a hungry one, a comrade at that, and a student, and by a man with means—that is why they believed me. This action, no doubt, seems more contemptible to you than the murder of my chum. Isn't that so? I, on the contrary, recall that I felt jolly because I could do it so well and adroitly, and I looked into the eyes, directly into the eyes of those to whom I so boldly and freely lied. My eyes are dark, beautiful, frank—and they were believed. Above all, I was proud because I had felt no remorse. To this day I recall with particular gratification the menu of the unnecessarily festive dinner which I had ordered with the stolen money and had eaten with appetite.

Do I experience remorse even now—repentance of the act? Not a bit.

I feel sad. I feel intensely sad, as no other person in this world feels; and my hairs are turning grey; but that is something else. *Something else.* Something terrible, unanticipated, incredible in its fearful simplicity.

2

Here was my problem. It was necessary not only that I should kill Alexis, but that Tatiana Nikolavevna should know that I had slain her husband and that I should evade the punishment provided by the law. Aside from the fact that it might give Tatiana Nikolayevna another occasion for mirth, the idea of penal servitude did not at all appeal to me. I love life exceedingly.

I love to see the golden wine play in the thin glass; I love, when weary, to drag myself towards the clean bed; I love to breathe in the pure air of the springtime, to see the beautiful sunset, to read interesting and clever books. I love myself, the strength of my muscles, the strength of my thought, clear and exact. I am happy that I am alone, and that not a single curious look has penetrated the depth of my soul with its dark caves and abysses, at the edge of which the head grows dizzy. Never have I understood or known that which people call the weariness of life. Life is interesting, and I love it for the grand mystery imprisoned within it; I love it even for its rigors, for its ferocious vindictiveness and its satanically-gay play with people and events.

I was the sole person whom I respected. How then could I risk to send this person off to prison, where he would be deprived of all possibility to lead the so-essential to him, variegated, complete and deep existence? Even from your viewpoint I was right in desiring to escape prison. I am good at doctoring. Having means, I cured many poor people. I am useful—surely more useful than the murdered Saveloff.

It would not have been difficult to have escaped punishment. A thousand devices exist whereby to kill a man unnoticed, and I, in my physician's role, could have resorted easily to one of these. Among my thought out and discarded plans, which consumed a great deal of time, was this one: to inoculate Alexis with an incurable and loathsome disease. The objections to the plan are evident: the lingering sufferings of the victim himself, the something ugly about it all, its coarseness, and its somewhat too—well, it's not exactly clever; and finally, not even the illness of her husband would have deprived Tatiana of joy. One imperative demand of my problem was that Tatiana should know whose hand smote her husband. Only cowards shrink before obstacles; such as I they only draw on.

An accident, that great ally of able men, came to my help. And I wish to call your especial attention, gentlemen experts, to this detail: *Precisely an accident, i.e.,* something external, not depending upon me, served as the basis and motive for what followed. In a newspaper I stumbled upon an item concerning a cashier, or some clerk or other, (the clipping is probably at my home or in the district attorney's office), who simulated a fit of epilepsy and made a pretence of having lost money during the attack—actually, of course, having stolen it. The clerk proved a coward, and confessed, revealing even the place of the stolen money; but the idea itself was not stupid but could be realised.

To simulate insanity and kill Alexis in a moment of aberration, and then "to become cured"—this was the plan which, conceived in a moment, needed much time and labour to assume a more definite and concrete form. At that time, I was acquainted with psychiatry only superficially, like any physician not a specialist, and I spent about a year in consulting authorities and in reflection. In the end I became convinced that my plan was altogether feasible. First of all, the attention of the experts should be directed to hereditary influences—and my heritage, to my great joy, seemed altogether consistent. My father was a drunkard; one uncle, his brother, ended his life in the hospital for the insane, and finally, my only sister, Anna, now dead, suffered from epilepsy.

It is true, that on my mother's side all were healthy; still a single drop of the poison of madness is sufficient to affect several generations. In physical health I resembled my mother, but I was possessed of some harmless eccentricities which could be depended upon to do me service. My relative unsociableness; which is simply an indication of a healthy mind, preferring to spend its time in solitude, with self and books, rather than upon idle and empty chatter; could be mis-interpreted as an unhealthy misanthropy; my soberness of tempera-ment—non-seeking coarse, sensual pleasures—as a manifestation of degeneracy. My stubbornness itself in reaching a once resolved upon goal—plenty examples could be drawn upon in my rich life—would have received, in the language of the experts, the terrible name of monomania, the domination of fixed ideas.

The ground for simulation was, therefore, unusually favourable—the statics of madness were upon the face of things, it remained for dynamics to do the work. To the unintentional touches of nature, it would be necessary to add two or three successful brush strokes to make the picture of madness complete. And I delineated very clearly to myself how it should all be, not with programmic thoughts, but with live images: even though I do not write stupid stories, I am far from deficient in artistic sense and imagination.

I saw that I was in a position to enact my role. A tendency to dis-semble has been always in my character and was one of the forms whereby I strove to inner freedom. Yet in the gymnasia I simulated friendship: walked the corridor embracing someone, as do real friends, artfully making a frank, friendly utterance, and at the same time sound-ing the fellow. When the softened comrade revealed himself entirely, I cast aside from me his little soul and walked away with the proud consciousness of my own strength and inner freedom. This same dual-ity maintained at home among kin; as a home of the Starover Sect has special dishes for strangers, so I also had everything special for various people—a special smile, special conversations and candour. I observed that people commit against themselves much that is stupid, injurious and unnecessary, and it seemed to me that if I should begin to tell the truth about myself, I would become, as they, and all this stupidity and superficiality would dominate me.

It has pleased me always to be deferential towards those whom I despised and to kiss those whom I abhorred, which made me free and a lord over others. Hence, I never was conscious of a lie before myself—that more general and lowest form of human subjection. The more I lied to people the more unsparingly just I became before my-self—a dignity at which few have arrived.

Generally speaking, I think that within me was concealed an un-common actor, capable of enacting the naturalness of the play—reach-ing at times a complete merging with the character personified—with an indefatigable, cold control of mind. Even when reading a book I would enter entirely into the psychology of the represented character, and—would you believe it?—grown man that I am, I have wept bitter tears over *Uncle Tom's Cabin*. How wonderful this faculty of the supple, sharpened, cultured mind—that of reincarnation! You live through a thousand lives; now you descend into the darkness of Hades; now you ascend the clear mountain heights; with one glance you observe the infinite universe. If man is destined to become a God, his throne shall be a book. . . .

Yes. That is how it is. Incidentally, I wish to make a complaint about the rules here. They put me to bed when I wish to write, *when I must write*. The doors are permitted to remain open, and I am compelled to listen how some madman bawls. He bawls and he bawls: it is simply unendurable. Here you really can make a man go out of his mind, and then say that he was insane previously. And have they no extra candle that I must injure my eyes with electric light?

Well then. I once even thought of going on the stage, but cast aside the stupid idea: simulation, which everyone knows to be simulation, has little value. Likewise, the cheap laurels of the official actor on government pay attracted me but little. As to the quality of my art you can judge from the fact that many donkeys consider me even now the most sincere and veracious of men. And what is strange: I have been always successful in deceiving not so much the donkeys—I said that in haste—as especially clever people; on the other hand, there exist two classes of beings of a lower order, whose confidence I never could succeed in obtaining. I refer to women and dogs.

Do you know that the respectable Tatiana Nikolayevna never believed in my love, and does not yet believe in it, I think, even after I had killed her husband. According to her logic I did not love her, but killed Alexis because she loved him. And this nonsense, doubtless, seems to her sound and convincing. Yet she is a clever woman!

The role of a madman did not strike me as being very difficult of enactment. Some of the necessary directions I got from books; others I had to obtain—like any actor worthy of the name—through my own creative faculty; the rest had to be left to be recreated by the public itself, whose emotions had been developed through constant contact with books and the theatre, where, by means of two or three vague contours, it had been taught to recreate live types. There still remained certain gaps to be filled; there was the prospect of a stern and erudite investigation by experts to which I should be subjected, but I looked for no serious danger even here. The extensive realm of

74

psychopathology has been so little explored; there is yet so much that is dark and accidental, so much freedom for the imagination and subjectivity, that I boldly committed my fate into your hands, gentlemen experts. I trust I have not offended you. I do not wish to reflect upon your scholarly authority, and am confident that you will coincide with me, as men accustomed to conscientious scientific thought.

....At last, that fellow has ceased bawling. It is simply unendurable.

During the period that my plan still remained a project, a thought struck me, which hardly could have penetrated an insane mind. *This thought was concerning the danger of my experiment.* Do you comprehend? Madness is a fire dangerous for jesting. Having thrown a match into a powder magazine, one may feel greater safety than if but the slightest thought of madness should steal into one's head. And I knew this, I knew—yet did danger ever daunt a brave man?

Moreover, was I not conscious of my thought, firm and clear, as of hammered steel, and absolutely obedient to me? As a rapier of keen edge, it bent, pricked, bit, pierced through the web of facts; truly, as a serpent it glided noiselessly in unexplored and dark depths, concealed for ages from the light of day; I held its hilt in my hand; it was the iron hand of a deft and experienced fencer. How obedient, expeditious and rapid was my thought, and how I loved it, my slave, my terrible power, my sole treasure!

....He howls again, and I am unable to continue. How awful to hear a man howl. I have heard many terrible sounds, but none so terrible as this, none so awful. There is nothing it resembles—it is the voice of a wild animal, passing through a human throat. It is something ferocious and frightened; free and yet piteous to abjectness. The mouth twists to one side, the muscles of the face become rigid, like ropes, the teeth show, doglike, and from the dark opening of the mouth issues forth this disgusting, bellowing, whistling, laughing, wailing sound...

Yes. Yes. Such was my idea. Incidentally you will direct your attention, doubtless, to my handwriting, and I request you not to attach significance to the fact that at times it trembles and seems to change. It is a long time since I have written; certain recent occurrences and insomnia have weakened me—whence the hand trembles occasionally. *It is something which used to occur even before.*

3

Now you understand the significance of the terrible fit into which I had fallen one evening at the house of the Kurganoffs. That was my first experiment and successful beyond all expectation. It is as if they really knew beforehand what was going to happen—as if the sudden madness of a person in full health were altogether natural, and to be expected at any time. No one was astonished, and each tried to outdo the other in colouring my play with the play of his own fantasy. It is a rare gastriloquist who has such a fine *troupe* of *naïve*, stupid, credulous people. Did they tell you how pale I was and how terrible? How cold—yes, precisely cold—sweat covered my entire body? How my eyes gleamed with an insane flame? When they told me later their impressions, I seemed morose and depressed, but in truth I trembled from head to foot with pride, happiness and derision.

Tatiana Nikolayevna and her husband were not there that evening—I do not know whether you made note of that. It was not an accident; I feared to frighten her; or, still worse, to arouse her suspicion. If there existed a person who could see through my play, it was she and none other.

Nothing that occurred that evening was accidental. On the contrary, every detail, the most petty, was planned with care. I timed my fit to occur after supper; I chose that moment because there was sure to be a gathering, and those present would be affected somewhat by wine. I sat at the edge of the table, a little distance from the candelabra with the lighted candles, as I did not want to cause a fire or to burn my nose. At my side sat Pavel Petrovich Pospeloff, that fat pig whom for a long time I desired to play a trick. He is especially disgusting when eating. When I first saw him at this occupation, the thought came into my head that eating is an immoral business. Everything occurred opportunely. Apparently, no one noticed that the plate flying in fragments from the blow of my fist was covered with a napkin, so that I should not cut my hands.

The whole trick was astoundingly clumsy, even stupid, but I counted on that. They could not have comprehended a more subtle prank. I began by swinging my arms and talked "excitingly" with Pavel Petrovich, until that individual opened wide his eyes in amazement; I followed this by falling into "concentrated thought," which called forth the question from the solicitous Irene Pavlovna:

"What is the matter with you, Anton Ignatyevich? Why are you so sad?"

When they all turned their faces upon me, I smiled tragically.

"Are you ill?"

"Yes. Just a trifle. My head feels dizzy. But do not concern yourself, please. It will pass away shortly."

That reassured the hostess, but the suspicious Pavel Petrovich looked disapprovingly askance. And when, a moment later, smiling with gratification, he lifted a glass of wine to his lips, I quickly struck the glass from under his nose—then my fist descended on the plate with a crash. The fragments flew, Pavel Petrovich sprawled and grunted, the women shrieked, and I, showing my teeth, pulled the table cover containing all—it was an exceedingly humorous picture.

Then I was surrounded and held; someone brought water, another led me to an armchair; and I roared like a lion confined in a "Zoo," and glared with my eyes. It was all so absurd, and they all were so stupid that, believe me, the desire was born in me to smash a few of those jaws in earnest, taking advantage of the privileges of my condition. Naturally I restrained myself.

Gradually I grew calmer, while my breast heaved convulsively; and I rolled my eyes and gnashed my teeth and asked weakly such questions as:

"Where am I? What is the matter with me?"

Even that absurd French phrase "Where am I?" succeeded with this folk, and not less than three imbeciles made haste to say:

"At the Kurganoffs." Then in a sweetened voice: "Do you know, dear doctor, who is Irene Pavlovna Kurganoff?"

Seriously, they were too petty for big play!

After a day—having given sufficient time for reports to reach the Saveloffs—I talked with Tatiana Nikolayevna and Alexis. The latter dismissed the matter with a single question:

"What was that rumpus you raised at the Kurganoffs?"

Saying this, he turned on his heels and entered his working chamber—from which I gathered that if I had become actually mad, he wouldn't have choked himself on account of it. To make up for it, his spouse proved especially loquacious, fervid and, of course, insincere, in the expression of her sympathy. And then. . . . not that I regretted what I had begun, the question simply occurred to me: Is it worthwhile?

"Do you love your husband intensely?" I said to Tatiana Nikolayevna, whose gaze followed Alexis. She turned quickly.

"Yes. What of it?"

"Oh, nothing, only—" and after momentary silence, cautious and full of unuttered thoughts, I added: "Why have you no confidence in me?"

She quickly and directly looked into my eyes, without replying. During this minute I forgot that sometime in the past she laughed, and my mind was free from malice against her, and that which I was doing seemed to me unnecessary and strange. It was my weariness, natural after a severe ordeal of the nerves, and it lingered but a single moment.

"And may one trust you?" asked Tatiana Nikolayevna after a prolonged silence.

"Of course not!" I replied in jesting tone, while within me flared up an extinguished flame. A force, a courage, a determination stopping before no obstacle—these I felt in me. Proud of the success thus far achieved, I resolved to go boldly to the end. In combat is the joy of life.

The second fit occurred a month after the first. There was less premeditation upon this occasion, and this was really unnecessary in view of the general plan. Indeed, I had no especial intention to arrange the matter for this evening, but when circumstances are favourable it is foolish not to make use of them.

And I remember clearly how it all happened. We sat in the drawing-room, when I became very sad. With great mental vividness I realised—this was a rare occurrence—that I was a stranger to all these people and that I was alone in the world—I, forever confined within this head, within this prison. They all became disgusting to me. And in my rage I shot out my fist and shouted something coarse and saw with joy the fright in the paled countenances.

"Good-for-nothings!" cried I. "Miserable, contented good-for-nothings! Liars, hypocrites, vipers! I hate you!"

It is true that I wrestled with them, then with the lackeys and coachmen. I was conscious, however, that I wrestled, and knew that it was for a purpose. I felt pleasant in punishing them, telling them straight to their faces the truth about themselves, what sort they were. Is everyone who dares tell the truth mad? I assure you, gentlemen experts, that I was altogether conscious that, when striking, I felt the contact of my hand with a live body experiencing pain. Later at home, where I was alone, I laughed and thought what a wonderful, excellent actor I was. Then I went to bed and spent the night reading a book; I even can recall the author—it was Guy de Maupassant. I enjoyed him, as always, and afterward slept like an infant. Do madmen read books and enjoy them? Do they sleep like infants?

Madmen do not sleep. They suffer, and in their head everything revolves. Yes, revolves and falls. . . . And they desire to howl, to scratch themselves with their nails. They desire to go down on all fours and

crawl softly, softly, and then to spring up all at once and to shriek out:
"Aha!"

And to laugh. And to howl. To raise up one's head and to howl
long—long, protractedly—protractedly, piteously—piteously.

Yes. Yes.

And I slept like an infant. Do madmen sleep like infants?

4

Nurse Masha asked me last evening:

"Anton Ignatyevich! Do you never pray to God?"

She spoke seriously and she believed that I would answer sincerely
and seriously. And I replied, without a smile, as she wished:

"No, Masha, never. But if it will afford you pleasure, you may make
the sign of the cross over me."

Maintaining the same grave demeanour, she made the sign of the
cross over me thrice, and I was very glad that I afforded a minute of
joy to this excellent woman. Like all highly-bred and free people, you,
gentlemen experts, do not direct your attention to the servant; but to
us prisoners and "madmen" it is given to observe her closely and to
make astonishing discoveries occasionally. I may take it for granted
that it never has occurred to you that the nurse Masha, hired by you
to look after the insane, *is herself insane?* But such is the fact.

Observe her walk, noiseless, gliding, somewhat timid and aston-
ishingly guarded and graceful—it is as if she were walking between
invisible, drawn swords. Examine her face well, when she is not observing and is unaware of your presence. When Masha sees one of
you approach her face assumes a serious, grave aspect, and smiles indulgently—the very same expression which dominates your face at
the moment. The explanation is that Masha possesses the strange and
significant faculty of reflecting involuntarily in her face the expression
of other faces. Occasionally she will look at me and smile. It is a pale,
reflected smile—not her own.

And I surmise that I must have smiled when she looked at me. At
times Masha's countenance will express suffering, will seem morose,
her brows will contract at the nose, the corners of the mouth will descend; the entire face will age ten years and grow sombre—evidently
my own face is thus at times. Now and then I frighten her with my
gaze. You know how strange and somewhat awesome is the gaze of
every deeply thoughtful man. Seeing me thus the eyes of Masha will
open wide, the pupils will grow darker, and, approaching me noise-

lessly, with uplifted hand, she will do something friendly and unexpected—smooth my hair or arrange my dress.

"Your belt will become undone," she will say, while her face will maintain its frightened expression.

However, there are moments when I see her alone. And when she is alone her face strangely seems to lack all expression. It is pale, handsome and enigmatic, like the face of a corpse. Cry out: "Masha!" and she will turn, smiling with *her own* gentle and timorous smile, and ask:

"Is there anything I can bring you?. . . ."

She is always bringing or taking away something, and if there is nothing to bring, take away or arrange, she will show signs of worriment. Her noiselessness is remarkable. Not once have I noticed her drop anything, or make a noise. I have attempted to talk with her about life, and she is strangely indifferent to everything, even to murders, conflagrations and other horrors which affect uncultured people.

"Do you realise they are being killed, wounded, and they leave behind them at home little hungry children?" said I to her concerning war.

"Yes, I understand," she replied, and then, as if lost in thought, asked: "Had I not better bring you some milk; you have eaten so little today?"

When I laugh, she responds with a somewhat frightened laugh. Never has she been in a theatre, she does not know that Russia is an empire and that there are other empires; she cannot read, and her acquaintance with the New Testament is limited to the quotations she has heard read in the church. Every evening she goes down on her knees and prays at length.

For a long time, I considered her simply a limited, blunt being, born for bondage, but a single incident compelled me to change my view. You probably know, you must have been informed, that I have lived through one nasty minute here, which, of course, doesn't demonstrate anything except weariness and a temporary collapse of one's strength. *I refer to the towel incident.* Being stronger than Masha I could have killed her, as there was no one present but us two, and if she had cried out or caught my hand. . . .but she did nothing of the kind. She merely said:

"No need of that, *golubchik.*"[2]

I have thought often about this phrase and till now cannot grasp the astonishing power concentrated in it and felt by me. It is not in the words, which in themselves are meaningless and empty; rather is it somewhere in the unknown to me and unfathomable depths of Masha's soul. She knows something. Yes, she knows, but cannot or will not say. I have tried often to secure from Masha an explanation of her words, but she cannot explain.

"Do you think suicide a sin? That it is forbidden by God?" I asked.

"No."

"Then why no need of that?"

"Just so. Simply no need for it," she said smilingly, and inquired: "May I bring you something?"

Without a doubt she is insane, but quiet and useful, like many insane people. Please do not molest her.

I have permitted myself to depart from my narrative, as something Masha did yesterday has recalled to me memories of childhood. I do not remember my mother, but I had an aunt named Anphisa, who made the sign of the cross over me every night. She was a taciturn old maid, with pimples on her face, and she felt ashamed when my father joked with her about a husband. I was still a youngster aged eleven when she strangled herself in the tiny barn where we kept our coals. Later she continued to appear to father, and that jolly atheist ordered prayers and masses.

My father was very clever and talented, and his speeches in court made not only nervous women, but also serious and balanced people weep. Only I did not weep, listening to him, because I knew him and knew that he himself understood little of what he was saying. He possessed considerable knowledge, many ideas and even more words; and his words and ideas and knowledge frequently combined themselves successfully and beautifully; but of this he had no comprehension. *I often even doubted as to whether he existed*—to such an extent did he exist in sounds and gestures that it sometimes occurred to me that this was not a human being, but an image flashed by a cinematograph, combined with a gramophone. He did not comprehend that he was a human being, that today he lived and that tomorrow he might die, and he sought nothing. And when he went to bed he ceased to move and fell into a slumber; to all appearances he had no dreams and ceased to exist. With his tongue—he was an attorney—he earned his thirty thousand a year, and not once was he astonished or thoughtful over this circumstance. I recall having visited with him a newly-purchased estate, and pointing at the trees in the grounds I remarked:

"Clients?"

He smiled indulgently and replied:

"Yes, my boy, talent is a big thing."

He drank much, and his intoxication found expression in more rapid movements, which finally would cease altogether, and he would end invariably by falling into a deep slumber. Everyone considered him extraordinarily endowed, and he often asserted that had he not become a famous attorney he would have been equally distinguished as an artist or as an author. Unfortunately, this is true.

Least of all he understood me. Once we were threatened with the loss of all our property. The thought gave me anguish. Nowadays, when only wealth gives freedom, I do not know what I should have become if fate had placed me in the ranks of the proletariat. I cannot picture to myself without anger anyone daring to place his hand upon me, compelling me to do that which I do not wish, purchasing for money my labour, my blood, my nerves, my life. This horror, however, I experienced only for one minute, as it immediately dawned upon me that such as I never remain poor. But father did not understand that. He sincerely considered me a dull youth and viewed with apprehension my supposed helplessness.

"Oh, Anton, Anton, what will become of you?" he would say. He himself seemed weary; his long, unkempt hair descended over the forehead; his face was yellow. I replied:

"Don't worry about me, papa. As I am not talented, I will kill Rothschild or rob a bank."

My father became angry, as he accepted my answer as an untimely and flat jest. He saw my face, he heard my voice and nevertheless accepted it as a jest. Wretched pasteboard clown, through misapprehension thou art called a man!

He did not know my soul, although the outward order of my life perturbed him, as he did not enter into its understanding. I was an apt pupil at the gymnasia, and this distressed him. Once when we had visitors—lawyers, litterateurs and artists—he directed his finger at me and said:

"I have a son; he is the first in his class. What have I done that God should punish me so?"

And they all laughed at me, and I laughed at them all. Even more than by my successes he was distressed by my conduct and attire. He would enter my room purposely to rearrange, unnoticed by me, the books on the table, and to create even a little bit of disorder. My neat way of combing my hair robbed him of his appetite.

"The superintendent has ordered a close haircut," I would say seriously and respectfully.

He scolded vehemently, but my entire inner being throbbed with contemptuous laughter.

Nothing, however, aroused my father's ire so much as my copybooks. Once, when drunk, he looked through them, seeming very hopeless and comical in his despondency.

"Haven't you ever made a blot?" he asked.

"Yes, papa, it happened once. It was when I was doing my trigonometry."

"Did you lick it up?"

"What do you mean by 'lick it up?'"

"Just what I said—did you lick up the blot of ink?"

"No, papa, I applied blotting paper."

My father waved his hand with a drunken gesture and growled as he arose:

"No, you are no son of mine. . . .No! No!"

Among my despised copybooks, however, was one which afforded him gratification—notwithstanding the fact that it contained not a single crooked line, not a blot or erasure. It contained, however, approximately the following: *My father is a drunkard, a thief and a coward.*

This was followed by some details, which, out of respect to my father's memory and to the law, I consider unnecessary to state.

I now recall one forgotten fact, which I think should prove of interest to you, gentlemen experts. I am very happy to have recalled it, very happy. How could it have slipped my memory?

We had in our house a maidservant named Katia, who was the mistress of my father, and simultaneously my mistress. She loved father because he gave her money, and me because I was young, had beautiful dark eyes and did not give her money. The night that my father's corpse lay in the parlour I entered Katia's room. It was not far from the parlour, whence could be heard clearly the voice of the chanter.

I think that the immortal spirit of my father must have experienced complete gratification!

This is really an interesting fact, and I don't understand how I could have forgotten it. To you, gentlemen experts, it may seem a small matter, a childish prank, having no serious significance, but that isn't so. It was a hard struggle, gentlemen experts, and the victory was not bought cheaply. My life was at stake. Had I trembled, turned back, proved thyself a fainthearted lover, I should have killed myself. *I recall, that was decided.*

What I did was not an easy matter for a youth of my years. Now I know that I fought with a windmill, but at that time it appeared to me in a different light. It is difficult for me to relate now all that I had lived through, but I can recall the feeling—it seemed as if with one act I had demolished all laws, divine and human. And I trembled terribly, to the point of the ridiculous; nevertheless, I nerved myself, and when I entered Katia's room I was prepared for her kisses like a Romeo.

At that time, I was yet a romanticist. Happy time, how distant it is! I remember, gentlemen experts, that returning from Katia I stepped before the corpse, crossed my arms on my chest like Napoleon, and with laughable pride gazed upon the corpse. Then I shuddered, frightened at seeing the shroud stir. Happy, distant time!

I fear to think upon it, but it is possible that I never have ceased to be a romanticist. And I came near being an idealist. I believed in human thought and its boundless force. The entire history of man seemed to me as one triumphant thought, and that was not so long ago. It is terrible for me to reflect that my entire life has been an illusion, that all life long I have been a fool like that crazy actor once confined in the next ward. He had gathered from everywhere strips of blue and red paper, and he had designated each strip a million *roubles*; he had begged them from visitors; had stolen and carried them from the closet, to the amusement of the keepers, whom it gave an opportunity to indulge in vulgar jests. He sincerely and deeply detested them, but me he liked, and upon parting handed me a million.

"It's a trifle," said he, "only a million, but you will forgive me, I have such expenses, such expenses."

Taking me aside, he explained in a whisper:

"I am about to start to Italy. I want to banish the Pope and to introduce new moneys into the country—these. Then, on Sunday, I will declare myself a Saint. The Italians will rejoice; they are always happy when given a new Saint."

Have I not lived upon this million?

It is strange for me to reflect upon the fact that my books—my companions and friends—have remained in their cases and silently guard that which I considered the wisdom of the earth, its hope and happiness. I am aware, gentlemen experts, that whether or not I am insane, from your viewpoint I am a good-for-nothing and a scamp— you should see this good-for-nothing when he enters his library!

Go, gentlemen experts, examine my house—you will find it interesting. In the left-hand upper drawer of my writing-table you will discover a detailed catalogue of my books, pictures and trifles; there also you will find the keys to the cases. You are men of culture, and I am confident that you will conduct yourself toward my property with due respect and care. *I also request you to see that the lamp doesn't smoke.* There is nothing worse than this smoke; it gathers everywhere, and it then takes the hardest kind of labour to get rid of its effects.

★★★★★★★★★★★★★★★★★★

Remark.

The assistant doctor Petroff has refused me *chloralamide* in the dose which I demand. I am a physician and know what I am doing, and if it is refused me I will take decisive measures. I have not slept two nights, and do not in the least desire to become insane. I demand that *chloralamide* be given me. I demand it. It is *infamous* to make one insane.

5

After my second attack they were afraid of me. In many houses the doors were quickly closed at my approach. At accidental meetings acquaintances shrank from me, smiled meanly and inquired significantly:

"Well, *golubchik*, how is your health?"

The situation developed to such a degree that I could have committed the most unlawful act and would not have lost the respect of those present. I looked at people and thought: If I so wish it, I may kill this one and that one, and nothing will happen to me. That which I experienced at this thought was something new, pleasant and a bit terrifying. Man ceased to be something strongly defended, a something which we fear to touch; in a word, some sort of shell fell from him; he seemed naked, and to kill him seemed easy and even tempting.

Fear, like a dense wall, protected me from inquisitive eyes, so that the necessity for a third preliminary attack was avoided. Only in this instance did I depart from the formulated plan; for the strength of genius does not build itself a frame for its confinement, and, to conform with changing conditions, does not even hesitate to alter the entire course of battle. It yet remained for me to obtain official absolution from past sins and sanction for those of the future—I refer to the necessity of securing scientifico-medical testimony of my illness.

At this time a happy concurrence of circumstances made it possible for me to turn to a psychiatrist, without it seeming more than by merest chance, or by obligation. This, perhaps, was an unnecessary but artistic touch in the interpretation of my role. It was Tatiana Nikolayevna and her husband who sent me to the psychiatrist.

"Do, please, go to the doctor, dear Anton Ignatyevich," said Tatiana Nikolayevna. Never before did she call me "dear." Apparently, it was necessary to pass for mad to receive this meaningless caress.

"Very good, dear Tatiana Nikolayevna, I'll go," I replied submissively. We three—Alexis also being present—sat in the drawing-room, subsequently the scene of the murder.

"Yes, Anton, you must go without fail," reiterated Alexis in a tone of authority, "or else you might do some mischief."

"What sort of mischief could I do?" I timidly protested before my stern friend.

"Who knows? You may break someone's head."

I fondled in my hand a heavy, cast-iron paperweight. Looking now at that object, now at Alexis, I asked:

"Head? You say—head?"

"Yes, head. Catch a thing like that on your head and you're done for."

It was becoming interesting. *It was precisely the head, and precisely with that thing that I had planned to crush it, and now that same head was telling how it would all end.* It was telling and smiling, as without care. And yet there: are people who believe in presentiments, and that death sends before it invisible heralds. What nonsense!

"One can't do much with this thing," said I. "It is altogether too light."

"So, you think it's too light!" returned Alexis hotly, as he snatched the paperweight from my hand and flourished it by its thin handle several times in the air. "Just try it!"

"Yes, I know. . . ."

"No, take hold and see."

I smiled, as unwillingly I took the heavy object. Just then Tatiana Nikolayevna interfered. Pale, her teeth chattering, she said, or rather shrieked:

"Stop that, Alexis, stop that!"

"Why, Tanya? What is the matter with you?" said he in an astonished tone.

"Stop that! You know I don't like such jokes."

We laughed, and the paperweight was replaced on the table.

On my visit to Professor T— everything happened as I had anticipated. He was cautious, controlled in his utterances and grave; he inquired whether I had any relatives in whose care I could trust myself; he counselled me to go home, take a rest and live quietly. Assuming the privilege due me as a member of the medical profession, I made a slight attempt at remonstrance. My boldness removed whatever doubts may have remained in the physician's mind, and he definitely placed me in the ranks of the demented. I trust, gentlemen experts, you will not attribute undue significance to this harmless jest aimed against one of our colleagues. As a scholar, Professor T— undoubtedly deserves respect and honour.

The few days which followed were among the happiest of my life. Sympathy was extended me in my role of invalid, visits were paid me, and everyone addressed me in a broken, clumsy tongue. Only I knew that I was perfectly healthy, and I enjoyed to the full the well-planned, mighty labour of my mind. In a consideration of all that is wonderful and incomprehensible of life's riches, nothing can be found to equal the human mind. There is divinity in it, a pledge of immorality and an indomitable force acknowledging no obstacles. People are overcome with ecstasy and wonderment when they behold the snowy summits of huge mountains. If they only would understand themselves, neither mountains, nor all the wonders and beauties of the earth, could transport them to such a degree as the consciousness of the power of thought. The simple mental process of the labourer as he expediently lays one brick upon the other—that is the supreme marvel and the deepest mystery.

I enjoyed my thought. Innocent in her beauty, she gave herself up to me with passion as a mistress; served me like a slave; and upheld me like a friend. Don't take it for granted that all these days spent at home between the four walls were employed only in thinking about my project. No, that was all clear and prepared. I meditated upon many things. I and my thought played with life and death and soared high, high above them. Among other things I solved during those days two very interesting chess problems over which I had laboured for a long time without success. Probably you are aware of the fact that three years ago I participated in the international chess tourney and was second only to Lasker. Had I not been an avowed enemy of publicity and continued to contend, *Lasker would have been compelled to surrender his kingdom.*

From the moment that the life of Alexis was delivered in my hands I was strangely disposed towards him. It was pleasant for me to think that he lived, drank, ate and rejoiced, simply because I permitted it. It was a feeling akin to that of a father toward a son. What alarmed me was his health. Notwithstanding his ill health, he was unpardonably careless, refusing to wear a waist-jacket and venturing outdoors without galoshes in the most threatening, raw weather. Tatiana Nikolayevna reassured me. She paid me a visit and told me that Alexis was in sound health and even slept well, which was unusual for him. Overjoyed, I requested Tatiana Nikolayevna to take with her a gift I had intended to make Alexis—a rare volume which accidentally fell into my hands and had struck for some time the literary man's fancy. Possibly the gift was a mistake from the standpoint of my plan. My action could be suspected as a premeditated manoeuvre; but I wished so much to afford Alexis pleasure that I decided to run a small risk. I even ignored the circumstance that the gift sacrificed something of the artistic effect of my play.

Upon this occasion I was very amiable and frank, and made a favourable impression on Tatiana Nikolayevna. Neither she nor Alexis had witnessed a single one of my attacks, and hence it was difficult, even impossible, for them to imagine me as mad.

"Come and see us," said Tatiana Nikolayevna at parting.

"Musn't do it," said I smilingly. "Doctor forbade."

"Oh, fiddlesticks! That doesn't mean us. In our house you are at home. And Alexis misses you."

I promised, and *never did I make a promise with such assurance of fulfilment as this one.* When reflecting upon these happy coincidences, does it not strike you, gentlemen experts, that Alexis had been condemned not by me alone, but also *by someone else?* In truth, however, there was no one else. Nothing could be more simple or logical.

The cast-iron paperweight lay in its place, when on the eleventh of December, five o'clock in the afternoon, I entered the drawing-room of the Saveloffs. Both Alexis and Tatiana had been accustomed to rest the hour preceding dinner, which usually occurred at seven o'clock. They greeted me effusively.

"Thanks for the book, brother," said Alexis, grasping my hand. "I was about to visit you, when Tanya told me that you were quite well again. We are going to the theatre this evening. Will you join us?"

A conversation began. I decided not to dissemble at all that evening—it was an occasion when the absence of dissembling was the subtlest kind of dissembling—and giving myself up to the mental exhilaration of the moment, I spoke at length and well. If the admirers of Saveloff's glories only knew how many of "his" best ideas had their inception and development in the brain of one unknown Doctor Kerzhentseff!

I spoke clearly, precisely, emphasizing each phrase, at the same time keeping my eye on the hand of the clock, thinking that when it should point at six, I would become a murderer. I said something funny and they laughed, and I made an effort to retain an impression of the sensation of one who was about to become a murderer. I understood the life process in Alexis not in the abstract, but rather in the physical sense—the beating of his heart, the coursing of the blood through the veins, the suppressed vibrations of the brain, and then—the interruption of this process, the cessation of the heart and the blood flow, and the death of the brain.

What would be its last thought?

Never did the clearness of my consciousness reach such height and power. Never was the sensation of the many-sided, harmoniously-working and *I* so complete. Truly a god: not seeing, I saw; not listening, I heard; not thinking, I understood.

Seven minutes remained, when Alexis lazily arose from the divan, stretched himself and went out.

"I'll be right back," he called after him.

I did not want to look upon Tatiana Nikolayevna, so I made my way to the window, threw aside the draperies and stood still. Without looking, I was conscious that Tatiana Nikolayevna had glided quickly through the room and was standing beside me. I heard her breathing, and knew that she was not looking through the window, but upon me, and I was silent.

"How beautifully the snow sparkles!" said Tatiana Nikolayevna, but I remained unresponsive. Her breath came quicker, then seemed to cease.

"Anton Ignatyevich!" said she, and stopped short.

I remained silent.

"Anton Ignatyevich!" she repeated in the same irresolute tone, and now I looked at her. Suddenly she tottered back, almost fell, as if she had been thrust back by the terrible force that was in my glance. She tottered and threw herself towards her husband, who had entered the room.

"Alexis!" she mumbled. "Alexis. . . .He. . . ."

"Well, what about him?"

Without smiling, but in a jesting tone, I said:

"She thinks that I want to kill you with that thing."

Then, in an unperturbed manner, without attempt at concealment, I picked up the paperweight, and, raising it in my hand, calmly approached Alexis. He, without blinking, gazed upon me with his pale eyes and repeated:

"She thinks. . . ."

"Yes, she thinks."

Slowly, easily, I began to raise my hand, and Alexis also slowly began to raise his, without removing his eyes from me.

"Hold a moment!" said I sternly.

The hand of Alexis remained where it was, while he, pale, still keeping his eyes upon me, smiled incredulously with his lips alone. Tatiana Nikolayevna uttered a strange cry, but it was too late. I struck him with the sharp edge nearer the temple than the eye. And when he fell, I bent over and struck him two times more. The district attorney declared that I had struck him several times, because his head was badly crushed. But that is untrue. I struck him only *three times*: once when he was standing, and twice on the floor.

It is true that the blows were very hard, but there were *only three*. That I remember for certain—*three blows*.

6

Please do not attempt to make clear what is crossed out at the end of the fourth part, and in general do not attach undue significance to my markings or accept them as evidences of deranged thought. In the strange position in which I find myself, I admit I am forced to exercise the greatest care, as you may well understand.

The dusk of night always acts strongly upon an exhausted nervous system, and that is why we are visited so frequently at night by horrible thoughts. On that night, following the murder, my nerves were, of course, in a particularly tense state. Despite my self-control, it is no jest to kill a man. After tea, having made my toilet, manicured my nails and changed my dress, I called in Maria Vasilyevna to keep me company. She was my housekeeper and a substitute for a wife. I think she had a lover on the side, but she is a pretty woman, gentle and not greedy, and I easily reconciled myself with this slight fault, which is almost unavoidable when a man obtains love for money. This stupid woman was the first to strike me a blow.

"Kiss me!" said I.

She smiled stupidly and remained unmoved.

"Come, now!"

All of a sudden, she trembled, blushed and with frightened eyes drew herself appealingly toward me from across the table and said:

90

"Anton Ignatyevich, little soul, go to the doctor!"

"What next?" I exclaimed angrily.

"Oh, please, don't shout so, I'm afraid! I'm so afraid of you, little soul mine, little angel!"

Yet she knew nothing of my fits, nor of the murder, and I had been always kind with her and reasonable. It was to be inferred that there was something in my person that other people did not have—something that frightened. The thought flashed through my mind and was gone quickly, leaving a strange sensation of cold in the legs and spine. It dawned upon me that Maria Vasilyevna must have learned something from the servant-maid or had stumbled across some spoiled apparel discarded by me, and this altogether naturally explained her fright.

"Leave me!" I commanded.

Then I retired to the divan in my library. I had no desire to read; my entire body felt weary, and my condition in general was such as experienced by an actor after a brilliantly played role. It was pleasant to gaze upon the books and pleasant to think that sometime later I would read them. I was pleased with my entire apartment, with the divan and with Maria Vasilyevna. There flashed through my mind fragments of phrases from my role. Mentally I re-enacted certain motions which I had made, and occasionally critical thoughts glided languidly: In such and such a situation it could have been better said or done. However, I was much gratified with my improvised "Hold a moment!" This will seem flimsy to him who himself has not experienced such an incredible instance of the power of inspiration.

"Hold a moment!" I repeated, closing my eyes, and smiled. My eyelids began to grow heavy, and I wanted to sleep, when languidly, very simply, like the other thoughts, there entered into my head a new thought, dominating with all the qualities of my thought: clearness, preciseness and simplicity. Languidly it entered and remained. Here it is, speaking, as it were, in the third person:

"It is very possible that Dr. Kerzhentseff is really insane. He thought that he simulated, but he is really insane—insane at this very instant."

Three or four times this thought reappeared, but I still smiled, uncomprehending:

"He thought that he simulated, but he is really insane—insane at this very instant."

When I realised. . . . at first, I thought that Maria Vasilyevna had uttered this phrase, because it seemed as if there were a voice, and this voice appeared to be hers. Then I thought it was the voice of Alexis.

Yes, Alexis, who was dead. Then I understood that it was my thought, and this was terrifying. Clutching my hair, I found myself somehow standing in the middle of the room. I mumbled:

"So that's how it is. All is ended. That which I feared has happened. I approached too closely to the border line, and now there is only one thing before me—madness."

When they came to arrest me, I appeared, according to their words, in an awful state—dishevelled, in torn apparel, pale and terrible. But, Oh Lord! To live through such a night and not to go out of one's mind—does it not indicate the possession of an invincible brain? And, really, I only tore my attire and broke a mirror. *Apropos*, permit me to make a suggestion. If it ever falls to the lot of any of you to live through that which I had lived through this night, hang a mirror in the room where you will toss about. Hang it the same as you do when there is a corpse in the house. *Hang a mirror!*

It is terrible for me to write about it. I fear that which I must recall and tell. But I dare not delay it longer, and perhaps with half-words I may only heighten the terror.

That evening!

Imagine to yourselves a drunken snake, yes, yes, precisely a drunken snake: it has saved its venom; it has increased its agility and swiftness, and its teeth are sharp and poisonous. It is drunk, and it is in a closed room, where are many trembling people. With its cold body it savagely glides among them, coils around their legs, buries its fangs in the very face, in the lips, and coils itself into a ball and stings into its own body. And it seems that it is not alone, but a thousand snakes toss about and sting and devour themselves. Such was my thought, the same in which I believed, and in the sharpness and poison of whose teeth I saw my salvation and safeguard.

The single thought scattered in a thousand thoughts, each of which was strong and hostile. They circled in a wild dance, and their music was a monstrous voice, sounding as from a horn, and issuing from some invisible depth. *This was an evasive thought, the most terrible of all snakes, as it concealed itself in the darkness.* From within my head, where I held it strongly, it entered into the secret recesses of the body, into its dark and invisible depths. And from thence it cried out, like a stranger, like an escaping slave, insolent and bold, in the consciousness of his security:

You thought that you simulated, but you were insane. You are small, you are bad, you are stupid, you, Dr. Kerzhentseff. Some sort of a Dr. Kerzhent-

seff, insane Dr. Kerzhentseff!. . . Thus, it cried out and I did not know whence came that monstrous voice. I do not even know who uttered it; I call it a *thought*, but perhaps it was not a thought. The other thoughts, like birds hovering over flames, circled in the head, while this one cried from somewhere below, above, the sides, where I could not see it or catch it.

And the most terrible thing which I experienced was the consciousness that I did not know myself and never did. As long as my *I* found itself within my brilliantly lighted head, where all moved and lived in law-conforming order, I had understood and known myself, had reflected upon my character and plans, and was, as I had thought, a lord. Now, however, I saw that I was not a lord, but a slave, wretched and helpless. Imagine to yourself that you are living in a house containing many rooms, that you occupy one room and think that you dominate the entire house. And suddenly you discover that the other rooms are occupied. *Yes, occupied.* Occupied by some mysterious beings, perhaps people, perhaps something else, and the house belongs to them. You wish to learn who they are, but the door is locked, and no sound issues therefrom, no voice. At the same time, you are conscious that precisely there, behind the silent door, your fate is being decided.

I approach the mirror. . . . Hang a mirror. Hang one!

I do not remember what happened afterward, until the arrival of the court authorities and the police. I asked what hour it was, and was told it was nine o'clock. For a long time, I found it difficult to realise that only two hours had elapsed since my return home, and only three since the murder of Alexis.

I ask your forgiveness, gentlemen experts, for treating of a moment so important from your standpoint, of the terrible state following the murder, in such general and indefinite terms. That, however, is all I remember and all that I can express by means of the human tongue. It is impossible for me to express in human language the terror I experienced in that brief space of time. Aside from this, I cannot vouch for the actuality of that which so vaguely impressed itself upon my mind. Perhaps it was not that which happened, but something else. Only one thing I remember distinctly—it was a thought, or a voice, or perhaps something else:

"*Dr. Kerzhentseff thought that he simulated madness, but he is actually insane.*"

I have just felt my pulse: 180! And that at the mere recollection of it!

In the preceding pages I have written much that was unnecessary and absurd, and unfortunately you have received and read them. I fear that it will give you a false conception of my person, as well as of the actual condition of my mental faculties. However, I have faith in your knowledge and in your clear intellect, gentlemen experts.

You understand, of course, that only grave reasons could have induced me, Dr. Kerzhentseff, to reveal the entire truth concerning the murder of Saveloff. And you will easily understand and appreciate them when I tell you that I do not know even now whether I feigned madness to kill and go unpunished, or killed because I was actually mad; that, probably, I shall never know. The nightmare of that evening is gone, but it has left in its wake sparks of fire. I have no absurd fears but I feel the terror of a man who has lost all. I have the cold consciousness of the fall of perdition, deceit and insolubility.

You learned men will argue about me. Some of you will say that I am mad, others will demonstrate that I am normal, and will admit only certain limitations in the name of degeneracy. With all your learning, however, you cannot demonstrate my madness or my normality as clearly as I can. My mind has returned to me, as you shall be convinced. It lacks neither in power nor in keenness. Excellent, energetic thought, giving even its enemies their due!

I am mad. Shall I give you reasons?

First of all, I will be judged by hereditary influences, those same influences the discovery of which rejoiced me so exceedingly when I first conceived my plan. The fits I had in my childhood… Guilty, gentlemen. I wished to conceal from you this detail about the fits, and have written that from childhood on I have enjoyed perfect health. Not that these trifling, short-lived attacks alarmed me to any extent. Candidly, I did not wish to encumber my account with unimportant details. Now this detail becomes necessary to a strictly logical structure, and, as you see, I give it unhesitatingly.

Therefore, hereditary influences and the attacks testify to my susceptibility to psychic illness. It began, unknown to myself, considerably prior to my plan. Dominating, however, as *all madmen*, with an unconscious cunning and a faculty to conform insane acts to norms of sober reflection, I began to deceive, not others, as I had thought, but myself. Borne along by a strange power, I made it appear that I went of my own accord. One can finish the model from the remaining evidence as from wax. You will agree with me.

It is not worthwhile to show that I did not love Tatiana Nikolayev-na—that a true motive for the crime did not exist, but was invented. Whether in the strangeness of my plan, in the cold-bloodedness of its execution, or in the attention to the innumerable details, one may detect easily the same unreasoning will. The very cunning and development of my thought preceding the crime demonstrate my abnormality.

"Wounded, death awaiting, in the arena I played, The dying gladiator enacting. . . ."

Not a single detail out of my life did I leave unrevealed. I searched through my entire life. I gave the aspect of madness to all my steps, to all my words; and in each case I made the mood fit the word and the thought. It seems, and this is the most astonishing thing of all, that even until tonight I have entertained the thought: perhaps I am actually mad. Yet somehow or other I have avoided the thought and ignored it.

While demonstrating my madness do you know what I have perceived? That *I am not mad*—that is what I have perceived. I will explain.

The leading fact behind my hereditary impulses and my fits is degeneracy. I am of the degenerate, whose like can be found in large numbers if only sought for more diligently, even amongst you, gentlemen experts. This gives a substantial key to the rest. My moral views you may attribute not to conscious reflection but to degeneracy. Truly, moral instincts are lodged so deeply that only in some deviation from the normal type is complete freedom from them possible. As to science, it maintains a too bold attitude in its generalizations, relegating all such deviations to the domain of degeneracy, even where physically the man may boast of the perfections of an Apollo, or the health of the lowest idiot. So be it. I have nothing against degeneracy—it brings me among excellent company.

Nor will I defend my motive for the crime. I tell you altogether candidly that Tatiana Nikolayevna really had wounded me by her laughter, and the offence lodged very deeply, as it happens with hidden, solitary natures such as mine. Suppose this is untrue. Suppose even that I did not love her. Is it not possible to admit that by killing Alexis I simply had attempted to test my powers? Do you not freely admit the existence of men who, risking their lives, clamber inaccessible summits simply because they are inaccessible; and yet you do not call them mad? You dare not pronounce as mad Nansen, that mighty

95

man of the expiring century! Moral life also has its poles, and one of these I tried to reach.

You are confused by the absence of jealousy, vengeance, cupidity and similar really stupid motives, which you have become accustomed to consider as the only ones that are real and normal. Hence, you men of science judge Nansen together with those fools and ignoramuses who even consider his enterprise as madness.

My plan. . . .It was unusual, it was original, it was bold to audacity; but then was it not intelligent from the viewpoint set by my purpose? It was precisely my inclination to dissimulation, already explained reasonably and fully, that inspired the plan. Madness? Is then genius really insanity? Cold-bloodedness? But is it absolutely necessary that a murderer should tremble, grow pale and be agitated? Cowards always tremble, even when embracing their servant-maids. Is then bravery madness?

How simply my own doubts of my health explain themselves! Like a true artist I threw myself too deeply into my role, identified myself temporarily with the represented character and for a moment lost my aptitude for self-account. Will you say that even in the courts, there is none who, pleading among the lawyer-actors, struggling daily Othello, has felt the actual need to slay?

Sufficiently convincing, isn't it, most learned gentlemen? Do you not experience a strange consciousness of my seeming sanity when I try to prove my madness and the converse feeling of seeming madness—when I try to prove my normality?

Yes. That is because you do not believe me. . . .I, too, do not believe myself, as I do not know *whom* in me to believe. Shall it be in thought, dastardly and worthless—that unfaithful servant who waits upon all? It is good only with which to clean one's boots, and I made it my friend, my god. Off with you from the throne, wretched, impotent thought!

What am I then, gentlemen experts—insane or not?

Masha, charming woman, you know something that I do not know. Tell me, of whom shall I seek help?

I know your answer, Masha. *No, I don't mean that.* You are a good and gracious woman, Masha, but you know neither physics nor chemistry. Not once have you been to the theatre, and, busily bent upon your daily tasks, you do not so much as suspect that the object upon which you live twirls. It twirls, Masha, it twirls, and we twirl with it. You are a child, Masha, a dull-witted creature, almost a plant, and I envy you exceedingly, nearly as much as I contemn you.

No, Masha, not you shall answer me. It is untrue; you do not know anything. Within one of the dark chambers of your ingenuous domicile lives something very useful to you, but in my house this chamber is empty. That something which had lived there died long ago, and on its grave, I have erected a magnificent monument. *It died, Masha, died, without hope of resurrection.*

What am I then, gentlemen experts, insane or not? Pardon me if I, with such rude persistence, dog you with this question; but then you are "men of science," as my father called you when he wished to flatter you; you possess books and you dominate, with clear, precise and infallible human thought. It is likely that half of you will maintain one opinion, the other half of you will maintain another; but I will believe you, learned gentlemen, believe the one and the other. Tell me, then. . . . .and to assist your enlightened minds I will reveal an interesting little fact.

During one calm and peaceful evening passed between these white walls I observed that Masha's countenance, each time it met my eyes, expressed fear, confusion and a subjection to something irresistible and terrible. Presently she departed, and I sat on the made bed and continued to think about one thing and another. And I yearned to do strange things. I, Dr. Kerzhentseff wished to howl. Not shout, but howl, like that fellow. I wished to tear my clothes and to scratch myself with my nails. I wished to seize my shirt at the collar, and at the start go slowly, slowly, and then tear it asunder, with one quick jerk, to the very bottom. And I, Dr. Kerzhentseff, wished to go down on all fours and crawl. All around was calm, and the snow beat against the window, and somewhere not far off silently prayed Masha. And I reflected long upon what to do. If I should howl, I would be heard, and trouble would ensue. If I should tear my shirt, it would be noticed on the morrow. So very shrewdly I chose the third: I would crawl. No one could hear me, and if caught I would say that a button came off and I was looking for it.

As long as I tried to hit upon a choice the feeling was that of contentment; it was not at all terrible, it was even pleasant; so that I recall I dangled my foot. Presently I reflected:

"But why crawl? Am I really insane?"

All at once a terrible feeling came upon me, and simultaneously I wished to do all: crawl, howl, scratch. And I became angry.

"Do you wish to crawl?" asked I. But it was silent. The desire was gone.

"No, you do wish to crawl," insisted I. And it was silent.

"Well, crawl then!"

So, tucking up my sleeves, I went down on my fours and crawled. And when I had traversed about half of the room in this manner, the absurdity of it aroused my risibility, so I sat me down on the floor and laughed, laughed, laughed.

With my habitual and unextinguished faith in the possibilities of knowledge, I thought that I had discovered the source of my insane desires. Evidently the desire to crawl, as well as other desires, were the result of autosuggestion. The persistent thought that I was a madman had called forth the insane desires, and as soon as I had gratified them it seemed that such desires were absent and I was not insane. The argument, as you see, is very simple and logical. But. . . .

But then I did crawl? I did crawl? What am I—a madman justifying himself, or a normal man leading himself out of his mind?

So, help me, oh, erudite men! Let your authoritative word incline the scales to one side or the other and solve this terrible, ferocious dilemma. And so, I wait! . . . .

Vainly I wait. Oh, my dear dull-heads—are you not I? Does not the same dastardly human thought, ever lying, treacherous, illusory, labour within your bald heads as within mine? And wherein is mine inferior to yours? If you should venture to prove me insane, I shall prove to you that I am normal; if you should try to prove me normal, I shall prove to you that I am insane. You will say that it is forbidden to steal, kill and deceive because it is immoral and criminal, and I will demonstrate that one may kill and plunder and that it is very moral. And you will think and speak, and I will think and speak, and we all shall be right, and none of us shall be right. Where is the judge who can decide between us and find the truth?

You have one formidable advantage which confers upon you the possession of truth: you did not commit a crime, you are not under judgment, and you have been invited, with substantial fees, to investigate my psychic condition. Ergo, I am insane. On the other hand, if you had been placed in confinement here, Professor Derzhembitzky, and I had been invited to observe you, then you would have been the madman and I the privileged bird—an expert, a liar, who differs from other liars only in that he lies not otherwise than under oath.

It is true, you have killed no one, have not stolen for the sake of stealing; and when you hire a cabby you consider it obligatory to haggle him out of a small coin, which demonstrates your spiritual health. You are not insane. However, something might happen, altogether unexpectedly....

Suddenly on the morrow, now, this moment, after you had read these lines, there comes into your head a stupid, but unwary thought: Perhaps I am insane? What will be your position then, professor? What a stupid, absurd thought—what reason is there to go out of one's mind? But try if you will to banish it. You have drank milk and thought it pure until someone said that it was mixed with water. Then an end—no more pure milk.

You are insane. Have you no desire to crawl on all-fours? Of course, you have none. What normal man wants to crawl? Well, for all that?... are you not disturbed by the appearance of just a slight desire, altogether slight, altogether trifling, mirth-provoking, to glide off the chair, and to crawl a little, just a little? Of course, no such desire appears. Whence could it appear within a normal man, who only a moment ago drank tea and chatted with his wife? Yet, do you not experience a something unusual in your legs, though previously you had not experienced it, and a strange feeling in your knees: a heavy numbness wrestling with the desire to bend the knees, and then.... *And actually, Professor Derzhembitzky, is there anyone to restrain you if you wish to crawl a bit?*

No one.

But don't crawl yet for a little while, I need you still. My battle is not yet ended.

8

One of the manifestations of the paradoxicalness of my nature is that I exceedingly love children, altogether small children, just when they are beginning to lisp and resemble all tiny animals: pups, kittens and diminutive snakes. Even snakes can be attractive when young. One serene, sunny day in autumn, I witnessed the following little scene: A very small girl, in a wadded overcoat and a broad-brimmed bonnet, from under which were visible only her rosy cheeks and her little nose, wished to approach a very little, thin-limbed, slender-headed dog, standing tremblingly with its tail between its legs. And suddenly the tot became scared, turned on her heels, and, looking like a little white ball, scampered over to her nurse, in whose lap she hid her face, making no outcry and shedding no tears. As to the pup, it blinked affectionately and bent its tail as if frightened, while the face of the nurse seemed so good and simple.

"Do not fear," said the nurse, as she looked smilingly at me, and her face seemed so good and simple.

I do not know why, but I have recalled often the little maiden, while yet free, while planning the murder, and here. Gazing upon that lovely group, under the bright autumn sun, I experienced the strange feeling of one who possessed the solution to something, and my projected murder seemed to me like a cold lie from out of another, altogether different world. That both of them, the little girl and the little dog, were so small and lovely, and that they laughably feared each other, and that the sun shone so brightly—all was so simple and full of benign and deep wisdom, as if namely here, in this group, was located the key to existence. Such was the feeling I experienced. And I said to myself: "I shall have to think about this"—but I thought about it no more.

I do not remember now the meaning of the incident; painfully I try to grasp it, but cannot. Nor do I know why I have related this amusing and unnecessary tale, when I have so much that is more serious and important to tell. *It is urgent that I should finish.*

The dead we will permit to rest in peace. Alexis is dead; it is a long time since he began to decompose; he is no more—the devil with him! There is something pleasant in being dead.

Nor will we speak of Tatiana Nikolayevna. She is unhappy, and I eagerly join in the general sympathy; but what is her unhappiness and all the unhappiness of the earth compared with that which I, Dr. Ker-zhentseff, am living through now! Not a few wives in the world lose their beloved husbands, and more husbands remain to be lost! We will leave them—let them weep!

But here, within this head. . . .

You comprehend, gentlemen experts, the terrible happening. I loved no one on earth except myself, and if was not the vile body, loved by the vulgar, that I loved in myself—I loved my human thought, my freedom. I never have known anything surpassing my thought; I worshipped it—and did it not deserve it? Did it not, like a giant, wrestle with the entire world and its delusions? It lifted me upon the summit of a high mountain, and I saw how far below me swarmed little people with their animal passions, with their eternal dread of life and death, with their churches, liturgies and prayers.

How mighty I felt, how free, how happy! Like a medieval baron secluded in his impregnable castle, truly an eagle in his nest, proudly and imperiously surveying the valleys below—so I was, invincible and proud in my castle, behind these bones of the cranium. A lord over myself, I also was a lord over the world.

I have been betrayed—basely, insidiously; thus, women betray, and slaves—and thought. My castle became my prison. My enemies fell upon me in my castle—where's salvation? In the impregnability of the castle, in the thickness of its walls is my perdition. My voice cannot penetrate outside, and who is so strong as to save me? No one. For none is stronger than I—and I am the sole enemy of my "I."

Base thought has betrayed me who so intensely believed in thought and loved it. It has not lost in beauty; it is not a whit less bright, keen or elastic—it is still like a rapier, but its hilt is no longer in my hand. And it is slaying me, its creator, its lord, with the same stolid indifference with which I once employed it to slay others.

Night comes on and I am seized with unspeakable terror. I was strong and my feet stood firmly upon the earth, and now I am thrown into the emptiness of boundless space. Exceeding great and terrible is my solitude—behind me, before me and around me a yawning emptiness. It is the fearful loneliness of one who lives, feels and thinks, and is incomprehensibly alone; how small I seem, absurdly null, and so weak that I expect to be extinguished any moment. It is an ill-boding solitude; in myself I constitute but an infinitesimal part; within myself I am surrounded and suffocated by enemies, morosely silent and mysterious. Whither I go they go with me; I am solitary midst a vast emptiness, and cannot confide in myself. It is the solitude of madness, and I have no means of knowing who I am, because my lips, my mind, my voice, are all given to utter the thoughts of the unknown *they*.

One cannot live thus. Meanwhile the world slumbers and husbands kiss their wives and learned men read their lectures, and the beggar rejoices in the penny thrown his way. Oh, stupid world, happy in thy stupidity, terrible will be thy awakening!

Who amongst the strong shall come to my aid? None! None! Where shall I seek that eternal something to which I may cling with my piteous, powerless, awesomely solitary "I?" Nowhere! Nowhere! Oh, dear, dear little girl, why is it that towards thee I stretch my blood-stained hands? Art thou not human like myself, and equally insignificant and lonely and subject to death? Is it that I pity thee or that I invite thy pity; but I would, as behind a shield, hide me behind thy helpless little body, from the hopeless void of ages and space. But no, no, it is all a lie!

I will ask you, gentlemen experts, to confer upon me a great and important service, and if you are possessed even of a little humanity, you cannot refuse me. I trust we understand each other sufficiently not to believe each other. And if I should request you to say in court that I am in a normal state least of all, shall I believe you. You may decide for yourselves, but no one can decide for me the question:

Did I simulate madness in order to slay, or did I slay because I was mad?

But the judges will believe you and sentence me to that which I wish: hard labor. Please do not place a false construction upon my intentions. I do not repent of slaying Saveloff; I do not seek in punishment an expiation of sin; and if it is essential that in order to demonstrate my well-being, I should kill someone, presumably for plunder, I shall kill and plunder with pleasure. But in penal servitude I seek something else, I myself do not know what.

I am being drawn toward these people by a vague hope, that in their midst, among violators of your laws—murderers and thieves—I shall find unknown sources of life and once again be on terms of friendliness with myself.

Supposing that I am doomed to disappointment, that hope should deceive me—I still desire to be with them. Oh, I know you well! You are cowards and hypocrites; your peace of mind is your first concern, and you would gladly confine in the insane asylum every thief who has stolen a loaf of bread—in your overzealousness you would acknowledge yourself as madmen rather than disturb your pet theories. I know you well. The criminal and the crime—that is your perpetual anxiety; that is the terrible voice coming from an unknown abyss; that is the inexorable condemnation of your wise and moral life, and howsoever you wad your ears with cotton that voice penetrates—it penetrates! And I wish to go to them. I, Dr. Kerzhentseff wish to take a place in the ranks of this much-dreaded army—as an eternal reproach, as one who asks and awaits an answer.

I do not cringe before you, but I demand that you report me as in normal health. Lie, if you do not believe it. However, if you pusillanimously wash your learned hands and sentence me to the insane asylum, or open the doors to freedom, I forewarn you in a friendly way that I'll commit some considerable unpleasantries.

I acknowledge no judge, no law, no forbidden thing. All is permissible. Can you imagine a world, having no laws of gravitation, having no above nor below, in which everything is a matter of whim and chance?

I, Dr. Kerzhentseff, am that new world. All is permissible. And I, Dr. Kerzhentseff, shall prove that. I will simulate normality. I will attain freedom. I will spend the remainder of my life in learning. I will surround me with your books, I will take from you all the might of your knowledge, of which you are so proud, and will seek the one thing of which the world has stood in need for so long a time. *That will be the explosive essence.* The equal of its force has not been seen: it is more powerful than dynamite, than nitro-glycerine, more powerful than the very thought of it. I possess talent, I am persistent, I will find it. *And when I do find it, I shall scatter in the air your accursed earth, which has so many gods and not one eternal God.*

★★★★★★★★★★★★★★★★★

Upon his appearance in the court room. Dr. Kerzhentseff maintained a very calm demeanor, and remained during the entire proceedings in one and the same non-expressive attitude. He replied to questions indifferently and impassively, occasionally calling for their repetition. Once he aroused the mirth of the select public that crowded that court room in large numbers. It was when the presiding judge turned with some order to the usher, and the accused, evidently not having heard or because of abstraction, arose and asked loudly:

"What? You tell me to go?"

"Go where?" asked the astonished presiding official.

"I don't know. I thought you said something."

The crowd laughed, and the presiding judge explained to Kerzhentseff what was the matter.

Four expert psychiatrists were called to the stand, and their opinions were equally divided. After the speech of the district attorney, the presiding judge turned to the accused, who had refused to accept the services of an attorney.

"Accused, what have you to say in your justification?"

Dr. Kerzhentseff arose. He slowly surveyed the judges with his dull, unseeing-like eyes and glanced at the public. And those upon whom fell that heavy, unseeing gaze experienced a strange and painful sensation: it was as if out of the hollow orbs of a skull there had glanced upon them nothing less than death itself, mute and impassive.

"Nothing!" replied the accused.

Having cast another look upon the people gathered in judgment upon him, he repeated:

"Nothing!"

A Present

1

"So, you'll come, won't you?" Senista repeated this for the third time, and for the third time Sazonka answered hastily:

"Sure, I'll come, sure I'll come. Why shouldn't I? Sure, I'll come."

And again, they were silent. Senista was lying on his back, covered up to the chin with a grey hospital blanket, and was looking steadily at Sazonka. He did not want Sazonka to go away, wanted him to say again that he would come to see him, and not leave him a prey to loneliness, disease, and fear. Sazonka, on the other hand, was anxious to get away, but he did not know how to do it without giving offense to the boy. He would blow his nose every little while, slide off the chair, and then sit straight and firmly again, as though resolved to remain there for all time.

He would have stayed longer if there were anything to talk about. But there was no subject he could converse upon and the thoughts that came to his head were so foolish, that he felt ashamed of himself. He wanted all the time to call Senista by his full name, Semyon Erofeyevich, which, of course, would have been preposterous. Senista was only a boy, a mere apprentice, while he was a full master in his trade and a drunkard into the bargain. Everybody called him Sazonka merely through force of habit. Only two weeks ago, he had given Senista his last box on the ear, which, of course, was very bad of him; but he could not talk about that in the hospital.

Sazonka began to slide off his chair determinedly, but before getting off halfway he suddenly slid back again, and said half-reproachfully, half-sympathetically:

"So that's the way it goes. Hurts, don't it?"

Senista nodded and answered quietly:

"Well, I guess it's time for you to go. You'll get it, if you don't."

"That's so, too," answered Sazonka cheerfully, glad to have found a

105

good excuse. "As it is, he told me to get back as soon as I could. 'Take it over,' said he, 'and get back the same moment. And see that you don't touch whiskey on the way.' The devil!"

But, together with the realisation that he could leave any moment, Sazonka began to feel a great pity for the large-headed Senista. The whole environment predisposed him to pity. The room was filled with beds placed close to each other, on which lay pale, gloomy men. The air was spoiled to the last ounce with the nauseating odours of medicines and human perspiration. Everything reminded him of his own health and strength. No longer trying to avoid Senista's questioning glance, Sazonka bent over him and said:

"Don't be afraid Semyon... Senia, I mean. I'll come, all right. Soon as I have time, I'll come right over. Ain't I human? My Lord, I can understand something, too. D'you believe me?"

And Senista answered with a smile on his black, parched lips:

"Yes, I believe you."

"Now you see!" Now Sazonka felt light and comfortable. He could even talk of the box on the ear he had given Senista two weeks ago. He mentioned it casually, touching Senista's head.

"And if people hit you on the head, it wasn't because they meant you harm. Lord, no! Only because your head is so handy. It's so big, and the hair is all cut so low."

Senista smiled again and Sazonka got up from his chair. He was very tall, and his curly hair, combed with a fine comb, rose like a soft cap. His shining eyes with their swollen eyelids, smiled at the boy.

"Well, good-a-bye," said he, without moving away from his place, however. He purposely said "good-a-bye," instead of "goodbye," because he thought it would sound more sincere and heartfelt. But it did not seem enough. He felt that he ought to do something even more sincere, something good and big, after which Senista would not mind remaining at the hospital, and he, himself, could go away with a light heart. And he stood there in childish embarrassment, when Senista again helped him out:

"Goodbye," said he in a thin childish voice, for which he was nicknamed "flute," and freed his hand from under the blanket and quite simply, as though he were Sazonka's equal, extended it to the man. And Sazonka, feeling that this was precisely what he was looking for, gently clasped the thin fingers with his large hand, held them for a while, and then let them go. There was something sad and mysterious in the slight pressure of those fingers, as though Senista were not only an equal of all men on earth, but above them all, freer than all. And it seemed so because he now belonged to an unknown, though terrible and powerful master. Sazonka felt that he could call him Semyon Erofeyevich.

"So, you'll come, won't you?" For the fourth time Senista begged of him, and this plaintive appeal drove away that something awful and magnificent, which but a moment ago had enveloped the boy in its noiseless wings. Senista again became for Sazonka a poor, sick boy, and he was again full of pity for him.

When Sazonka walked away from the hospital, he thought that he was followed for some time by the odour of medicines and the piteous appeal:

"So, you'll come, won't you?"

And Sazonka answered his absent implorer,

"Sure, I'll come. Ain't I human?"

2

Easter was coming on, and there was so much work in the tailor's shop that Sazonka got a chance to get drunk only once, on a Sunday. He had to sit all day long near his window. He had a sort of platform, on which he sat Turkish fashion. The spring days were very light and very long, and Sazonka sat there sewing, gloomily whistling a melancholy tune. In the morning there was no sun in Sazonka's window, and streams of cool air forced their way through the loose woodwork. But towards midday a sharp yellow band appeared in the window, and in it particles of dust were dancing merrily. And half an hour later, the whole windowsill, with the scissors and the scraps of cloth scattered over it, was already burning with a blinding light, and it became so hot that the window had to be opened.

And together with a stream of fresh air, mixed with the odours of manure, drying mud, and opening buds, a weak, early fly flew into the room, followed by the confused noises of the street. Chickens were pecking the ground near the house wall, or cackling contentedly, lying in the round holes they had made for themselves in the soft ground. On the opposite side of the street, children were playing "knucklebones," and their loud, joyous voices, mixed with the sounds of small iron boards hitting the bones, rang with vigour and freshness. There was very little traffic in this street, situated on the outskirts of the city of Orel, and only occasionally a peasant cart would rattle by slowly, jumping from one deep rut still filled with mud, to another. The parts of the cart, loosely made, constantly struck against each other, producing dull sounds that reminded one of the coming summer and the vast expanses of fields.

When Sazonka's back bones would begin to ache, and his tired fingers would be able to hold the needle no longer, he would jump out into the street, barefooted as he was, make a couple of gigantic leaps over the pools of water, and join the playing children.

"Come on, let me try it," he would say, and a dozen dirty hands would extend the boards towards him, and a dozen eager voices would beg him:

"Do it for me, Sazonka! For me!"

Sazonka would choose a heavy board, roll up his sleeve and, assuming the posture of the athlete hurling the disk, he would begin measuring the distance with his eyes. Then the heavy board would leave his hand with a soft "swish," and, bounding up and down on the ground, would cut its way into the very centre of the long cone, scattering the bones all around. The feat would be applauded by the enthusiastic shouts of the children. After a couple of throws, Sazonka would sit down to rest and say to the children:

"And Senista is still in the hospital, boys."

But the children, busy with their own affairs, would take this piece of news coolly and indifferently.

"I ought to take him some present. Well, just wait, I'll do it."

The word "present" aroused the interest of several of the boys. Little Mishka, nicknamed the Suckling Pig, holding his breeches with one hand, and with the other his upturned shirt in which lay the sheep-bones, advised him:

"You give 'im a dime."

A dime was the sum that Mishka's grandfather had promised him for Easter, and the boy's conception of human happiness did not go beyond this. But there was no time for discussing the question of the present. A couple of gigantic leaps brought Sazonka back to the other side of the street, and to his work.

His eyelids were still swollen, but his face became pale-yellow and the freckles on his nose and around the eyes became even more numerous and darker than before. Only his carefully combed hair still had the appearance of a fine cap, and whenever his employer, Gabriel Ivanovich, looked at Sazonka's head, he was, for some reason or other, reminded of a small saloon and of whiskey—which recollection would cause him to spit, and curse furiously.

Sazonka's head was heavy. Sometimes the same thought would roll over in his mind for hours; and it would be either about his new boots, or his new harmonica. But he often thought of Senista and the present he was going to take over to him. The sewing machine was running monotonously, the proprietor cursed everybody, but Sazonka's tired brain could only conceive of the picture of how he would come to the hospital and give Senista a present, wrapped up in a red handkerchief. Sometimes a heavy drowsiness would come over him and then he would not be able to recall even Senista's face. He only saw clearly the red handkerchief, and it seemed to him all the time that the knots were not well tied. He told everybody that he would go to see Senista on the first day of Easter.

"Got to do it," he would repeat. "I'll comb my hair and run straight over. 'Here you are, kid, that's for you!'" But as he would be saying this, another scene would come before him. He would see the open doors of the saloon, with the counter wet with spilled whiskey, inside. A bitter realization of his own weakness, against which he could not struggle, would overwhelm him, and an irresistible desire would come over him to shout out:

"I'll go to Senista! To Senista!"

And his brain would again become heavy and irresponsive to everything, except the red handkerchief. But there was no joy in this one thought that persisted in his brain; rather a stern lesson, a terrible warning.

3

On the first day of Easter, Sazonka was drunk. On the second day, he was still more drunk, got into a fight, and had to spend the night in jail. It was only on the fourth day that he finally decided to visit Senista.

The sunlit street was bright with red shirts and the brilliant glitter of white teeth shelling the sunflower seeds. Harmonicas were heard here and there; iron boards struck piles of knuckle-bones, scattering them in all directions; a rooster was crowing bravely, challenging another rooster to combat. But Sazonka paid attention to none of these things. His face, with one eye blackened, and the lip cut, was gloomy and serious, and his hair was dishevelled, no longer having the appearance of a fine cap. He was ashamed of his debauch, ashamed because he had broken his word, because he could not go to see Senista in the holiday array he had planned—wearing a red woollen shirt and a vest—ashamed because he was going, dirty, unkempt, his breath reeking with liquor. But the nearer he came to the hospital, the calmer he grew. More and more his eyes sought the bundle containing the present which he was carrying carefully in his left hand. And Senista's face, with its appealing look and parched lips seemed to be constantly before him, as clear and as lifelike as though the boy himself were there.

"Ain't we human, kid? Oh, Lord!" Sazonka kept on saying to himself, as he hurried along. Now he is in front of the large yellow hospital-building, with its black-framed windows, which look like gloomy eyes. Now he is in the long corridor, in the midst of the medicine odours and an atmosphere of indistinct fear and unpleasantness. Now he is in the ward, right by Senista's bed. . . .

But where is Senista?

"Whom are you looking for," asked the nurse, following him into the ward.

"There was a boy here, Semyon. Semyon Erofeyev. Right in this place." And Sazonka pointed to the empty bed.

"You ought to ask first, and not break in like this," said the nurse rudely. "It wasn't Semyon Erofeyev, either, but Semyon Pustoshkin."

"Erofeyev, that's according to his father. His father's name was Erofey, so he is Erofeyich," explained Sazonka, slowly turning paler and paler.

"Oh, he's dead, your Erofeyich. And we don't care for his father's name. For us, he's Semyon Pustoshkin. He's dead, I say."

"Is that so?" There was reverent astonishment in Sazonka's voice, as he stood there, so pale that the freckles on his face appeared almost like ink stains. "When did he die?"

"Last night."

"And may I. . . ." Sazonka did not finish his stammered request.

"Why not?" answered the nurse indifferently. "Just ask where the morgue is, they'll show you. If I were you, I wouldn't be so upset about it. He was sickly anyhow; couldn't live long."

Sazonka's tongue inquired about his way, very politely. His legs bore him in the direction indicated, but his eyes saw nothing. Only when the face of the dead Senista was directly in front of him did his eyes begin to see. Then, too, he began to feel the coldness of the morgue. The walls of the dreary room were bespotted with moisture, the single window was covered with a thick layer of spiders' webs. No matter how brightly the sun shone outside, its rays never penetrated through this window, and the sky always appeared grey and gloomy, as in autumn. A fly was buzzing somewhere. Drops of water were falling from the ceiling. After each drop, the air would reverberate with a pitiful, ringing noise.

Sazonka stepped back and said aloud:

"Goodbye, Semyon Erofeyich."

Then he knelt down, touched the wet floor with his forehead, and rose up again.

"Forgive me, Semyon Erofeyich," said he, just as loudly and distinctly, and then knelt down again, and pressed his head against the floor.

The fly stopped buzzing, and everything was still, with that peculiar stillness which sets in when a dead man is in the room. At regular intervals drops of water fell into a metal basin, striking the bottom gently and softly.

4

The hospital stood on the outskirts of the city, and immediately beyond it began a large field. Sazonka went there. The level field, uninterrupted by a single tree or building, stretched in all directions, and the light breeze seemed to be its warm, even breath. Sazonka followed a dry road at first, but after a while he turned to the left and began to walk across the field itself, towards the river. In some places the ground was still wet and his boots left deep marks in it.

Reaching the river, Sazonka lay down on its bank in a spot where the air was warm and perfectly still, as in a greenhouse. He closed his eyes. The rays of the sun passed through his lowered eyelids in red waves. A lark was pouring forth its song in the blue sky, and it was so pleasant to lie there without a single thought in his head. The spring waters had already subsided, leaving the marks of their recent activity in the form of large pieces of ice, stranded on the opposite shore. The white triangular pieces of ice were steadily disappearing under the merciless, hot rays of the sun. Sazonka lay there half asleep, and, accidentally, threw out one arm. His hand came in contact with a hard object, covered with cloth.

The present!

Jumping up to a sitting position, Sazonka exclaimed:

"God! What is this?"

He had forgotten his bundle entirely and now looked at it with frightened eyes. It seemed to him that the bundle had come there by its own will, and he was afraid to touch it. Sazonka gazed at it, without lifting his eyes, and a stormy, rumbling pity, a furious wrath was rising in him. He looked at the bundle, and he seemed to see how on the first day, and the second, and the third, Senista was waiting for him, turning his head towards the door, expecting him in vain. And he died lonely, forsaken, like a puppy thrown out into the backyard. Only one day sooner, and the boy's closing eyes might have seen the present, and his childish heart might have been filled with joy, and his soul might have soared to Heaven without suffering the torment of loneliness.

Sazonka began to sob, tearing his fine hair, and rolling on the ground. He cried aloud, lifting his hands to Heaven in pitiful justification:

"O God! Ain't we human?"

And then he fell on the ground, his cut lip touching the earth. And there he remained, overwhelmed with dumb grief. The new grass tickled his face gently; a sweet, quieting odour came from the ground, and the earth seemed to exhale a feeling of mighty power, of a passionate appeal for life. The eternal mother earth was enfolding a sinning son in her embrace, and was filling his suffering heart with warmth, love, and hope.

And far away, in the city, the joyful holiday bells were ringing their discordant melody.

A Story Which Will Never Be Finished

Exhausted with the painful uncertainty of the day, I fell asleep, dressed, on my bed. Suddenly my wife aroused me. In her hand a candle was flickering, which appeared to me in the middle of the night as bright as the sun. And behind the candle her chin, too, was trembling, and enormous, unfamiliar dark eyes stared motionlessly.

"Do you know," she said, "do you know they are building barricades on our street?"

It was quiet. We looked straight into each other's eyes, and I felt my face turning pale. Life vanished somewhere and then returned again with a loud throbbing of the heart. It was quiet and the flame of the candle was quivering, and it was small, dull, but sharp-pointed, like a crooked sword.

"Are you afraid?" I asked.

The pale chin trembled, but her eyes remained motionless and looked at me, without blinking, and only now I noticed what unfamiliar, what terrible eyes they were. For ten years I had looked into them and had known them better than my own eyes, and now there was something new in them which I am unable define. I would have called it pride, but there was something different in them, something new, entirely new. I took her hand; it was cold. She grasped my hand firmly and there was something new, something I had not known before, in her handclasp.

She had never before clasped my hand as she did this time.

"How long?" I asked.

"About an hour already. Your brother has gone away. He was apparently afraid that you would not let him go, so he went away quietly. But I saw it."

It was true then; the time had arrived. I rose, and, for some reason, spent a long time washing myself, as was my wont in the morning before going to work, and my wife held the light. Then we put out the light and walked over to the window overlooking the street. It was spring; it was May, and the air that came in from the open window was such as we had never before felt in that old, large city. For several days the factories and the roads had been idle; and the air, free from smoke, was filled with the fragrance of the fields and the flowering gardens, perhaps with that of the dew. I do not know what it is that smells so wonderfully on spring nights when I go out far beyond the outskirts of the city. Not a lantern, not a carriage, not a single sound of the city over the unconcerned stony surface; if you had closed your eyes, you would really have thought that you were in a village. There a dog was barking. I had never before heard a dog barking in the city, and I laughed for happiness.

"Listen, a dog is barking."

My wife embraced me, and said:

"It is there, on the corner."

We bent over the window-sill, and there, in the transparent, dark depth, we saw some movement—not people, but movement. Something was moving about like a shadow. Suddenly the blows of a hatchet or a hammer resounded. They sounded so cheerful, so resonant, as in a forest, as on a river when you are mending a boat or building a dam. And in the presentiment of cheerful, harmonious work, I firmly embraced my wife, while she looked above the houses, above the roofs, looked at the young crescent of the moon, which was already setting. The moon was so young, so strange, even as a young girl who is dreaming and is afraid to tell her dreams; and it was shining only for itself.

"When will we have a full moon?...."

"You must not! You must not!" my wife interrupted. "You must not speak of that which will be. What for? *It* is afraid of words. Come here."

It was dark in the room, and we were silent for a long time, without seeing each other, yet thinking of the same thing. And when I started to speak, it seemed to me that someone else was speaking; I was not afraid, yet the voice of the other one was hoarse, as though suffocating for thirst.

"What shall it be?"

"And—they?"

"You will be with them. It will be enough for them to have a mother. I cannot remain."

"And I? Can I?"

I know that she did not stir from her place, but I felt distinctly that she was going away, that she was far—far away. I began to feel so cold, I stretched out my hands—but she pushed them aside.

"People have such a holiday once in a hundred years, and you want to deprive me of it. Why?" she said.

"But they may kill you there. And our children will perish."

"Life will be merciful to me. But even if they should perish—"

And this was said by her, my wife—a woman with whom I had lived for ten years. But yesterday she had known nothing except our children, and had been filled with fear for them; but yesterday she had caught with terror the stern symptoms of the future. What had come over her? Yesterday—but I, too, forgot everything that was yesterday.

"Do you want to go with me?"

"Do not be angry"—she thought that I was afraid, angry—"Don't be angry. Tonight, when they began to knock here, and you were still sleeping, I suddenly understood that my husband, my children—all these were simply temporary. . . .I love you, very much"—she found my hand and shook it with the same new, unfamiliar grasp—"but do you hear how they are knocking there? They are knocking, and something seems to be falling, some kind of walls seem to be falling—and it is so spacious, so wide, so free. It is night now, and yet it seems to me that the sun is shining. I am thirty years of age, and I am old already, and yet it seems to me that I am only seventeen, and that I love someone with my first love—a great, boundless love."

"What a night!" I said. "It is as if the city were no more. You are right, I have also forgotten how old I am."

"They are knocking, and it sounds to me like music, like singing of which I have always dreamed—all my life. And I did not know whom it was that I loved with such a boundless love, which made me feel like crying and laughing and singing. There is freedom—do not take my happiness away, let me die with those who are working there, who are calling the future so bravely, and who are rousing the dead past from its grave."

"There is no such thing as time."

"What do you say?"

"There is no such thing as time. Who are you? I did not know you. Are you a human being?"

She burst into such ringing laughter as though she were really only seventeen years old.

"I did not know you, either. Are you, too, a human being? How

115

strange and how beautiful it is—a human being!"

That which I am writing happened long ago, and those who are sleeping now in the sleep of grey life and who die without awakening— those will not believe me: in those days there was no such thing as time. The sun was rising and setting, and the hand was moving around the dial—but time did not exist. And many other great and wonderful things happened in those days.... And those who are sleeping now the sleep of this grey life and who die without awakening, will not believe me.

"I must go," said I.

"Wait, I will give you something to eat. You haven't eaten anything today. See how sensible I am: I shall go tomorrow. I shall give the children away and find you."

"Comrade," said I.

"Yes, comrade."

Through the open windows came the breath of the fields, and silence, and from time to time, the cheerful strokes of the axe, and I sat by the table and looked and listened, and everything was so mysteriously new that I felt like laughing. I looked at the walls and they seemed to me to be transparent. As if embracing all eternity with one glance, I saw how all these walls had been built, I saw how they were being destroyed, and I alone always was and always will be. Everything will pass, but I shall remain. And everything seemed to me strange and queer—so unnatural—the table and the food upon it, and everything outside of me. It all seemed to me transparent and light, existing only temporarily.

"Why don't you eat?" asked my wife.

I smiled:

"Bread—it is so strange."

She glanced at the bread, at the stale, dry crust of bread, and for some reason her face became sad. Still continuing to look at it, she silently adjusted her apron with her hands and her head turned slightly, very slightly, in the direction where the children were sleeping.

"Do you feel sorry for them?" I asked.

She shook her head without removing her eyes from the bread.

"No, but I was thinking of what happened in our life before."

How incomprehensible! As one who awakens from a long sleep, she surveyed the room with her eyes and all seemed to her so incomprehensible. Was this the place where we had lived?

"You were my wife."

116

"And there are our children."

"Here, beyond the wall, your father died."

"Yes. He died. He died without awakening."

The smallest child, frightened at something in her sleep, began to cry. And this simple childish cry, apparently demanding something, sounded so strange amid these phantom walls, while there, below, people were building barricades.

She cried and demanded—caresses, certain queer words and promises to soothe her. And she soon was soothed.

"Well, go!" said my wife in a whisper.

"I should like to kiss them."

"I am afraid you will wake them up."

"No, I will not."

It turned out that the oldest child was awake—he had heard and understood everything. He was but nine years old, but he understood everything—he met me with a deep, stern look.

"Will you take your gun?" he asked thoughtfully and earnestly.

"I will."

"It is behind the stove."

"How do you know? Well, kiss me. Will you remember me?"

He jumped up in his bed, in his short little shirt, hot from sleep, and firmly clasped my neck. His arms were burning—they were so soft and delicate. I lifted his hair on the back of his head and kissed his little neck.

"Will they kill you?" he whispered right into my ear.

"No, I will come back."

But why did he not cry? He had cried sometimes when I had simply left the house for a while: Is it possible that IT had reached him, too? Who knows? So many strange things happened during the great days.

I looked at the walls, at the bread, at the candle, at the flame which had kept flickering, and took my wife by the hand.

"Well—'till we meet again!"

"Yes—'till we meet again!"

That was all. I went out. It was dark on the stairway and there was the odour of old filth. Surrounded on all sides by the stones and the darkness, groping down the stairs, I was seized with a tremendous, powerful and all-absorbing feeling of the new, unknown and joyous something to which I was going.

At the Roadside Station

It was early spring when I went to the bungalow. On the road still lay last year's darkened leaves. I was unaccompanied; and alone I wandered through the still empty bungalows, the windows of which reflected the April sun. I mounted the broad bright terraces, and wondered who would live here under the green canopy of birch and oak. And when I closed my eyes, I seemed to hear quick, cheerful footsteps, youthful song, and the ringing sound of women's laughter.

I used often to go to the station to meet the passenger trains. I was not expecting anyone: there was no one to come and see me; but I am fond of those iron giants, when they rush past, rolling their shoulders, tearing along the rails with colossal momentum, and carrying somewhither persons unknown to me, but still my fellow creatures. They seem to me alive and uncanny. In their speed I recognise the immensity of the world and the might of man, and when they whistle with such abandon and in so imperious a manner, I think how they are whistling in the same way in America, and Asia, may be in torrid Africa.

The station was a small one, with two short sidings, and when the passenger train had left, it became still and deserted. The forest and the streaming sunshine dominated the little low platform, and the desolate track, and blended the rails in silence and light. On one of the sidings under an empty sleeping-car fowls wandered about, swarming round the iron wheels, and one could hardly believe, as one watched their peaceful, fussy activity, that it would be much the same in America, in Asia, or in torrid Africa. . .

In a week I became acquainted with all the inhabitants of this little corner, and saluted as acquaintances the watchmen in their blue blouses, and the silent pointsmen with their dull countenances, and their brass horns, which glittered in the sun.

Every day I saw at the station a *gendarme*. He was a healthy, strong fellow, as are they all, with broad back, in a tightly stretched blue uniform, with enormous arms and a youthful countenance, upon which, from behind a severe official dignity, there still looked out the blue-eyed *naïveté* of the country. At first, he used to scan me all over with a gloomy suspicion, and put on a look of unapproachable severity without a touch of indulgence, and when he passed me would clank his spurs in a peculiarly sharp and eloquent manner. But he soon became used to me, just as he had become used to the pillars which supported the roof of the platform, to the desolate track, and to the discarded sleeping-car under which the fowls kept running about. In such quiet corners a habit is soon formed.

And when he left off observing me, I perceived that this man was bored—bored as no one else in the world. He was bored with the wearisome station, bored by the absence of thoughts, bored by his strength-devouring inactivity, bored by the exclusiveness of his position, somewhere in the void between the station-master, who was unapproachable to him, and the lower *employés* to whom he was himself unapproachable. His soul lived on breaches of the peace, but at this tiny station no one ever committed a breach of the peace, and every time the passenger train departed without any adventure there passed over the face of the *gendarme* the expression of annoyance and vexation of a person who has been deprived of his due.

For some minutes he would stand still in indecision, and then with listless gait walk to the other end of the platform without any aim or object. On his way he might stop for a second in front of some peasant woman who had been waiting for the train—but she was only a peasant woman like any other—and so knitting his brows the *gendarme* would pass on his way. Then he would sit down stout and listless, as though he had been boiled soft, and felt how soft and flabby were his useless arms under the cloth of his uniform, and how his powerful body, created for work, grew weary with the torturing fatigue of doing nothing. We are bored only in head, but he was bored in every part of him, from head to foot: his cap, cocked on one side with youthful lack of purpose, was bored, his spurs were bored and tinkled inharmoniously and irregularly as though muffled.

Then he began to yawn. How he yawned! his mouth became contorted, expanded from ear to ear, grew broader and broader, till it swallowed up his whole face, it seemed that in another second, through the ever enlarging aperture, you would be able to survey his very inside, choke-full of crowdy and greasy soup. How he yawned! He went away in a hurry, but for long that awful yawn seemed to put my jawbone out of joint, and the trees were broken and bobbing about to my tear-filled eyes.

Once from the mail train they took a passenger travelling without a ticket, and this was a very festival for the bored *gendarme*. He drew himself up, his spurs jingled with precision and austerity, his face became concentrated and angry; but his happiness was but short-lived. The passenger paid his fare, and with a hasty oath got back into the car, and in the rear the metal rowels of the *gendarme's* spurs gave a disconcerted and piteous rattle, as his enervated body swayed feebly over them. And at times when he yawned, he became to me something terrible.

For some days workmen had been busy about the station clearing the site, and when I returned from town after a stay of a couple of days, the masons were laying the third row of bricks; a brand-new building was arising. These masons were numerous and worked quickly, and skilfully; and it was a strange pleasure to watch the straight, even wall springing up out of the ground. When they had covered one row with mortar, they laid on a second row, adjusting the bricks according to their dimensions, laying them now on the broad side, now on the narrow, and cutting off the corners to make them fit. They worked meditatively, and though the course of their meditation was evident enough, and their problem clear, still it gave an additional charm and interest to the work. I was looking at them with enjoyment when an authoritative voice at my elbow shouted:

"Look here, you. What's your name! Why don't you put this right?"

It was the voice of the *gendarme*, squeezing himself through the iron railings, which separated the asphalt platform from the workmen; he was pointing to a certain brick and insisting: "You with the beard! lay that brick properly. Don't you see, it's a half-brick?"

The mason with the beard, which was in places whitened with lime, turned round in silence—the *gendarme's* face was severe and imposing—in silence he followed the direction of the *gendarme's* finger, took up the brick, trimmed it, and in silence put it back in its place. The *gendarme* gave me a severe look and went away; but the seductive interest in the work was stronger than his, sense of dignity. When he had made a couple of turns on the platform, he again came to a standstill in front of the workmen adopting a somewhat careless and contemptuous pose. But his face no longer showed signs of boredom.

I went to the wood, and when I was returning through the station it was one o'clock, the workmen were resting, and the place was empty as usual. But someone was busying himself about the unfinished wall; it was the *gendarme*. He was taking up bricks, and finishing the fifth row. I could only catch a sight of his broad, tightly stretched back, but it was expressive of intent thought, and indecision. Evidently the work was more complicated than he had imagined. His unaccustomed eye was playing him false; he stepped back, shook his head, stooped for a fresh brick, striking the ground with his sabre as he bent down. Once he raised his finger, in the classic gesture of one who has discovered the solution of a problem, such as might have been used by Archimedes himself, and his back once more assumed the erect attitude of greater self-confidence and certainty. But immediately it became once more doubled up in the consciousness of the undignified nature of the work undertaken. There was in his whole, full-grown figure something secretive as with children, when they are afraid they will be found out.

I carelessly struck a match to light a cigarette, and the *gendarme* turned round startled. For a moment he looked at me in confusion, and suddenly his youthful countenance was illumined by a slightly solicitous, confiding, and kindly smile. But the very next moment he resumed his austere, unapproachable look, and his hand went up to his little thin moustache—but in it, in that very hand, there still lay that unlucky brick! And I saw how painfully ashamed he was of that brick, and of his involuntary, compromising smile. Apparently, he did not know how to blush, otherwise he would have become as red as the brick which he still held helplessly in his hand.

They had carried the wall up half way, and it was no longer possible to see what the skilful masons were doing on their scaffolding. Once more the *gendarme* oscillated from end to end of the platform, yawning, and when he turned round and passed me, I could feel that he was ashamed—and that he hated me. And as I looked at his powerful arms listlessly swinging in their sleeves, at his inharmoniously jingling spurs, and trailing sabre, it seemed to me that it was all unreal—that in the scabbard there was no sabre at all, with which he might cut a man down, in the case no revolver, with which he might shoot a man dead. And his very uniform, that too was unreal, and seemed as though it was all just some strange masquerade taking place in full daylight, in the face of the honest April sun, and amidst ordinary working people, and busy fowls picking up grains under the sleeping-car.

But at times—at times I began to fear for someone. He was so terribly bored.

Bargamót and Garas'ka

It would be unjust to say that Nature had injured Iván Akindínytch Bargamótov, who in his official capacity was called "Constable No. 20," and unofficially simply Bargomótov. The inhabitants of one of the out-skirts of the provincial towns of Aryól (Orel), who in their turn were nicknamed "gunners," from the name of their abode (Gunner Street) and, from the moral side were characterized as "broken-headed gun-ners," when they dubbed Ivan Akindínytch "Bargamót," were without doubt not thinking of the qualities which belong to such a delicate and delicious fruit as the *bergamót*. By his exterior Bargamót reminded one rather of the mastodon, or of any of those engaging, but extinct creatures, which for want of room have long ago deserted a world al-ready filling up with flacid little humans. Tall, stout, strong, loud-voiced Bargamót loomed big on the police horizon, and certainly would long ago have attained notable rank, if only his soul, compressed within those stout walls, had not been sunk in an heroic sleep.

Outward impressions in passing to Bargamót's soul by means of his little fat-encased eyes, lost all their sharpness and force, and arrived at their destination only in the form of feeble echoes and reflexions. A person of sublime requirements would have called him a lump of flesh; his superior officers called him a "stock," but a useful one—while to the "gunners," the persons most interested in this question, he was a staid, serious matter-of-fact man, one worthy of every respect and consideration. What Bargamót knew he knew well, were it only a policeman's instructions, which he had assimilated some time or other with all the energy of his mighty frame, and which had sunk so deep into his sluggish brain, that it would have been impossible to rout them out again, even with vitriol. Nevertheless, certain truths occu-pied a permanent position in his soul, truths acquired by way of life's experience, and unconditionally dominating the situation.

Of that which Bargamót did not know he kept such an imperturbably stolid silence, that people who did know it became somehow or other somewhat ashamed of their knowledge. But the chief point was this, that Bargamót was enormously powerful; and might was right in Gunner Street, a slum inhabited by shoemakers, tailors who worked at home, and the representatives of other "liberal" professions. Owning two public houses, uproarious on Sundays and Mondays, Gunner Street devoted all its leisure hours to Homeric fights, in which the women, bare-headed and dishevelled, took immediate part (as they separated their husbands), and also the little children, who gazed with delight on the daring of their papas.

All this rough wave of drunken "gunners"; beat against the immovable Bargamót, as against a stone breakwater, while he would deliberately seize with his mighty hands a pair of the most desperate rowdies, and personally conduct them to the "lock up," and the rowdies would obediently submit their fate to the hands of Bargamót, protesting merely for the sake of appearances.

Such was Bargamót in the domain of international relations. In the sphere of home politics, he held himself with no less dignity. The small tumble-down cottage, in which Bargamót lived with his wife and two young children, and which with difficulty afforded room for his mighty body, and trembled with craziness and with fear for its own existence whenever Bargamót round turned, might be at ease, if not with regard to its own wooden structure, at all events in respect of the family unity.

Domestic, careful, and fond of digging in his garden on free days, Bargamót was severe. He instructed his wife and children through the same medium of physical influence, not conforming so much to the actual requirements of science as to certain indefinite prescriptions on that score which existed in the ramifications of his big head. This did not prevent his wife Máriya, who was still a young and handsome woman, on the one hand from respecting her husband as a steady, sober man, and on the other, in spite of all his massiveness, from twisting him round her finger with that ease and force of which only weak women are capable.

At about ten o'clock on a warm spring evening Bargamót stood at his usual post at the corner of Gunner Street and the 3rd Garden Street. He was in a bad humour. Tomorrow was Easter Day and soon people would be going to church, while he would have to stand on duty till 3 o'clock in the morning, and would only get home in time for the conclusion of the fast. (First meal after the Lenten fast). Bargamót did not feel any need of prayer, but the bright holiday air which permeated the unusually peaceful and quiet street affected even him.

He did not like the spot on which he had stood still every day for a matter of ten years. He felt a desire to do something of a holiday character such as others were doing. And in view of these uneasy feelings there arose within him a certain discontent and impatience. Moreover, he was hungry. His wife had given him no dinner at all that day, and so he had had to put up with a few sups of *kuass* and bread. His great stomach was insistently demanding food; and how long it was still to the conclusion of the fast!

Ptu!—spat Bargamót, as he made a cigarette and began reluctantly to suck at it. At home he had some good cigarettes, presented to him by a local shop-keeper, but he was reserving them till the conclusion of the fast.

Soon the "gunners" drew along towards the church, clean and respectable in jackets and waistcoats over red and blue flannel shirts, and in long boots with innumerable creases, and high pointed heels. Tomorrow all this splendour was destined to disappear behind the counter of the "pub" (pawned), or to be torn in pieces in a friendly struggle for harmony.

But for today the "gunners" were resplendent. Each one carefully carried a parcel of *paschal* cakes. None took any notice of Bargamót, neither did he look with especial love on his "god-children," and uneasily prognosticated how many times he would have to make a journey tomorrow to the police station.

In fact, he was jealous that they were free and could go where it was bright, noisy and cheerful, while he was stuck there like a penitent.

"Here I have to stand because of you, drunkards," muttered he, summing up his thoughts, and spat once more—he felt a hollow in the pit of his stomach.

The street was becoming empty. The Eucharistic bell had ceased. Then the joyful changes of the treble peal, so cheerful after the melancholy tolling of the Lenten bells, spread over the world the joyful news of Christ's Resurrection. Bargamót took off his hat and crossed himself. Soon he would be going home. He became more cheerful as he imagined to himself the table laid with a clean cloth, the *paschal* cakes and the eggs. He would without hurry give to all the Easter salutation. They would wake up Jack and bring him in, and he would at once demand the coloured egg, about which he had held circumstantial conversations the whole week through with his more experienced little sister. Oh, how he'll open wide his mouth when his father brings him, not the bright dyed egg, but the real marble one, which the same obliging shop-keeper had presented to Bargamót!

"Amusing little fellow!" said Bargamót with a smile, feeling a sort of paternal tenderness welling up from the depths of his soul.

But Bargamót's placidity was broken in on in the most abject manner. Round the corner were heard uneven footsteps and low mutterings.

"Who the devil is coming here?" thought Bargamót, looking round the corner and feeling injured in his very soul.

"Garas'ka! Yes, drunk as usual! Well, that's a finisher!"

It was a mystery to Bargamót how Garas'ka could have managed to get drunk before daylight, but of the fact of his drunkenness there was no doubt. His behaviour, mysterious as it would have been to an outsider, was perfectly clear to Bargamót, who was well acquainted with the "Gunner" soul in general, and with the low nature of Garas'ka in particular. Attracted by an irresistible force from the middle of the street, in which he had the habit of walking, he was pressed close to the hording. Supporting himself with both hands, and contemplating the wall with a concentrated air of enquiry, Garas'ka staggered, while he gathered up his strength for a fresh struggle with any unexpected impediments he might meet with.

After a short but intense meditation he pushed himself energetically from the wall, and staggered backwards into the middle of the street, made a deliberate turn, and set out with long strides into space, which turned out to be not quite so endless as it has been said to be, but was in fact bounded by a mass of lamps.

With the first of these, Garas'ka came into the closest relations, and clasped it in the firm embrace of friendship.

"A lamp! Stop!" said he curtly, as he established the accomplished fact. Quite unusually, of course, Garas'ka was in an excessively good humour. Instead of heaping well-deserved objurgations upon the lamppost he turned to it with mild reproaches, which contained some touches of familiarity.

"Stand still, you silly ass, where are you going to?" he muttered as he staggered away from the lamppost, and again fell with his whole chest upon it, almost flattering his nose against its cold, damp surface.

"That's right! eh?" and by clinging with half his length along the post he managed to hold on, and sank into a reverie.

Bargamót contemptuously compressed his lips, as he looked down on Garas'ka from his superior height. Nobody annoyed him so much in the whole of Gunner Street as this wretched toper. To look at him—one would not have thought there was any strength in him, and yet he was the greatest scandal in the whole neighbourhood.

He's not a man, but an ulcer! A "gunner" gets drunk, makes a disturbance, spends the night in the lock-up, and he gets over all this like a gentleman—but Garas'ka always does it stealthily, and of malice prepense. He may be beaten half to death or nearly starved at the police station, still they can never break him of bad language, of his most offensively foul tongue.

He will stand under the windows of any of the most respectable people in Gunner Street, and begin to swear without rhyme or reason. The shopmen seize Garas'ka and beat him—the crowd laughs and advises them to give it him hot. Garas'ka would revile even Bargamót himself in such fantastically realistic language, that without understanding all the subtleties of his wit, he felt himself more insulted, than if he had been whipped.

How Garas'ka got his living, remained to the "gunners" one of those mysteries which enveloped his whole existence. Certainly no one had ever seen him sober. He lived, or rather camped about in the orchards, or the river-bank, or under shrubs. In winter he disappeared to somewhere or other, and with the first breath of spring he re-appeared.

What attracted him to Gunner Street, where it was everyone's business to beat him, was again a profound mystery of Garas'ka's soul, but get rid of him they could not. They strongly suspected, and that not without reason, that he was a thief, but they could not take him in the act, so he was beaten on merely circumstantial evidence.

On this occasion Garas'ka had evidently a difficult path to negotiate. The rags, which made a pretence of seriously covering his emaciated body, were all over still undried mud.

His face, with its big, bulbous red nose, which was incontestably one of the causes of his unstable equilibrium, was covered with an irregularly distributed watery growth, and gave substantial evidence of its close relations with alcohol and a neighbour's fist. On his cheek near the eye was a scratch of evidently recent origin.

He succeeded at last in parting company with the lamppost, and when he observed the dignified silent figure of Bargamót he was overjoyed.

"Our best respects to you Bargamót Bargamótytch—we hope we see you well!" said he with a polite wave of the hand, but he staggered, and was fain to prop himself up with his back against the lamppost.

"Where are you going to?" growled Bargamót saturninely.

"We're orl righ'!"

"On the old lay, eh? Or do you want a doss in the cells. You wretch, I'll run you in at once."

"No, you don't!"

Garas'ka was just going to make a gesture of defiance, when he wisely restrained himself, spat and rubbed his foot about on the ground as though to rub out the spittle.

"You can talk when you get to the police station! March!"

Bargamót's mighty hand stretched out to Garas'ka's collar, so greasy in fact that it was evident that Bargamót was not his first guide on the thorny path of well-doing. Giving the drunken man a slight shake, and propelling his body in the required direction, and at the same time giving it a certain stability, Bargamót dragged him towards the above-mentioned goal, just as a strong hawser might tow after it a very light schooner, which had met with an accident outside the harbour. He considered himself deeply injured, instead of enjoying his well-earned rest, to have to drag himself with this drunkard to the station.

Ugh! Bargamót's hands itched—but the consciousness that on such a high festival it would be unseemly to let them have their way, restrained him. Garas'ka strode on bravely, mingling in a remarkable manner self-confidence, and even insolence, with meekness. He evidently harboured some thought of his own, which he began to approach by the Socratic method.

"Tell me, Mr. Policeman, what is today?"

"Won't you shut up!" Bargamót replied in contempt. "Drunk before daylight!"

"Has the bell at Michael the Archangel's rung yet?"

"Yes, what's that to you?"

"Then Christ is risen!"

"Well, He is risen."

"Then allow me——" Garas'ka was carrying on this conversation half twisted towards Bargamót, and with his face resolutely turned to him. Bargamót, interested by the strange questions, mechanically let go the greasy collar. Garas'ka, losing his support, staggered and fell before he could show to Bargamót an object which he had just taken out of his pocket. Raising his great shoulders, as he supported

128

himself on his hands, Garas'ka looked on the ground, then fell face downwards, and began to wail, as a peasant woman wails for the dead.

Garas'ka howling! Bargamót was surprised, but deciding that it must be some new joke of his, he still felt interested as to developments. The development was that Garas'ka continued howling without words, just like a dog.

"What's up now? Off your nut, eh?" said Bargamót as he gave him a shove with his foot. He went on howling. Bargamót was in a dilemma.

"What's got yer, eh?"

"The eg—g."

"Well?"

Garas'ka went on howling, but less noisily, he sat down and lifted up his hand. The hand was covered with something sticky, to which adhered pieces of coloured egg-shell. Bargamót still in doubt, began to have an inkling that something untoward had taken place.

"I—like a gentleman—to present—Easter egg—but you—" blubbered Garas'ka disconnectedly; but Bargamót understood.

It was evident what had been Garas'ka's intention. He wished to present him with an Easter egg according to Christian usage, and Bargamót was for taking him to goal. Perhaps he had brought the egg a long way, and now it was broken—and he was crying. Bargamót imagined to himself that the marble egg he was keeping for Jack was broken, and how sorry it made him.

"'Ere's a go!" said Bargamót shaking his head, as he looked at the wallowing drunkard, and pitied him as intensely as he would have pitied a man cruelly wronged by his own brother.

"He was going to present——"

"He is also a living soul," muttered the policeman, striving albeit clumsily to render the state of affairs clear to himself, and feeling a mixture of shame and pity, which became more and more oppressive.

"And you would have run him in! Shame on yer!"

Sighing heavily as he bent down, he knocked his short sword against a stone, and sat down on his heels near to Garas'ka.

"Well," he muttered in confusion, "perhaps it is not broken."

"Not broken! Why yer was ready to break my snout for me. Brute!"

"But what did you shove for!"

"What for——" mimicked Garas'ka. "I was going—like a gentleman to—and him to—the lock up. Think that's my last egg? Yer lump!"

129

Bargamót sniffed. He did not feel in the least hurt by Garas'ka's abuse; through his whole ill-organised interior he felt a sort of half pity, half shame, while in the remotest depths of his stout body something kept tiresomely wimbling and torturing.

"Can one help giving you a thrashing?" said Bargamót, more to himself than to Garas'ka.

"Not you, you garden scarecrow! Now look 'ere."

Garas'ka was evidently falling into his usual groove. In his somewhat clearing brain, he was picturing to himself a whole perspective of the most compromising terms of abuse, and most insulting epithets, when Bargamót cleared his throat with a sound which left not the slightest doubt as to the firmness of his determination and declared:

"We'll go to my house, and break the fast."

"What! go to your house you tubby devil!"

"Let's go, I say."

Garas'ka's surprise was boundless. Quite passively he allowed himself to be lifted up and led by the hand, and he went—but whither? Not to the lock-up, but to the house of Bargamót himself—actually to eat his Easter breakfast there! A seductive thought came into his head—to give Bargamót the slip, but though his head had become cleared by the very unusualness of the situation his feet still remained in such evil case, that they seemed sworn to perpetually cling to one another, and to prevent each other from walking.

Then, too, Bargamót was such a wonder that Garas'ka, truth to tell, did not want to get away.

Bargamót, twisting his tongue, and searching for words and stuttering, now propounded to him the instructions for a policeman, and now reverting to the special question of thrashing, and the lockup, deciding in his own mind in the positive, and at the same time in the negative.

"You say truly, Iván Akindínytch, we must be beaten," acknowledged Garas'ka, feeling even a sort of awkwardness. Bargamót was a sore wonder!

"No, I don't mean to do that," mumbled Bargamót, evidently understanding, even less than Garas'ka, what his woolly tongue was babbling.

They arrived at last at Bargamót's house—and Garas'ka had already ceased to wonder. Máriya at first opened her eyes wide at the sight of the unwonted couple, but she guessed from her husband's perturbed look, that there was no room for objections, and in her womanly kind-heartedness, quickly understood what she was expected to do.

Quieted and confused, Garas'ka sat down at the decorated table. He felt ashamed enough to sink into the ground. Ashamed of his rags, of his dirty hands, ashamed of his whole self, torn, drunken, disgusting as he was. Scalding himself with the deuced hot soup, swimming with fat, he spilt it on the tablecloth, and although the hostess with delicacy pretended not to have noticed it, he grew confused and spilt still more. So unbearably did those shrivelled fingers tremble with those great dirty nails, which Garas'ka now noticed for the first time.

"Ivan Akindínytch, what surprise have you for Jacky?" asked Máriya.

"Never mind later on," hurriedly replied Bargamót. He was scalding himself with the soup, blew on his spoon, and stolidly wiped his moustache—but through all this solidity the same amazement was apparent, as in the case of Garas'ka.

Máriya hospitably pressed her guest to eat:

"Garásim," (full name of Garas'ka), she said, "how are you called after your father's name?"

"Andréitch."

"Welcome, Garásim Andréitch."

Garas'ka, in endeavouring to swallow, choked, and throwing down his spoon, dropped his head on the table, right on the greasy spot which he had just made. From his breast there escaped again that rough, piteous howl, which had before so disturbed Bargamót.

The children, who had almost left off taking any notice of the guest, dropped their spoons and joined their treble to his tenor. Bargamót looked at his wife with a troubled and woeful expression.

"Now, what's the matter with you, Garásim Andréitch. Leave off," said she, trying to quiet the perturbed guest.

"By my father's name! Since I was born no one ever called me so!"

Carelessness

1

The father arrived at the station two hours before the train was supposed to leave. He left the house when the sun had only just risen, travelled thirty miles through hemp fields, forests, and meadows, and now smelled of hemp, flowers and odorous roadside dust. The station smelled of coal, oil, and sun-baked iron. The workman, who smelled just like the father, and, furthermore, of horse manure and tar, sharply turned the carriage on its two back wheels, adjusted the seat, and left, and the father was left alone with his little bag, umbrella, and sweet flatbreads. For a minute the father felt sad, and he cried out in a frail tenor:

"Ivan! Ah Ivan!"

But the workman was far away and did not hear him. And suddenly, happiness overcame the father, and this was because he was alone in such a strange and unusual place, and it was also because he was traveling to the city, and because of the clear, cloudless sky, a wide, calming azure above the iron roof. At first, he sat leisurely on the bench, pleasantly sensing that he was already in command of that complex and curious thing they call the train and the railway; but because there was not a soul on the station, he dared to take a careful peek into all the places around him. He took a peek into the buffet: there was a long table there covered by a marbled oilcloth, and on the oilcloth, flies were crawling around. Respectfully he took a peek into the telegraph room: there was also nobody there, and a machine was tapping something out by itself, letting out a long, white ribbon. The father shook his head, cleared his throat, and said:

"Ingenuity!"

He stood for a bit by the ticket office, but, since the office was closed and there was nobody there except for him, he went to the platform.

133

The platform too he found to his liking: it was long, clean, business-like, tarred in some places, and in others covered with asphalt—just what is needed for big and important business. Shiny rail tracks ran from it in various directions, keeping precise trail of countless thundering trains; and, if one went in one direction, then one would arrive in one unknown corner of the world, and in the other—in another corner of the world, just as unknown and mysterious. This thought agitated the father to such an extent that he almost ran back to the ticket office, but it was still closed and there was not a soul around. Still too early.

"Remarkable! Remarkable!" said the father importantly, even sternly, and energetically shook his head, causing roadside dust to fall unnoticeably from his hair and clothes. It is likely that because this dust has softened the rustle of his clothes, his movements were made soundless, and only his large boots with hobnailed heels made loud taps as he walked, which were almost indecently loud. That is why he stepped off the platform onto a path, onto soft, rustling sand. There he saw the train engine.

It was a large, black, dirty engine. It stood on a reserve line and looked as if it was sleeping—but, clearly, it was only pretending. In all of its motionlessness and silence it seemed like the real overlord of these parts, a severe, iron monster, full of hidden power and limitless, unstoppable ambition. That is him, who, if only he desires, could fly to this or that corner of the world. That is him, who, with thunder, rumble, and whistle, rushes day and night atop slippery rails, screaming, dispersing crowds, running over the careless, and lighting up green and red lights all along his path—he, the motionless, dirty wad of iron, an incomprehensible tangle of wheels, pipes, and levers.

"Remarkable!" said the father with emphasis.

"Remarkable!"

And over his head the sky was blue and boundless, and was calling him somewhere.

2

But, it appears, it really was sleeping. No smoke, no rustle—very much as dead. And there was nobody aboard. Now was his chance to stick out a hand and carefully stroke its very wheel. The father did just that, although not before putting some spit on his hands, as if he was afraid of burning himself. And then some more spit ....

He looked around nervously—there is an old woman walking

across the path, staring at him. He frowned, pretended to straighten his beard, took out a blue checkered handkerchief and proceeded to spend a long time wiping his face: let the old woman think I am sweating. He really was sweating—dirty streaks of sweat and dust were left on the handkerchief. The tricked old woman left, and the father was overcome by an intolerable urge to wink at somebody. He winked and laughed: if only my congregation could see me now—a priest, and look what he is up to. But then the father realized that all this was very serious and not at all funny, and the ticket office might be open already. No, still closed, and still an hour and a quarter left until the train was to leave. A watchman walked across the hallway and looked at the father; the father gave him a nod of his head and the watchman bowed.

"Polite people, learned, not like our lot," thought the father approvingly and, filled with courage, went straight over to the sleeping engine. And now it appeared to him in some way like a kind, calm horse, and the father spoke to it in the same tender way as he would to a horse before work:

"Well, well, get some rest, get some rest. Soon you'll carry us again, brother."

The engine remained genially silent. If one was to approach it from the other side then one would be hidden from the station. The father grabbed a rail, started to climb, but slipped. He flushed and spent a long time shaking his head, sprinkling dust and smiling into empty space. He took a moment to think, then placed his umbrella and his little bag on the sand, then picked them up again, and again put them down, and, pulling up his robe, carefully climbed up. There were only three steps but to the father it seemed as high as a belfry.

"Remarkable. Re-mar-kable," said the father in a stern, thoughtful tone, in which he would normally speak about mysterious science and its wonders. And, already feeling himself a little like a scientist, he casually stroked something with his hand. But, in actual fact, he did not understand anything at all, he only believed: the manifold parts of the machine, the unclear relationship between them, arrows, numbers, levers—it all spoke of a great enterprise, of difficult and arduous thought, of something considerable and very promising. And it was especially pleasant that he himself, a rural backwater priest, was somehow involved in all of this—by way of his human nature and respect for science.

"That's quite something they've come up with! This—this is

something! Remarkable," said the father and looked askance with contempt at the little bag and umbrella. When he first bought the umbrella he would read lectures about it, but now even it did not seem to him very important. Of course, it is nothing compared to what we have going on here. He touched a lever—nothing. He touched another—suddenly something gave out a loud hiss, and the engine somehow mysteriously came to life. Somewhere something was hissing. He turned his head around, bent down—hissing. The father grew pale, and his heart began to beat: thump-thump—what if the driver comes, what would he tell him? He carefully pressed something—the hissing definitely stopped, but it started shaking: *raz-raz, raz-raz*. This is even worse. He glanced helplessly at the umbrella and pulled a lever— something pushed him back, and then forward, and then stood him up straight on his feet spread out wide. The father did not get to celebrate having been saved, he looked outside: everything was swimming by; a telegraph pole was swimming by, and, looking back, there were the umbrella and the little bag swimming away.

"I'm off."

3

It strums, rumbles, jerks, snuffles heavily, and rolls around—a pure beast. And there is nothing to grab onto, everything has become so confused. The father turned something and the engine leaped forward, like a cat, and it began to sprint at such a pace that the wind started howling in his ears. And again, he turned something else, yanked the wrong thing. A wild, deafening whistle sounded above his head, a roar even, something terrible and utterly unbearable. At least before this he was traveling in silence, but now he has raised a roar over the whole world.

"Oh God!" the father began to pray. But there was no prayer for such a case! "Oh God, Oh God. . . . What next?"

He stuck out his head. The wind ripped the hat off his head and his dusty hair began spinning around his face, going into his mouth, beating against his eyes. His heart had stopped beating a long time ago—how he remained alive the father did not know himself. After he untangled himself from his hair there was no hat, there was nothing. There was some forest. An insane forest, relentlessly rushing back, straight into a bottomless pit.

"Oh God!" A bridge... And now the bridge is gone, all gone. And the earth has been lowered down somewhere, and the father and the engine are flying upwards—upwards.

"Oh God!" There is a lad near a herd. "Hey lad, lad!" There is a watchman, the watchman is waving a red flag, his face pale with horror. "Hey watchman, watchman!" And again, there is nothing, and the earth is up above, and bushes are rushing overhead.

It is becoming clear now that this is all a trick, that this cannot be happening—otherwise, what are the flatbreads? The umbrella and the flatbreads. But where are they?

"My flatbreads! My flatbreads," mutters the father, twisting his face from tears. It was happiness, it was paradise, it was a feeling of boundless, incredible bliss when he held them under his arm. Why did he have to nose around, why did he touch things, why did he climb aboard? He slipped once—what joy it was when he slipped—slipped!

"Fool! Vermin," the father scolds himself forcefully, while also adding: "Re-mar-kable!"

It thunders, it rumbles, it stares at him with its white dials and, wrapping him in iron, carries him somewhere, carries him on. Again, a red flag darts past, like the tongue of a flame—that means danger, that means terror ahead, terror. The end.

And the father can no longer see, can no longer hear, can no longer think. The clatter of the wheels, the clanging, the trees flying past, the tremors, the swaying of a tired body, the shreds of thoughts still running through his mind—it is all blending into a single feeling of an unstoppable, terrible, rabid flight. Everything in him is being emptied, everything is being frozen and blown out by the wind. Is it he himself that is rushing forward, or is it the engine that is carrying him—he does not know.

And this is no longer a train engine. That engine was left at the station, but this—this is something deaf and relentless, pushing out from somewhere down below in its terrible nakedness. Neither prayers nor curses have any power over it for it is utterly unyielding, and it gives the world that terrible and unusual appearance, the appearance of the world seen through the eyes of a man passing away.

For an instant, during an unusually powerful jolt, the father recovers his senses and cries out in a strangely inappropriate voice, a voice in which one hails a cab: "Stop!"

And then he curses in words just as strangely unsuitable:

"Just stop, you fool. You fool. You beast. You beast."

And again, he freezes, absorbed by the feeling of the terrible, rabid flight. And he stands, swaying, so crushed and bewildered; his head is dangling helplessly, and the dusty wrinkles on his face are darkening timidly and pitifully. The wrinkles of pleasant laughter, quiet pleasures, grief for the sick.

It is empty, dead, and perhaps even peaceful—in the din and rumble of the torrent carrying him away. And, faintly twinkling, like a quiet, distant glow of a lighthouse, when only black waves and storms lie ahead, a faint, intermittent glimmer of the last thought of those sweet flatbreads, now far away.

Dies Irae

1.

....This free song of the stern days of justice and retribution I have composed myself, as well as I could, I, Geronimo Pascagna, a Sicilian bandit, murderer, highwayman, criminal.

Having composed it to the best of my ability, I meant to sing it loudly, as good songs should be sung, but my jailer would not allow it. My jailer's ear is overgrown with hair; it has a strait and a narrow channel: fit for words that are untruthful, sly, words that can crawl upon their bellies like reptiles.

But my words walk erect, they have deep chests, broad backs—ah, how painfully they tore at the tender ear of the jailer which was over-grown with hair!

"If the ear is shut, seek another entrance, Geronimo," I said to myself amicably; and I pondered, and I sought, and finally I succeeded and found it, for Geronimo is no fool, let me tell you. And this is what I found: I found a stone. And this is what I did: I chiselled my song into the stone, and with the blows of my wrath I set aflame its icy heart. And when the stone came to life and glanced at me with the fiery eyes of wrath, I cautiously took it away and placed it at the very edge of the prison wall.

Can you not see what I have in mind? I am wise, I figure that a friendly quake will soon again set the earth aquiver, and once again it will destroy your city; and the walls will crumble, and my stone will drop and shatter the jailer's head. And having shattered it, it will leave upon his soft waxy blood-grey brain the impress of my song of free-dom, like the seal of a king, like a new commandment of wrath—and thus will the jailer go down to his grave.

I say, jailer, shut not your ear, for I shall enter through your skull!

2.

If I am then alive, I shall laugh with joy; and if I chance to be dead, my bones shall dance in their insecure grave. That will be a merry Tarantella!

Can you say upon your oath that such things can never be? The same quake might cast me back upon the face of the earth: my rotting coffin, my decayed flesh, my whole body, dead and buried for keeps, tightly clamped down. For such things have happened upon great days: the earth opening up about the cemeteries, the still coffins crawling out into the light.

Those still coffins, uninvited guests at the banquet!

3.

These be the names of the comrades with whom I made friends in those fleeting hours: Pascale, a professor; Giuseppe, Pincio, Alba. They were shot by firing squads. There was also another one, young, obliging, and so handsome. It was a pity to look at him. I esteemed him as a son, he reverenced me as a father, but I did not know his name. I had not chanced to ask him, or perhaps I have forgotten it. He, too, was shot by the soldiers. There may have been one or two more, also friends, I do not remember them. When the youngster was being put to death, I did not run far away, I hid right here, back of the wall—now crumbled—near the trampled cactus. I saw and heard everything. And when I started to leave, the trampled cactus pierced me with its thorn. Was it not planted near the wall to keep away the thieves? How faithful are the servants of the rich!

4.

The firing squad put them to death. Remember the names which I have mentioned; and with regard to those whom I have not mentioned by name, remember merely that they were put to death. But don't go and make a sign of the cross upon your brow, or worse than that—don't go and order a requiem mass—they did not like such things. Honour the dead with the silence of truth, and if you must lie, lie in some merrier fashion, but never by saying mass: they did not like that.

5.

That first quake that destroyed the prison and the city had a voice of rare power and of queer, superhuman dignity: it roared from below, from beneath the ground, it was vast and hoarse and menacing; and everything shook and crumbled. And ere I grasped what was going on, I knew that all was over, that it was perhaps the end of the earth. But I was not particularly frightened: why should I be especially frightened even if it were the end of the world? Long did he roar, that deaf subterranean trumpeter.

And all at once politely opened the door.

6.

I had sat a long time in prison, without hope. I had tried to flee and failed. Nor could you have managed to escape, for that accursed prison was very well built.

And I had become accustomed to the iron of the bars and to the stone of the walls, and they seemed to me eternal, and he who had built them the strongest in the world. And it was no use to think whether he was just or not, so strong and eternal he was. Even in my dreams I saw no freedom—I did not believe, expect or feel it. And I feared to call it. It is perilous to call freedom; while you keep still, you may live; but call freedom once, ever so softly, you must either gain it or die. This is true, so said Pascale, the professor.

And thus, without hope I sat in prison, and suddenly opened the door. Politely and of its own accord. At any rate it was no human hand that opened it.

7.

The streets were in ruins, in a terrible chaos. All the material of which people build was resolved to its elements and lay as it had been in the beginning. The houses were crumbling, bursting, reeling like drunken, squatting down upon the ground, on their own crushed legs. Others were sulkily casting themselves down upon the ground, with their heads upon the pavement—crash! And opened were the little boxes in which human beings live—pretty little boxes, all plastered with paper.

The pictures still hung on the walls, but the people were no more; they had been thrown out, they were lying beneath masses of stone. And the earth was twitching convulsively—for, you must know that the subterranean trumpeter had started to roar again, that deaf devil who can never have enough noise because he is so deaf. Sweet, painstaking, gigantic devil!

But I was free and I did not understand it yet. I hesitated to walk away from that accursed prison. I was standing there, blinking stupidly at the ruins. And the comrades had also assembled, none attempting to leave, crowding distractedly, like the children about the figure of a dissipated, drunken mother that had fallen to the ground. A fine mother, indeed!

Suddenly Pascale, the professor, said:

"Look!"

One of the walls which we had deemed eternal had burst in two; and the window, with its iron bars, had split in two as well. The iron was twisted and torn like a rotten rag—think of it, the iron! In my hands it had not even rattled, it had pretended to be eternal, the most powerful thing on earth, and now it was not worth to be spat upon— the iron, think of it!

Then I, and the rest of us, understood that we were free.

8.

Free!

9.

It is harder for you to bend a grass blade than for him to bend three iron rails one atop the other. Three or a hundred, it is all the same to him. It is more difficult for you to raise a cup of water to your lips than for him to raise a sea of water, to shake it up, to lift the dregs thereof and to cast them out upon the shore; to bring the cold to boiling. It is harder for you to gnaw through a piece of sugar than for him to gnaw through a mountain. It is more difficult for you to tear a thin and rotting thread than for him to break three wire ropes twisted into one braid. You will perspire and flush with exertion before you manage to stir up an anthill with your stick—and he with one push destroys your city. He has picked up an iron steamship as you with your hand pick up a tiny pebble, and has cast it ashore—have you ever seen the like of such strength?

10.

All that had been open he has shut; the door of your house has grown into its walls, and together they have choked you: your door, your walls, your ceiling. And he likewise has opened the doors of the prison which you had shut so carefully.

You, rich man, whom I hate!

11.

If I gather from all over the world all the good words which people use, all the tender sayings, all the ringing songs and fling them all into the joyous air;

If I gather all the smiles of children, the laughter of women whom none has yet wronged, the caresses of grey-haired mothers, the faithful handshakes of a friend—and weave of them all an incorruptible wreath for someone beautiful head;

If I pass over the face of the earth and garner all the flowers that grow upon it: in the forests and in the fields, in the meadows and in the gardens of the rich, in the depths of the waters, upon the azure bottom of the ocean; if I gather all the precious sparkling stones, bringing them forth out of hidden crevices, out of the gloomy depths of mines, tearing them from the crowns of kings and from the ears of the rich—and pile them all, the stones and the flowers, into one radiant mountain;

If I gather all the fires that burn in the universe, all the lights, all the rays, all the flashes, flares and silent glows, and in the glare of one mighty conflagration illumine the quaking worlds;

Even then I shall be unable to name thee, to crown thee, to laud thee—O Freedom!

12.
Freedom!

13.
Over my head was the sky, and the sky is always free, always open to the winds and to the movement of the clouds; under my feet was the road, and the road is always free; it was made to walk on, it was made for the feet to move over its surface, going back and forth, leaving one spot and finding another. The road is the sweetheart of him who is free; you have to kiss it on meeting, to weep over it on parting.

And when my feet began to move upon the road, I thought that a miracle had occurred. I looked, and Pascale's feet were also moving, the professor! I looked, and the youngster was also moving with youthful feet, hurrying, stumbling, and suddenly he ran.

"Whither?"

But Pascale sternly reproved me.

"Don't throw questions at him; you'll break his limbs. For you and I are old, Geronimo."

And we wept. And suddenly the deaf trumpeter roared out anew.

CHANT THE SECOND

1.
A long time we walked about the city and saw much that was striking, strange and sinister.

2.

Neither can you shut in the fire—I was saying this, I, Geronimo Pascagna. If you would be at peace, put it out altogether, but do not lock it up in stone, in iron or in glass; it will escape, and your strongly built house will come to a bad end. When your mighty house is fallen, and your life is extinct, it alone will burn, retaining the heat and the blazing ruddiness and all the force of the flame. It may lie awhile on the ground, it may pretend even to be dead; then it will lift its head upon a slender neck and look about—to the right and to the left, forward and backward. And it will leap. And it will hide again, and will look again, it will straighten up, throw back its head, and suddenly it will grow terribly stout.

And it will no longer have one head upon one slender neck: it will have thousands. And it will no longer crawl slowly, it will run, it will make gigantic bounds. It had been silent, now it is singing, whistling, yelling, giving orders to stone and to iron, driving all from its path.

And suddenly it will begin to circle.

3.

We saw more dead people than living; and the dead were calm; they did not know what had happened to them, and they were calm. But what about the living? Just think what a ridiculous thing was told us by a madman for whom, too, in those days of stern equality the door had opened!

Do you think he was amazed? He looked on attentively and benignly, and the grey stubble on his yellow face bristled with proud joy—as though he had done it all himself. I do not like madmen, and was going to walk past him, but Pascale, the professor, stopped me, and respectfully asked the proud madman:

"What makes you so pleased, *signor*?"

Pascale was far from being short of stature, but the madman searched for him a long time with his eyes, like for a grain of sand that has suddenly spoken out aloud from amidst of a sand heap, and finally he discovered him. And hardly parting his lips—so proud was he—he repeated the question:

"What makes me so pleased?"

And he waved his hand majestically and said:

"This is perfect order. We have so long craved for order."

He called that order! I laughed out aloud, but just at that moment a corpulent and altogether insane monk came up, and proved even

144

more ridiculous.

4.

For a long time, they played their comedy among the ruins, the lunatic and the monk, while we sat on a heap of stones, laughing and encouraging them, shouting "bravo."

"Fraud! I have been deceived!" cried the fat monk.

He was so fat, I don't think you've ever seen any one as fat. It was repulsive to watch him, the yellow fat of his cheeks and of his belly quivered and shook so with wrath and fear.

"There's perfect order for you!" cried the lunatic approvingly, hardly deigning to part his lips.

"Fraud!" yelled the monk.

And suddenly he commenced to curse God. The monk! Think of it!

5.

. . . .

6.

He assured us all that God had deceived him and he wept. He swore like a crooked gambler that this was poor recompense for his prayers and his faith. He stamped his feet and he cursed like a mule driver who comes out of a gin mill and suddenly discovers that his mules had scattered to the four winds.

And suddenly Pascale, the professor, lost his temper. He demanded that I give him my knife and said to the monk who had sat down for a rest after his outburst of curses:

"Listen, in a minute I will slit your belly, and if I find there but one drop of wine or one atom of a pullet. . . ."

"And if you don't?" angrily retorted the monk.

"Then we shall count you among the saints. Hold his legs, Geronimo!"

The monk was frightened and departed mumbling:

"And I thought you were Christians! Blasphemy! Blasphemy!"

But the lunatic gazed after him benignly and spoke approvingly:

"This is what I call perfect order. We have been so long waiting for perfect order."

7.

And we walked a long time about the city and saw many odd things. But the day was short, and the night fell upon earth earlier than ever before; and when the firing squad was killing Pascale, the soldiers had lighted their torches.

8.

When Pascale was put against the wall, against the portion of it which had remained uninjured, and the soldiers raised their rifles, the officer said to him:

"You will die in a moment. Tell me why are you not afraid? That which has happened is terrible, and we are all pale with horror, but you are not. Why is that?"

Pascale was silent; he waited for the officer to ask him more questions so that he might reply to all of them in one.

"And whence comes your boldness: to stoop and to take that which belongs to others at a time when people in terror forget even themselves and their children? And are you not sorry for those women and children who have perished? We have seen cats that have lost their mind through terror, and you are a human being. I will have you shot instantly."

This was well spoken, but our Pascale could speak every bit as well. He has been shot dead. He is dead, but some day when all the dead arise you will hear his speech, and you will shed tears, if by that time all the tears are not exhausted, O Man.

He said:

"I take that which is another's because I have nothing that is my own. I took the raiment off a dead man in order to clothe my living flesh, but you have seen me do it, and so you have stripped me; and now I stand naked in front of your rifles. Soldiers, fire!"

But the officer did not suffer them to fire and asked him to speak further.

9.

"Naked I stand in front of your rifles and fear nothing, not even your rifles. But you are pale with fear, and you fear everything, even your own rifles, even my naked body. When the quake was heard, it destroyed and killed your city, your fortunes, your children and wives—but it opened a prison for me. What then shall, I fear? I have nothing of my own upon the face of the earth. I am, naked.

10.

"And if the whole earth crumbled into ruin, and the very beasts howled with horror, and the fish found a voice to express their grief, and the birds fell to the ground with dread, even then I would not fear.

146

For all others it means the ruin of the earth, for me it opens the doors of a prison. What then shall, I fear? I am naked.

11.

"And if the universe crumbled, with heaven and hell, and horror were enthroned over the infinity of living creatures, even then I would know no fear. For all it would be the end of the universe, for me the opening of a prison. What then shall, I fear? I am naked.

12.

"And now, when with one salvo of your rifles you will destroy for me the earth and the universe, even now I know no fear. For all of you it will be the destruction and the fall of a human body, but for me a prison will open its gates. Soldiers, fire! I am naked."

13.

The torches blazed. It was the shortest day which I had ever seen. Night fell upon the earth more quickly than ever before.

"It is your turn now," ordered the officer, when Pascale, the professor, had fallen.

True, I had not been caught in any wrongdoing, and there was nothing to kill me for. But can you argue with them? And so, I stood up. And I lamented the night. Do you understand me? the night! Here the torches and the fires were ruining it, and there, behind the torches and the fire, it stood out strong, and firm, and dark as the nights of my youth. I love the night, for then I do not see myself and can think what I will.

The day reaches my garments, but can go no further. It stops at the darkness of my body and turns blind. But the night reaches my very heart. That is why it is so easy to love at night; anybody will tell you that. Ah, to spend only one hour in the shade of the faithful, of the black and beautiful night, only one hour. But can you argue with them? So, I stood up.

But it is well to love also in the day time, when the sun is shining. Love itself is like the night, it reaches the heart, don't you see. And in love you fail to see your own self, even as in the midst of night. And if you only look into its eyes—straight into its black eyes—and look without tearing your gaze away. . . .

Suddenly for some reason the officer shouted angrily at the soldier and snapped at me:

"Get out of here!"

14.

Another day passed. And on that day the soldiers shot that young-ster who had called me father.

15.

Night sank upon the earth and I departed from that city of the dead.

16.

Dies irae—the day of wrath, the day of vengeance and of stern ret-ribution, the day of Horror and of Death.

17.

. . . . That procession which I had watched from behind the wall was a strange and a terrible sight. They were bearing the statues of their saints, but did not know whether to raise them still higher over their heads or to cast them upon the ground, trampling the fragments underfoot. Some were still cursing, while others were already saying their prayers, but they walked on together, the children of the same father and the same mother, or Horror and of Death. They leaped over the crevices and disappeared in abysses. And the saints reeled like drunkards.

Dies irae. . . . Some were singing, others were weeping, and still others were laughing. Some howled like lunatics. And they were wav-ing their hands, and all were in a hurry. The fat-bellied monks were running. From whom were they running away? Not a soul was seen behind them. Meekly lolled the ruins in the warm glow of the sun, and the fire was disappearing into the ground, smoking wearily.

18.

From whom were they fleeing? There was not a soul behind them.

19.

You barely touched a tree, and a ripe orange fell at your feet. First one, then another, a third. . . . The crop bids fair to be fine. A good orange is like a little sun, and when there is an abundance of them, you feel like smiling, as though the sun shone brightly. And the leaves are so dark, just like the night back of the sun. No, they are green, dark green. Why are you telling untruths, Geronimo?

But how cautious is that deaf devil, that subterranean trumpeter, who is never content because of his deafness: he has destroyed a city, but has left an orange suspended on a branch, to wait for Geronimo. You barely touch the tree, and a ripe orange drops at your feet. First one, then another, then a third. . . . They will be taken overseas to strange lands. And in those lands, where reign the cold and the fogs, people will look at them and say: "Yes, there is a sun for you!"

20.

Pascale, the professor—we called him "*il professore*" because he was so wise, he could write verses, and he discoursed so nobly on all sorts of subjects. He is dead.

21.

Why am I terrified? Why do I walk faster and faster? I had been afraid there. . . .

22.

I never knew that my feet so loved to walk. They love every step which they make. They part so sadly with every step; they seem to want to turn back. And so greedy are they that the longest road seems short to them, that the widest road seems narrow. They regret—fancy!—that they cannot at once walk backward and forward, to the right and to the left. Let them have their will and they will cover the earth with their traces, not leaving a patch: and still, they would seek more.

And another thing I did not know: I did not know about my eyes that they can breathe.

Afar off I see the ocean.

23.

What else can I tell you? I was seized by the *gendarmes*.

24.

Once more thou hast locked the doors of my prison, O Man! When didst thou have time to build it? Still in ruins lies thy house, the bones of thy children are not yet bare in the grave, but thou art already at work, tapping with thy hammer, patching together with cement the obedient stone, rearing before thy face the obedient iron. How fast dost thou build thy prisons, O Man!

Still in ruins are thy churches, bu thy prison is all finished.

Still shaking with terror are thy hands, but already they grasp the key, and rattle the lock, and slip the bolt. Thou art a musician: to the jingle of gold, thou requirest the accompanying rattle of fetters—let that be the bass.

Grim death is still in thy blanched nostrils, and already thou art sniffing at something, turning thy nose this way and that way. How fast buildest thou thy prisons, O Man!

25.

The iron does not even rattle—so strong it is. And it is cold to the touch like someone's icy heart. Silent is also the stone of the walls—so proud it is, so everlasting and mighty. At the appointed time comes the jailer and flings at me my food like at a savage beast. And I show my teeth—why should I not show my teeth? I am starved and naked. And the clock is striking.

Art thou content, O Man, my master?

26.

But I do not believe in thy prison, O Man, my master! I do not believe in thy iron; I do not believe in thy stone, in thy power, O Man, my master! That which I have once seen destroyed, shall never be knit together again.

Thus, would have spoken even Pascale, the professor.

27.

Set thy clock a-going, it marks well the time until it stops. Rattle thy keys, for even thy paradise thou hast shut with lock and key. Rattle thy keys and shut the door, they shut well while there is a door. And walk around cautiously.

And when all is still, thou wilt say: it is well now, it is quite still now. And thou wilt lie down to sleep. It is quite still now, thou wilt say, but I hear how he is gnawing at the iron with his teeth. But thou wilt say that the iron is too strong for him, and thou wilt lie down to sleep. And when thou hast fallen asleep, holding tight thy keys in thy happy hands, suddenly the subterranean trumpeter will roar out loudly, awaking thee with his thunder, raising thee to thy feet with the force of terror, holding thee erect with a mighty arm: so that dying thou shalt see death. Wide as the day will open thy eyes; terror will tear them wide open. Ears will come to thy heart, so that dying thou shalt hear death.

And thy clock will stop.

28.
Freedom!

His Excellency the governor

1

Fifteen days had passed since that memorable occurrence, and yet it filled his mind—as though Time itself had lost its ascendancy over thought and things, or else had stopped like a broken clock. Wherever he might turn his fancy, in whatever strange and distant channels, still his hunted thoughts returned to that same incident, and ran, helpless, against it; as upon a great silent prison wall in a blind alley. And what strange paths these fancies took. He thought, for instance, of an Italian trip of long ago—a journey full of sunshine, youth and song. He pictured one of those Italian beggars, and directly rose before his vision the mob of workmen, the volley of musketry, the smell of powder, and the blood! Or perhaps a perfume rose to his brain, and at once he remembered his handkerchief—*that* had been perfumed too—and with *that* he had signalled for the filing!

At first the sequence of his thought had been logical—quite comprehensible; and though burdensome had caused him no uneasiness. But soon everything reminded him of that occasion, abruptly and with most painful untimeliness: like a blow from around the corner. He laughs, and suddenly he seems to hear general laughter on all sides, and sees with hideous clearness the face of one of the dead—although at the time he had not really thought of laughing: nor had the others laughed! .... Or else he hears the swallows twittering in the twilight; or sees a chair—just a common oak chair; or reaches for the—everything calls to his mind one and the same indelible scene—the white waving handkerchief, the shots, the blood! As though he lived in a room with a thousand doors, and whichever one he tried to open, the same fixed picture met his gaze: the signal—the smoke—the blood!

The affair was simple enough of itself—though sad, of course. The workmen in a suburban factory, after a three weeks' strike, had gathered—some thousand strong—together with their women and children, their old and disabled, and had appeared before him with demands which he as governor could not grant. And they had carried themselves impudently and defiantly; had screamed; insulted the officials—and one woman, who seemed quite beside herself, had plucked at his sleeve till the seam gave way. Then when his staff had led him back on to the balcony (he still only wanted to speak with them and pacify them) the workmen had begun to throw stones, had broken a number of windows, and wounded the Chief of Police. Then his rage got the better of him and he gave the signal with his handkerchief!

The people were so turbulent that they had to be shot at a second time; and so there were many dead—forty-seven, according to the count;—among them nine women and three children, singularly enough all girls! .... The number of the wounded was even greater.

Drawn by a strange, unconquerable passion of curiosity, and against the advice of his people, he had gone to see the dead where they were laid out in the engine-house shed of the Police Station No. 3. Naturally there was no urgent reason for his going, but he felt that in some unaccountable way they would be the better for it if he saw to them himself; as someone who has shot carelessly and at random feels moved to find where the bullet had lodged, and to handle it.

It was dark and cool in the long engine-house, and the bodies lay under a strip of grey canvas, in two precise rows, like a strange display of curious wares. They had probably been arranged for the governor's visit, and were laid in careful order, shoulder to shoulder, with faces up. The canvas covered only their heads and the upper part of their bodies; the legs were exposed as though to facilitate their counting—these stiff, immovable legs, some in old worn boots, some with tattered little shoes, and others bare and dirty, the sunburned skin showing strangely enough through the grime. The women and children were laid by themselves; and here, too, one felt there had been an attempt to simplify the count.

And it was still, far too still for such a throng of people; and the living who entered were unable to dispel the silence. From behind a wooden partition came the sound of a groom at work. He evidently thought himself alone—but for the dead—and talked to his horses with careless joviality: "Whoa there, you devil! Stand still while I curry you!"

The governor glanced at the rows of legs that lost themselves in the gloom, and said, in his smothered bass, almost a whisper: "How many are there?"

The Assistant Police Commissioner, a young, beardless fellow with a pimply face, stepped up from behind and, saluting, announced, in a loud voice: "Thirty-five men, nine women and three children, Your Excellency!"

The governor frowned involuntarily, and the Assistant Police Commissioner bowed himself into the background. He would gladly have called the governor's attention to the neat lane between the corpses that had been carefully strewn with sand, but the governor had no eyes for this, though he was staring fixedly at the floor.

"Three children?"

"Three, Your Excellency. Would Your Excellency wish the canvas removed?"

The governor was silent.

"There are all sorts of persons here, Your Excellency," continued the commissioner, deferentially but briskly, while he took the governor's silence for consent, and commanded, in hasty whispers: "Ivanoff! quick, Isidorshuck, take the other end—here, pull away now!"

With a soft, sliding rustle the dingy canvas came away and one after the other the white spots of faces dawned into view—bearded and old, young and smooth—all different, but united in the common likeness of death. One hardly saw the wounds and the blood, they were mostly hidden under their clothes; only in one face the eye appeared unnaturally dark and sunken, shedding strange black tears that looked in the dusk like tar. The majority had the same pale, blank stare; some had kept their identical twinkle, and one covered his face with his hand as though to shield it from the glare. But the Assistant Commissioner gazed with a pained expression at these corpses that so disturbed his sense of order.

The governor felt that these pale faces had been among the mob that morning—in the foremost ranks, he knew; and many of them he had seen personally as he parleyed with them. But now they were all beyond his recognition. This new community with death had lent them a most singular expression! They lay there lifeless and motionless on the floor; like plaster casts made flat on the back that they might rest more firmly. Yet this immovability seemed counterfeited—one could hardly believe it real. They were dumb, and the silence seemed as artificial as their rigid pose; but something about them of anxious expectancy made it painfully impossible for the observers to speak. If a busy city had suddenly been turned to stone, and all its inhabitants petrified at one blow; if the sun had stood still, and the leaves had hushed their rustling, and all that walked or moved had stiffened—they might have shown this same strange look of interrupted effort, of breathless expectancy and mysterious alertness for what was yet to come.

"May I ask if Your Excellency wishes to order coffins or whether they shall be buried in a common trench?" asked the Assistant Commissioner, with loud *naïveté*: the exigencies of the emergency impressed him with a certain deferential self-confidence—and furthermore he was very young.

"What sort of a trench?" asked the governor perfunctorily.

"You just dig a large ditch, Your Excellency—" The governor turned abruptly and left the place. As he entered the carriage, he heard behind him the heavy grating of the rusty hinges—they were shutting in the dead.

Next morning, he visited the wounded in the city hospital, still driven by that same tormenting curiosity: the longing to undo the inevitable, and to blot out the past. The dead at least stared at him, but these would not deign him a glance! And in the stubbornness with which they averted their eyes, he read the immutability of his accomplished act. It was finished! Something monstrous had been done, and it was idle and useless to strive to alter the fact.

And from that very moment, Time for him had stood still, and this certain something inexplicable and unspeakable had come over him. It was not remorse, for he felt himself in the right; nor was it pity, that gentle feeling that softly veils the heart and calls forth tears. He could think of these dead quite calmly; even of the little children. Their pain and their sorrows hardly moved him. But he could not rid his thoughts of them—they were constantly before his mind in sharpest outline—these puppets, these broken dolls! And therein lay the horrid mystery—a something, like the tales of magic of one's nursery days. According to others, four—five—seven—days had elapsed since the catastrophe—but for him in the meantime not one single hour had gone by. His thoughts played yet about that time—those shots—that signalling handkerchief!—the realisation that something irrevocable was about to happen—*had* happened!

He was convinced that he could far more easily be calm, and forget the things which no vain regrets could alter, if the people about him would be less pointed in their attentions. By their actions, looks and gestures; their respectful, sympathetic manner, and their voices as though soothing a fretful invalid, they firmly fastened in his brain the thought of that ineradicable occurrence.

The Chief of Police announced the next day, in soothing tones, that two or three more of the wounded had been dismissed, cured, from the hospital; each morning his wife, Maria Petrovna, pressed her lips to his forehead to see whether he had a fever—as though he were a child! and those dead bodies—unripe fruit, of which he had eaten too freely! What nonsense!

And eight days after the event the Right Reverend Bishop Micael himself called upon him, and at his first words clearly showed that he had the same notion as all the others, and had come to lighten the governor's conscience. He spoke of the workmen as sinners, and called him a peacemaker—and all this without introducing a single one of his well-worn Bible texts—for he knew the governor was not particularly fond of clerical prating. The old man appeared to distressing disadvantage as he lied so aimlessly in the face of his God.

During the interview the bishop turned his deaf ear toward his companion, and, purple with rage (he could feel himself how the blood mounted to his brow) the governor pouted his lips and trumpeted into that great bloodless ear that was turned toward him from that soft, grey bush of hair: "Sinners they may be, Your Eminence; nevertheless, if I were in your place I should certainly say a Mass for their departed souls."

The bishop turned away his ear, smoothed down his waistcoat with a bony hand, and nodded his head as he answered, in his softest voice: "Each station has its own cross. Had I been in Your Excellency's place I should never have ordered them shot, nor burdened the Holy Office with Masses for their souls. But that is neither here nor there— they were undoubtedly sinners!" With a parting benediction he swept to the door—his gown rustling and swaying—bowing to each object that he passed as though blessing it. In the vestibule he fussed a long time with his barge-like goloshes, turning first one ear and then the other to the impatient governor, who was helping him, with unwilling politeness: "Don't trouble, Your Excellency! Oh, please don't trouble yourself!" And these words of his sounded to the governor as if he were a helpless invalid to whom the least exertion might be fatal.

That same day the governor's son, an officer in a St. Petersburg regiment, came home for his Sunday furlough, and though he was in gay good humour, and gave no special reason for his unusual visit, it was evident that the same incomprehensible anxiety for the governor had induced him to come. He made light of the whole affair, and assured them that in St. Petersburg they were delighted with the pluck and energy of Peter Iljitch; and yet he strongly urged that they should ask for another Cossack regiment and double then precautionary measures. "What sort of precautionary measures?" asked the governor, stern and amazed—but there was no answer. These apprehensions seemed all the more absurd as perfect calm had reigned in the city from that day on. The workmen had resumed their labours: even the interment had passed off undisturbed, though the Chief of Police had felt some anxiety, and ordered out all the reserves. Yet nothing indicated the possibility of a repetition of the incident of August seventeenth.

Finally he received from St. Petersburg a flattering acknowledgment of his detailed report of the occurrence. One would have thought that this would lighten the load and sink his burden in the sea of the past! But the fact will not sink! As though deriving its power from Time and Death, it stands rigid in his remembrance—the unburied corpse of a vanished event. Stubbornly, night after night, he seeks to bury it; the darkness passes, day breaks, and there again—the beginning and end of all things, between him and the world stands that indelible picture: the signal with the white handkerchief, the crack of rifles, the blood!

2

The governor's audience has long been ended, and he is about to drive out to his villa, waiting on for his *aide-de-camp* Kosloff, who is shopping for Her Excellency. He sits in his study, his papers before him, and yet he cannot work—he broods. Then, rising, he thrusts his hands deeper into the pockets of his red-striped trousers, throws back his great grey head, and paces the room with heavy, soldierly tread. He pauses at the window, spreads the strong, thick fingers of his hand, and says, in strident tones: "But what is it all about?" And he fancies that as long as he sat and thought he was an ordinary man like any other; simply Peter Iljitch—but with the first sound of his own voice, that gesture—he has suddenly become the governor, the Major-General! An uneasy feeling creeps over him, his thoughts whirl and tangle; and with a curt official shrug of his left shoulder-strap he turns from the window and paces the floor again.

"*This* is the *way* the *Gov*-er-nors walk!" The rhythm jerks through his brain, keeping time with his heavy footfall until he seats himself again, carefully avoiding all movement that shall recall his official capacity.

The sound of a bell.

"Has he come yet?"

"If you please, no, Your Excellency."

And while the lackey speaks the title softly and respectfully, he suddenly recollects: "Ah yes! They broke the windows there that day, and I have not seen them yet." . . . .

"Call me when he comes. I shall be in the drawing-room."

The high old-fashioned windows had eight small panes, which gave the room the gloomy look of an office: the appearance of a Court of Chancery, or of a jail. The three windows nearest the balcony had new panes, which still showed the marks of putty-daubed fingers; apparently it had never entered into the idle brains of any of the countless servants that all traces of that disturbance must be wiped away. It was the same old story—if you ordered them they would do it; if not they'd never lift a finger of their own accord . . . .

"Let this be cleaned directly! I can't stand this disorder!"

"Yes, Your Excellency!"

He would have liked to step out onto the balcony, yet it seemed unwise to draw the attention of the passers-by, so he stared through the glass at the Square, where the mob had surged that day, where the rifles had crashed—and forty-seven restless people had been turned to dumb, still corpses!—row on row—shoulder to shoulder—feet to feet—like a parade seen from below.

Now all was still out there. Close by the window stands a poplar with ragged bark, already in autumn colouring, and behind it lies the Square, peaceful and sleepy in the sun. Hardly a stone stirring, and the cobblestones lying in even rows like beads, with here and there a bit of grass between, greener in the hollows and along the gutters. Empty and deserted the Square was—but rather smiling; yet, perhaps because he saw it through the dingy panes, it appeared dismal and squalid, brooding in sullen apathy over its hopeless grey misery. And although it was broad daylight, yet all these things—the poplar with its ragged bark, the vacant, even rows of cobblestones—seemed craving for the night to come and wrap their useless being in its darkness.

"Has he not come yet?"

"No, Your Excellency."

"When he comes bring him here."

The drawing-room had been furnished in the time of the previous governor, or possibly earlier still, judging from the soiled and faded condition of its costly hangings. About the brassbound chimney hole

157

were traced dark yellow stains, like lines about the drooling mouth of age. These were masked by hangings, and in winter when the rooms were lighted, one hardly noticed these defects; but now they crowded into view in all their shabby elegance, making a most painful impression. For instance, that landscape—a moonlight scene in Italy: it hangs crooked, yet no one gives it a straightening touch, and it seems to have hung so throughout the rule of successive governors. The furniture, too, is costly, but worn and moth-eaten: like an apartment in a luxurious villa whose owner has suddenly died of a stroke, and whose estate has long lain in litigation, cared for by quarrelling heirs.

And nothing in the room was the property of its occupants; not even the photographs. Either they were official belongings or had been forgotten by some predecessor. Instead of portraits of friends and relatives, there was an album with views of the city: the seminary, the district court; then four unknown officials, two seated and two standing behind them; a weather-beaten bishop, and finally a round hole that ended at the cover.

"Hideous!" said the governor aloud, and threw the album aside, with a gesture of loathing. He had been standing to look at the pictures, and now he turned again with a shrug and started his customary pacing. "*This*-is-the-*way*-the-*Gov*-er-nors-*walk*, -the-*Gov*-ev-nors-*walk*! the-*Gov*-er-nors-*walk*!"

—So trod the former governor, and his predecessor, and *his*, and all the other unknown governors. They rose from somewhere, paced these halls with firm, square steps; while over them hung the crooked Italian landscape—held receptions, even gave balls—and then vanished again somewhere. Perhaps they too had ordered the people shot—at least something similar had occurred under his third predecessor.

A workman was crossing the deserted square, splashed with paint, and carrying his paint and brushes—then all was empty again. Down from the ragged poplar fell a shrivelled leaf, floating aimlessly to the ground—and instantly the thought whirled through his head: that signal with the white handkerchief—the shots—the blood!

Trivial detail occurred to him now; how he had prepared to give the signal. He had pulled his handkerchief from his pocket beforehand and held it tightly clutched in a ball in his right hand; then he unfolded it carefully and waved it hastily, not up and down, but forward and out, as though he were tossing something—as though he were flinging bullets! Then it came to him that he had taken a stride—had crossed an invisible threshold—the iron door had clanged behind him with a loud grating of its iron hinges, and there was no return.

"Ah, you at last, Leo Andrejevitch. I've waited—the Lord knows how long!"

"I'm sorry, Peter Iljitch, but you never can find anything in this beastly hole."

"Now, let's be off! Come! Yes, but listen!" The governor stood still and continued, pursing his lips: "Why are all our public offices so dirty? Take, for instance, our government office; or—I was in the police department the other day—I tell you it's a pothouse, a stable—and decent men sit there in good, fresh uniform, with the dirt about in heaps!"

"But there's no money!"

"Nonsense! Quibbles! And here"—the governor waved his hand to indicate the walls—"look at that now—disgusting!"

"Yes, but, Peter Iljitch, what's to hinder your doing it over to suit yourself? How often have I said that very thing to Maria Petrovna, and Her Excellency agrees with me thoroughly."

The governor strode to the door, muttering: "It's not worth while!"

His *aide* cast a pitying glance at the broad back, at his stringy, muscular neck like a double column supporting the head, and, striving to keep anxiety out of his voice, he remarked: "By the way, I've just seen 'the Pike'; he tells me that the last of the wounded was dismissed from the hospital yesterday. He was the worst of the lot, and seemed to have very little chance. But these peasants have the most astonishing vitality!" In private the Chief of Police was known as "the Pike" because of his pale, bulgy eyes, and his long, lank body, with its narrow, fin-like back.

The governor made no answer. He was enjoying the autumn sunshine and the keen autumn air—a mixture of languor and crispness, as though each could be enjoyed by itself; here freshness, and there a wave of heat:—and the heavens were so lovely—tender, distant, and such a wonderful, startling blue. How perfect it must be in the country now!

He had already seated himself in the carriage, and moved over to make room for the *aide*, when a man passed by with a peculiar stoop. As he pulled off his cap he shielded his face with his elbow, so that the governor had only a glimpse of a shock of curly fair hair and a tanned young throat—he noticed that he trod carefully and noiselessly, as though he had been barefooted, and that he bent over as if looking backward. "What a singularly unpleasant person!" thought he.

159

Evidently the two men following the governor thought so too. They were stepping into a carriage close at hand. With the rapid glance of professional keenness, they turned simultaneously to note the fellow, but finding nothing questionable about him, hurried on to precede the governor.

They were in a smart rubber-tyred trap—the wheels leaped, the body swayed, and they sat leaning forward on account of the rapid motion, and had soon left the governor far behind in order not to annoy him with their dust.

"Who are those two?" he asked his *aide*, looking at him suspiciously from the corner of his eye—and the other answered carelessly: "Secret Police."

"What's that for?" asked the governor abruptly.

"I don't know," said Leo Andrejevitch evasively; "that's the Pike's affair."

At the corner stood the beardless young Police Commissioner, strutting and admiring his shiny lacquered boots—the same one who had accompanied the governor on his inspection of the bodies; and as they passed the police headquarters two mounted guards rode out from under the arch, their horses' hoofs pounding behind in the dust. Their faces beamed with officious zeal, and they both gazed steadily at the governor's back. The *aide* pretended not to notice, but the governor threw a lowering glance at the men, and then, with his white-gloved hands tightly clenched on his knees, he lost himself in gloomy thought.

The road to the villa circled the outskirts of the town, through a lane called Kanatnaja alley, where factory hands and their families lived, crowded by all sorts of miserable beings from the city—some in wretched tumble-down huts, and some in two-story brick tenements of barrack-like uniformity. The governor would gladly have bowed if he had seen anyone; but the street was empty, as though it were late at night—not even the children about. Only one little lad appeared for a moment behind a fence, among the red leaves of a rowan-tree, but even he slid hastily from the trunk and hid in the gateway. Through the summer the alley had been crowded with chickens and lean, dirty pigs, but there were none left now—apparently, they had all been eaten in the three weeks' famine.

Nothing even indirectly recalled the catastrophe, but in the empty silence of the street, so indifferent to the governor's passing, lay something heavy, sullen, brooding—and a light cloud of incense seemed to hang in the transparent air.

"Listen!" cried the governor suddenly, grasping his companion's knee. "That man there—"

"What man?"

The governor did not answer. Firmly clutching his knee, he gazed at the *aide* with a face like a barred and shuttered house whose doors and windows have suddenly been thrown open. Then he knit his heavy grey brows, deliberately turned his ponderous back, and gazed intently out of the carriage. The horses of the guard pounded down the road, and the dismal, lonely lane, dark on one side, bright sunlight on the other, was also sunk in dreary brooding . . . .

Like a stampeded herd the cottages huddled together; with their riddled roofs, their broken benches, and their overhanging windows—like greybeards' chins thrust out. Then came a vacant lot, with a broken fence and an old well, sunk about the rim and boarded over; then a row of great lime-trees behind a high broken wall, and a stately old house that had drifted somehow to these wastes, but was now long since abandoned. Its shutters were closed, and on a sign could be read: "This House for Sale." Then beyond came cottages again, and a row of brick houses—large, bleak and hideous, with deep-set narrow windows. They were quite new—you could still see the caked plaster lying about, and the holes where the scaffolding had been; but they were already squalid and neglected. They looked like prisons, and life in such a place must be fully as sad, as hopeless, and as narrow as a life in jail!

There is the gateway to the open fields, and the last little house—no trace of vegetation about it, no fence. It stands there leaning forward, walls and roof both, as though someone had shoved it violently from behind—and neither in the windows nor anywhere about a single person visible.

"After the fall rains you'll have trouble, Peter Iljitch, getting the carriage through here. I should think you'd literally sink in the mud!"

3

Laughter and song and merry games—for tomorrow Peter Iljitch's son, the officer, returned to St. Petersburg, and friends had gathered to say goodbye. Uniforms and gay frocks were scattered about in the open glades and meadows, under the purple and gold of the autumn foliage, and in the sapphire clearness of the woodland ways. As the red wintry sunset faded and the stars moved by in the heavens, they set off fireworks—rockets that burst with a loud report, star-mines and pinwheels. A stifling smoke crept under the great old trees that stood there, so earnestly watching; and when they started the Bengal lights, hurrying figures were changed to ghosts—to fluttering, flitting shadows!

Commissioner "Pike," who had pretty freely quenched his thirst at dinner, gazed indulgently at the gay throng, strutted comically about among the ladies, and enjoyed himself. And when presently he heard the governor's voice close beside him in the smoky darkness, he was taken with a wild desire to kiss him on the shoulder, to hug him carefully—or any little thing of that kind—as an expression of his devotion. Instead of this, however, he laid his hand on the left breast of his uniform, threw away a cigarette he had just lighted, and said: "Ah! Your Excellency, what a charming *fête*!" ....

"Listen, Illawion Wassiljevitch," interrupted the governor, with a suppressed growl. "Why do you always set these spies here? What does it mean?"

"Some rascal might plan an attack on Your Excellency's sacred person," said the Pike, with deep emotion, and laying both hands on his heart. "And then, besides .... it is my duty!"

Popping of firecrackers, shrieks of terror, and loud laughter drowned his words. Then a sudden rain fell, extinguishing the red and green fires which had illuminated the smoky darkness, and made the governor's buttons and epaulets shine out.

"I know the reason, Illawion Wassiljevitch—that is, I think I can guess it. But I think it can hardly be serious."

"It is most exceedingly serious, your Excellency! The whole town is talking of it. Astonishing how busily they talk about it! I have already arrested three men—but they were the wrong ones."

A fresh outburst of firing and gay shouts interrupted him, and when the noise had subsided the governor had gone.

After supper they all drove off, marshalled by the young Assistant Commissioner. Everything: the fireworks which he had seen from behind the trees, the carriages and the people, seemed to him extraordinarily lovely, and his own fresh voice astonished him with its beauty and its power. The Pike was horribly drunk, cracked jokes, laughed, and even sang the first few bars of the Marseillaise:

"*Allons, enfants de la patrie, Le jour de gloire est arrivé!*" ....

At last, they had all gone. "What are you worrying about so, father?" said the lieutenant, laying his hand on Peter Iljitch's shoulder with patronising kindliness. The governor was very much loved by his family, and the governor's lady even feared him a trifle; but they all felt that he had aged sadly in these last few weeks, and their fondness was not without a tinge of contempt.

"Nonsense! Nothing but nonsense!" answered Peter Iljitch hesitatingly. For some reasons he would gladly have unburdened himself to his son, but then again, their views differed so radically that he had feared this explanation. Yet now this very difference of opinion might be of use. "The thing is this, you see," he continued, with some embarrassment, "this trouble with the workmen makes me somewhat uneasy."

Their eyes met square—but the son's face was blank with astonishment as he dropped his hand from his father's shoulder, saying: "But I thought you had your 'Honourable Mention' from St. Petersburg!"

"Certainly—and it pleased me very much. And yet . . . .Aljosha!" He gazed into his son's fine eyes with the clumsy tenderness of a stern old man. "They aren't Turks after all, are they? They're as much Russians as we—their names are Ivan and Peter, like ours.—And yet I treated them like Turks! 'Hm? How does the thing strike you now?"

"It strikes me that you are a Revolutionist!"

"But they wear the cross upon their breasts, Aljosha! And I"—he raised his finger—"I ordered them to fire at those crosses!"

"As far as I've seen you, father, you've never shown any particular religious scruples before. What have the crosses to do with it? That might be a telling point if you were addressing your regiment in the Square, or for some such occasion, but—"

"To be sure! Of course!" agreed the governor hastily; "the crosses are aside from the argument. The point I want to make is this—that they are fellow-beings. Do you understand, Aljosha; fellow-countrymen! Yes, if I were some German now, called August Karlovitch Schlippe-Detmold! . . . .but my name is Peter—and Iljitch besides!"

The lieutenant's voice was rather dry. "You have such distorted notions, father! What have the Germans to do with this affair? And then, for that matter, haven't Germans shot down Germans, and Frenchmen the French—and so on? Why shouldn't Russians fire on Russians? As a representative of the Government, you certainly know that law and order must be supported at all costs; and whoever it may be who disturbs them—the same rule applies. If I were the guilty one, it would be your *duty* to have me shot down like a Turk!"

"That's true," said the governor, nodding thoughtfully, and beginning to pace the floor. "That's quite true!" And then he stopped. "But they were driven by hunger, Aljosha. If you could have seen them!"

"There were the peasants in Sensivjejvo—they rose because they were famished too—but that didn't keep you from giving them a good dose of the knout!"

"Flogging is a very different thing from—That fool laid them all out in a row! Like game at the end of a hunt! And I looked at their poor thin legs, and thought: 'These legs will never walk again!' You cannot understand, Alexey! Of course, as a matter of State, an executioner is a necessity—but to *be* the executioner!"

"What are you talking about, father?"

"I know—I feel it—they will kill me yet!—It's not that I fear death"—the governor raised his grey head and looked steadily at his son—"but I know . . . .they will surely kill me! I never understood before. I only thought: 'What is it all about?'"—he stretched his powerful fingers and then doubled them into a fist. "But now I understand: they mean to kill me! Don't laugh; you are young yet. But I have felt death today—here, in my head. Yes, in my head!"

"Father, I beg of you, send for the Cossacks! Demand a bodyguard! They'll grant you anything! I beg of you, as your son, and I ask it in the name of Russia, to whom your life is precious!"

"And who is to kill me but this same Russia? And why should I have the Cossacks? . . . .To defend me from Russia—in the *name* of Russia! And after all, could Cossacks, spies or guards, save a man with death branded on his forehead? You've been drinking a good deal this evening, Alexey, but you are sober enough to understand this: I feel the hand of death! Even there in the storehouse, where they laid the bodies, I felt it; yet then I did not realise what it was. This I've just been telling you, about crosses and Russians, is nonsense, of course—has nothing to do with the thing. But do you see this handkerchief?" Eagerly he drew a handkerchief from his pocket, unfolded it, and held it up for inspection like a conjurer: "Alexey Petrovitch, now look here!" He waved it hastily and a subtle perfume was wafted to the lieutenant, who sat there looking anxious. "There, you doubting scientist! you *fin de siècle* thinker! You believe in nothing—but I believe in the old law: Blood for blood! You will see!"

"Father, send in your resignation, and travel."

He seemed to have expected this advice, and was not at all surprised. "No—not for the world," he answered firmly; "you can see for yourself that would be tantamount to flight. Nonsense! Not for the world!"

"Forgive me, father, but you seem so unreasonable!" The lieutenant cocked his head and shrugged his shoulders. "I don't know really what to think. Mother groans and you talk of death—and what is it all about? I'm ashamed of you, father! I've always considered you a man of discernment and force, and now you're like a child or a hysterical woman. Forgive me! But I cannot understand it at all!"

He himself was not in the least hysterical, nor in the slightest degree womanish—this handsome young fellow, with his fresh, smooth-shaven face and the calm, finished manner of a man who not only respects himself but reveres himself! He always seemed to be the sole individual in a crowd; and you must be a most distinguished person (a general at the very least) to have him aware of you and to make him overcome that slight constraint and reserve that the average public inspired in him. He was a good swimmer and loved the sport, and when he went to the baths on the Neva in the summertime, he noted his own perfect symmetry as coolly and complacently as though he were quite alone . . . .One day a Chinaman appeared at the baths, and everyone stared at him—some with a sneaking curiosity and some quite openly and unabashed. He alone did not vouchsafe him a glance—considering himself far more interesting and more important than any Chinaman . . . .

Everything in the world was clear and simple to him; everything could be reduced to a formula—and he knew that with the Cossacks things would certainly go better than without the Cossacks.

His reproaches had a ring of righteous indignation, only tempered by politeness and the fear of wounding the old man's vanity. All this that his father had told him was not entirely unexpected. He had always known him to be a dreamer. But it struck him as something coarse, barbarous, atavistic. "Crosses! Blood for blood! Ivan and Peter!" How absurd it all was!

"You're a poor stick of a governor, even if they have given you an 'Honourable Mention,'" thought he slowly, as he followed his father's retreating figure with his handsome eyes . . . .

"Well, what is it, father—are you vexed with me?"

"No," answered the governor simply. "I am grateful for your sympathy, and you'll do well to quiet your mother. As to myself I am perfectly convinced! I've explained my impressions to you now. This is my view of it, and yours is different. We shall see which is correct!—But now, be off to bed. It's time you went to sleep."

"I'm not tired yet. Shan't we take a turn in the garden?"

"That suits me."

They went out into the darkness and disappeared from each other's view—only their voices and an occasional hasty touch disturbing their sense of a strange, all-embracing loneliness. The stars, on the other hand, were numberless, and sparkled in bright companionship, and when they reached the open, out from under the close-set trees, Alexey Petrovitch could distinguish at his side the tall, heavy silhouette of his father. The night, the air and the stars had called up a tenderer feeling for this dark shadowy presence, and he repeated his reassuring explanations.

"Yes, yes," answered Peter Iljitch from time to time—though it was not quite clear whether he agreed or not.

"But how dark it is!" said Alexey Petrovitch, and stood still. They had come to a shady walk where the darkness was complete. "You should have lanterns put here, father!"

"What for? Tell me."

They both stood still, and now that the sound of their steps was hushed, the loneliness reigned unbroken—unbounded!

"Well, what is it?" asked Alexey Petrovitch impatiently.

"Does this darkness mean anything to you?"

"Dreaming again!" thought the lieutenant, and observed, with jaunty gaiety: "It means that you are not to wander about here alone! Anywhere in these woods they might have laid an ambush."

"An ambush! Yes, that's what the darkness tells me too. Imagine! Behind each one of these trees sits a man—an invisible man—watching! So many men—forty-seven—as many as we killed that day! And they sit there and hear what I say—and spy!"

The lieutenant had grown nervous. He searched the darkness round about and took a step forward. "How unnecessary to excite yourself so!" he exclaimed involuntarily.

"No—but wait a moment!" The son started as he felt a light touch of the hand. "Picture to yourself that everywhere—there in the town even, and wherever I go—they are lying in wait. If I walk—he walks too; and watches me! Or I get into the carriage, and a man passes and pulls off his cap—he is spying on me!"

The darkness grew sinister, and the invisible speaker's voice sounded strange and distant.

"That will do, father, let's go!" said the lieutenant, striding hastily off without waiting for his father.

"You see now, my dear boy!" came in Peter Iljitch's deep voice, with a startling ring of mockery. "You wouldn't believe me when I told you! There he sits in your own head!"

The lights in the house seem so far and dim that the lieutenant feels a mad impulse to run. If he might only reach them! . . . .He almost doubts his own courage, and at the same time develops a feeling of respect for his father, who strides so calmly along through the darkness.

But fear and respect both vanish as soon as he enters the well-lighted rooms; and nothing remains but the impression of rage against his father, who will not listen to the voice of Reason, and refuses the Cossack guard with the stubbornness of senility!

4

Summer and winter, the governor rose at seven, had his cold tub, drank his milk, and took his two-hour walk—no matter what the weather. He had given up smoking early in life, hardly drank at all, and at fifty-six years, for all his white hair, he was as sound and fresh as a stripling. His teeth were even, powerful, and slightly yellowed with tartar, like those of an old horse. The eyes were a bit puffy, but full of fire still; and his great fleshy old nose bore the marks of his glasses. He never wore a *pince-nez*, but for reading or writing used a pair of gold-rimmed spectacles with powerful lenses.

In the country he busied himself very much with his garden. He cared very little for flowers, or the purely aesthetic side of horticulture, but had built fine conservatories and a forcing house, where he cultivated peaches. Since the day of the catastrophe, he had only glanced into the hothouse one single time, and then had come hastily away—there was something so pleasant, so peaceful, and consequently so grievous in the warm, damp air.

The greater part of his days, when he was not busy in town, he spent in the vast park, pacing with firm, direct steps down the long avenues that traversed its fifteen *dessiatines*. He was not much given to reflection. Now and again lively and interesting thoughts came to him, never with any particular sequence, and wandered through his brain like an unshepherded flock. And sometimes for hours he strode along, lost in thought and oblivious to his surroundings; yet could not have told what matters he had been pondering.

Occasionally he was made aware of a deep and mighty working of his soul; at times tormenting, at times exalting—but to what it

167

all tended he never understood. And only his changing moods, from grave to gay, from tender to severe, gave index in his character of this mysterious, secret expansion in the depths of his being. Since the catastrophe his moods (no matter what his clearer thoughts might be) were gloomy, wild, hopeless; and whenever he woke from his deep brooding, he felt that he passed this interval through a long and horrible night.

In his youth he had once been caught by the fierce current of a river, and almost drowned; and for years he carried the impress on his soul of that strangling darkness, his faintness, the eager, greedy sucking depths. And what he now endured was that same feeling!

One sunny, windless morning, two days after his son's departure, he was out again on the avenue, pacing in silent thought. The yellow leaves that had fallen in the night had already been swept away, and across the marks of the broom, the tracks of his large feet, with their high heels, and broad, square soles, showed clear—deep pressed into the soil; as though to the weight of the man himself had been added the burden of his ponderous thought, pressing him to the earth! Now and again, he paused, and over his head in the tangle of sunlit branches was heard the rhythmic hammer of a woodpecker. Once while he stood still a little squirrel ran across the path. He darted from tree to tree like a fluffy ball of red fur.

"They will certainly kill me with a revolver—you can buy such good revolvers now," he thought. "They don't understand much about bombs here yet—and then bombs are only for the man who runs; Aljosha, for instance!—when he is made governor, they'll kill him with a bomb!" thought Peter Iljitch, and his bearded lip curled with a slight ironical smile, though his eyes were fixed and gloomy. "I wouldn't run—no, bad as it is, I wouldn't run!"

He halted and brushed a cobweb from his fatigue jacket. "A pity, though, that no one will ever know of my notion of honour and my pluck. They know all the rest, but that they can never know. They'll shoot me down like any old scoundrel. Too bad! But there's nothing for it—I shan't speak of it! Why try to rouse the Judge's pity? It's not honourable to work on his feelings—his position is hard enough at best—and now they come and whine for mercy! I am a man of honour, I tell you—honourable!" . . . .

It was the first time he had thought of a judge; and he wondered how he had happened to think of it. It came to him as if the question had long ago been settled. As though he had slept, and in his dreams, someone had explained most convincingly all the necessary details about the judge, and when he awoke he had forgotten the particulars, but only remembered that there was a judge—a law-abiding justice, panoplied with authority, and encompassed with threatening might! And now, after the first moment of astonishment, he met the thought of this unknown judge as though he were an old and valued friend . . . . "Aljosha could never understand that! According to him everything must be 'for reasons of State.'

But what sort of statesmanship was that: shooting a hungry mob? Interests of State demand that the starving be *fed*—and not shot at! He is young and inexperienced yet, and easily influenced." . . . .But before he had quite finished this complacent thought, he suddenly realised that he himself, and not Aljosha, had ordered the firing!. . . .The air suddenly grew close, and he heard (absurdly enough) a single mighty, awful thunder: "Too late!" . . . .He was not sure whether it were simply a thought or a feeling, or if he had pronounced it. It rang on every side, and menaced him like lightning overhead. Then came a long time of bewilderment; hasty disbanding of thoughts, and painful shattering of ideas—finally, a calm—so complete that it seemed indifference!. . . .

The windows of the forcing house twinkled in the sunshine among the trees, and the wild grapevine's red leaves glowed like bloodstains against the white angles of its walls. Following his custom, the governor turned down the narrow path between the empty hotbeds and stepped into the forcing-house. Only one workman was pottering about, old Jegor.

"Is the gardener not here?"

"No, Your Excellency. He has gone to town for cuttings today; this is Friday."

"Aha!. . . .And is everything doing well?"

"Thanks be!"

The sunshine streamed through the open windows, driving out the close, heavy dampness. You felt how hot and strong the sun was, and yet how gentle—how beneficent! The governor sat down, the light sparkling on the metal of his uniform. He undid his jacket and, watching the old man attentively, said: "Well, how goes it, Brother Jegor?"

The old fellow answered this friendly but somewhat indefinite question with a polite smile. He stood up and rubbed his dirty hands together.

"Tell me, Jegor—I hear they're going to kill me—on account of the workmen that time, you know!" Jegor kept on smiling politely, but no longer rubbed his hands—he hid them behind his back and was speechless! "What do you think about it, my man—will they kill me, or not? Can you read and write? . . . .Then tell me what you think . . . .We two old fellows can talk it over frankly, can't we?"

Jegor shook his head until a lock of soft grey fell over his eyes, stared at the governor, and answered: "Who can tell? It may be so, Peter Iljitch!"

"And who is to kill me?"

"Why, the people, to be sure! 'The Community,' as they say in the village."

"And what does the gardener think about it?"

"I don't know, Peter Iljitch . . . .I haven't heard."

Both sighed deeply.

"It looks rather bad for us, doesn't it, old fellow?. . . . But sit down!"

Jegor did not accept the invitation, and was silent.

"And I thought I was doing the right thing! . . . .the shooting, I mean. They were throwing stones, insulting me. They almost hit me!"

"They only do that when they're in trouble. The other day again, on the marketplace, a drunken man—an apprentice or some such thing—who knows!—began to cry and cry; and then he picked up a stone, and bang! he let it fly! . . . .and only just because he was in trouble!"

"They will kill me, and then they'll be sorry themselves," said the governor thoughtfully, trying to call to his mind the face of his son Alexey Petrovitch.

"Sorry they'll surely be—that's certain . . . .Oh, how sorry they'll be! Bitter tears they'll shed!"

A ray of hope dawned.

"Then why do they want to kill me? . . . .That's nonsense, old man!"

The workman gazed wide-eyed into space, with veiled pupils and a rigid attitude. For an instant he seemed petrified; the soft folds of his worn cotton shirt, the fuzzy hair, the grimy hands, all seemed like an enchantment brought about by a skilful artist who had wrapped the hard stone in soft, downy raiment.

"Who can tell!" answered Jegor, without looking at him. "The people seem to wish it! . . . .But don't trouble about it anymore, Your Excellency. You know we have to have our foolish gossip.... And they'll take a long time—and talk; and then forget it themselves!"

The ray of hope vanished.

What Jegor had said was nothing new, nor especially clever; but his words had a singular ring of conviction, like those dreams that came to the governor as he paced his long lonely avenues. The one phrase, "The people wish it," was a clear expression of what Peter Iljitch had felt—it was convincing, irrefutable! But perhaps this strange conviction lay not so much in the words of Jegor as in his set look—his fuzzy hair, and his broad, earth-stained hands! ....And the sun still shone!

"Well, goodbye, Jegor ....Have you any children?"

"Good health to you, Peter Iljitch!"

The governor shrugged his shoulders, buttoned his coat, and pulled a *rouble* from his pocket. "Here, take that, old man! Buy yourself something with it."

With a nod of thanks, Jegor held out his old flat hand, where the silver balanced as on a roof.

"What singular beings they are!" mused the governor, as he strode down the walk in the flickering shade; his own figure checkered by sun and shadow as he went. "Very strange creatures! ...They wear no wedding rings, and you can never tell whether they are married or not.... However—No! They do wear rings, but they are silver.... or tin maybe! How odd! Tin rings!.... These fellows get married and cannot even afford gold wedding rings for three *roubles*—What misery! ....I didn't notice! Those bodies in the storeroom probably had tin rings on too. Yes, now I recollect: tin rings with a very thin band!"

Lower and lower, in ever-narrowing circles, swung his fancy; like a hawk hovering over a field, and swooping down to pick up one small grain! ....A woodpecker hammered, a shrivelled leaf fell and floated away, and he himself floated off in a painful, troubled daydream ....A workman—his face is young and handsome, but in all the wrinkles black grime of toil has settled—iron filings that have eaten into the skin, and worn the hair prematurely. His broad mouth is hideously wide open.... he screams! He is calling something. His shirt is torn over his chest, and he tears it yet more open—easily, noiselessly, like soft paper; baring his breast. His chest, and half his throat, are white; but above that line he is dark—as though his figure were like all other men's, but they had put another sort of head upon it.

"Why do you tear your shirt? It is horrible to see your naked body!" But the bare, white breast is thrust wildly toward him. "Here, take it! Here it is! ....But give us justice! ....We want justice! ...."

"But where shall I find justice? How singular you are!"

A woman speaks.

"The children are all dead! The children are all dead! The children ....the children....the children have all died!"

"That is why it is so lonely down your lane!"

"The children! The children! The children are all dead! The children!"

"But it is impossible that a child should die of hunger! A child ... a little creature who cannot even reach the cupboard door itself! You do not love your children! If my child were hungry, I should give it food! ....But you even wear tin rings!"

"Ah! We wear iron rings! Our bodies are bound. Our souls are bound. We wear iron rings!"

On the back steps in the shed a maid was brushing Maria Petrovna's skirt. The kitchen windows stood open: one could see the cook in his spotless jacket. It smelled of refuse ....it was dirty. "What have I come to!" said the governor, in amazement .... "Why, it's the kitchen. What was I thinking of? Ah yes! I wanted to see the time! How soon will luncheon be ready? It's early yet ....ten o'clock ....But it seems to disturb them to have me here ....I must go!" And he turned into his accustomed path, and wandered up and down, thinking steadily.

And the manner of his thought was of one who fords a great and unknown river. Now the water reaches to his knees ....he presses on! But finally sinks from sight; only to struggle up later, breathless and pale! ....He thought of his son Alexey Petrovitch—tried to think of his office and his affairs; but wherever he led his fancies they always harked back unexpectedly to the catastrophe, and burrowed there as in an inexhaustible mine. It seemed strange that nothing happening before that event had the power to hold his attention ....the past all seemed so trivial, so superfluous!

It was in the second year of his governorship, some five years ago, that he had ordered the knout for the peasants of Sensiwjejewo. On that occasion also he had received an Honourable Mention from the Minister; and from that event dated the rapid and glittering career of Alexey Petrovitch, who was regarded with some attention as the son of an energetic and farsighted man. He dimly remembered (it was so long ago) that the peasants had taken some grain from the proprietors by force, and he had come, with a detachment of soldiers and police, to restore it to the owners of the estates. The affair was nothing terrible, nothing threatening in itself, but rather farcical!

The soldiers dragged away the sacks of grain, and the peasants lay down on them and were dragged too, amid the laughter and jeers of the force, to whom the whole thing was a huge lark! But the fellows began to shriek and fight; striking out and running amuck against the fences—the walls—the soldiers! . . . .One of them, torn from his sack of grain, fumbled silently in the grass with his trembling hands, looking for a stone to throw. Not a stone could he find, but he kept on hunting till a policeman, at a signal from his chief, kicked him in the rear, so that he fell on all fours, and crawled away.

But they all, these peasants, seemed to be made of wood. They were so clumsy, almost creaking in their movements! To turn one of them forward where he belonged took two men. Then, faced about, he still was uncertain where to look; and when he was finally settled, he could not tear himself away again, so that it took two men to force him back.

"Here, uncle, off with your clothes! You're going swimming!"

"What!" asked the peasant, dumbfounded. "How?"—although the thing was so perfectly clear and simple. A rough hand loosened the single button, the clothes fell, and the lean, bare peasant back stood out, unabashed. They laid the lash on lightly, more as a threat than as a punishment, and the mood of the whole affair was simply comical. On the homeward march the soldiers raised a jolly chorus, and those about the carts where the peasants were bound winked at them genially.

It was autumn. Windswept clouds hung over the bare stubble fields, and they all marched off to the city . . . .to the light! But the village behind them still lay as before; under its depressing sky, in the midst of its dark, sodden, loamy fields, with their short, spare stubble. . . .

"The children are all dead! The children are all dead!. . . .The children! The children! . . . ."

★★★★★★★★★★★★★★

The gong sounded for luncheon. Its clear, penetrating tones rang cheerily through the park. Abruptly the governor faced about and glanced sharply at his watch. "Ten minutes to twelve!" He put the watch back and stood still. "Disgraceful!" he cried, in a rage, his mouth trembling with emotion. "Disgraceful! I'm almost afraid I'm a coward!"

After luncheon he went to his study to look through the mail from town. Grumbling, and wool-gathering and blinking through his glasses, he sorted the envelopes, laying some aside and cutting others carefully, to skim through their contents. Presently he came upon a note in a narrow envelope of cheap, thin paper, pasted over with yellow stamps of one *copek*. He opened it as carefully as he had the others. When he laid the envelope to one side, he unfolded the thin, ink-splotched sheet, and read:

"Butcher of our Children!"

Whiter and whiter grew his face, till it was almost as white as his hair. And his dilated pupils stared through the thick convex glasses at the words:

"Butcher of our Children!"

The letters were large, crooked and pointed, and terribly black—they staggered uncertainly across the rough, coarse paper and cried:

"Butcher of our Children!"

5

Already the city knew that the governor was to be killed. They had heard it at dawn of the day after the shooting. None spoke of it openly, but all felt it; as though while the living lay in their uneasy sleep, the dead were stretched out quietly in careful order. . . . .shoulder to shoulder, in the engine-room, a dark shape had floated over the city, shadowing it with its wings. And the people spoke of the assassination of the governor as a foregone conclusion—an irrevocable fact. Some accepted it at once; others, more conservative, not till later. Some took it carelessly for granted as a thing that concerned them but slightly; like an eclipse, only visible in another hemisphere, and hardly interesting the inhabitants of this one. Others, a small minority, rose and agitated the question whether the governor deserved this fearful sentence—whether the death of one single individual, no matter how dangerous, could have any effect while the general conditions of the living were unchanged. Opinions differed, but even the most heated arguments were impersonal, as though the question were not a possibility of the future, but already an accomplished fact which no discussion might alter.

Among the better educated the arguments took a broader theoretical stand, and the governor's personality was forgotten, as though he were already dead. The debate proved that the governor had more friends than enemies, and many even of those who believed ethically in political assassination found excuses for him. Had a vote been taken in the city, probably an overwhelming majority, on various practical or theoretical grounds, would have cast then ballot against the death—or as some called it, the "execution"!

But the women, generally so merciful and timid at the sight of blood, showed in this case a surprising grimness—a pitiless spite. Nearly all demanded his death—the most hideous death! Reasoning had no power over them; they held their opinions stubbornly, with a certain brute force. A woman might be convinced by evening that the assassination was unnecessary, but next morning she would awake firm in her original conviction; as though she had slept off the effects of the argument overnight!

Bewilderment and confusion reigned supreme. A disinterested listener, hearing their talk, could not have gathered whether the governor should be killed or not, and might have asked, in amazement: "But where did you get the idea that he must die? . . . .And who is to kill him?". . . .But there would be no answer. Soon, however, he would see, as all the others did, that the governor *must* be killed—that his death was imperative! . . . .yet he would have known as little as all the rest from what source this knowledge came. Everyone—friend or foe of the governor—partisan or prosecutor—all gave themselves up to the one unswerving thought of his death. Ideas differed, and words differed, but the feeling was the same: a mighty, all-pervading conviction, strong and immutable as death itself!

Born in the dark, itself a part of the unfathomable darkness, it reigned triumphant and menacing. . . .and all in vain men sought to illuminate it with the feeble light of then intelligence. As though the hoary withered law, "A death for a death," had waked from its torpid sleep, opened its glazed eyes, gazed on the slaughtered children, the men and the women, and had stretched its remorseless arm over the head of their slayer. And the people, thinking and unthinking, inclined themselves to this law, and avoided the sinner. He was at the mercy of any death that might come. And from all sides—from dark corners, from fields, woods and hollows—they pressed about him: reeling, limping, dull and abject—not even interested!

So it might have been in those far-distant times while still there were prophets among men; when thoughts and words were scarcer, and this same hoary Law, that punished death with death, was young. When the beasts made friends with man, and the lightning was his brother! In those strange days of old, the guilty must pay for death in kind. The bee stung him, the ox gored him, the overhanging stone awaited his coming to fall and crush his defenceless head; disease gnawed him, as the jackal gnaws the carrion; arrows turned in their flight, only to strike his black heart or his downcast eyes; and rivers changed their course only to wash the sands from beneath his feet—even the majestic ocean dashed its tattered waves on high and threatened him with its roar—till he fled to the desert. A thousand deaths—thousand graves! The desert buried him under her soft sands; she wept and smiled, and over him her winds blew, whistling. And the sun itself—that life-giver—seared his dead brain with careless laugh, and softly beamed on the creatures that swarmed in the hollows of his miserable eyes. The heavy masses of the hills lay upon his breast, and in their eternal silences they buried the secret of his expiation!. . . . But that was long ago, when this great Law was young—a stripling that punished death with death—and seldom in those days did his cold, keen eyes swerve in the performance of his duty! . . . .

Within the town discussion soon died out, poisoned by its own unripeness. One must either accept the assassination as a sacred fact and meet all argument as the women did with the one incontrovertible phrase: "What right had he to murder children?" or else be reduced to helpless contradictions, to vacillation, to shifting grounds—as a drunken group might gravely exchange their hats, yet get no farther on their homeward way!

Speculation wearied them finally, so they stopped talking; and nothing on the surface reminded one of that fatal day. But amid the silence and the calm grew a great cloud of grim suspense. All waited—those who were indifferent to the catastrophe and its consequences, those who looked eagerly forward to the execution, and those who were uneasy about it—all!. . . .all waited for the inevitable, with the same vast, breathless suspense! Had the governor died of a fever in these days, or from an accident, none would have taken it for mere chance, but behind the given reason would have found a primary cause—invisible, unacknowledged.

Among the masses, as the foreboding grew, their thoughts turned often to the Kawatnaja lane. The lane itself was still and calm, as was the city; and the swarming spies peered vainly for any signs of new uprising or criminal attempts. Here, as elsewhere, they heard rumours of the assassination of the governor, but could never discover their source. All spoke of it, but in such an uncertain, even foolish way, that one could find no key to their talk.

"Some mighty man—oh, a very mighty man, who could never possibly fail!—would undoubtedly kill the governor one of these days!" That was all one could make of it.

The secret agent, Grigorjeff, overheard some such gossip one day as he sat in a low gin-shop pretending to be drunk. Two workmen, who had already been drinking rather freely, sat at the next table, their heads together. Clumsily clinking their glasses, they talked in suppressed murmurs. "They'll kill him with a bomb!" said the first, evidently well informed. "What! with a bomb!" said the other, amazed.

"Certainly, with a bomb—what else?" reiterated the other. He puffed at his cigarette, blew the smoke in his companion's face, and added sternly: "It will blow him to a thousand little bits!"

"They said it would be on the ninth day."

"No," said the other, with a frown which expressed the highest degree of scornful negation. "Why the ninth day? That's superstition—that idea of the ninth day! They'll simply kill him early in the morning—that's all!"

"When?"

Shielding his face with his outspread hand, he lurched suddenly forward and hissed into his companion's ear: "Next Sunday week!"

Silently they stared into each other's grim, bleary eyes, both swaying to and fro. Then the first lifted a threatening finger and said, with impressive secrecy:

"Do you understand?"

"They'll never miss him ....O! They're not that kind."

"No," said the other, with lowering brows. "How could we miss? The pack is stacked.....We hold four aces."

"A whole handful of trumps—" added the other.—"You understand, don't you?"

"Yes, of course I understand!"

"Then, if you understand, we'll drink to it. Aren't you afraid of me now, Wanja?"

They whispered for some time, blinking and nodding, and upsetting the empty bottles in their eagerness ....That same night they were arrested, yet nothing suspicious was found upon them, and the preliminary examination showed that they did not know the slightest thing, and had only repeated vague rumours.

"But how did you happen to know the very day ....that Sunday!" asked the angry officer who was conducting the examination.

"Can't say," said the man, somewhat cowed—he had been three days without drinking or smoking—"I was drunk!"

"I'd like to send you all to—" fumed the lieutenant—but he did not finish his remark.

Even the ones who were sober were no better. They spoke freely of the governor in the workshops and on the streets, raged at him, and exulted at his approaching death—yet never anything definite—and soon they stopped talking and waited patiently. Now and again passing labourers exchanged comments.—"He drove by again yesterday without any guard."

"He's walking into the trap himself!" And they went about their work. But next day a whisper ran through the shops:

"Yesterday he drove down the lane!"

"Let him drive!"

They counted each day of his life . . . .their number seemed too great! . . . .Twice the rumour of his death was started. It spread suddenly in the Kawatnaja lane, and immediately grew to certainty in the factories. It was impossible to say how it arose but, scattered in little groups, they told each other the details of the murder: the street, the hour, the number of the murderers—the weapon! Some could have sworn they heard the explosion. And all stood there, pale, determined; outwardly neither glad nor sorry: till at last word came that it was a false alarm. Then they separated, just as calmly, and without disappointment—as though it were not worthwhile to be excited over an affair that was postponed but for a few days at most . . . .or perhaps a few hours—or even minutes!

Both in the city and in the Kawatnaja lane the women were the harshest, most unrelenting judges. They produced no evidence, they gave no verdict—they simply bided their time! And on then waiting, they laid the coals of their unshakable belief; the whole burden of their unhappy lives; and the hideousness of their depraved, hungry, smothered thoughts. They had in their daily lives one special adversary that the men did not know . . . .the oven!—the ever-hungry, open-mouthed oven; more awful than the glowing fires of hell! From morning till night, throughout their days, and every day, it held them in its sway; eating their soul, casting out from their brains all thought, save that which concerned itself.

The men knew nothing of this. When a woman waked at dawn and saw the stove—the oven door half open—it worked on her fancy like a ghost; gave her a sickening sense of disgust and fear, and dull, brutish terror!

Robbed of her thoughts, she hardly knew what had robbed her; and in her confusion humbly offered up her soul again each day before this altar; black, deadly misery wrapping her as in a veil. And thus, the women in the Kawatnaja lane became so fierce and hard! They beat their children—beat them nearly to death!—quarrelled amongst themselves, and with their husbands, and their mouths streamed with abuse, complaints and wantonness.

In those three terrible weeks of famine, when for days no fires were made—then at last, the women rested . . . .that strange, calm rest of the dying whose pains have ceased some moments before the end! Their thoughts, freed for an instant from those iron bands, fastened with all their passion and power to the vision of a new life . . . .as though this strike were not about the monthly wages of the men, but about a full and glad release of their eternal bonds. And in those heavy days when they buried their little children . . . .dead from exhaustion! . . . .and numb with pain, weariness and hunger—bewailed them with bloody tears—the women grew kind and gentle as never before! They were convinced that such horrors could not have been sent without a purpose—that some vast reward must follow their sufferings.

So, when on the 17th of August the governor stepped out before them, into the Square shimmering in the sunlight, they took him for the dear Lord Himself—with his grey beard.. . . .And he said:

"You must go back to your work! I cannot talk to you till you have gone back to your work."

Then: "I will see what I can do for you. Get to work and I shall write to Petersburg!"

Then: "Your employers are not robbers, but honourable men, and I forbid you to speak so of them. And if you are not back at your work by tomorrow, I shall lock up the shops and send you all to the workhouse!"

Then: "It is your own fault that the children died! Take up your work again!"

Then: "If you act like this, and do not disperse, I'll have you driven off!". . . .

Then followed a chaos of howls; babies crying; the whine of bullets; pushing; and a wild flight! They do not know themselves where they are fleeing to—they fall! Up again and on—children and home are lost! . . . .Then suddenly again, in the twinkling of an eye, there sits the cursed oven!—stupid, insatiable, with its everlasting open mouth!. . . .And the same old round begins again from which they thought to have torn themselves forever; and to which they have returned . . . .forever!

Perhaps the idea of the governor's assassination emanated from the women's brains. The well-worn words in which man had been wont to clothe his hatred for man no longer sufficed them. Loathing! Contempt! Rage!—it transcended all these . . . .it was a feeling of calm, unqualified condemnation . . . .If the axe in the headsman's hands could feel, it might have this emotion—that cool, sharp, shining, steady blade! The women waited quietly; without wavering and without doubts.

And while they wait, they take their fill of the good, fresh air—the same air that the governor breathes! . . . .They are like children. If a door chances to slam, or someone runs clattering down the lane, they rush out—bareheaded and excited . . . ."Is he dead yet?"

"No—it was only Ssenjka running to the shop for vodka."

And so, it goes till another knock comes, or a sudden rush of feet, to break the deadly silence of the street.

When the governor drives by, they peer at him eagerly from behind the curtains; and when he has passed, go back to their ovens again. It did not surprise them that the governor, who had always been followed by guards, suddenly appeared without an escort . . . .the headsman's axe, if it could feel, would not be astonished at the sight of a bare throat! It was quite in the order of things that the throat should be bare.

They sat and spun their gruesome threads—these grey, dismal women with their grey, dismal lives—and it was they who awakened that hoary old Law that punished death with death.

Their sorrow for their dead was suppressed and torpid; it was only a part of their great general pain, and they gulped it down as the great, briny ocean would swallow one small briny tear. But on Friday of the third week after the deluge of blood, Nastassja Saasnova, whose little girl (Tanja, only seven) had been killed, went suddenly mad! For three weeks she had worked over her oven like all the rest; had quarrelled with her neighbours, had beaten her other children—and all at once, without any warning, she went insane.

It began in the morning. Her hand trembled, and she broke a cup; then it all came over her with a sickening shock, and she forgot what she was about, ran from one thing to another, and repeated foolishly. "God, what am I doing?" . . . .Then finally she was quite silent! And dumb, with stealthy tread, she slid from corner to corner, taking things up and putting them down—moving them from place to place—and even, in the beginning of her madness, hardly able to tear herself away from the stove. The children were in the garden flying their kites, and when little Petjka ran in for a piece of bread he found his mother stealthily hiding all sorts of things in the oven—a pair of shoes, an old coat, and his cap! At first the boy laughed, but when he caught sight of his mother's face, he ran shrieking into the street. "A—a—ai!" he screamed as he ran, and set the lane in wild alarm.

The women gathered and began to whimper over her like frightened dogs. But she only widened her circles, breaking through their detaining arms; gasped for air and mumbled to herself. Piece by piece she jerked off her rags till, stripped to the waist, her lean and haggard body, with its withered, dangling breasts, showed yellow against the wall. Then with a long and hideous wail she repeated, over and over: "I can't! Oh, my dear, I can't—I can't—I can't—I can't!" and ran out into the street, the others following.

Then the whole lane was transformed for one instant into a single shrill howl; it was impossible to tell who was crazy and who was not. The panic subsided when the men ran out from the shops, bound the maniac hand and foot, and poured a bucket of water over her. She lay there in a puddle by the roadside, her naked bosom pressed to the earth, her fists and the blue, mottled arms stretched stiffly forward.

She had turned her face to the side, and her eyes were wild and glaring; her wet grey hair was pressed close to her head, making it seem pitifully small; her whole body was shaken with convulsive jerks. Out from the factory ran her husband, in a fright. He had not washed his sooty face, his shirt was shiny with oil and grime, and a burned finger on his left hand was tied up with a greasy rag.

"Nastja!" he called, bending over her, stern and harsh. "What do you mean? What is the matter with you?" She turned her dumb glassy stare at him and shuddered. He saw the purple bloodshot arms they had so pitilessly bound; loosened the ropes and smoothed her naked yellow shoulder . . . . Then came the police! . . . .

When the crowd dispersed two men among them neither went back to the factory nor stayed in the lane: but they went their way slowly to the city. They walked along keeping step; silent and pondering. At the outlet of the Kawatnaja lane they parted.

"What a scene!" said one. "Are you going my way?"

"No!" said the other curtly, and strode along. He had a young tanned throat, and under his cap a shock of curly yellow hair.

6

Sooner or later the news of the governor's assassination had crept into the palace, but here they took it with an extraordinary indifference. As the close presence of the strong man in his full powers hindered their knowledge of the fact that this death meant *his* death!... .they regarded it only as a temporary hallucination. Toward the middle of September, the household returned to town, at the urgent request of The Pike who had convinced Maria Petrovna that the country was not safe. And there, life took on its accustomed aspect... .the routine of many years.

Kosloff, the *aide*, who loathed the dirt and the banal decorations of the governor's mansion, had personally supervised its refurnishing. He bought fresh hangings for the walls and reception-rooms, had the ceilings retinted, and ordered new furniture ... .green oak in the style of the Decadence! He quite took upon himself the supervision of the house, to the delight of all; from the servants who were infused with his energy, to Maria Petrovna, who hated all domestic cares, in spite of its roominess the palace was most inconveniently arranged. The bathrooms were next to the reception-rooms, and the lackeys had to carry their dishes down a long cold corridor past the windows of the dining-hall, where one could see them quarrelling and nudging each other as they went. All this Kosloff wished to change, but he had to postpone his plans till summer.

"He will be pleased," he said to himself, meaning the governor— but strangely enough this image did not call forth in his mind Peter Iljitch, but some other! Yet in his eager bustle of reform, he was not at all conscious of this thought.

As usual Peter Iljitch was the centre of his family, and the expressions, "His Excellency ordered it," "His Excellency wishes ... ." "His Excellency would be angry ... ." were now as ever the household words; and yet, had they set up a puppet in his place, dressed in the governor's uniform, and let it speak a few words, it would have made no difference—so much of the office was but empty form!

If he fell into a rage and shouted at a man, and that man trembled, it looked as though the rage and the trembling both were simulated, and that nothing of the sort had really taken place. Even had he committed a murder in these days, that very death would have seemed counterfeited. As far as concerned himself, he still lived; but to the others he had already died, and they handled the dead carelessly, and felt the cold and the gloom that emanated from him without quite understanding what it meant.

Thought can kill in time! Drawing its strength from the Eternal

Sources, it is mightier than engines, weapons, or powder! It robs men of their will, and makes even the instinct of self-preservation blind. It clears a free space for its deadly stroke; as the forest underbrush is cleared about the tree that must be felled! So, this thought was killing the governor! . . . .As the child, when the time of its fruition is complete, struggles from its mother's womb, this imperious death-dealing thought—till now giving evidence of its being only by the muffled beating of its heart—strove irresistibly toward the light, and began to lead an individual life. Imperiously it called up those from the dark who should do the deed, and hailed them as saviour!

Unconsciously the people held themselves aloof from the one dedicated to death, and robbed him of that invisible but mighty shield that the life of the mass forms for the life of the individual.

After the first anonymous letter calling the governor "Butcher" a few days passed without any such missives. Then, as if with silent accord, they began literally to shower upon him, as though they had poured from a slit in the postbag; and each morning the stack of envelopes on his desk grew higher. In different quarters of the town, out of different post-boxes, these letters were segregated from the other mail by different people; gathered into a heap, and brought to their common destination—this one man! Formerly the governor had received anonymous letters, sometimes with abuse and veiled threats, mostly denunciations and complaints, but he had never read them. Now, however, he felt himself impelled to read them; as he was forced, too, to think constantly of his own death . . . .And reading and reflection both required solitude! . . . .

Seldom through the day, but oftener towards evening, he sat at his disordered desk with a glass of tea untasted by his side, shrugged his broad shoulders, put on his strong, gold-rimmed spectacles, examining the envelopes of the letters as he opened them. He had learned to know them at a glance. For, in spite of differences in writing, paper, and postmarks, they had something in common—like the dead in the engine-house! . . . .and not only he, but the lodge-keeper, who took in Peter Iljitch's private correspondence, recognised them unerringly.

The governor read each letter attentively—earnestly—from beginning to end; and if any words were illegible, he puzzled over them long, as to their meaning. Uninteresting ones, or those that contained only filthy abuse, he destroyed; also, those which gave him friendly warning of his coming assassination. All others he numbered and filed, for some reason unknown to himself. In general, their contents were wearisomely monotonous. Friends warned, foes threatened—and the matter dwindled into a series of inconclusive "Ayes" and "Noes."

From constant repetition he was quite used to the words "Murderer" on the one hand. . . .and "Steadfast Defender of Order" on the other, and to a certain extent had accustomed himself to that other thought . . . .that friend and foe alike believed in the inevitable approach of his death! . . . .A cold shudder ran over him. He would gladly have warmed himself, but there was nothing to warm him . . . .The tea was cold! . . . .they always brought him cold tea lately, for some reason!. . . .and even the high tiled stove was cold!. . . .Long ago—soon after he had come here—he had intended to build a fireplace, but he had put it off, and the old Dutch oven gave very little heat, no matter how much coal you burned! . . . .In vain he hugged the lukewarm tiles, then paced the floor up and down, saying, in his deepest regimental tones: "I've grown to be a perfect hothouse plant!" . . . .Then he sat down to his letters again, looking for something important or decisive.

"Your Excellency!—You are a general, but generals are mortal too. Some generals die a natural death, and some by violence. You, Your Excellency, will die a violent death!

"I have the honour to subscribe myself, Your Excellency's most obedient servant . . . ."

The governor smiled—at that time he could still smile—and was about to tear the carefully written page when he bethought himself, made a marginal note: "No. 43, Sept. 22, 190-," and filed it.

"My Lord governor! (Or to be more correct, My Lord Turkish Pasha!)—You are a thief and a hired assassin! . . . .

"I'd swear to God you turned a pretty penny on that transaction when you murdered the working men. . . . ."

The governor turned purple, crumpled the note in his fist, pulled off his spectacles and roared, with the roll of a big bass drum:

"R-r-r-r-apscallion!"

Then he dug his hands into his pockets, stuck out his elbows and began to pace the floor in a feverish rage. . . .keeping time with the rhythm of: "This-is-the-way-the-Gov-ern-ors walk!"

When he had quieted himself he smoothed out the letter, read it to the end, numbered it with an unsteady hand, and filed it carefully. "He must certainly see that," he said, thinking of his son.

That same evening Fate sent him another letter. It was signed "A Labourer." Apart from the signature, however, nothing in the letter denoted the brawny craftsman—miserable and uneducated—which was the governor's conception of "labourer."

"Here in the works, and in town, they say that you are to be killed soon. I don't know precisely who will do it, but I think it will not be the agents of any organisation; but rather a volunteer from among the citizens, who are roused by your brutal proceedings against the workmen on August 17th. I frankly say that I and some of my party are against this resolution, not because we pity you—had you yourself any pity on the women and the children that day?—and I think that no one in the place has any pity for you! . . . .but simply because I am opposed in principle to any violent death. I am against War, Capital Punishment, Political Execution. . . .and against murder in general!

"In the battle for our ideals—Liberty, Fraternity and Equality—we should make use only of such weapons as do not contradict these ideals. Death is a weapon of that evil, old-world order whose device is Slavery, Privilege and Enmity. Good can never come from evil, and in the battle where force is the weapon, the victor can never be 'the Right,' but 'Might'; that is, the one is more pitiless, more inhuman . . . .no respecter of persons, and not above using any weapons—in one word, a Jesuit!

"If a scrupulous man were forced to shoot, he would certainly either shoot in the air, or else commit some folly that would get him into trouble; because his soul would revolt at the work of his own hands. I hold that many of the well-known unsuccessful political assassinations have been wrecked on this point, because the victims have been rogues capable of taking every advantage, while the instruments have been men of honour, who have perished for the cause. You may be sure, my Lord governor, that if all the people who attempt the lives of your kind were rascals, they would surely find such loopholes and methods as would not enter into an honest man's head, and you would all long since have been dispatched.

"From my point of view the Revolution can merely be a propaganda of ideas—in the sense in which the Christian Martyrs were revolutionists. For even if the labourers did win a battle, the Rascals would only pretend to be beaten to gain time for new trickery, and to get back at their foe. We must conquer with our heads, not with our fists; for as regards the head, the Rascals are rather weak! For this reason, they even hide books from the poor man, condemning him to darkness of ignorance because they fear for their existence. Do you know why they won't allow the workmen the eight-hour labouring day? Do you think the gentlemen did not know themselves that in eight hours of intelligent work the production would be no less than in eleven now? But the thing is this—that with the eight-hour law, the men would have time to learn as much as their masters, and would take the work out of their hands. These people only think they are wise, because they have made all the others stupid—against a really clever man they would not be worth a *sou*!

"I have gone so deeply into the discussion of these questions, in order that you should not misunderstand my first words against your assassination, and consider me a traitor to the common cause of all other honourable men. I must furthermore add that I and my mates who share my convictions were not in the Square on the 17th, because we knew very well what the end would be, and did not care to stand there like the fools who believed that Justice was to be had from one of your kind!

"Now, naturally the others agree with us and say: 'If we go there again, we won't ask, we'll strike!' According to my mind that's equally foolish . . . .because, as I say: why go there at all? You yourself will come to us soon enough with friendly words and bows—and then we'll show you! . . . .

"Honoured Sir, Forgive my boldness, that I should have come to you with my workingman's talk—for I have learned by myself all I know out of books—but it seems strange to me that an educated man who is not such a rascal as all the rest, could act so to the miserable working men who trusted him . . . .that he could order them shot! . . . Maybe you will have a guard of Cossacks, a detachment of the Secret Service, or take a trip somewhere—and so save your life; and then my words may be of some use, and point out to you the right way to serve the true interests of the nation.

"They say here in the works that you were bought by Capital! . . . .but I don't believe that, for our employers aren't so stupid as to throw away their money. . . .and besides that, I know you can't be bribed. . . .and are no thief either, like the others in the service who need the money for their chorus-girls and champagne and truffles. I might even say that in the main you are a man of honour . . . ."

The governor laid the letter carefully upon the table, triumphantly took his moist spectacles from off his nose, polished them ceremoniously with the corner of his handkerchief, and said, with stately deference:

"I thank you, young man."

Slowly he walked down the room and turned to the cold tile stove, saying impressively: "You may take my life, it belongs to you ....But my honour—"

He did not end the phrase, but held his head high, and stalked back to the writing-table, a trifle absurd in his ponderous dignity.....

"I might even say that in the main you are a man of honour... ....in the main a man of honour ....in the main a man of honour—who wouldn't hurt a chicken without cause, but how could you, an honourable man, be responsible for such an order? That is the question, honoured sir! The people are not chickens! The people are sacred! And if you could understand the masses and their sufferings, you would go out into that same Square, bow yourself humbly to the earth and beg for forgiveness.

"Think, from generation to generation—from kindred to kindred, since that time of the first slaves, who, at the bidding of their tyrannical princes built the Pyramids, we have led this existence! As there are among you hereditary nobles—that is, oppressors—so among us there are hereditary labourers, hereditary slaves. And consider further, that in all these ages we have been only beaten and oppressed, and as far back into the past as I can trace my ancestry, I see nothing but tears, despair, ill-treatment. And all this is stamped upon the soul—and all this has been kept as the sole heritage, from father to son, from mother to daughter. Attempt to look into the soul of a simple peasant or labourer—a shuddering horror! While we are yet unborn, we have suffered a thousand wrongs. When we finally crawl forth into life we stumble into a sort of cavern, where we are nourished on wrongs and clothe ourselves in our wrongs!

"They tell me that somewhere, five years ago, you ordered the knout for the peasants—do you realise what you did then? You thought you had only flayed their backs. No, you stripped their souls, enslaved for ages. You flogged the dead, and the yet unborn! And though you may be a General and an Excellency—yet I make bold to say you are not fit to lay your lips in adoration on one of those sacred peasant backs, much less to lay the lash!

"And when the workmen came to you, who was it, do you think, who came? ....Those were the slaves who built the Pyramids—they rose and came with their thousands of years of chafings and groans, to ask for kindness, for help, for counsel! Came to you, as to an enlightened and humane man of the twentieth century. And how did you treat them? Ah! You! ....Your forefather perhaps was an overseer over these same slaves and beat them with stripes, and then handed down to you this foolish hatred for the working classes!

"Honoured Sir! The masses are awakening. At present they are only turning in their sleep, and already the pillars in your house are tottering; but wait till they are quite awake. These words of mine are new to you—think them over! . . . .Furthermore, I ask your pardon that I have troubled you so long, and in the name of the 'Brotherhood,' I hope they may not kill you."—

"They will kill me, though," thought the governor, as he folded up the letter. For an instant the picture of old Jegor, with his steel-grey hair, rose in his mind, only to vanish in the boundless darkness of its void.

No vestige of thought was left in him, nothing either of contradiction or of assent. He stood by the burnt-out stove—on the table the lamp glowed under its green silk shade—in another room his daughter was playing the piano; someone seemed to be teasing Her Excellency's pug, for he began to bark viciously—and still the lamp burned . . . .

The lamp burned!

7

In the next few days, no letters came. The sendings stopped abruptly, as by preconcerted action, and the silence that followed held something sinister and unusual. The sudden cessation gave the feeling that the end was not yet come, that somewhere in the void something was taking its course; that a new phase had entered into the Thought, and was shaping things in secret. And time sped by, with a swoop of its mighty pinions—each upward swing a day, each downward sweep a night!

Twice the Pike had interviewed Her Excellency at a most unusual hour. He scolded the man in the anteroom who helped him off with his coat, rowing him in energetic whispers as though he were one of his own policemen, or a cabby. And when the coat was off and he was drawing on his fresh white gloves, he bent his sleek head condescendingly to the fellow's side-whiskers, gnashed his musty-tobacco-stained teeth, and held his half-gloved hand, with fingers dangling limp, close over his nose. (He always did this at the slightest contact with a lackey.). . . .Then, assuming the manner of a man of the world, he mounted the stairs.

Formerly he would never have dared to scold the governor's servants, but now things were come to such a pass that he not only did, but must. Last night a highly suspicious character had been arrested by one of the secret agents, close to the entrance of the palace! At a distance he had followed the governor on his accustomed morning stroll; then had hung about the palace all day, peering in at the basement windows, hiding behind the trees, and conducting himself in a most suspicious manner. On his arrest they found neither weapons, papers, nor any other treasonable articles about him; and they recognised him as the suburbanite Ipatikoff—furrier by trade. His statements were vague and shifty. He asserted that he had only passed the house once, and seemed to be hiding something. On searching his quarters, they found but a few rotten skins, a boy's fur coat unfinished, and other appurtenances of his trade. Household goods there were none—no weapons, no papers. The case seemed in the highest degree mysterious. None of the governor's household—the lodge-keeper nor anyone else—had observed him, though he had passed the main entrance at least a dozen times.

In the night a spy tried the door to test the matter and, finding it unlocked, walked into the porter's lodge, scratched his name on the wall as a proof of his presence, and then walked out again unnoticed. The gatekeeper pleaded forgetfulness as his excuse for not locking up .... "But at such a time, when such an attempt was to be expected, that sort of carelessness was unpardonable!"

"I'm in an awful fix, Your Excellency," complained the Pike to the governor's lady, laying his white-gloved hand on his scented breast. "His Excellency won't listen to the idea of a bodyguard! The Secret Service men are dog-tired (excuse the expression) with their everlasting trotting after him .... and to tell you the truth, it's all nonsense anyway, because the first scoundrel that comes along could catch him around the corner, or hit his Excellency with a stone over the wall. . ...If anything should happen—which God forbid!—people will say: 'The Chief of Police is to blame! The Chief of Police did not watch out!' What can I do against His Excellency's damned stubbornness? Excuse the expression, Your Excellency, but fancy the position I'm in! It really is too—I'll bid you good day, Your Excellency!"

It developed that the Pike had prepared a programme. The governor was to get a few months' furlough and travel for his health—any one of the foreign baths would do. Things were quiet in the city now, and he was in high favour at St. Petersburg—there would be no trouble on that score!

"Otherwise, I can guarantee nothing, Your Excellency!" continued the Chief, with feeling.. . . ."Human powers have their limits, your Excellency, and I tell you frankly I cannot answer for anything!. . . . After two or three months it will all happily be forgotten, and then— Welcome home, your Excellency. It will be just the season of the Italian Opera. We'll give a gala performance—and then His Excellency can take his walks abroad to his heart's content."

"What nonsense about the opera!" said the governor's lady, yet she approved of the proposition, as she herself was most uneasy.

On his way out the Chief of Police stopped at the lodge to bully the porter again.

"I'll teach you! I'll make your chin-whiskers stand up, you fat-faced fool! He grows chin-whiskers like a Lord Chancellor—the son of a gun! . . . .and thinks he doesn't have to lock the door! I'll make you dance. You—"

That evening Maria Petrovna begged her husband to take her abroad with the children.

"Oh, please, Pievna, won't you?" she said in her tired voice, her eyes drooping under their long dark lashes. Her face was thickly powdered, and her yellow, flabby cheeks dangled like a pointer's as she shook her head. "You know I've not been at all well lately, and really I must go to Carlsbad."

"Can't you and the children go without me?"

"Ah, but no, Pievna! What makes you talk like that? I'd be so worried if you were not there. Please."

She did not say what would worry her—her object was clear without that. To her great surprise, Peter Iljitch readily agreed to the plan—though under ordinary circumstances her mere mention of a wish called forth his opposition . . . .At least that used to be their way!

"They certainly can't lay that to cowardice," thought the governor. "It isn't any plan of mine—and maybe she really does need a cure. She looks as yellow as a lemon . . . .Besides, there's always plenty of time for them to kill me. . . .and if they don't attempt anything it will prove that I am right, and they are wrong!. . . .Then I'll resign—and then I shall build the finest kind of a conservatory . . . ."

Even while these thoughts were passing, he was convinced that he would neither have the trip nor the conservatory! That was why he had given such prompt assent. And after he had consented, he forgot the circumstances immediately as though they did not concern him in the least. He hesitated for a long time about the arrangements for his furlough, set the date, changed it, and then forgot the thing completely till two days after the time he had appointed. Then again, he named a day . . . .but again he forgot it deliberately. Moreover, his wife, whose mind was completely set at rest at the mere idea of their departure, did not urge him to hurry—she had her fall wardrobe to finish, and tailors and dressmakers took all her time . . . .besides, Cissy was not nearly ready.

In the lonely silence surrounding the governor since the sudden stopping of the letters, he felt something incomplete—like the echo of a soft voice in the distance—as if he sat in an empty room, with someone speaking behind the wall, the vibrations of whose voice could be felt but not heard. And when another letter came—a final belated letter—he went forward to take it as though he had long been expecting it, and was much surprised to see that it was in a slender, delicately tinted envelope with a forget-me-not stamped on the back. But it did not come in the morning like all the other letters which had been posted the night before, but with the evening mail—showing that it had been written the same day.

The notepaper was of the same pale shade, and was also stamped with the blue forget-me-not. The writing was painstaking and distinct; the lines slanted heavily, as though the writer were not quite sure of her syllables and, rather than divide the words, ran them down the page in a small, cramped hand. At times she began to write downhill long before the end of the line, in tiny little letters, in the evident fear that she would not have room for the rest of the sentence. And the words all seemed to be coasting down the snowy page—the smallest one in front, on their little sleds.

The letter was signed "A Schoolgirl."

Last night I dreamed about your funeral, and I am going to write you about it—even if it isn't right, and if it does harm the poor workmen, and the little girls that you killed! But you're a poor old man yourself, and so I'm writing you this letter.
I dreamed that you were not buried in a black coffin, as all older people are, but in a white one, like the ones for little girls—and it was policemen that went down Moscow Street carrying your coffin—and they didn't carry it with their hands, but on their heads. And a great crowd of policemen walked behind. But none of your friends were there; and none of the people in the city. And all the doors and windows were barred when you were carried by—as they are at night!

I was so frightened that I waked up, and began to think about it—and that is what I am going to write you about ....I thought maybe there is no one at all who will cry for you when you are dead. The people in your house are all hard and selfish, and only care about themselves; and perhaps when you die, they'll be glad, because they think then they can be governor! I do not know your wife, but I don't believe there can be very many gentle and kind ladies in those circles of pleasure and pride.

No respectable people would ever go to your funeral, of course, for they are all angry at the way you treated the workmen ... .and one man even said they wanted to put you out of the club, but they were afraid of the Government! ....Masses won't do any good, because you know yourself our bishop would just as soon say a Mass for a dead dog if he got money enough for it.... And when I think that you probably know all this without my telling you, then I feel very sorry for you—as if you were really a friend of mine. I've only seen you twice: once on Moscowa Street—but that was long ago—and the second time at our school exhibition, when you drove up with the bishop....but, of course, you wouldn't remember me then....and I promise you faithfully that I'll pray for you, and that I'll cry over you as though I really had been your daughter, because I am very, very sorry for you.

P.S.—Please burn this letter! But I am so awfully sorry for you.

He loved that little schoolgirl.

Late that night, just before going to bed, he stepped out on to the balcony—that same balcony from which he had given the signal with his white handkerchief! ....The cold fall rains had already set in, and the night was black and dismal. In this heavy autumnal darkness, one felt how far away the sun was, how long it had been gone, and how late the dawn would be. Far to the left in the driveway burned two bright lanterns with reflectors, and their white light penetrated the darkness, yet did not banish it......There it still lay—quiet, close, ponderous.

The city doubtless slept already, for not a lighted window was to be seen, and no wheels sounded in the dim-lit streets. Under one of the lanterns something gleams vaguely—probably a puddle ....

School had closed for the day, and she no doubt has long since done her lessons, and now sleeps quietly somewhere in this black, silent space—from whence they send their letters with their threats—from whence his death is about to come . . . .But there, too, lives this little child, who sleeps just now, but who will weep for him when his time comes.

How quiet it is, how dark—how silent.

8

Two weeks before the governor's death, a linen-covered package was handed in to the Government House—its value declared at three roubles. It proved to be an infernal machine—a bomb intended to explode on being opened. But it was badly made by the unskilled hands of one who had only read of such things—so it missed fire. Yet in the very homemade simplicity of the outfit there was something sinister and terrifying, as if blind Death had stretched forth his hand and was fumbling clumsily about in the dark.

The police sounded the alarm, and Maria Petrovna insisted upon her husband's wiring to St. Petersburg that very day, to ask for sick leave. She herself drove first to the tailor's, and then wrote her son a long letter full of horrors—all in French . . . .

A strange and radical change had come over the governor. In place of the man, they used to know appeared an entirely new figure. No one knew precisely when the change came about, and in the main he seemed the same; but upon his face had dawned such an expression of righteousness it seemed a new countenance. He smiled where formerly he would have been grave, and frowned where he had been wont to smile; he was bored and indifferent where he used to be attentive and animated. He was horribly candid in the expression of his feelings. When he chose, he was silent; left the room when he felt inclined, and turned his back when people bored him.

Those who had counted for years on his liking and friendship, who knew all his thoughts and moods, felt themselves suddenly neglected—quite shoved aside—and could no longer understand his feelings and fancies. All the bows and smiles and cordial greetings had suddenly disappeared—the little ceremonious form of politeness: "If you will be so good, my dear fellow!"—"I am vastly obliged to you, my dear sir!"—which had seemed like second nature to him, he dropped completely; and people were taken aback at the remarkable, even alarming originality of his new manner. So, animals, accustomed to looking on a man's apparel as the person himself, might be taken aback at the sight of a naked figure.

He had simply ceased to be polite—and directly the bond was broken which had held him throughout many years to his wife, his children, his associates—as though it had only been made of smiles and compliments, and had vanished together with the ceremonious kissing of the hand. He did not judge them, he did not hate them; found nothing new or repulsive in them—they simply fell out of his soul; as decayed teeth crumble in the mouth. . . .as the hair falls out . . . .as a dead skin is sloughed off—painlessly, quietly, without an effort. When the veil of custom and politeness fell from him, he stood there forsaken and aloof; yet he did not even feel it—as though loneliness had been his natural state throughout his long, eventful life.

He forgot his morning greetings, he forgot to say goodnight; and when his wife held out her hand, or his daughter Cissy lifted her smooth forehead to his lips, he was not quite sure what to do with the hand or the forehead. When guests came to luncheon—the Vice-governor and his wife, or Kosloff—he did not rise, or bow, or smile, but went hastily on with his meal—and when he had finished, he did not ask to be excused, but simply rose and left the room.

"Where are you going, Pievna? Please stay with us, we are so lonely. They'll bring the coffee soon." He answered calmly: "No! I'd rather go to my study. I don't want any coffee," and the rudeness of the answer was lost in its candour and simplicity.

He cared nothing about Cissy's new clothes, did not greet the guests of the house, let Her Excellency invent excuses for his absence, had nothing to do with society, and refused to accept statements without an explanation of motives. Twice a week he received petitioners, and listened to each attentively, with an interest that seemed even a trifle rude, as he inspected the petitioner from head to foot. "Are you convinced that it will be better so?" he asked, after he had listened patiently; and when the astonished man had given an affirmative answer, he promised immediately to grant his request. In these days he never considered the possibility of overstepping the limits of his powers, or else he had an exaggerated impression of them; at all events, he often decided matters which were quite out of his province. The new governor, in consequence, had many difficulties with the entanglements that resulted—all the more so as some of the questions were of the most complex and illegal character.

In order to dispel her husband's gloom, Maria Petrovna often came to his study, felt of his forehead to see if he were feverish, and began to talk about their trip. But he held her off with blunt directness. "Yes, very well, run along now! I would rather be alone. You have your own room, and I don't bother you there."

"Ah, how you have changed, Pievna!"

"Nonsense! Nonsense!" he said, in his gruffest tones, leaning his back up against the cold stove. "Do go and make that pug of yours shut up. You can't hear a thing in the whole house for his barking!"

Of all his former habits, card-playing was the only one which he still enjoyed. Twice a week he had his whist, and he played for small stakes with keen and evident pleasure. He was a thoughtful, clever player, and if his partner revoked, he called him down in proper shape. "What are you thinking of, my dear sir! I led diamonds!" flashed out his cool, clear voice—hard and cutting as the diamond itself. . . .and Maria Petrovna, in the next room, hearing her husband's voice, would smile her tired smile and shake her head sadly. Her yellow cheeks hung flabby as a pointer's; the powder stood out on her face, and her heavy, bulging, brownish lids rose and fell like iron shutters in a shop window. At this moment it seemed to her, as it did to all the others, utterly impossible that a person who could play cards like that could be assassinated.

Through the two long weeks before his death, he simply waited. Doubtless he had other feelings beside—thoughts of the daily routine, his surroundings, his past; the stale, old thoughts of a man whose body and mind are long since fossilised. Probably he thought of the work-men and that sad, awful day—but all these reflections were vague and superficial, and vanished as they came—like the light wind's ripple on the river—and again as before, the still, dark waters of his fathomless soul stood calm in silent waiting. It was as though politeness and habit only had united him to his mental processes, and when ceremony and custom vanished his ideas fled too. He was as isolated in his brain as he was in his family.

As usual he rose at seven, had his cold shower, drank his milk, and at eight o'clock took his accustomed stroll. Each time he crossed the threshold of his palace he felt that he should never return—that the two hours' walk would prolong itself into an eternal wander-ing through the unknown . . . .With his red-lined general's cloak; tall, broad-shouldered, his grey head high with soldierly bearing; he marched through the city for two long hours like a stately ghost— past wooden houses dark with mould, past countless gates and empty squares, past shops whose clerks, shivering in the brisk morning air, bowed slavishly.

195

Whether the pale October sun shone out, or the fine cold rain trickled down, unfailingly he rose and followed his orbit—a sad, majestic wanderer of the town, seeking death at the head of his column. Forward he marched through mire and puddle, the scarlet lining of his overcoat reflected in the mud; forward through the streets, not noticing policemen's salutes nor horses—and a bird's-eye view of his daily Road of Suspense would have shown an extraordinary tracery of short, straight lines, crossing and recrossing in a hopeless tangle. He seldom glanced to right or left, and never looked behind; yet scarcely even saw what was before him, so sunk was he in the depths of his dark forebodings. He rarely acknowledged greetings, and many a startled eye encountered his passing glance—direct, unseeing, and yet so penetrating.

Long after he was dead and buried, and the new governor, a smiling young man surrounded by Cossack guards, drove rapidly through the city in his equipage of state, many recalled these last two long weeks of his pilgrimage—the grey-haired ghost in the General's uniform marching through the mire with upright carriage, the scarlet lining of his cloak glancing in the puddles; and followed by the hoary old law: "A life for a life!"

The crush and the jostling curiosity of the main streets wearied him, and he preferred to lose himself in the silent, squalid alleys, with their tiny three-room cottages, their broken fences, and slippery wooden sidewalks. Throughout these days he had but one desire—to go the length and breadth of Kawatnaja lane. But he could not bring himself to gratify this wish: it seemed too horrible, too painful, more painful than death itself. And a thrill of wonder came over him as he thought of that earlier September, he had driven down the lane quite fearlessly, and had even wished that he might meet some one of the people, to speak to them in passing.

But one spot he never neglected. This was the street that led to the seminary, where each morning, just at nine, it swarmed with little schoolgirls. Forgetting his usual haste, he strode along here like some good-natured, whimsical old general, out for his morning walk. He nodded to them as they came: the big girls first, stately, tall and dignified; then the little ones, with their short brown skirts and their huge knapsacks; and they shyly answered his greeting. His near-sighted eyes could not distinguish their faces. Large and small, in groups they came, and they seemed to him like a cluster of rosy petals. As the last one passed, he smiled his quiet, ironical smile, a sly twinkle in his eye meanwhile, and then at the next corner he was transformed again into the silent, stately ghost, seeking death at the head of his column.

At first two spies, at their chief's secret command, trailed him at a distance; but he did not observe them, as he never looked back. For some days they conscientiously followed his devious paths, but soon tired of it—it seemed so foolish to run after a man who was hanging about the most dangerous spots in such an idiotic way. So, they stopped now and again at some friendly shop to gossip with a policeman, dropped in at an alehouse, and often lost sight of their charge for hours at a time.

"It's all the same—there's nothing to do anyway!" said one of them apologetically. He had the smug, shaven face of a priest, and seemed a prosy old fool. He was gulping down a hot *pâté*, and although he had not quite swallowed the first, he was already reaching for the second. "When a man's in his dotage and runs into the trap himself, what are you going to do with him . . . .will you kindly tell me?"

"Oh, it's only for form's sake," said the barkeeper.

"And how about the Pike?" asked the second spy, a gloomy man who had seen better days, but was given to drink, and had been caught cheating at cards. Growling like a dog over his bone, he devoured everything in sight, drinking vodka steadily meanwhile; and though he was never drunk, yet he never stopped drinking.

"What about the Pike? He knows well enough that we aren't angels from heaven!"

"He acts like a horse in a fire . . . .take him out of his stall and he rears and plunges. He'd sooner burn up than leave the stable," said the barkeeper.

"No, he knows we aren't angels," repeated the first, with a sigh. And in fact, they had very little in common with angels—these two poor devils—and it was quite beyond their feeble power to arrest the course of events!

Home again over the familiar threshold, even then the governor felt no thrill of relief, nor any surety of one more day of life. He took things as they came, and forgot the sense of his past wanderings in the awakening dread of what the day would yet bring forth. And the empty, idle days passed by with frightful haste—yet time stood still; as if the mechanism that turned up each new day had been jarred and, instead of the following one, the same old day came round again. Even the calendar on his desk that he used to turn—usually at night, as though he were calling up the advancing day—even this stood pointing to that long-past date, and when occasionally he looked at that back number, his breast heaved, he knew not why, and a feeling of sickness came to him as he turned his eyes away.

"Nonsense!" he exclaimed angrily. Nowadays when he was alone, he often broke into short ejaculations, indefinite and disconnected. He was especially apt to say "Nonsense!" or "Disgusting!"

He did not fear death in the least, and viewed it quite impersonally. They would shoot at him; he would fall . . . .And then would come the funeral with the bands, and his Orders carried behind the coffin, etc. He'd go bravely forward to meet it. He did not even think of a life beyond the grave; for him it all ended here. And he ate with his usual appetite and slept soundlessly and dreamlessly.

Yet once in the night—and it was three days before his end—he must have had a heavy dream; for he awoke with the sound of his own hoarse, muffled groans. And as he recognised this strange, dull voice of his, and his eyes encountered the darkness, he felt the shudder and weakness of death. He huddled the clothes up over his head, drew up his bony knees, knotted himself into a bundle in the bed and, reviewing his whole past life, from infancy to age, he began to sob bitterly and softly; and whispered to the damp, white, silent pillow: "Have pity on me! Help me someone, whoever it is! Have mercy! ——!"

But no one was there to pity him; and soon he was conscious through his tears of his great shaken frame in its strange, cramped attitude, and his rough, hoarse voice, and he mastered himself and lay still. And long he lay there silent, in the same tense pose, staring up wide-eyed into the dark . . . .And in the morning, he started out again in his military cloak. For two days more its scarlet lining was reflected in the puddles by the wayside, and the tall, stately ghost stalked through the streets, seeking his grave at the head of his column.

★★★★★★★★★★★★★★★★

The affair came about very simply and quickly—like a picture in a biograph.

At the crossing of two streets was a dingy hay-market, open on Fridays; and here a hesitating voice arrested the governor.

"Your Excellency!"

"Yes?"

He stood still and faced about.

From behind a lonely hedge across the street two men came hastily striding through the mud: one in high boots, the other in gaiters without overshoes, his trousers rolled up. These wet feet must make him very cold, for his face is greenish pale, and his thick blond hair stands out very stiffly from his head . . . . In his left hand he holds a folded paper, and the right is thrust deep into his pocket.

And directly all is clear; the victim knew that death had come, and they knew that he had seen it.

"If you please," said the man, and a convulsive tremor passed over his face.

"A petition? . . . . What is it about?" the governor asked superfluously too, but strangely impelled to play the scene out. Yet he did not reach for the petition. The fellow still held out his left hand with the bit of paper that would have deceived no one, and without handing it to the governor he fumbled with his right hand for the revolver; knitting his brows in his endeavour to free it from the lining of his pocket.

The governor cast one quick glance about. The squalid marketplace, the mud littered with straw, the lonely hedge—Ah! But it was too late. He gave one short, deep, gasping sigh, and straightened up. . . . without terror, and quite without defiance. Yet still there lay somewhere—perhaps in the deep-set wrinkles about his heavy nose—a quiet, almost imperceptible pleading for mercy—just a trace of remorse. But he himself was unconscious of this, and neither of the men observed it.

His death came in three quick shots, sounding together in rapid succession like a single loud report. Three minutes later a policeman hurried up, followed by the Secret Service men, and then the people, as though they had all been hanging about the neighbourhood, behind the corner, awaiting the end.

. . . . And the corpse was covered over . . . .

Some ten minutes later the ambulance drove slowly through the streets with its red cross—and throughout the city questions and answers flew like stones:

"Is he dead?" "On the spot!" "Who was it—did they arrest him?" "No; they got away. No one knows who it was. There were three men."

And all day long they spoke only of the assassination, some with censure, some with joyful approbation. But through all their talk, whatever its character, one felt the shiver of a mighty terror. Something powerful and annihilating swept like a cyclone over their daily lives; and from behind their dreary counters, their samovars, their beds and wheaten cakes, peered forth through the dimness of the commonplace the threatening figures of that hoary old Law of Revenge.

. . . .And the little schoolgirl wept! . . . .

In the Basement

1

He drank hard, lost his work and his acquaintances, and took up his abode in a cellar in the company of thieves and unfortunates, living on the last things he had.

His was a sickly, anaemic body, worn out with work, eaten up by sufferings and vodka. Death was already on the watch for him, like a grey bird-of-prey blind in the sunshine, sharp eyed in the black night. By day death hid itself in the dark corners, but at night it took its seat noiselessly by his bedside, and sat long, till the very dawn, and was quiet, patient, and persistent. When at the first streak of light he put out his pale head from under the blankets, his eyes gleaming like those of a hunted wild animal, the room was already empty.

But he did not trust this deceptive emptiness, which others believe in. He suspiciously looked round into all the corners; with crafty suddenness he cast a glance behind his back, and then leaning upon his elbows he gazed intently before him into the melting darkness of the departing night. And then he saw something, such as ordinary people do not see: the rocking of a monster grey body, shapeless, terrible. It was transparent, embraced all things, and objects were seen in it as behind a glass wall. But now he feared it not; and it, leaving behind it a cold impression, departed until the next night,

For a short time, he was wrapped in oblivion, and terrible, extraordinary dreams came to him. He saw a white room, with white floor and walls, illumined by a bright white light, and a black serpent which was creeping away under the door with a gentle rustling-like laughter. Pressing its sharp flat head to the floor, it wriggled and quickly glided away, and was lost somewhere or other, and then again, its black flattened nose appeared through a crevice under the door, and its body drew itself out in a black ribbon—and so again and again. Once in his sleep he dreamed of something pleasant, and laughed, but the sound

201

seemed strange, and more like a suppressed sob, it was terrible to hear it—his soul somewhere in the unknown depths laughing, or perhaps weeping, while the body lay motionless as the dead.

By degrees the sounds of nascent day began to invade his consciousness: the indistinct talk of passers-by, the distant squeaking of a door, the swish of the *dvornik's* broom as he brushed away the snow from the window-sill—all the undefined bustle of a great city awakening. And then there came upon him the most horrible, mercilessly clear consciousness that a new day had arrived, and that he would soon have to get up, in order to struggle for life without any hope of victory.

One must live.

He turned his back to the light, threw the blanket over his head, so that not the minutest ray might penetrate to his eyes, squeezed himself together into a small ball, drawing his legs up to his very chin, and so lay motionless, dreading to stir and to stretch out his legs. A whole mountain of clothes lay upon him as a protection against the cold of the basement, but he did not feel their weight, and his body remained cold. And at every sound speaking of life, he seemed to himself to be monstrous and unveiled, and he hugged himself together all the tighter, and silently groaned—neither with voice nor in thought—since he feared now his own voice and his own thoughts.

He prayed to someone that the day might not come, so that he might always lie under the heap of rags, without movement or thought, and he concentrated his whole will to keep back the coming day, and to persuade himself that it was still night. And more than anything in the world he wished that someone from behind would put a revolver to the back of his head, just at the place where there is a cavity, and blow his brains out.

But daylight unfolded, broad, irresistible, calling forcibly to life, and all the world began to move, to talk, to work, to think. The first in the basement to wake was the landlady, the old Matryóna. She got up from the side of her 25-year-old lover, and began to stamp about the kitchen, clatter with the buckets, and busy herself about something close to Khijhnyakóv's very door. He felt her approach, and lay quiet, determined not to answer if she called him. But she kept silence, and went away somewhere. In the course of an hour or two the two other lodgers woke up, an unfortunate named Dunyásha, and the old woman's lover Abrám Petróvitch. He was so called in spite of his youth out of respect, because he was a daring and skilful thief, and something else besides, which was guessed at, but not spoken about.

The waking up of these terrified Khijhnyakóv more than anything, since they had a hold on him, and the right to come in and sit on his bed, to touch him, and recall him to thought and speech. He had become intimate with Dunyásha one day when he was drunk, and had promised her marriage, and although she had laughed and slapped him on the back, she sincerely considered him as her lover, and patronized him, although she was herself a stupid, dirty, unwashed slut, who had spent many a night at the police-station. With Abrám Petróvitch he had only the day before yesterday been on the drink, and they had kissed one another and sworn eternal friendship.

When the fresh loud voice of Abrám Petróvitch and his quick steps resounded near the door, Khijhnyakóv's heart's blood curdled with fear and suspense, and he could not help groaning aloud, and then was all the more frightened. In one distinct picture that drinking-bout passed before him: how they had sat in some dark tavern or other, illumined by a single lamp, amid dark people who kept whispering together about something, while they themselves also whispered together. Abrám Petróvitch was pale and excited, and complained of the hardships of a thief's life; for some reason or other he had bared his arms and allowed him to feel the badly-mended bones of his once broken arm, and Khijhnyakóv had kissed him and said:

"I love thieves, they are so bold," and proposed to him that they should drink to "brotherhood," although they had for long been on quite intimate terms.

"And I love you, because you are educated, and understand us so well," replied Abrám Petróvitch.

"Look again at my arm; here it is, eh?"

And again, the white arm had passed before his eyes, seeming to be sorry for its own whiteness, and suddenly realising something (which he did not now remember or understand), he had kissed that arm, and Abrám Petróvitch had proudly cried:

"Indeed, brother, death before surrender!"

And then something dirty whirling round and round, howls, whistles, and jumping lights. Then he had felt cheerful, but now when death was hiding in the corners, and when day was rushing in upon him from every direction with the inexorable necessity to live and do something, to struggle after something and ask for something—he felt tortured and inexpressibly frightened.

"Are you asleep sir?" Abrám Petróvitch enquired sarcastically through the door, and receiving no answer, added:

"Well, then, sleep away; devil take you!"

Many acquaintances visited Abrám Petróvitch, and throughout the day the door squeaked on its hinges, and bass voices were to be heard. And it seemed to Khijhnyakóv, at every sound, that they were coming for him, and he buried himself the deeper in his bedclothes, and listened long to catch to whom the voice belonged. He waited and waited in agony, trembling all over his body, although there was no one in the whole world who would come to fetch him.

He had once had a wife—long ago—but she was dead. Still further back in the past he had had brothers and sisters, and still earlier—something indistinct and beautiful, which he called Mother. All these were dead, or possibly some one of them might be still alive, only so lost in the wide, wide world, that he was as though dead. And he himself would soon be dead too—he knew it. When he should get up today his legs would tremble and give way under him, and his hands would make uncertain strange motions—and this was death. But meanwhile, he must needs live, and that is such a serious task for a man who has neither money, health, nor will, that Khijhnyakóv was seized with despair. He threw off his blanket, clasped his hands, and breathed out into the void such prolonged groans, that they seemed to proceed from a thousand suffering breasts, therefore was it that they were so full, brimming over with insupportable torture.

"Open, you devil!" cried Dunyásha from the other side of the door, pounding it with her fists. "Or I'll break the door down!"

Trembling with tottering steps, Khijhnyakóv reached the door, opened it, and quickly lay down again, nay almost fell, on his bed. Dunyásha already befrizzled and bepowdered, sat down at his side, shoving him against the wall, and crossing her legs, said with an air of importance:

"I have brought you news. Kátya expired yesterday."

"What Kátya?" asked Khijhnyakóv, using his tongue clumsily and uncertainly, as though it did not belong to him.

"Come, now, you can't have forgotten!" laughed Dunyásha. "The Kátya who used to live here. How can you have forgotten her, when she has been gone only a week?"

"Died?"

"Why, of course died, as all die." Dunyásha moistened the tip of her little finger and wiped the powder from her thin eyelashes.

"What of?"

"What all die of. Who knows what? They told me yesterday at the *café*, Kátya was dead."

"Did you love her?"

"Certainly, I loved her! What are you talking about!"

Dunyásha's stupid eyes looked at Khijhnyakóv in dull indifference as she swung her fat leg. She did not know what more to say, and tried to look at him, as he lay there, in such a manner as to show to him her love, and with that intent she gently winked her eye, and dropped the corners of her full lips.

The day had begun.

2

That day, a Saturday, the frost was so severe that the boys did not go to school, and the horseraces were postponed for fear of the horses' catching cold. When Natálya Vladímirovna came out from the lying-in hospital, she was for the first moment glad that it was evening, that there was no one on the embankment, that none met her—an unmarried girl, with a six-day-old child in her arms. It had seemed to her that, as soon as she should cross the threshold, she would be met by a shouting, hissing crowd, among whom would be her senile, paralytic, and almost blind father, her acquaintances, students, officers and their young ladies; and that all these would point the finger at her and cry:

"There goes a girl who has passed through six classes at the high-school, had acquaintances among the students both intellectual and of good birth, who used to blush at a word spoken unadvisedly, and who six days ago gave birth to a child, in the lying-in hospital, side by side with other fallen women."

But the embankment was deserted. Along it the icy wind travelled unrestrained, lifted a grey cloud of snow, ground by the frost into a biting dust, and covered with it everything living and dead which met it in its path. With a gentle whistle it wove itself round the metal pillars of the railings, so that they shone again, and looked so cold and lonely that it was a pain to look at them. And the girl felt herself to be just such a cold thing, an outcast from mankind and life She had on a little short jacket, the one which she usually wore skating, and which she had hurriedly thrown on when she left her home suffering the premonitory pains of childbirth.

And when the wind seized her, and wrapped her thin skirt about her ankles, and chilled her head, she began to fear that she might be frozen to death; and her fear of a crowd disappeared, and the world expanded into a boundless icy wilderness, in which was neither man, nor light, nor warmth. Two burning teardrops gathered in her eyes, and froze there. Bending her head down, she wiped them away with the formless bundle she was carrying, and went on faster. Now she no longer loved herself nor the child, and both lives seemed to her worthless; only certain words, which had, as it were, sunk into her brain, persistently repeated themselves, and went before her calling:

"Nyemtchínovskaya Street, the second house from the corner. Nyemtchínovskaya Street, the second house from the corner."

These words she had repeated for six days as she lay on the bed and fed her infant. They meant, that she must go to Nyemtchínovskaya Street, where her foster-sister, an unfortunate, lived, because only with her, and with no one else, could she find an asylum for herself and her child. A year ago, when all was still well, and she was continually laughing and singing, she had visited Kátya, who was ill, and had helped her with money, and now she was the only human being remaining before whom she was not ashamed.

"Nyemtchínovskaya Street, the second house from the corner. Nyemtchínovskaya Street, the second house from the corner."

She walked on, and the wind whirled angrily round her; and when she came upon the bridge it greedily dashed at her bosom, and dug its iron nails into her cold face. Vanquished, it dropped noisily from the bridge, and circled along the snow-covered surface of the river, and again swept upwards, overshadowing the road with cold, trembling wings, Natalya Vladimirovna stood still, and in utter weakness leaned against the rail. From the depth below, there looked up at her a dull black eye—a spot of unfrozen water—and its gaze was mysterious and terrible. But before her resounded and called persistently the words:

"Nyemtchínovskaya Street, the second house from the corner. Nyemtchínovskaya Street, the second house from the corner."

Khijhnyakóv—dressed, and lay down again on. his bed rolled to the very eyes in a warm overcoat, his sole remaining possession. The room was cold, there was ice in the corners, but he breathed into the astrakhan collar, and so became warm and comfortable. The whole day long he kept deceiving himself, that tomorrow he would go and seek work, and ask for something; but meanwhile he was content not to think at all, but merely to tremble at the sound of a raised voice the other side of the wall, or at the sound of a sharply slammed door. He had lain long in this way, perfectly still, when at the entrance door he heard an uneven rapping, timid, and yet hurried and sharp, as if someone was knocking with the back of the hand. His room was the one next to the entrance door, and by craning his head and pricking up his ears he could distinguish everything which took place near it. Matryóna went to the door and opened it, let someone in and closed it again. Then followed an expectant silence.

"Whom do you want?" asked Matryóna in a hoarse, unfriendly tone. A stranger's voice, gentle and broken, bashfully replied:

"I want Kátya Nyetchayeva. She lives here?"

"She did. But what do you want with her?"

"I want her very badly. Is she not at home?" and in her voice there was a note of fear.

"Kátya is dead. She died, I say—in the hospital."

Again, there was a long silence, so long indeed that Khijhnyakóv felt a pain in his back; but he did not dare to move it, while the people there kept silence.

Then the stranger's voice pronounced gently, and without expression, the one word:

"Goodbye!"

But evidently she did not go away, since in the course of a minute Matryóna asked: "What have you there? Have you brought something for Kátya?"

Someone knelt down, striking her knees on the floor, and the stranger's voice, convulsed with suppressed sobs, uttered quickly the words:

"Take it, take it! For the love of God, take it! And then I—I'll go away."

"But what is it?"

Again, there was a long silence, and then a gentle weeping, broken, and hopeless. There was in it a deadly weariness, and a black despair, without a single gleam of hope. It was as though a hand had impotently drawn the bow across the overtightened, the last remaining, string of an expensive instrument, and when the string snapped the soft wailing note had been silenced for ever.

"Why, you have nearly smothered it!" exclaimed Matryóna in a rough, angry tone. "You see what sort of people undertake to bear children. How could you do it? Whoever would wrap up babies like that? Come now, come along; do, I say. How could you do such a thing?"

Once more all was silent near the door.

Khijhnyakóv listened a little longer and then lay down, delighted that no one had come to fetch him, and not taking the trouble to guess the truth about what he had not understood in that which had just taken place. He began already to feel the approach of night, and wished that someone would turn the lamp up higher. He became restless, and, clenching his teeth, he endeavoured to restrain his thoughts. In the past there was nothing but mire, falls, and horror, and—there was the same horror in the future. He was just beginning by degrees to snuggle himself together, and draw up his hands and feet, when Dunyásha came in, dressed to go out in a red blouse, and already slightly intoxicated. She plopped down on the bed, and said with a gesture of surprise:

"Oh Lord!" She shook her head and smiled. "They have brought a little baby here. Such a tiny one, my friend, but he shouts just like a police-inspector. By God, just like a police-inspector!" (Known in Russia for shouting at the top of their voices.)

She swore whimsically, and *coquettishly* flipped Khijhnyakóv's nose.

"Let's go and see. Why not, indeed! Yes, we'll just take a look at him. Matryóna is going to bath it; she is boiling the *samovar*. Abrám Petróvitch is blowing up the charcoal with his boot. How funny it all is. And the baby is crying: '*Wa, wa, wa!*'"

Dunyásha made a face which she meant to represent the baby, and again went on puling: "'*Wa, wa, wa!*' Just like a police-inspector, by God! Let's go. Don't you want to?—well, then devil take you! Turn up your toes where you are, rotten egg, you!"

And she danced out of the room. But half an hour after Khijhnyakóv, tottering on his weak legs and hanging on to the doorposts, hesitatingly opened the door of the kitchen.

"Shut it! you've made a draught," cried Abrám Petróvitch.

Khijhnyakóv hastily slammed the door behind him, and looked round apologetically; but no one took any notice of him, so he calmed down. The combined heat of the stove, the urn, and the company made the kitchen pretty warm, and the vapour rose, and then rolled down the colder walls in thick drops. Matryóna with a severe and irritated mien was washing the child in a trough, and with pock-marked hands was splashing the water over him, while she crooned:

"Little lambkin, then, it s'all be clean. It s'all be white."

Whether it was because the kitchen was light and cheerful, or because the water was warm and caressing, at all events the child was quiet, and wrinkled up its little red face as though about to sneeze.

Dunyásha looked at the tub over Matryóna 's shoulder, and seizing her opportunity, splashed the little one with three fingers.

"Get away!" the old woman cried in a threatening tone, "where are you coming to? I know what to do without your help. I have had children of my own."

"Don't meddle. She's quite right, children are such tender things," said Abram Petróvitch, in support of her; "they want some handling."

He sat down on the table, and with condescending satisfaction contemplated the little rosy body. The baby wriggled its fingers, and Dunyásha with wild delight wagged her head and laughed.

"Just like a police-inspector, s'welp me Bob!"

"But have you seen a police-inspector in a trough?" asked Abrám Petróvitch.

All laughed, and even Khijhnyakóv smiled; but almost immediately the smile left his face in affright, and he looked round at the mother. She was sitting wearily on the bench, with her head thrown back, and, her black eyes, abnormally large from sickness and suffering, lighted up with a peaceful gleam, and on her pale lips hovered the proud smile of a mother. And when he saw this Khijhnyakóv burst into a solitary, belated laugh:

"He! he! he!"

He even looked proudly round on all sides. Matryóna took the baby out of the tub, and wrapped it in a bath-sheet. The child burst into loud crying, but was soon quieted again, and Matryóna, unrolling the sheet, smiled in confusion and said:

"What a dear little body, just like velvet."

"Let me feel," entreated Dunyásha.

"What next!"

Dunyásha began suddenly to tremble all over, and stamped her feet; choking with longing, and mad with the desire, which overwhelmed her, she cried in such a shrill voice as none had ever heard from her:

"Let me! let me!"

"Yes, let her," entreated Natálya Vladimirovna in a fright. And Dunyásha just as suddenly became quiet again. She cautiously touched the child's little shoulder with two fingers, and following her example, Abrám Petróvitch, with a condescending wink, also reached out to that little red shoulder.

"Yes, indeed, children are tender things," said he in self-justification.

Last of all Khijhnyakóv tried it. His fingers felt for a moment the touch of something living, downy like velvet, and withal so tender and

209

feeble that his fingers seemed no longer to belong to him, and became as tender as the something he touched. And thus, craning their necks, and unconsciously lighting up into a smile of strange happiness, stood the three, the thief, the prostitute, and the lonely broken man, and that little life, feeble as a distant light on the *steepe*, was vaguely calling them somewhither, and promising them something beautiful, bright, immortal. And the happy mother looked proudly on, while above the low ceiling the house rose in a heavy mass of stone, and in the upper flats the rich sauntered about, and yawned with *ennui*.

Night had come on, black, malign, as all nights are, and had pitched her tent in darkness over the distant snowy fields; and the lonely branches of trees became chilled with fear, just those branches which first welcomed the morning sun. With feeble artificial light man fought against her, but strong and malign she girded the isolated lights in a hopeless circle, and filled the hearts of men with darkness. And in many a heart she extinguished the feeble flickering sparks.

Khijhnyakóv did not sleep. Huddled up together into a little ball, he hid himself under a soft heap of rags from the cold and from the night, and wept, without effort, without pain or convulsion, as those weep whose heart is pure and without sin, as the heart of a little child. He pitied himself huddled up into a heap, and it seemed to him that he pitied all mankind and the whole of human life, and in this feeling, there was a secret, profound gladness. He saw the child, just born, and it seemed to him that he himself was reborn to a new life, and would live long, and that his life would be beautiful. He loved and yet pitied this new life, and he felt so happy, that he laughed so that he shook the heap of rags, and then asked himself:

"Why am I weeping?"

But he could not discover the answer to his own question, and so replied:

"So!"

And such a profound thought was conveyed by this short word, that this wreck of a man, whose life was so pitiable and lonely, was convulsed with a fresh burst of scalding tears.

But at his bedside rapacious death was noiselessly taking its seat, and waiting—quietly, patiently, persistently.

In the Train

We couldn't sleep. We entered the train car wanting to get some rest, in its illusive darkness, under the chatter of the wheels and the rhythmic swaying of soft beds, when drowsy thought steadily floats over a wavy dreamscape—but it just happened that we began to talk about something, about some faraway people and faraway things, and we ended up talking half the night away. I do not know why, but all people on journeys become philosophers; torn away from things of habit they are truly awakened and with surprise begin to look backwards and forwards, to recollect things that are very remote, and to dream of a future that is just as far away.

If human thought could take form, then every rushing train would become enveloped in a row of shadows, and you would no longer be able to hear its rumble under a thousand voices, drawn-out and dull. For the people in the train car the present does not exist—that damned present that holds its grip over one's thoughts and the movement of one's hands—perhaps this is why people in the train car become philosophers.

And we talked. We talked about people and we talked about life, about its beauty and riches, about its bottomless depths, above which float people-chips, blind and carefree. They know only its surface, and they are so light, too light, never descending down to the bottom. It happens that sometimes they are covered by a worldly wave, and for a moment life opens up to them its mysterious depths and will blind them, and frighten them—and then again to the surface, again the blue tent, what they call the sky when talking to children, again the sleepy, blind swaying, and like that until the end—until they rot.

We talked like this for a long time—in the illusive darkness of the train car, under the quiet ringing of the wheels, not being able to see each other but sensing our ever-growing proximity and gentle affection. Torn away from things of habit, people in the train car become sensitive to their ever-lonely hearts and greedily drink up the soft, fleeting kindness, like flowers sucking up water in the drought.

"We have to sleep," he said.

"It's about time," I replied.

Smiling, we shut our eyes, but half an hour later we found our-selves standing in the corridor outside our compartment, staring out the window. It's likely the moon was somewhere behind the clouds, and the night was bright, and the snowy murk of the earth merged seamlessly with the lunar murk of the night winter sky. The thick layer of snow smoothed out the mounds and irregularities, but we often travelled on this road and everything that passed before us appeared familiar and previously seen.

"But that's not true," I said. "We neither see nor know anything."

He understood me and, without breaking away from the window, pressed his head closer to mine and replied:

"It only seems familiar. The eyes deceive."

"The eyes deceive. When I travel this road, I always look out the window, and my sight covers it all as far as the horizon. And it seems a lot to me, but it's. . . . .it's only as far as the horizon. When I travel by several times my memory will retain only some houses and stations, and some faces, and the forest, and even individual trees. It seems to me like that's everything—but that's only a few houses, a few faces, and individual trees. I know one birch tree here. It stands at the edge of the forest, apart from the rest, as if it ran out of the forest and is star-ing greedily into the field. If it is felled, I won't find the place where it lived and, quite likely, won't even remember it.

"I know that birch tree. It looks like it's screaming."

"Yes. And do you remember where it is?"

"It's somewhere here. I don't know. I don't remember. And I haven't seen it for a while."

"Looks like it was felled."

The Russian winter forest passed us with a breath of cold, night, and loneliness. And again, the snowy murk and the same murky sky. And, because we've often travelled this route, the sky itself seemed familiar and long known to us, and you could not believe that this was a new sky, one which we have never seen before. A green light flew by, then some snow-covered roofs, and then the train stopped.

"Belyevo station," said the conductor.

We knew this station well because the train always stopped here for five minutes, but for some reason we didn't speak about it.

"Belyevo?" repeated someone behind us. "They make good pasties here. I know."

And he slammed the door. Our train stopped right in front of the telegraph, and through a wide window one could see the people working inside. They didn't know that they were being watched, indifferently getting on with their business, and the whole thing reminded one a little of a scene behind a raised curtain. One telegraphist, a young man with a moustache, was facing in our direction, and at one point his eyes even met mine, yet there was no expression in them. The station lights were reflected slightly by the large glass window, and because of this only the illuminated part of his face could be clearly seen; that which was in the shadow disappeared, as if it did not exist at all.

"Take a better look at the telegraphist," my companion told me.

I did. The telegraphist was still working with the same indifference. He then spoke something to his side, puffed on a cigarette, and stood up. He took one step away and at once disappeared behind the shining glass. And then he appeared again, and once more sat down to work. The cigarette between his teeth seemed to distract him, the illuminated part of his face was frowning, and eventually he ended up putting the cigarette down on the edge of the desk.

And that's it. The train began to move, and the station passed by in reverse order: station lamps, some snow covered roofs, a green light—and again the fields, the snowy murk, and the same murky sky. This is the way apparitions come to us: they come in one door and leave through the other, but the room stays the same—the same table, the same armchairs, the same silent flicker of the candle. And the pale, seemingly melting image, stays only in our eyes, and our frozen heart tries to tell us something.

"Well, that's the Belyevo we know," said my colleague.

"And if one was to go back, it would appear again."

"And disappear again!"

"And what if one was to stay there?"

"For how long?" he asked quietly. "For how long?" he repeated, smiling only in thought.

And again, we stood huddled together looking out the windows, and through them we could actually see that indifferent telegraphist behind the shining glass, racing over the snowy fields. But that was only an image. He was in our eyes—only in our eyes.

"He has a good face," I said, recalling.

"He is young. He is probably twenty-five. He has been working on the telegraph already for six or seven years, on this very telegraph. You could see something habitual and regular in the movement of his hands, in the expression of his face, in that cigarette, placed on the side of the desk."

"He didn't see us. It's brighter where they are, and he didn't see us."

"It's likely he saw only the silhouette of the train car. He can see only train cars and their silhouettes. Every day he is on duty at the telegraph, and by him pass tens.....hundreds of train cars. Many travel this route, and every day thousands of people go past him this way and back. Perhaps half of Russia passed by here—all past him. And he knows nothing about those who had passed."

"Leo Tolstoy often takes this route."

"Leo Tolstoy takes this route. Ministers, princes, great painters, writers, and singers take this route. By now thousands of eyes had rested on him with indifference, and he, with the same indifference, sat and worked. Who knows—it may be that Tolstoy looked at him, and at that time he was talking with someone and smoking, greedily sucking up the vile tobacco. He can see only the train cars and their silhouettes. From darkness or sunlight, train cars arrive at the empty lines and stand as if they were going to stand there forever. And in five minutes they depart, and the lines are empty again, and it is as if no one had ever stood here before. In summer faces flit in the windows, and in winter the train cars are shut and covered with hoarfrost and are as silent as if there is not a living man inside.

"Silent they come and, without opening, silent they leave—and he sits there working, and knows nothing about those who passed by. He is working, which means that he is passing on words. Even if the words are as clear as day, for him they are closed, like train cars—after all, he knows neither those who are speaking, nor those who are listening. And right by him, like train cars, the words pass by—someone's joy and someone's grief, someone's thoughts, ideas, orders. He only passes them on. And he has both eyes and ears, but he is deaf and blind, as if he has neither hearing nor sight."

"He has a life of his own."

"He lives in Belyevo in the house of some *petit bourgeois* woman with three windows above a ravine, where, if just for a moment one steps off the beaten path, one would drop head deep into the snow. The only dark spots are directly in sight: a small pile of ash and frozen waste, and a naked, crooked trunk of a willow tree. And then we have his small, hot little room with a stove bench, and on this bench, he sits during the holidays, in the mornings, and when he plays his guitar. He likes embroidered Russian shirts, which he receives as gifts on his birthdays, and he dreams of a new uniform jacket and a pair of polished boots. He doesn't drink yet, he's still young and full of dreams, which is why his room is clean, his clothes are covered with a sheet, and there are muslin covers over the window.

"And when he reads some old, tattered book with missing pages, he doesn't think for a moment that this book was also written by a man—it exists for him by itself and, like the crooked willow tree which he spends his time looking at, just as seldom evokes contemplation. When at night he makes his way home from duty he is very afraid of dogs, and when he is back at home he quickly undresses and, looking at his socks, worn out at the heel, falls asleep with thoughts of socks and the telegraph. Everything that happens in the world of the great, the loud, the dazzling, takes place somewhere on the side, and he does not suspect and does not think that the author of that tattered book is a passenger who was only yesterday traveling by, perhaps right past him.

"His human soul, as rich as a Stradivari violin, is given away to a street musician, who uses it to play shoddy polka, and it will never get to know itself, will never find its real voice, because the one who could extract it, the life-artist, the life-painter, the great life-musician, passes by somewhere on the periphery, and he will never discover it. And, letting the silent, closed train cars pass him by, he ends up passing himself by, just as closed, just as silent and transient." Thus said my companion and became lost in thought, and his cheek, pressed to mine, grew cold.

"But, it's possible he's not at all like that, and you've made all this up."

"It's possible. After all, we've only passed by."

The train car was swaying lightly and snowy fields were swimming by. They seemed familiar but were deceiving: I've never seen these fields! He stood next to me, and his cheek pressed to mine, and with this touch he too has deceived me: I don't know him! Tomorrow we will part company, and his image will remain only in my eyes, and other people will begin to pass by me—and I will pass by others. Maybe, by myself.

Judas Iscariot

CHAPTER 1

Jesus Christ had often been warned that Judas Iscariot was a man of very evil repute, and that He ought to beware of him. Some of the disciples, who had been in Judaea, knew him well, while others had heard much about him from various sources, and there was none who had a good word for him. If good people in speaking of him blamed him, as covetous, cunning, and inclined to hypocrisy and lying, the bad, when asked concerning him, inveighed against him in the severest terms.

"He is always making mischief among us," they would say, and spit in contempt. "He always has some thought which he keeps to himself. He creeps into a house quietly, like a scorpion, but goes out again with an ostentatious noise. There are friends among thieves, and comrades among robbers, and even liars have wives, to whom they speak the truth; but Judas laughs at thieves and honest folk alike, although he is himself a clever thief. Moreover, he is in appearance the strangest person in Judaea. No! he is no friend of ours, this foxy-haired Judas Iscariot," the bad would say, thereby surprising the good people, in whose opinion there was not much difference between him and all other vicious people in Judaea.

They would recount further that he had long ago deserted his wife, who was living in poverty and misery, striving to eke out a living from the unfruitful patch of land which constituted his estate. He had wandered for many years aimlessly among the people, and had even gone from one sea to the other—no mean distance—and everywhere he lied and grimaced, and would make some discovery with his thievish eye, and then suddenly disappear, leaving behind him animosity and strife. Yes, he was as inquisitive, artful and hateful as a one-eyed demon. Children he had none, and this was an additional proof that Judas was a wicked man, that God would not have from him any posterity.

None of the disciples had noticed when it was that this strange, foxy-haired Jew first appeared in the company of Christ: but he had for a long time haunted their path, joined in their conversations, performed little acts of service, bowing and smiling and currying favour. Sometimes they became quite used to him. so that he escaped their weary eyes; then again, he would suddenly obtrude himself on eye and ear, irritating them as something abnormally ugly, treacherous and disgusting. They would drive him away with harsh words, and for a short time he would disappear, only to reappear suddenly, officious, flattering and crafty as a one-eyed demon,

There was no doubt in the minds of some of the disciples that under his desire to draw near to Jesus was hidden some secret intention—some malign and cunning scheme.

But Jesus did not listen to their advice; their prophetic voice did not reach His ears. In that spirit of serene contradiction, which ever irresistibly inclined Him to the reprobate and unlovable, He deliberately accepted Judas, and included him in the circle of the chosen. The disciples were disturbed and murmured under their breath, but He would sit still, with His face towards the setting sun, and listen abstractedly, perhaps to them, perhaps to something else. For ten days there had been no wind, and the transparent atmosphere, wary and sensitive, continued ever the same, motionless and unchanged.

It seemed as though it preserved in its transparent depths every cry and song made during those days by men and beasts and birds—tears, laments and cheerful song, prayers and curses—and that on account of these crystallised sounds the air was so heavy, threatening, and saturated with invisible life. Once more the sun was sinking. It rolled heavily downwards in a flaming ball, setting the sky on fire. Everything upon the earth which was turned towards it: the swarthy face of Jesus, the walls of the houses, and the leaves of the trees—everything obediently reflected that distant, fearfully pensive light. Now the white walls were no longer white, and the white city upon the white hill was turned to red.

And lo! Judas arrived. He arrived bowing low, bending his back, cautiously and timidly protruding his bumpy head—just exactly as his acquaintances had described. He was spare and of good height, almost the same as that of Jesus, who stooped a little through the habit of thinking as He walked, and so appeared shorter than He was. Judas was to all appearances fairly strong and well knit, though for some reason or other he pretended to be weak and somewhat sickly. He had an uncertain voice. Sometimes it was strong and manly, then again shrill as that of an old woman scolding her husband, provokingly thin, and disagreeable to the ear, so that ofttimes one felt inclined to tear out his words from the ear, like rough, decaying splinters.

His short red locks failed to hide the curious form of his skull. It looked as if it had been split at the nape of the neck by a double sword-cut, and then joined together again, so that it was apparently divided into four pails, and inspired distrust, nay, even alarm: for behind such a cranium there could be no quiet or concord, but there must over be heard the noise of sanguinary and merciless strife. The face of Judas was similarly doubled. One side of it, with a black, sharply watchful eye, was vivid and mobile, readily gathering into innumerable tortuous wrinkles. On the other side were no wrinkles. It was deadly flat, smooth, and set, and though of the same size as the other, it seemed enormous on account of its wide-open blind eye. Covered with a whitish film, closing neither night nor day, this eye met light and darkness with the same indifference, but perhaps on account of the proximity of its lively and crafty companion it never got full credit for blindness.

When in a paroxysm of joy or excitement, Judas would close his sound eye and shake his head. The other eye would always shake in unison and gaze in silence. Even people quite devoid of penetration could clearly perceive, when looking at Judas, that such a man could bring no good. . . .

And yet Jesus brought him near to Himself, and once even made him sit next to Him. John, the beloved disciple, fastidiously moved away, and all the others who loved their Teacher cast down their eyes in disapprobation. But Judas sat on, and turning his head from side to side, began in a somewhat thin voice to complain of ill-health, and said that his chest gave him pain in the night, and that when ascending a hill, he got out of breath, and when he stood still on the edge of a precipice he would be seized with a dizziness, and could scarcely restrain a foolish desire to throw himself down. And many other impious things he invented, as though not understanding that sicknesses do not come to a man by chance, but as a consequence of conduct not corresponding with the laws of the Eternal. Thus, Judas Iscariot kept on rubbing his chest with his broad palm, and even pretended to cough, midst a general silence and downcast eyes.

John, without looking at the Teacher, whispered to his friend Simon Peter—

"Aren't you tired of that lie? I can't stand it any longer. I am going away."

Peter glanced at Jesus, and meeting his eye, quickly arose.

"Wait a moment," said he to his friend.

Once more he looked at Jesus; sharply as a stone torn from a mountain, he moved towards Judas, and said to him in a loud voice, with expansive, serene courtesy—

"You will come with us, Judas."

He gave him a kindly slap on his bent back, and without looking at the Teacher, though he felt His eye upon him, resolutely added in his loud voice, which excluded all objection, just as water excludes air—

"It does not matter that you have such a strange face. There fall into our nets even worse monstrosities, and they sometimes turn out very tasty food. It is not for us, our Lord's fishermen, to throw away a catch, merely because the fish have spines, or only one eye. I saw once at Tyre an octopus, which had been caught by the local fishermen, and I was so frightened that I wanted to run away. But they laughed at me. A fisherman from Tiberias gave me some of it to eat, and I asked for more, it was so tasty. You remember, Master, that I told you the story, and you laughed, too. And you, Judas, are like an octopus—but only on one side."

And he laughed loudly, content with his joke. When Peter spoke, his words resounded so forcibly, that it seemed as though he were driving them in with nails. When Peter moved, or did anything, he made a noise that could be heard afar, and which called forth a response from the deafest of things: the stone floor rumbled under his feet, the doors shook and rattled, and the very air was convulsed with fear, and roared. In the clefts of the mountains his voice awoke the inmost echo, and in the morning time, when they were fishing on the lake, he would roll about on the sleepy, glittering water, and force the first shy sunbeams into smiles,

For this apparently, he was loved: when on all other faces there still lay the shadow of night, his powerful head, and bare breast, and freely extended arms were already aglow with the light of dawn.

The words of Peter, evidently approved as they were by the Master, dispersed the oppressive atmosphere. But some of the disciples, who had been to the seaside and had seen an octopus, were disturbed by the monstrous image so lightly applied to the new disciple. They recalled the immense eyes, the dozens of greedy tentacles, the feigned repose—and how all at once: it embraced, clung, crushed and sucked, all without one wink of its monstrous eyes. What did it mean? But Jesus remained silent. He smiled with a frown of kindly raillery on Peter, who was still telling glowing tales about the octopus. Then one by one the disciples shame-facedly approached Judas, and began a friendly conversation, with him, but—beat a hasty and awkward retreat.

Only John, the son of Zebedee, maintained an obstinate silence; and Thomas had evidently not made up his mind to say anything, but was still weighing the matter. He kept his gaze attentively fixed on Christ and Judas as they sat together. And that strange proximity of divine beauty and monstrous ugliness, of a man with a benign look, and of an octopus with immense, motionless, dully greedy eyes, oppressed his mind like an insoluble enigma.

He tensely wrinkled his smooth, upright forehead, and screwed up his eyes, thinking that he would see better so, but only succeeded in imagining that Judas really had eight incessantly moving feet. But that was not true. Thomas understood that, and again gazed obstinately.

Judas gathered courage: he straightened out his arms, which had been bent at the elbows, relaxed the muscles which held his jaws in tension, and began cautiously to protrude his bumpy head into the light. It had been the whole time in view of all, but Judas imagined that it had been impenetrably hidden from sight by some invisible, but thick and cunning veil. But lo! now, as though creeping out from a ditch, he felt his strange skull, and then his eyes, in the light: he stopped and then deliberately exposed his whole face.

Nothing happened; Peter had gone away somewhere or other, Jesus sat pensive, with His head leaning on His hand, and gently swayed His sunburnt foot. The disciples were conversing together, and only Thomas gazed at him attentively and seriously, like a conscientious tailor taking measurement. Judas smiled; Thomas did not reply to the smile; but evidently took it into account, as he did everything else, and continued to gaze. But something unpleasant alarmed the left side of Judas' countenance as he looked round. John, handsome, pure, without a single fleck upon his snow-white conscience, was looking at him out of a dark corner, with cold but beautiful eye. And though he walked as others walk, yet Judas felt as if he were dragging himself along the ground like a whipped cur, as he went up to John and said: "Why are you silent, John? Your words are like golden apples in vessels of silver filigree; bestow one of them on Judas, who is so poor."

John looked steadfastly into his wide-open motionless eye, and said nothing. And he looked on, while Judas crept out, hesitated a moment, and then disappeared in the deep darkness of the open door.

Since the full moon was up, there were many people out walking. Jesus went out too, and from the low roof on which Judas had spread his couch he saw Him going out. In the light of the moon each white figure looked bright and deliberate in its movements; and seemed not so much to walk as to glide in front of its dark shadow. Then suddenly a man would be lost in something black, and his voice became audible. And when people reappeared in the moonlight, they seemed silent—like white walls, or black shadows—as everything did in the transparent mist of night. Almost everyone was asleep when Judas heard the soft voice of Jesus returning. All in and around about the house was still. A cock crew; somewhere an ass, disturbed in his sleep, brayed aloud and insolently as in daytime, then reluctantly and gradually relapsed into silence. Judas did not sleep at all, but listened surreptitiously. The moon illumined one half of his face, and was reflected strangely in his enormous open eye, as on the frozen surface of a lake.

Suddenly he remembered something, and hastily coughed, rubbing his perfectly healthy chest with his hairy hand: maybe someone was not yet asleep, and was listening to what Judas was thinking!

CHAPTER 2

They gradually became used to Judas, and ceased to notice his face. Jesus entrusted the common purse to him, and with it there fell on him all household cares: he purchased the necessary food and clothing, distributed alms, and when they were on the road, it was his duty to choose the place where they were to stop, or to find a night's lodging.

All this he did very cleverly, so that in a short time he had earned the goodwill of some of the disciples, who had noticed his efforts. Judas was an habitual liar, but they became used to this, when they found that his lies were not followed by any evil conduct; nay, they added a special piquancy to his conversation and tales, and made life seem like a comic, and sometimes a tragic, tale.

According to his stories, he seemed to know everyone, and each person that he knew had some time in his life been guilty of evil conduct, or even crime. Those, according to him, were called good, who knew how to conceal their thoughts and acts: but if one only embraced, flattered, and questioned such a man sufficiently, there would ooze out from him every untruth, nastiness, and lie, like matter from a pricked wound. He freely confessed that he sometimes lied himself;

but affirmed with an oath that others were still greater liars, and that if anyone in this world was ever deceived, it was Judas.

Indeed, according to his own account, he had been deceived, time upon time, in one way or another. Thus, a certain guardian of the treasures of a rich *grandee* once confessed to him, that he had for ten years been continually on the point of stealing the property committed to him, but that he was debarred by fear of the *grandee*, and of his own conscience. And Judas believed him—and he suddenly committed the theft, and deceived Judas. But even then, Judas still trusted him—and then he suddenly restored the stolen treasure to the *grandee*, and again deceived Judas. Yes, everything deceived him, even animals. Whenever he pets a dog, it bites his fingers; but when he beats it with a stick it licks his feet, and looks into his eyes like a daughter. He killed one such dog, and buried it deep, laying a great stone on the top of it—but who knows? Perhaps just because he killed it, it has come to life again, and instead of lying in the trench, is running about cheerfully with other dogs.

All laughed merrily at Judas' tale, and he smiled pleasantly himself, winking his one lively, mocking eye—and by that very smile confessed that he had lied somewhat; that he had not really killed the dog. But he meant to find it and kill it, because he did not wish to be deceived. And at these words of Judas, they laughed all the more.

But sometimes in his tales he transgressed the bounds of probability, and ascribed to people such proclivities as even the beasts do not possess, accusing them of such crimes as are not, and never have been. And since he named in this connection the most honoured people, some were indignant at the calumny, while others jokingly asked:

"How about your own father and mother, Judas—were they not good people?"

Judas winked his eye, and smiled with a gesture of his hands. And the fixed, wide-open eye shook in unison with the shaking of his head, and looked out in silence.

"But who was my father? Perhaps it was the man who used to beat me with a rod, or may be—a devil, a goat or a cock.... How can Judas tell How can Judas tell with whom his mother shared her conch. Judas had many fathers: to which of them do you refer?"

But at this they were all indignant, for they had a profound reverence for parents; and Matthew, who was very learned in the scriptures, said severely in the words of Solomon:

"'*Whoso slandereth his father and his mother, his lamp shall be extin-*

guished in deep darkness.'"

But John the son of Zebedee haughtily jerked out:

"And what of us? What evil have you to say of us, Judas Iscariot?"

But he waved his hands in simulated terror, whined, and bowed like a beggar who has in vain asked an alms of a passer-by: "Ah! they are tempting poor Judas! They are laughing at him, they wish to take in the poor, trusting Judas!" And while one side of his face was crinkled up in buffooning grimaces, the other side wagged sternly and severely, and the never-closing eye looked out in a broad stare.

More and louder than any laughed Simon Peter at the jokes of Judas Iscariot. But once it happened that he suddenly frowned, and became silent and sad, and hastily dragging Judas aside by the sleeve, he bent down, and asked in a hoarse whisper—

"But Jesus? What do you think of Jesus? Speak seriously, I entreat you."

Judas cast on him a malign glance.

"And what do you think?"

Peter whispered with awe and gladness—

"I think that He is the son of the living God."

"Then why do you ask? What can Judas tell you, whose father was a goat?"

"But do you love Him? You do not seem to love anyone, Judas."

And with the same strange malignity, Iscariot blurted out abruptly and sharply: "I do."

Some two days after this conversation, Peter openly dubbed Judas "my friend the octopus"; but Judas awkwardly, and ever with the same malignity, endeavoured to creep away from him into some dark corner, and would sit there morosely glaring with his white, never-closing eye.

Thomas alone took him quite seriously. He understood nothing of jokes, hypocrisy or lies, nor of the play upon words and thoughts, but investigated everything positively to the very bottom. He would often interrupt Judas' stories about wicked people and their conduct with short practical remarks:

"You must prove that. Did you hear it yourself? Was there any one present besides yourself? What was his name?"

At this Judas would get angry, and shrilly cry out, that he had seen and heard everything himself; but the obstinate Thomas would go on cross-examining quietly and persistently, until Judas confessed that he had lied, or until he invented some new and more probable lie, which provided the others for some time with food for thought. But when Thomas discovered a discrepancy, he would immediately come and calmly expose the liar.

Usually, Judas excited in him a strong curiosity, which brought about between them a sort of friendship, full of wrangling, jeering, and invective on the one side, and of quiet insistence on the other. Sometimes Judas felt an unbearable aversion to his strange friend, and, transfixing him with a sharp glance, would say irritably, and almost with entreaty—

"What more do you want? I have told you all."

"I want you to prove how it is possible that a he-goat should be your father," Thomas would reply with calm insistency, and wait for an answer.

It chanced once, that after such a question, Judas suddenly stopped speaking and gazed at him with surprise from head to foot. What he saw was a tall, upright figure, a grey face, honest eyes of transparent blue, two fat folds beginning at the nose and losing themselves in a stiff, evenly-trimmed beard. He said with conviction:

"What a stupid you are, Thomas! What do you dream about—a tree, a wall, or a donkey?"

Thomas was in some way strangely perturbed, and made no reply. But at night, when Judas was already closing his vivid, restless eye for sleep, he suddenly said aloud from where he lay—the two now slept together on the roof—

"You are wrong, Judas. I have very bad dreams. What think you? Are people responsible for their dreams?"

"Does, then, anyone but the dreamer see a dream?" Judas replied.

Thomas sighed gently, and became thoughtful. But Judas smiled contemptuously, and firmly closed his roguish eye, and quickly gave himself up to his mutinous dreams, monstrous ravings, mad phantoms, which rent his bumpy skull to pieces.

When, during Jesus' travels about Judaea, the disciples approached a village, Iscariot would speak evil of the inhabitants and foretell misfortune. But almost always it happened that the people, of whom he had spoken evil, met Christ and His friends with gladness, and surrounded them with attentions and love, and became believers, and Judas' money-box became so full that it was difficult to carry. And when they laughed at his mistake, he would make a humble gesture with his hands, and say:

"Well, well! Judas thought that they were bad, and they turned out to be good. They quickly believed, and gave money. That only means that Judas has been deceived once more, the poor, confiding Judas Iscariot!"

But on one occasion, when they had already gone far from a village, which had welcomed them kindly, Thomas and Judas began a hot dispute, to settle which they turned back, and did not overtake Jesus and His disciples until the next day. Thomas wore a perturbed and sorrowful appearance, while Judas had such a proud look, that you would have thought that he expected them to offer him their congratulations and thanks upon the spot. Approaching the Master, Thomas declared with decision: "Judas was right, Lord. They were ill-disposed, stupid people. And the seeds of your words have fallen upon the rock." And he related what had happened in the village.

After Jesus and His disciples left it, an old woman had begun to cry out that her little white kid had been stolen, and she laid the theft at the door of the visitors who had just departed. At first the people had disputed with her, but when she obstinately insisted that there was no one else who could have done it except Jesus, many agreed with her, and even were about to start in pursuit. And although they soon found the kid straying in the underwood, they still decided that Jesus was a deceiver, and possibly a thief.

"So that's what they think of us is it!" cried Peter, with a snort "Lord, will Thou that I return to those fools, and—"

But Jesus, saying not a word, gazed severely at him, and Peter in silence retired behind the others. And no one ever referred to the incident again, as though it had never occurred, and as though Judas had been proved wrong. In vain did he show himself on all sides, endeavouring to give to his double, crafty, hook-nosed face an expression of modesty. They would not look at him, and if by chance any one did glance at him, it was in a very unfriendly, not to say contemptuous, manner.

From that day on Jesus' treatment of him underwent a strange change. Formerly, for some reason or other, Judas never used to speak directly with Jesus, who never addressed Himself directly to him, but nevertheless would often glance at him with kindly eyes, smile at his rallies, and if He had not seen him for some time, would inquire: "Where is Judas?"

But now He looked at him as if He did not see him, although as before, and indeed more determinedly than formerly, He sought him out with His eyes every time that He began to speak to the disciples or to the people; but He was either sitting with His back to him, so that He was obliged, as it were, to cast His words over His head so as to reach Judas, or else He made as though He did not notice him at all.

And whatever He said, though it was one thing one day, and then next day quite another, although it might be the very thing that Judas was thinking, it always seemed as though He were speaking against him. To all He was the tender, beautiful flower, the sweet-smelling rose of Lebanon, but for Judas He left only sharp thorns, as though Judas had neither heart, nor sight, nor smell, and did not understand, even better than any, the beauty of tender, immaculate petals.

"Thomas! Do you like the yellow rose of Lebanon, which has a swarthy countenance and eyes like the roe?" he inquired once of his friend, who replied indifferently—

"Rose? Yes, I like the smell. But I have never heard of a rose with a swarthy countenance and eyes like a roe!"

"What? Do you not know that the polydactylous cactus, which tore your new garment yesterday, has only one beautiful flower, and only one eye?"

But Thomas did not know this, although only yesterday a cactus had actually caught in his garment and torn it into wretched rags. But then Thomas never did know anything, though he asked questions about everything, and looked so straight with his bright, transparent eyes, through which, as through a pane of Phoenician glass, was visible a wall, with a dismal ass tied to it.

Sometime later another occurrence took place, in which Judas again proved to be in the right.

At a certain village in Judaea, of which Judas had so bad an opinion, that he had advised them to avoid it, the people received Christ with hostility, and after His sermon and exposition of hypocrites they burst into fury, and threatened to stone Jesus and His disciples. Enemies He had many, and most likely they would have carried out their sinister intention, but for Judas Iscariot. Seized with a mad fear for Jesus, as though he already saw the drops of ruby blood upon His white garment, Judas threw himself in blind fury upon the crowd, scolding, screeching, beseeching, and lying, and thus gave time and opportunity to Jesus and His disciples to escape.

Amazingly active, as though running upon a dozen feet, laughable and terrible in his fury and entreaties, he threw himself madly in front of the crowd and charmed it with a certain strange power. He shouted that the Nazarene was not possessed of a devil, that He was simply an impostor, a thief who loved money as did all His disciples, and even Judas himself: and he rattled the money-box, grimaced, and beseeched, throwing himself on the ground. And by degrees the anger of the crowd changed into laughter and disgust, and they let fall the stones which they had picked up to throw at them.

"They are not fit to die by the hands of an honest person," said they, while others thoughtfully followed the rapidly disappearing Judas with their eyes.

Again, Judas expected to receive congratulations, praise, and thanks, and made a show of his torn garments, and pretended that he had been beaten; but this time, too, he was greatly mistaken. The angry Jesus strode on in silence, and even Peter and John did not venture to approach Him: and all whose eyes fell on Judas in his torn garments, his face glowing with happiness, but still somewhat frightened, repelled him with curt, angry exclamations.

It was just as though he had not saved them all, just as though he had not saved their Teacher, whom they loved so dearly.

"Do you want to see some fools?" said he to Thomas, who was thoughtfully walking in the rear. "Look! There they go along the road in a crowd, like a flock of sheep, kicking up the dust. But you are wise, Thomas, you creep on behind, and I, the noble, magnificent Judas, creep on behind like a dirty slave, who has no place by the side of his masters."

"Why do you call yourself magnificent?" asked Thomas in surprise.

"Because I am so," Judas replied with conviction, and he went on talking, giving more details of how he had deceived the enemies of Jesus, and laughed at them and their stupid stones.

"But you told lies," said Thomas.

"Of course, I did," quickly assented Iscariot. "I gave them what they asked for, and they gave me in return what I wanted. And what is a lie, my clever Thomas? Would not the death of Jesus be the great lie of all?"

"You did not act rightly. Now I believe that a devil is your father. It was he that taught you Judas."

The face of Judas grew pale, and something suddenly came over Thomas, and as if it were a white cloud, passed over and concealed the road and Jesus. With a gentle movement Judas just as suddenly drew Thomas to himself, pressed him closely with a paralysing movement, and whispered in his ear—

"You mean, then, that a devil has instructed me, don't you, Thomas? Well, I saved Jesus. Therefore, a devil loves Jesus and has need of Him, and of the truth. Is it not so, Thomas? But then my father was not a devil, but a he-goat. Can a he-goat want Jesus? Eh? And don't you want Him yourselves, and the truth also?"

Angry and slightly frightened, Thomas freed himself with difficulty from the clinging embrace of Judas, and began to stride forward quickly. But he soon slackened his pace as he endeavoured to understand what had taken place.

But Judas crept on gently behind, and gradually came to a standstill. And lo! in the distance the pedestrians became blended into a parti-coloured mass, so that it was impossible any longer to distinguish which among those little figures was Jesus. And lo! the little Thomas, too, changed into a grey spot, and suddenly—all disappeared round a turn in the road.

Looking round, Judas went down from the road and with immense leaps descended into the depths of a rocky ravine. His clothes blew out with the speed and abruptness of his course, and his hands were extended upwards as though he would fly. Lo! now he crept along an abrupt declivity, and suddenly rolled down in a grey ball, rubbing off his skin against the stones; then he jumped up and angrily threatened the mountain with his fist—

"You too, curse you!"

Suddenly he changed his quick movements into a comfortable, concentrated dawdling, chose a place by a big stone, and sat down without hurry. He turned himself, as if seeking a comfortable position, laid his hands side by side on the grey stone, and heavily leaned his head upon them. And so, for an hour or two be sat on, as motionless and grey as the grey stone itself, so still that he deceived even the birds. The walls of the ravine rose before him, and behind, and on every side, cutting a sharp line all round on the blue sky; while everywhere immense grey stones obtruded from the ground, as though there had been at some time or other, a shower here, and as though its heavy drops had become petrified in endless split, upturned skull, and every stone in it was like a petrified thought; and there were many of them, and they all kept thinking heavily, boundlessly, stubbornly.

A scorpion, deceived by his quietness, nobbled past, on its tottering legs, close to Judas. He threw a glance at it, and, without lifting his head from the stone, again let both his eyes reel fixedly on something—both motionless, both veiled in a strange whitish turbidness, both as though blind and yet terribly alert. And lo! from out of the ground, the stones, and the clefts, the quiet darkness of night began to rise, enveloped the motionless Judas, and crept swiftly up towards the pallid light of the sky. Night was coming on with its thoughts and dreams.

That night Judas did not return to the halting-place. And the disciples, forgetting their thoughts, busied themselves with preparations for their meal, and grumbled at his negligence.

CHAPTER 3

Once, about mid-day, Jesus and His disciples were walking along a stony and hilly road devoid of shade, and, since they had been more than five hours afoot, Jesus began to complain of weariness. The disciples stopped, and Peter and his friend John spread their cloaks and those of the other disciples, on the ground, and fastened them above between two high rocks, and so made a sort of tent for Jesus. He lay down in the tent, resting from the heat of the sun, while they amused Him with pleasant conversation and jokes. But seeing that even talking fatigued Him, and being themselves but little affected by weariness and the heat, they went some distance off and occupied themselves in various ways.

One sought edible roots among the stones on the slope of the mountain, and when he had found them brought them to Jesus; another, climbing up higher and higher, searched musingly for the limits of the blue distance, and failing, climbed up higher on to new, sharp-pointed rocks. John found a beautiful little blue lizard among the stones, and smiling brought it quickly with tender hands to Jesus. The lizard looked with its protuberant, mysterious eyes into His, and then crawled quickly with its cold body over His warm hand, and soon swiftly disappeared with tender, quivering tail.

But Peter and Philip, not caring about such amusements, occupied themselves in tearing up great stones from the mountain, and hurling them down below, as a test of their strength. The others, attracted by their loud laughter, by degrees gathered round them, and joined in their sport. Exerting their strength, they would tear up from the ground an ancient rock all overgrown, and lifting it high with both hands, hurl it down the slope. Heavily it would strike with a dull thud, and hesitate for a moment; then resolutely it would make a first leap, and each time it touched the ground, gathering from it speed and strength, it would become light, furious, all-subversive. Now it no longer leapt, but flew with grinning teeth, and the whistling wind let its dull round mass pass by. Lo! it is on the edge—with a last, floating motion the stone would sweep high, and then quietly, with ponderous deliberation, fly downwards in a curve to the invisible bottom of the precipice.

"Now then, another!" cried Peter. His white teeth shone between his black beard and moustache, his mighty chest and arms were bare, and the sullen, ancient rocks, dully wondering at the strength which lifted them, obediently, one after another, precipitated themselves into the abyss. Even the frail John threw some moderate-sized stones, and Jesus smiled quietly as He looked at their sport.

"But what are you doing, Judas? Why do you not take part in the game! It seems amusing enough?" asked Thomas, when he found his strange friend motionless behind a great grey stone.

"I have a pain in my chest. Moreover, they have not invited me."

"What need of invitation! At all events, I invite you; come! Look what stones Peter throws!"

Judas somehow or other happened to glance sideward at him, and Thomas became, for the first time, indistinctly aware that he had two faces. But before he could thoroughly grasp the fact, Judas said in his ordinary tone, at once fawning and mocking—

"There is surely none stronger than Peter? When he shouts, all the asses in Jerusalem think that their Messiah has arrived, and lift up their voices too. You have heard them before now, have you not, Thomas?"

Smiling politely, and modestly wrapping his garment round his chest, which was overgrown with red curly hairs, Judas stepped into the circle of players.

And since they were all in high good humour, they met him with mirth and loud jokes, and even John condescended to vouchsafe a smile, when Judas, pretending to groan with the exertion, laid hold of an immense stone. But lo! he lifted it with ease, and threw it, and his blind, wide-open eye gave a jerk, and then fixed itself immovably on Peter; while the other eye, cunning and merry, was overflowing with quiet laughter.

"No! you throw again!" said Peter in an offended tone.

And lo! one after the other they kept lifting and throwing gigantic stones, while the disciples looked on in amazement. Peter threw a great stone, and then Judas a still bigger one. Peter, frowning and concentrated, angrily wielded a fragment of rock, and struggling as he lifted it, burled it down; then Judas, without ceasing to smile, searched for a still larger fragment, and digging his long fingers into it, grasped it, and swinging himself together with it, and paling, sent it into the gulf. When he had thrown his stone, Peter would recoil and so watch its fall; but Judas always bent himself forward, stretched out his long vibrant arms, as though he were going to fly after the stone. Eventually both of them, first Peter, then Judas, seized hold of an old grey stone, but neither one nor the other could move it. All red with his exertion, Peter resolutely approached Jesus, and said aloud—

"Lord! I do not wish to be beaten by Judas. Help me to throw this stone."

Jesus made answer in a low voice, and Peter, shrugging his broad shoulders in dissatisfaction, but not daring to make any rejoinder, came back with the words—

"He says: 'But who will help Iscariot?'"

Then glancing at Judas, who, panting with clenched teeth, was still embracing the stubborn stone, he laughed cheerfully—

"Look what an invalid he is! See what our poor sick Judas is doing!"

And even Judas laughed at being so unexpectedly exposed in his deception, and all the others laughed too, and even Thomas allowed his pointed, grey, over-hanging moustache to relax into a smile.

And so, in friendly chat and laughter, they all set out again on the way, and Peter, quite reconciled to his victor, kept from time to time digging him in the ribs, and loudly guffawed—

"There's an invalid for you!"

All of them praised Judas, and acknowledged him victor, and all chatted with him in a friendly manner; but Jesus once again had no word of praise for Judas. He walked silently in front, nibbling the grasses, which He plucked. And gradually, one by one, the disciples craved laughing, and went over to Jesus. So that in a short time it came about, that they were all walking ahead in a compact body, while Judas—the victor, the strong man—crept on behind, choking with dust.

And lo! they stood still, and Jesus laid His hand on Peter's shoulder, while with His other He pointed into the distance, where Jerusalem had just become visible in the smoke. And the broad, strong back of Peter gently accepted that slight sunburnt hand.

For the night they stayed in Bethany, at the house of Lazarus. And when all were gathered together for conversation, Judas thought that they would now recall his victory over Peter, and sat down nearer. But the disciples were silent and unusually pensive. Images of the road they had traversed, of the sun, the rocks and the grass, of Christ lying down under the shelter, quietly floated through their heads, breathing a soft pensiveness, begetting confused but sweet reveries of an eternal movement under the sun. The wearied body reposed sweetly, and thought was merged in something mystically great and beautiful—and no one recalled Judas!

Judas went out, and then returned. Jesus was discoursing, and His disciples were listening to Him in silence.

Mary sat at His feet, motionless as a statue, and gazed into His face with upturned eyes. John had come quite close, and endeavoured to sit so that his hand touched the garment of the Master, but without disturbing Him. He touched Him and was still. Peter breathed loud and deeply, repeating under his breath the words of Jesus.

Iscariot had stopped short on the threshold, and contemptuously letting his gaze pass by the company, he concentrated all its fire on Jesus. And the more he looked the more everything around Him seemed to fade, and to become clothed with darkness and silence, while Jesus alone shone forth with uplifted hand. And then, lo! He was, as it were, raised up into the air, and melted away, as though He consisted of mist floating over a lake, and penetrated by the light of the setting moon, and His soft speech began to sound tenderly, somewhere far, far away. And gazing at the wavering phantom, and drinking in the tender melody of the distant dream-like words, Judas gathered his whole soul into his iron fingers, and in its vast darkness silently began building up some colossal scheme.

Slowly, in the profound darkness, he kept lifting up masses, like mountains, and quite easily heaping them one on another: and again, he would lift up and again heap them up; and something grew in the darkness, spread noiselessly and burst its bounds. His head felt like a dome, in the impenetrable darkness of which the colossal thing continued to grow, and someone, working on in silence, kept lifting up masses like mountains, and piling them one on another and again lifting up, and so on and on. . . whilst somewhere in the distance the phantom-like words tenderly sounded.

Thus, he stood blocking the doorway, huge and black, while Jesus went on talking, and the strong, intermittent breathing of Peter repeated His words aloud. But on a sudden Jesus broke off an unfinished sentence, and Peter, as though waking from sleep, cried out exultingly—

"Lord! to Thee are known the words of eternal life!"

But Jesus held His peace, and kept gazing fixedly in one direction.

And when they followed His gaze, they perceived in the doorway the petrified Judas with gaping mouth and fixed eyes. And, not under-standing what was the matter, they laughed. But Matthew, who was learned in the Scriptures, touched Judas on the shoulder, and said in the words of Solomon—

"*He that looketh kindly shall be forgiven; but he that is met within the gates will impede others.*"

Judas was silent for a while, and then fretfully and everything about him, his eyes, hands and feet, seemed to start in different directions, as those of an animal which suddenly perceives the eye of man upon him. Jesus went straight to Judas, as though words trembled on His lips, but passed by him through the open, and now unoccupied, door.

In the middle of the night the restless Thomas came to Judas' bed, and sitting down on his heels, asked—

"Are you weeping, Judas?"

"No! Go away, Thomas."

"Why do you groan, and grind your teeth? Are you ill?"

Judas was silent for a while, and then fretfully there fell from his lips distressful words, fraught with grief and anger—

"Why does not He love me? Why does He love the others? Am I not handsomer, better and stronger than they? Did not I save His life while they ran away like cowardly dogs?"

"My poor friend, you are not quite right. You are not good-look-ing at all, and your tongue is as disagreeable as your face. You lie and slander continually; how then can you expect Jesus to love you?"

But Judas, stirring heavily in the darkness, continued as though he heard him not—

"Why is He not on the side of Judas, instead of on the side of those who do not love Him? John brought Him a lizard; I would bring him a poisonous snake. Peter threw stones; I would overthrow a mountain for His sake. But what is a poisonous snake? One has but to draw its fangs, and it will coil round one's neck like a necklace. What is a mountain, which it is possible to dig down with the hands, and to trample with the feet? I would give to Him Judas, the bold, magnificent Judas. But now He will perish, and together with him will perish Judas."

"You are speaking strangely, Judas!"

"A withered fig-tree, which must needs be cut down with the axe, such am I: He said it of me. Why then does He not do it? He dare not, Thomas! I know him. He fears Judas. He hides from the bold, strong, magnificent Judas. He loves fools, traitors, liars. You are a liar, Thomas; have you never been told so before?"

Thomas was much surprised, and wished to object, but he thought that Judas was simply railing, and so only shook his head in the darkness. And Judas lamented still more grievously, and groaned and ground his teeth, and his whole huge body could be heard heaving under the coverlet.

"What is the matter with Judas? Who has applied fire to his body? He will give his son to the dogs. He will give his daughter to be betrayed by robbers, his bride to harlotry. And yet has not Judas a tender heart? Go away, Thomas; go away, stupid! Leave the strong, bold, magnificent Judas alone!"

Chapter 4

Judas had concealed some *denarii*, and the deception was discovered, thanks to Thomas, who had seen by chance how much money had been given to them. It was only too probable that this was not the first time that Judas had committed a theft, and they all were enraged. The angry Peter seized Judas by his collar and almost dragged him to Jesus, and the terrified Judas paled but did not resist.

"Master, see! Here he is, the trickster! Here's the thief. You trusted him, and he steals our money. Thief! Scoundrel! If Thou wilt permit, I'll—"

But Jesus held His peace. And attentively regarding him, Peter suddenly turned red, and loosed the hand which held the collar, while Judas shyly rearranged his garment, casting a sidelong glance on Peter, and assuming the downcast look of a repentant criminal.

"So that's how it's to be," angrily said Peter, as he went out, loudly slamming the door. They were all dissatisfied, and declared that on no account would they consort with Judas any longer; but John, after some consideration, passed through the door, behind which might be heard the quiet, almost caressing, voice of Jesus. And when in the course of time he returned, he was pale, and his downcast eyes were red as though with recent tears.

"The Master says that Judas may take as much money as he pleases." Peter laughed angrily. John gave him a quick reproachful glance, and suddenly flushing, and mingling tears with anger, and delight with tears, loudly exclaimed:

"And no one must reckon how much money Judas receives. He is our brother, and all the money is as much his as ours: if he wants much let him take much, without telling anyone, or taking counsel with any. Judas is our brother, and you have grievously insulted him—so says the Master. Shame on you, brother!"

In the doorway stood Judas, pale and with a distorted smile on his face. With a light movement John went up to him and kissed him three times. After him, glancing round at one another, James, Philip and the others came up shamefacedly; and after each kiss Judas wiped his mouth, but gave a loud smack as though the sound afforded him pleasure. Peter came up last.

"We were all stupid, all blind, Judas. He alone sees, He alone is wise. May I kiss you?"

"Why not? Kiss away!" said Judas as in consent.

Peter kissed him vigorously, and said aloud in his ear—

"But I almost choked you. The others kissed you in the usual way, but I kissed you on the throat. Did it hurt you?"

"A little."

"I will go and tell Him all. I was angry even with Him," said Peter sadly, trying noiselessly to open the door.

"And what are you going to do, Thomas?" asked John severely. He it was who looked after the conduct and the conversation of the disciples.

"I don't know yet. I must consider."

And Thomas thought long, almost the whole day. The disciples had dispersed to their occupations, and somewhere on the other side of the wall, Peter was shouting joyfully—but Thomas was still considering. He would have come to a decision more quickly had not Judas hindered him somewhat by continually following him about with a mocking glance, and now and again asking him in a serious tone—

"Well, Thomas, and how does the matter progress?"

Then Judas brought his money-box, and shaking the money and pretending not to look at Thomas, began to count it—

"Twenty-one, two, three. . . . Look, Thomas, a bad coin again. Oh! what rascals people are; they even give bad money as offerings. Twenty-four. . . . and then they will say again that Judas has stolen it . . . twenty-five, twenty-six. . . ."

Thomas approached him resolutely. . . for it was already towards evening, and said—

"He is right, Judas. Let me kiss you."

"Will you? Twenty-nine, thirty. It's no good. I shall steal again. Thirty-one. . . ."

"But how can you steal, when it is neither yours nor another's? You will simply take as much as you want, brother."

"It has taken you a long time to repeat His words! Don't you value time, you clever Thomas?"

"You seem to be laughing at me, brother."

"And consider, are you doing well, my virtuous Thomas, in repeating His words? He said something of His own, but you do not. He really kissed me—you only defiled my mouth. I can still feel your moist lips upon mine. It was so disgusting, my good Thomas. Thirty-eight, thirty-nine, forty. Forty *denarii*. Thomas, won't you check the sum?"

"Certainly, He is our Master. Why then should we not repeat the words of our Master?"

"Is Judas' collar torn away? Is there now nothing to seize him by? The Master will go out of the house, and Judas will unexpectedly steal three more *denarii*. Won't you seize him by the collar?"

"We know now, Judas. We understand."

"Have not all pupils a bad memory? Have not all masters been deceived by their pupils? But the master has only to lift the rod, and the pupils cry out, 'We know, Master!' But the master goes to bed, and the pupils say: 'Did the Master teach us this?' And so, in this case, this morning you called me a thief, this evening you call me brother. What will you call me tomorrow?"

Judas laughed, and lifting up the heavy rattling money-box with ease, went on:

"When a strong wind blows it raises the dust, and foolish people look at the dust and say: 'Look at the wind!' But it is only dust, my good Thomas, ass's dung trodden underfoot. The dust meets a wall and lies down gently at its foot, but the wind flies farther and farther, my good Thomas."

Judas obligingly pointed over the wall in illustration of his meaning, and laughed again.

"I am glad that you are merry," said Thomas, "but it is a great pity that there is so much malice in your merriment."

"Why should not a man be cheerful, who has been kissed so much, and who is so useful? If I had not stolen the three *denarii* would John have known the meaning of delight? Is it not pleasant to be a hook, on which John may hang his damp virtue out to dry, and Thomas his moth-eaten mind?"

"I think that I had better be going."

"But I am only joking, my good Thomas. I merely wanted to know whether you really wished to kiss the old obnoxious Judas—the thief who stole the three *denarii* and gave them to a harlot."

"To a harlot!" exclaimed Thomas in surprise. "And did you tell the Master of it?"

"Again, you doubt, Thomas. Yes, to a harlot. But if you only knew, Thomas, what an unfortunate woman she was. For two days she had had nothing to eat."

"Are you sure of that?" said Thomas in confusion.

"Yes! Of course, I am. I myself spent two days with her, and saw that she ate and drank nothing except red wine. She tottered from exhaustion, and I was always falling down with her."

Thereupon Thomas got up quickly, and, when he had gone a few steps away, he flung out at Judas:

"You seem to be possessed of Satan, Judas."

And as he went away, he heard in the approaching twilight how dolefully the heavy money-box rattled in Judas' hands. And Judas seemed to laugh.

But the very next day Thomas was obliged to acknowledge that he had misjudged Judas, so simple, so gentle, and at the same time so serious was Iscariot. He neither grimaced nor made ill-natured jokes; he was neither obsequious nor scurrilous, but quietly and unobtrusively went about his work of catering. He was as active as formerly, as though he did not have two feet like other people, but a whole dozen of them, and ran noiselessly without that squeaking, sobbing, and laughter of a hyena, with which he formerly accompanied his actions. And when Jesus began to speak, he would seat himself quickly in a corner, fold his hands and feet, and look so kindly with his great eyes, that many observed it. He ceased speaking evil of people, but rather remained silent, so that even the severe Matthew deemed it possible to praise him, saying in the words of Solomon:

"'*He that is devoid of wisdom despiseth his neighbour: but a man of understanding holdeth his peace.*'"

And he lifted up his hand, hinting thereby at Judas' former evil-speaking. In a short time, all remarked this change in him, and rejoiced at it: only Jesus looked on him still with the same detached look, although he gave no direct indication of His dislike. And even John, for whom Judas now showed a profound reverence, as the beloved disciple of Jesus, and as his own champion in the matter of the three *denarii*, began to treat him somewhat more kindly, and even sometimes entered into conversation with him.

"What do you think, Judas," said he one day in a condescending manner, "which of us, Peter or I, will be nearest to Christ in His heavenly kingdom?"

Judas meditated, and then answered—

"I suppose that you will."

"But Peter thinks that he will," laughed John.

"No! Peter would scatter all the angels with his shout; you have heard him shout. Of course, he will quarrel with you, and will endeavour to occupy the first place, as he insists that he, too, loves Jesus. But he is already advanced in years, and you are young; he is heavy on his feet, while you run swiftly; you will enter there first with Christ? Will you not?"

"Yes, I will not leave Jesus," John agreed.

On the same day Simon Peter referred the very same question to Judas. But fearing that his loud voice would be heard by the others, he led Judas out to the farthest corner behind the house.

"Well then, what is your opinion about it?" he asked anxiously. "You are wise; even the Master praises you for your intellect. And you will speak the truth."

"You, of course," answered Iscariot without hesitation. And Peter exclaimed with indignation, "I told him so!"

"But, of course, he will try even there to oust you from the first place."

"Certainly!"

"But what can he do, when you already occupy the place? Won't you be the first to go there with Jesus? You will not leave Him alone? Has He not named you the *Rock*?"

Peter put his hand on Judas' shoulder, and said with warmth: "I tell you, Judas, you are the cleverest of us all. But why are you so sarcastic and malignant? The Master does not like it. Otherwise, you might become the beloved disciple, equally with John. But to you neither," and Peter lifted his hand threateningly, "will I yield my place next to Jesus, neither on earth, nor there! Do you hear?"

Thus, Judas endeavoured to make himself agreeable to all, but, at the same time, he cherished hidden thoughts in his mind. And while he remained ever the same modest, restrained and unobtrusive person, he knew how to make some especially pleasing remark to each. Thus, to Thomas he said:

"The fool believeth every word: but the prudent taketh heed to his paths."

While to Matthew, who suffered somewhat from excess in eating and drinking, and was ashamed of his weakness, he quoted the words of Solomon, the sage whom Matthew held in high estimation:

"*The righteous eateth to the satisfying of his soul: but the belly of the wicked shall want.*"

But his pleasant speeches were rare, which gave them the greater value. For the most part he was silent, listening attentively to what was said, and always meditating.

When reflecting, Judas had an unpleasant look, ridiculous and at the same time awe-inspiring. As long as his quick, crafty eye was in motion, he seemed simple and good-natured enough, but directly both eyes became fixed in an immovable stare, and the skin on his protruding forehead gathered into strange ridges and creases, a distressing surmise would force itself on one, that under that skull some very peculiar thoughts were working. So thoroughly apart, peculiar, and voiceless were the thoughts which enveloped Iscariot in the deep silence of secrecy, when he was in one of his reveries, that one would have preferred that he should begin to speak, to move, nay, even, to tell lies. For a lie, spoken by a human tongue, had been truth and light compared with that hopelessly deep and unresponsive silence.

"In the dumps again, Judas?" Peter would cry with his clear voice and bright smile, suddenly breaking in upon the sombre silence of Judas' thoughts, and banishing them to some dark corner. "What are you thinking about?"

"Of many things," Iscariot would reply with a quiet smile. And perceiving, apparently, what a bad impression his silence made upon the others, he began more frequently to shun the society of the disciples, and spent much time in solitary walks, or would betake himself to the flat roof and there sit still. And more than once he startled Thomas, who has unexpectedly stumbled in the darkness against a grey heap, out of which the hands and feet of Judas suddenly started, and his jeering voice was heard.

But one day, in a specially brusque and strange manner, Judas recalled his former character. This happened on the occasion of the quarrel for the first place in the kingdom of heaven. Peter and John were disputing together, hotly contending each for his own place nearest to Jesus. They reckoned up their services, they measured the degrees of their love for Jesus, they became heated and noisy, and even reviled one another without restraint. Peter roared, all red with anger. John was quiet and pale, with trembling hands and biting speech.

Their quarrel had already passed the bounds of decency, and the Master had begun to frown, when Peter looked up by chance on Judas, and laughed self-complacently: John, too, looked at Judas, and also smiled. Each of them recalled what the cunning Judas had said to him. And foretasting the joy of approaching triumph, they, with silent consent, invited Judas to decide the matter.

Peter called out, "Come now, Judas the wise, tell us who will be first, nearest to Jesus, he or I?"

But Judas remained silent, breathing heavily, his eyes eagerly questioning the quiet, deep eyes of Jesus.

"Yes," John condescendingly repeated, "tell us who will be first, nearest to Jesus."

Without taking his eyes off Christ, Judas slowly rose, and answered quietly and gravely:

"I."

Jesus let His gaze fall slowly. And quietly striking himself on the breast with a bony finger, Iscariot repeated solemnly and sternly: "I, I shall be nearest to Jesus!" And he went out. Struck by his insolent freak, the disciples remained silent; but Peter suddenly recalling something, whispered to Thomas in an unexpectedly gentle voice:

"So that is what he is always thinking about! See?"

Chapter 5

Just at this time Judas Iscariot took the first definite step towards the Betrayal. He visited the chief priest Annas secretly. He was very roughly received, but that did not disturb him in the least, and he demanded a long private interview. When he found himself alone with the dry, harsh old man, who looked at him with contempt from beneath his heavy overhanging eyelids, he stated that he was an honourable man who had become one of the disciples of Jesus of Nazareth with the sole purpose of exposing the impostor, and handing Him over to the arm of the law.

"But who is this Nazarene?" asked Annas contemptuously, making as though he heard the name of Jesus for the first time.

Judas on his part pretended to believe in the extraordinary ignorance of the chief priest, and spoke in detail of the preaching of Jesus, of His miracles, of His hatred for the Pharisees and the Temple, of His perpetual infringement of the Law, and eventually of His wish to wrest the power out of the hands of the priesthood, and to set up His own personal kingdom. And so cleverly did he mingle truth with lies, that Annas looked at him more attentively, and lazily remarked: "There are plenty of impostors and madmen in Judah."

"No! He is a dangerous person," Judas hotly contradicted. "He breaks the law. And it were better that one man should perish, rather than the whole people."

Annas, with an approving nod, said—

"But He, apparently, has many disciples."

"Yes, many."

"And they, it seems probable, have a great love for Him?"

"Yes, they say that they love Him, love Him much, more than themselves."

"But if we try to take Him, will they not defend Him? Will they not raise a tumult?"

Judas laughed long and maliciously. "What, they? Those cowardly dogs, who run if a man but stoop down to pick up a stone. They indeed!"

"Are they really so bad?" asked Annas coldly.

"But surely it is not the bad who flee from the good; is it not rather the good who flee from the bad? Ha! ha! They are good, and therefore they flee. They are good, and therefore they hide themselves. They are good, and therefore they will appear only in time to bury Jesus. They will lay Him in the tomb themselves; you have only to execute Him."

"But surely, they love Him? You yourself said so."

"People always love their teacher, but better dead than alive. While a teacher's alive he may ask them questions which they will find difficult to answer. But, when a teacher dies, they become teachers themselves, and then others fare badly in turn. Ha! ha!"

Annas looked piercingly at the Traitor, and his lips puckered—which indicated that he was smiling.

"You have been insulted by them. I can see that."

"Can one hide anything from the perspicacity of the astute Annas? You have pierced to the very heart of Judas. Yes, they insulted poor Judas. They said he had stolen from them three *denarii*—as though Judas were not the most honest man in Israel!"

They talked for some time longer about Jesus, and His disciples, and of His pernicious influence on the people of Israel, but on this occasion the crafty, cautious Annas gave no decisive answer. He had long had his eyes on Jesus, and in secret conclave with his own relatives and friends, with the authorities, and the Sadducees, had decided the fate of the Prophet of Galilee. But he did not trust Judas, who he had heard was a bad, untruthful man, and he had no confidence in his flippant faith in the cowardice of the disciples, and of the people.

Annas believed in his own power, but he feared bloodshed, feared a serious riot, such as the insubordinate, irascible people of Jerusalem lent itself to so easily; he feared, in fact, the violent intervention of the Roman authorities. Fanned by opposition, fertilised by the red blood of the people, which vivifies everything on which it falls, the heresy would grow stronger, and stifle in its folds Annas, the government, and all his friends. So, when Iscariot knocked at his door a second time Annas was perturbed in spirit and would not admit him. But yet a third and a fourth time Iscariot came to him, persistent as the wind, which beats day and night against the closed door and blows in through its crevices.

"I see that the most astute Annas is afraid of something," said Judas when at last he obtained admission to the high priest.

"I am strong enough not to fear anything," Annas answered haughtily. And Iscariot stretched forth his hands and bowed abjectly.

"What do you want?"

"I wish to betray the Nazarene to you."

"We do not want Him."

Judas bowed and waited, humbly fixing his gaze on the high priest.

"Go away."

"But I am bound to return. Am I not, revered Annas?"

"You will not be admitted. Go away!"

But yet again and again Judas called on the aged Annas, and at last was admitted.

Dry and malicious, worried with thought, and silent, he gazed on the Traitor, and, as it were, counted the hairs on his knotted head. Judas also said nothing, and seemed in his turn to be counting the somewhat sparse grey hairs in the beard of the high priest.

"What? you here again?" the irritated Annas haughtily jerked out, as though spitting upon his head.

"I wish to betray the Nazarene to you."

Both held their peace, and continued to gaze attentively at each other. Iscariot's look was calm; but a quiet malice, dry and cold, began slightly to prick Annas, like the early morning rime of winter.

"How much do you want for your Jesus?"

"How much will you give?"

Annas, with evident enjoyment, insultingly replied: "You are nothing but a band of scoundrels. Thirty pieces—that's what we will give."

And he quietly rejoiced to see how Judas began to squirm and run about—agile and swift as though he had a whole dozen feet, not two.

"Thirty pieces of silver for Jesus!" he cried in a voice of wild madness, most pleasing to Annas. "For Jesus of Nazareth! You wish to buy Jesus for thirty pieces of silver? And you think that Jesus can be betrayed to you for thirty pieces of silver?" Judas turned quickly to the wall, and laughed in its smooth, white fence, lifting up his long hands. "Do you hear? Thirty pieces of silver! For Jesus!"

With the same quiet pleasure, Annas remarked indifferently:

"If you will not deal, go away. We shall find someone whose work is cheaper."

And like old-clothes men who throw useless rags from hand to hand in the dirty market-place, and shout, and swear and abuse each other, so they embarked on a rabid and fiery bargaining. Intoxicated with a strange rapture, running and turning about, and shouting, Judas ticked off on his fingers the merits of Him whom he was selling.

"And the fact that He is kind and heals the sick, is that worth nothing at all in your opinion? Ah, yes! Tell me, like an honest man!"

"If you—" began Annas, who was turning red, as he tried to get in a word, his cold malice quickly warming up under the burning words of Judas, who, however, interrupted him shamelessly:

"That He is young and handsome—like the Narcissus of Sharon, and the Lily of the Valley? What? Is that worth nothing? Perhaps you will say that He is old and useless, and that Judas is trying to dispose of an old bird? Eh?"

"If you—" Annas tried to exclaim; but Judas' stormy speech bore away his senile croak, like down upon the wind.

"Thirty pieces of silver! That will hardly work out to one *obolus* for each drop of blood! Half an *obolus* will not go to a tear! A quarter to a groan. And cries, and convulsions! And for the ceasing of His heartbeats? And the closing of His eyes? Is all this to be thrown in gratis?" sobbed Iscariot, advancing toward the high priest and enveloping him with an insane movement of his hands and fingers, and with intervolved words.

"Includes everything," said Annas in a choking voice.

"And how much will you make out of it yourself? Eh? You wish to rob Judas, to snatch the bit of bread from his children. No, I can't do it. I will go on to the market-place, and shout out: 'Annas has robbed poor Judas. Help!'"

Wearied, and grown quite dizzy, Annas wildly stamped about the floor in his soft slippers, gesticulating: "Be off, be off!"

But Judas on a sudden bowed down, stretching forth his hands submissively:

"But if you really. . . . . But why be angry with poor Judas, who only desires his children's good. You also have children, young and handsome."

"We shall find someone else. Be gone!"

"But I—I did not say that I was unwilling to make a reduction. Did I ever say that I could not too yield? And do I not believe you, that possibly another may come and sell Jesus to you for fifteen *oboli*—nay, for two—for one?"

And bowing lower and lower, wriggling and flattering, Judas submissively consented to the sum offered to him. Annas shamefacedly, with dry, trembling hand, paid him the money, and silently looking round, as though scorched, lifted his head again and again towards the ceiling, and moving his lips rapidly, waited while Judas tested with his teeth all the silver pieces, one after another.

"There is now so much bad money about," Judas quickly explained.

"This money was devoted to the Temple by the pious," said Annas, glancing round quickly, and still more quickly turning the ruddy bald nape of his neck to Judas' view.

"But can pious people distinguish between good and bad money! Only rascals can do that."

Judas did not take the money home, but went beyond the city and hid it under a stone. Then he came back again quietly with heavy, dragging steps, as a wounded animal creeps slowly to its lair after a severe and deadly fight. Only Judas had no lair; but there was a house, and in the house, he perceived Jesus. Weary and thin, exhausted with continual strife with the Pharisees, who surrounded Him every day in the Temple with a wall of white, shining, scholarly foreheads, He was sitting, leaning His cheek against the rough wall, apparently fast asleep. Through the open window drifted the restless noises of the city. On the other side of the wall Peter was hammering, as he put together a new table for the meal, humming the while a quiet Galilean song. But He heard nothing; he slept on peacefully and soundly. And this was He, whom they had bought for thirty pieces of silver.

Coming forward noiselessly, Judas, with the tender touch of a mother, who fears to wake her sick child—with the wonderment of a wild beast as it creeps from its lair suddenly, charmed by the sight of a white flowerlet—he gently touched His soft locks, and then quickly withdrew his hand. Once more he touched Him, and then silently crept out.

"Lord! Lord!" said he.

And going apart, he wept long, shrinking and wriggling and scratching his bosom with his nails and gnawing his shoulders. Then suddenly he ceased weeping and gnawing and gnashing his teeth, and fell into a sombre reverie, inclining his tear-stained face to one side in the attitude of one listening. And so, he remained for a long time, doleful, determined, from everyone apart, like fate itself.

★★★★★★★★★★★★★★★★★

Judas surrounded the unhappy Jesus, during those last days of His short life, with quiet love and tender care and caresses. Bashful and timid like a maid in her first love, strangely sensitive and discerning, he divined the minutest unspoken wishes of Jesus, penetrating to the hidden depth of His feelings, His passing fits of sorrow, and distressing moments of weariness. And wherever Jesus stepped, His foot met something soft, and whenever He turned His gaze, it encountered something pleasing. Formerly Judas had not liked Mary Magdalene and the other women who were near Jesus. He had made rude jests at their expense, and done them little unkindnesses. But now he became their friend, their strange, awkward ally.

With deep interest he would talk with them of the charming little idiosyncrasies of Jesus, and persistently asking the same questions, he would thrust money into their hands, their very palms—and they brought a box of very precious ointment, which Jesus liked so much, and anointed His feet. He himself bought for Jesus, after desperate bargaining, an expensive wine, and then was very angry when Peter drank nearly all of it up, with the indifference of a person who looks only to quantity; and in that rocky Jerusalem almost devoid of trees, flowers, and greenery he somehow managed to obtain young spring flowers and green grass, and through these same women to give them to Jesus.

For the first time in his life, he would take up little children in his arms, finding them somewhere about the courts and streets, and unwillingly kiss them to prevent their crying; and often it would happen that some swarthy urchin with curly hair and dirty little nose, would climb up on the knees of the pensive Jesus, and imperiously demand to be petted. And while they enjoyed themselves together, Judas would walk up and down at one side like a severe jailor, who had himself, in springtime, let a butterfly in to a prisoner, and pretends

246

to grumble at the breach of discipline.

On an evening, when together with the darkness, alarm took post as sentry by the window, Iscariot would cleverly turn the conversation to Galilee, strange to himself but dear to Jesus, with its still waters and green banks. And he would jog the heavy Peter till his dulled memory awoke, and in clear pictures in which everything was loud, distinct, full of colour, and solid, there arose before his eyes and ears the dear Galilean life. With eager attention, with half-open mouth in child-like fashion, and with eyes laughing in anticipation, Jesus would listen to his gusty, resonant, cheerful utterance, and sometimes laughed so at his jokes, that it was necessary to interrupt the story for some minutes. But John told tales even better than Peter. There was nothing ludicrous, nor startling, about his stories, but everything seemed so pensive, unusual, and beautiful, that tears would appear in Jesus' eyes, and He would sigh softly, while Judas nudged Mary Magdalene and excitedly whispered to her—

"What a narrator he is! Do you hear?"

"Yes, certainly."

"No, be more attentive. You women never make good listeners."

Then they would all quietly disperse to bed, and Jesus would kiss His thanks to John, and stroke kindly the shoulder of the tall Peter.

And without envy, but with a condescending contempt, Judas would witness these caresses. Of what importance were these tales and kisses and sighs compared with what he, Judas Iscariot, the red-haired, misshapen Judas, begotten among the rocks, could tell them if he chose?

CHAPTER 6

With one hand betraying Jesus, Judas tried hard with the other to frustrate his own plans. He did not indeed endeavour to dissuade Jesus from the last dangerous journey to Jerusalem, as did the women; he even inclined rather to the side of the relatives of Jesus, and of those amongst His disciples who looked for a victory over Jerusalem as indispensable to the full triumph of His cause. But he kept continually and obstinately warning them of the danger, and in lively colours depicted the threatening hatred of the Pharisees for Jesus, and their readiness to commit any crime if, either secretly or openly, they might make an end of the Prophet of Galilee. Each day and every hour he kept talking of this, and there was not one of the believers before whom Judas had not stood with uplifted finger and uttered this serious warning:

"We must look after Jesus. We must defend for Jesus, when the hour comes."

But whether it was the unlimited faith which the disciples had in the miracle-working power of their Master, or the consciousness of their own uprightness, or whether it was simply blindness, the alarming words of Judas were met with a smile, and his continual advice provoked only a grumble. When Judas procured, somewhere or other, two swords, and brought them, only Peter approved of them, and gave Judas his meed of praise, while the others complained:

"Are we soldiers that we should be made to gird on swords? Is Jesus a captain of the host, and not a prophet?"

"But if they attempt to kill Him?"

"They will not dare when they perceive how all the people follow Him."

"But if they should dare! What then?"

John replied disdainfully—

"One would think, Judas, that you were the only one who loved Jesus!"

And eagerly seizing hold of these words, and not in the least offended, Judas began to question impatiently and hotly, with stern insistency:

"But you love Him, don't you?"

And there was not one of the believers who came to Jesus whom he did not ask more than once: "Do you love Him? Dearly love Him?"

And all answered that they loved Him.

He used often to converse with Thomas, and holding up his dry, hooked forefinger, with its long, dirty nail, in warning, would mysteriously say:

"Look here, Thomas, the terrible hour is drawing near. Are you prepared for it? Why did you not take the sword I brought you?"

Thomas would reply with deliberation:

"We are men unaccustomed to the use of arms. If we were to take issue with the Roman soldiery, they would kill us all, one after the other. Besides, you brought only two swords, and what could we do with only two?"

"We could get more. We could take them from the Roman soldiers," Judas impatiently objected, and even the serious Thomas smiled through his overhanging moustache.

"Ah! Judas! Judas! But where did you get these? They are like Roman swords."

"I stole them. I could have stolen more, only someone gave the alarm, and I fled."

Thomas considered a little, then said sorrowfully—

"Again, you acted ill, Judas. Why do you steal?"

"There is no such thing as property."

"No, but tomorrow they will ask the soldiers: 'Where are your swords?' And when they cannot find them, they will be punished though innocent."

The consequence was, that after the death of Jesus the disciples recalled these conversations of Judas, and determined that he had wished to destroy them, together with the Master, by inveigling them into an unequal and murderous conflict. And once again they cursed the hated name of Judas Iscariot the Traitor.

But the angry Judas, after each conversation, would go to the women and weep. They heard him gladly. The tender womanly element, that there was in his love for Jesus, drew him near to them, and made him simple, comprehensible, and even handsome in their eyes, although, as before, a certain amount of disdain was perceptible in his attitude towards them.

"Are they men?" he would bitterly complain of the disciples, fixing his blind, motionless eye confidingly on Mary Magdalene. "They are not men. They have not an *oboles'* worth of blood in their veins!"

"But then you are always speaking ill of others," Mary objected.

"Have I ever?" said Judas in surprise. "Oh, yes, I have indeed spoken ill of them; but is there not room for improvement in them? Ah! Mary, silly Mary, why are you not a man, to carry a sword?"

"It is so heavy, I could not lift it!" said Mary smilingly.

"But you will lift it, when men are too worthless. Did you give Jesus the lily that I found on the mountain? I got up early to find it, and this morning the sun was so beautiful, Mary! Was He pleased with it? Did He smile?"

"Yes, He was pleased. He said that its smell reminded Him of Galilee."

"But surely, you did not tell Him that it was Judas—Judas Iscariot—who got it for Him?"

"Why, you asked me not to tell Him."

"Yes, certainly, quite right," said Judas, with a sigh. "You might have let it out, though, women are such chatterers. But you did not let it out; no, you were firm. You are a good woman, Mary. You know that I have a wife somewhere. Now I should be glad to see her again; perhaps she is not a bad woman either. I don't know. She said, 'Judas was a liar and malignant,' so I left her. But she may be a good woman. Do you know?"

"How should I know, when I have never seen your wife?"

"True, true, Mary! But what think you, are thirty pieces of silver a large sum? Is it not rather a small one?"

"I should say a small one."

"Certainly, certainly. How much did you get when you were a harlot, five pieces of silver or ten? You were an expensive one, were you not?"

Mary Magdalene blushed, and dropped her head till her luxuriant, golden hair completely covered her face, so that nothing but her round white chin was visible.

"How bad you are, Judas; I want to forget about that, and you remind me of it!"

"No, Mary, you must not forget that. Why should you? Let others forget that you were a harlot, but you must remember. It is the others who should forget as soon as possible, but you should not. Why should you?"

"But it was a sin!"

"He fears who never committed a sin, but he who has committed it, what has he to fear? Do the dead fear death; is it not rather the living? No, the dead laugh at the living and their fears."

Thus, by the hour would they sit and talk in friendly guise, he—already old, dried-up and misshapen, with his bulbous head and monstrous double-sided face; she—young, modest, tender, and charmed with life as with a story or a dream.

But time rolled by unconcernedly, while the thirty pieces of silver lay under the stone, and the terrible day of the Betrayal drew inevitably near. Already Jesus had ridden into Jerusalem on the ass's back, and the people, strewing their garments in the way, had greeted Him with enthusiastic cries of "Hosanna! Hosanna! He that cometh in the name of the Lord!"

So great was the exultation, so unrestrainedly did their loving cries rend the skies, that Jesus wept, but His disciples proudly said:

"Is not this the Son of God with us?"

And they themselves cried out with enthusiasm: "Hosanna! Hosanna! He that cometh in the name of the Lord!"

That evening it was long before they went to bed, recalling the enthusiastic and joyful reception. Peter was like a madman, as though possessed by the demon of merriment and pride. He shouted, drowning all voices with his leonine roar; he laughed, hurling his laughter at their heads, like great round stones; he kept kissing John and James, and even gave a kiss to Judas. He noisily confessed that he had had great fears for Jesus, but that he feared nothing now, that he had seen the love of the people for Him.

Swiftly moving his vivid, watchful eye, Judas glanced in surprise from side to side. He meditated, and then again listened, and looked. Then he took Thomas aside, and pinning him, as it were, to the wall with his keen gaze, he asked in doubt and fear, but with a certain confused hopefulness:

"Thomas! But what if He is right? What if He be founded upon a rock, and we upon sand? What then?"

"Of whom are you speaking?"

"How, then, would it be with Judas Iscariot? Then I should be obliged to strangle Him in order to do right. Who is deceiving Judas? You or he himself? Who is deceiving Judas? Who?"

"I don't understand you, Judas. You speak very unintelligently. 'Who is deceiving Jesus?' 'Who is right?'"

And Judas nodded his head and repeated like an echo:

"Who is deceiving Judas? Who?"

And the next day, in the way in which Judas raised his hand with thumb bent back, and by the way in which he looked at Thomas, the same strange question was implied:

"Who is deceiving Judas? Who is right?"

And still more surprised, and even alarmed, was Thomas, when suddenly in the night he heard the loud, apparently glad voice of Judas:

"Then Judas Iscariot will be no more. Then Jesus will be no more. Then there will be Thomas, the stupid Thomas! Did you ever wish to take the earth and lift it? And then, possibly hurl it away?"

"That's impossible. What are you talking about, Judas?"

"It's quite possible," said Iscariot with conviction, "and we will lift it up some day when you are asleep, stupid Thomas. Go to sleep. I'm enjoying myself. When you sleep your nose plays the Galilean pipe. Sleep!"

But now the believers were already dispersed about Jerusalem, hiding in houses and behind walls, and the faces of those that met them looked mysterious. The exultation had died down. Confused reports of danger found their way in; Peter, with gloomy countenance, tested the sword given to him by Judas, and the face of the Master became even more melancholy and stern. So swiftly the time passed, and inevitably approached the terrible day of the Betrayal. Lo! the Last Supper was over, full of grief and confused dread, and already had the obscure words of Jesus sounded concerning someone who should betray Him.

"You know who will betray Him?" asked Thomas, looking at Judas with his straight-forward, clear, almost transparent eyes.

"Yes, I know," Judas replied harshly and decidedly. "You, Thomas, will betray Him. But He Himself does not believe what He says! It is full time! Why does He not call to Him the strong, magnificent Judas?"

No longer by days, but by short, fleeting hours, was the inevitable time to be measured. It was evening; and evening stillness and long shadows lay upon the ground—the first sharp darts of the coming night of mighty contest—when a harsh, sorrowful voice was heard. It said:

"Dost Thou know whither I go, Lord? I go to betray Thee into the hands of Thine enemies."

And there was a long silence, evening stillness, and swift black shadows.

"Thou art silent, Lord? Thou commandest me to go?"

And again silence.

"Allow me to remain. But perhaps Thou canst not? Or darest not? Or wilt not?"

And again silence, stupendous, like the eyes of eternity.

"But indeed, Thou knowest that I love Thee. Thou knowest all things. Why lookest Thou thus at Judas? Great is the mystery of Thy beautiful eyes, but is mine less? Order me to remain! But Thou art silent. Thou art ever silent. Lord, Lord, is it for this that in grief and pains have I sought Thee all my life, sought and found! Free me! Remove the weight; it is heavier than even mountains of lead. Dost Thou hear how the bosom of Judas Iscariot is cracking under it?"

And the last silence was abysmal, like the last glance of eternity.

"I go."

But the evening stillness woke not, neither uttered cry nor plaint, nor did its subtle air vibrate with the slightest tinkle—so soft was the fall of the retreating steps. They sounded for a time, and then were silent. And the evening stillness became pensive, stretched itself out in long shadows, and then grew dark;—and suddenly night, coming to meet it, all atremble with the rustle of sadly brushed-up leaves, heaved a last sigh and was still.

There was a bustle, a jostle, a rattle of other voices, as though some-one had untied a bag of lively resonant voices, and they were falling out on the ground, by one and two, and whole heaps. It was the disciples talking. And drowning them all, reverberating from the trees and walls, and tripping up over itself, thundered the determined, power-ful voice of Peter—he was swearing that never would he desert his Master.

"Lord," said he, half in anger, half in grief: "Lord! I am ready to go with Thee to prison and to death."

And quietly, like the soft echo of retiring footsteps, came the in-exorable answer:

"I tell thee, Peter, the cock will not crow this day before thou dost deny Me thrice."

Chapter 7

The moon had already risen when Jesus prepared to go to the Mount of Olives, where He had spent all His last nights. But He tar-ried, for some inexplicable reason, and the disciples, ready to start, were hurrying Him. Then He said suddenly:

"He that hath a purse, let him take it, and likewise his scrip; and he that hath no sword, let him sell his garment and buy one. For I say unto you that this that is written must yet be accomplished in me: 'And he was reckoned among the transgressors.'"

The disciples were surprised and looked at one another in confu-sion. Peter replied:

"Lord, we have two swords here."

He looked searchingly into their kind faces, lowered His head, and said softly:

"It is enough."

The steps of the disciples resounded loudly in the narrow streets, and they were frightened by the sounds of their own footsteps; on the white wall, illumined by the moon, their black shadows appeared—and they were frightened by their own shadows. Thus they passed in silence through Jerusalem, which was absorbed in sleep, and now they came out of the gates of the city, and in the valley, full of fantastic, mo-tionless shadows, the stream of Kedron stretched before them. Now they were frightened by everything. The soft murmuring and splash-ing of the water on the stones sounded to them like voices of people approaching them stealthily; the monstrous shades of the rocks and the trees, obstructing the road, disturbed them, and their motionlessness seemed to them to stir.

But as they were ascending the mountain and approaching the garden, where they had safely and quietly passed so many nights before, they were growing ever bolder. From time to time they looked back at Jerusalem, all white in the moonlight, and they spoke to one another about the fear that had passed; and those who walked in the rear heard, in fragments, the soft words of Jesus. He spoke about their forsaking Him.

In the garden they paused soon after they had entered it. The majority of them remained there, and, speaking softly, began to make ready for their sleep, outspreading their cloaks over the transparent embroidery of the shadows and the moonlight. Jesus, tormented with uneasiness, and four of His disciples went further into the depth of the garden. There they seated themselves on the ground, which had not yet cooled off from the heat of the day, and while Jesus was silent, Peter and John lazily exchanged words almost devoid of any meaning.

Yawning from fatigue, they spoke about the coolness of the night; about the high price of meat in Jerusalem, and about the fact that no fish was to be had in the city. They tried to determine the exact number of pilgrims that had gathered in Jerusalem for the festival, and Peter, drawling his words and yawning loudly, said that they numbered 20,000, while John and his brother Jacob assured him just as lazily that they did not number more than 10,000. Suddenly Jesus rose quickly.

"My soul is exceedingly sorrowful, even unto death; tarry ye here and watch with Me," He said, and departed hastily to the grove and soon disappeared amid its motionless shades and light.

"Where did He go?" said John, lifting himself on his elbow. Peter turned his head in the direction of Jesus and answered fatiguedly:

"I do not know."

And he yawned again loudly, then threw himself on his back and became silent. The others also became silent, and their motionless bodies were soon absorbed in the sound sleep of fatigue. Through his heavy slumber Peter vaguely saw something white bending over him, some one's voice resounded and died away, leaving no trace in his dimmed consciousness.

"Simon, are you sleeping?"

And he slept again, and again some soft voice reached his ear and died away without leaving any trace.

"You could not watch with me even one hour?"

"Oh, Master! if you only knew how sleepy I am," he thought in his slumber, but it seemed to him that he said it aloud. And he slept again. And a long time seemed to have passed, when suddenly the figure of Jesus appeared near him, and a loud, rousing voice instantly awakened him and the others:

"You are still sleeping and resting? It is ended, the hour has come— the Son of Man is betrayed into the hands of the sinners."

The disciples quickly sprang to their feet, confusedly seizing their cloaks and trembling from the cold of the sudden awakening. Through the thicket of the trees a multitude of warriors and temple servants was seen approaching noisily, illumining their way with torches. And from the other side the disciples came running, quivering from cold, their sleepy faces frightened; and not yet understanding what was going on, they asked hastily:

"What is it? Who are these people with torches?"

Thomas, pale faced, his moustaches in disorder, his teeth chattering from chilliness, said to Peter:

"They have evidently come after us."

Now a multitude of warriors surrounded them, and the smoky, quivering light of the torches dispelled the soft light of the moon. In front of the warriors walked Judas Iscariot quickly, and sharply turning his quick eye, searched for Jesus. He found Him, rested his look for an instant upon His tall, slender figure, and quickly whispered to the priests:

"Whomsoever I shall kiss, that same is He. Take Him and lead Him cautiously. Lead Him cautiously, do you hear?"

Then he moved quickly to Jesus, who waited for him in silence, and he directed his straight, sharp look, like a knife, into His calm, darkened eyes.

"Hail, Master!" he said loudly, charging his words of usual greeting with a strange and stern meaning.

But Jesus was silent, and the disciples looked at the traitor with horror, not understanding how the soul of a man could contain so much evil. Iscariot threw a rapid glance at their confused ranks, noticed their quiver, which was about to turn into a loud, trembling fear, noticed their pallor, their senseless smiles, the drowsy movements of their hands, which seemed as though fettered in iron at the shoulders—and a mortal sorrow began to burn in his heart, akin to the sorrow Christ had experienced before. Outstretching himself into a hundred ringing, sobbing strings, he rushed over to Jesus and kissed

His cold cheek tenderly. He kissed it so softly, so tenderly, with such painful love and sorrow, that if Jesus had been a flower upon a thin stalk, it would not have shaken from this kiss and would not have dropped the pearly dew from its pure petals.

"Judas," said Jesus, and with the lightning of His look He illumined that monstrous heap of shadows which was Iscariot's soul, but he could not penetrate into the bottomless depth. "Judas! Is it with a kiss you betray the Son of Man?"

And He saw how that monstrous chaos trembled and stirred. Speechless and stern, like death in its haughty majesty, stood Judas Iscariot, and within him a thousand impetuous and fiery voices groaned and roared:

"Yes! We betray Thee with the kiss of love! With the kiss of love, we betray Thee to outrage, to torture, to death! With the voice of love, we call together the hangmen from their dark holes, and we place a cross—and high over the top of the earth we lift love, crucified by love upon a cross."

Thus stood Judas, silent and cold, like death, and the shouting and the noise about Jesus answered the cry of His soul. With the rude irresoluteness of armed force, with the awkwardness of a vaguely understood purpose, the soldiers seized Him and dragged Him off—mistaking their irresoluteness for resistance, their fear for derision and mockery. Like a flock of frightened lambs, the disciples stood huddled together, not interfering, yet disturbing everybody, even themselves. Only a few of them resolved to walk and act separately. Jostled from all sides, Peter drew out the sword from its sheath with difficulty, as though he had lost all his strength, and faintly lowered it upon the head of one of the priests—without causing him any harm. Jesus, observing this, ordered him to throw away the useless weapon, and it fell under foot with a dull thud, and so evidently had it lost its sharpness and destructive power that it did not occur to anyone to pick it up. So, it rolled about underfoot, until several days afterwards it was found on the same spot by some children at play, who made a toy of it.

The soldiers kept dispersing the disciples, but they gathered together again and stupidly got under the soldiers' feet, and this went on so long that at last a contemptuous rage mastered the soldiery. One of them with frowning brow went up to the shouting John; another rudely pushed from his shoulder the hand of Thomas, who was arguing with him about something or other, and shook a big fist right in front of his straightforward, transparent eyes.

John fled, and Thomas and James fled, and all the disciples, as many as were present, forsook Jesus and fled. Losing their cloaks, knocking themselves against the trees, tripping up against stones and falling, they fled to the hills terror-driven, while in the stillness of the moonlight night the ground rumbled loudly beneath the tramp of many feet. Someone, whose name did not transpire, just risen from his bed (for he was covered only with a blanket), rushed excitedly into the crowd of soldiers and servants. When they tried to stop him, and seized hold of his blanket, he gave a cry of terror, and took to flight like the others, leaving his garment in the hands of the soldiers. And so, he ran stark-naked, with desperate leaps, and his bare body glistened strangely in the moonlight.

When Jesus was led away, Peter, who had hidden himself behind the trees, came out and followed his Master at a distance. Noticing another man in front of him, who walked silently, he thought that it was John, and he called him softly:

"John, is that you?"

"And is that you, Peter?" answered the other, pausing, and by the voice Peter recognised the traitor. "Peter, why did you not run away together with the others?"

Peter stopped and said with contempt:

"Leave me, Satan!"

Judas began to laugh, and paying no further attention to Peter, he advanced where the torches were flashing dimly and where the clanking of the weapons mingled with the footsteps. Peter followed him cautiously, and thus they entered the court of the high priest almost simultaneously and mingled in the crowd of the priests who were warming themselves at the bonfires. Judas warmed his bony hands morosely at the bonfire and heard Peter saying loudly somewhere behind him:

"No, I do not know Him."

But it was evident that they were insisting there that he was one of the disciples of Jesus, for Peter repeated still louder: "But I do not understand what you are saying."

Without turning around, and smiling involuntarily, Judas shook his head affirmatively and muttered:

"That's right, Peter! Do not give up the place near Jesus to anyone."

And he did not see the frightened Peter walk away from the courtyard. And from that night until the very death of Jesus, Judas did not see a single one of the disciples of Jesus near Him; and amid all that multitude there were only two, inseparable until death, strangely bound together by sufferings—He who had been betrayed to abuse and torture and he who had betrayed Him. Like brothers, they both, the Betrayed and the betrayer, drank out of the same cup of sufferings, and the fiery liquid burned equally the pure and the impure lips.

Gazing fixedly at the wood-fire, which imparted a feeling of warmth to his eyes, stretching out his long, shaking hands to the flame, his hands and feet forming a confused outline in the trembling light and shade, Iscariot kept mumbling in hoarse complaint:

"How cold! My God, how cold it is!"

So, when the fishermen go away at night leaving an expiring fire of drift-wood upon the shore, from the dark depth of the sea might something creep forth, crawl up towards the fire, look at it with wild intentness, and dragging all its limbs up to it, mutter in hoarse complaint:

"How cold! My God, how cold it is!"

Suddenly Judas heard behind him a burst of loud voices, the cries and laughter of the soldiers full of the usual sleepy, greedy malice; and lashes, short frequent strokes upon a living body. He turned round, a momentary anguish running through his whole frame—his very bones. They were scourging Jesus.

Has it come to that?

He had seen the soldiers lead Jesus away with them to their guardroom. The night was already nearly over, the fires had sunk down and were covered with ashes, but from the guardroom was still borne the sound of muffled cries, laughter, and invectives. They were scourging Jesus.

As one who has lost his way, Iscariot ran nimbly about the empty courtyard, stopped in his course, lifted his head and ran on again, and was surprised when he came into collision with heaps of embers, or with the walls.

Then he clung to the wall of the guardroom, stretched himself out to his full height, and glued himself to the window and the crevices of the door, eagerly examining what they were doing. He saw a confined stuffy room, dirty, like all guardrooms in the world, with bespitten floor, and walls as greasy and stained as though they had been trodden and rolled upon. And he saw the Man whom they were scourging. They struck Him on the face and head, and tossed Him about like a soft bundle from one end of the room to the other.

And since He neither cried out nor resisted, after looking intently, it actually appeared at moments as though it was not a living human being, but a soft effigy without bones or blood. It bent itself strangely like a doll, and in falling, knocking its head against the stone floor it did not give the impression of a hard substance striking against a hard substance, but of something soft and devoid of feeling. And when one looked long, it became like some strange, endless game—and sometimes it became almost a complete illusion.

After one hard kick, the man or effigy fell slowly on its knees before a sitting soldier, he in turn flung it away, and turning over, it dropped down before the next, and so on and on. A loud guffaw arose, and Judas smiled too—as though the strong hand of someone with iron fingers had torn his mouth asunder. It was the mouth of Judas that was deceived.

Night dragged on, and the fires were still smouldering. Judas threw himself from the wall, and crawled to one of the fires, poked up the ashes, rekindled it, and although he no longer felt the cold, he stretched his slightly trembling hands over the flames, and began to mutter dolefully:

"Ah! how painful, my Son, my Son! How painful!"

Then he went again to the window, which was gleaming yellow with a dull light between the thick grating, and once more began to watch them scourging Jesus. Once before the very eyes of Judas appeared His swarthy countenance, now marred out of human semblance, and covered with a forest of dishevelled hair. Then someone's hand plunged into those locks, threw the Man down, and rhythmically turning His head from one side to the other, began to wipe the filthy floor with His face. Right under the window a soldier was sleeping, his open mouth revealing his glittering white teeth; and some one's broad back, with naked, brawny neck, barred the window, so that nothing more could be seen. And suddenly the noise ceased.

"What's that? Why are they silent? Have they suddenly divined the truth?"

Momentarily the whole head of Judas, in all its parts, was filled with the rumbling, shouting and roaring of a thousand maddened thoughts! Had they divined? They understood that this was the very best of men—it was so simple, so clear! Lo! He is coming out, and behind Him they are abjectly crawling. Yes, He is coming here, to Judas, coming out a victor, a hero, arbiter of the truth, a god. . . .

"Who is deceiving Judas? Who is right?"

But no. Once more noise and shouting. They are scourging Him again. They do not understand, they have not guessed, they are beating Him harder, more cruelly than ever. The fires burn out, covered with ashes, and the smoke above them is as transparently blue as the air, and the sky as bright as the moon. It is the day approaching.

"What is day?" asks Judas.

And lo! everything begins to glow, to scintillate, to grow young again, and the smoke above is no longer blue, but rose-coloured. It is the sun rising.

"What is the sun?" asks Judas.

CHAPTER 8

They pointed the finger at Judas, and some in contempt, others with hatred and fear, said:

"Look, that is Judas the Traitor!"

This already began to be the opprobrious title, to which he had doomed himself throughout the ages. Thousands of years may pass, nation may supplant nation, and still the air will resound with the words, uttered with contempt and fear by good and bad alike:

"Judas the Traitor!"

But he listened imperturbably to what was said of him, dominated by a feeling of burning, all-subduing curiosity. Ever since the morning when they led forth Jesus from the guardroom, after scourging Him, Judas had followed Him, strangely enough feeling neither grief nor pain nor joy—only an unconquerable desire to see and hear everything. Though he had had no sleep the whole night, his body felt light; when he was crushed and prevented from advancing, he elbowed his way through the crowd and adroitly wormed himself into the front place; and not for a moment did his vivid quick eye remain at rest. At the examination of Jesus before Caiaphas, in order not to lose a word, he hollowed his hand round his ear, and nodded his head in affirmation, murmuring:

"Just so! Thou hearest, Jesus?"

But he was a prisoner, like a fly tied to a thread, which, buzzing, flies hither and thither, but cannot for one moment free itself from the tractable but unyielding thread.

Certain stony thoughts lay at the back of his head, and to these he was firmly bound; he knew not, as it were, what these thoughts were; he did not wish to stir them up, but he felt them continually. At times they would come to him all of a sudden, oppress him more and more, and begin to crush him with their unimaginable weight, as though the vault of a rocky cavern were slowly and terribly descending upon his head.

Then he would grip his heart with his hand, and strive to set his whole body in motion, as though he were perishing with cold, and hasten to shift his eyes to a fresh place, and again to another. When they led Jesus away from Caiaphas, he met His weary eyes quite close, and, somehow or other, unconsciously he gave Him several friendly nods.

"I am here, my Son, I am here," he muttered hurriedly, and maliciously poked to some gaper in the back who stood in his way.

And now, in a huge shouting crowd, they all moved on to Pilate for the last examination and trial, and with the same insupportable curiosity Judas searched the faces of the ever-swelling multitude. Many were quite unknown to him; Judas had never seen them before, but some were there who had cried, "Hosanna!" to Jesus, and at each step the number of them seemed to increase.

"Well, well!" thought Judas, and his head spun round as if he were drunk, "the worst is over. Directly they will be crying: 'He is ours, He is Jesus! What are you about?' and all will understand, and—"

But the believers walked in silence. Some hypocritically smiled, as if to say: "The affair is none of ours!" Others spoke with constraint, but their low voices were drowned in the rumbling of movement, and the loud delirious shouts of His enemies.

And Judas felt better again. Suddenly he noticed Thomas cautiously slipping through the crowd not far off, and struck by a sudden thought, he was about to go up to him. At the sight of the traitor, Thomas was frightened, and tried to hide himself. But in a little narrow street, between two walls, Judas overtook him.

"Thomas, wait a bit!"

Thomas stopped, and stretching both hands out in front of him solemnly pronounced the words:

"*Avaunt*, Satan!"

Iscariot made an impatient movement of the hands.

"What a fool you are, Thomas! I thought that you had more sense than the others. Satan indeed! That requires proof."

Letting his hands fall, Thomas asked in surprise:

"But did not you betray the Master? I myself saw you bring the soldiers, and point Him out to them. If this is not treachery, I should like to know what is!"

"Never mind that," hurriedly said Judas. "Listen, there are many of you here. You must all gather together, and loudly demand: 'Give up Jesus. He is ours!' They will not refuse you, they dare not. They themselves will understand."

"What do you mean! What are you thinking of!" said Thomas, with a decisive wave of his hands. "Have you not seen what a number of armed soldiers and servants of the Temple there are here? Moreover, the trial has not yet taken place, and we must not interfere with the court. Surely, he understands that Jesus is innocent, and will order His release without delay."

"You, then, think so too," said Judas thoughtfully. "Thomas, Thomas, what if it be the truth? What then? Who is right? Who has deceived Judas?"

"We were all talking last night, and came to the conclusion that the court cannot condemn the innocent. But if it does, why then—"

"What then!"

"Why, then it is no court. And it will be the worse for them when they have to give an account before the real Judge."

"Before the real! Is there any 'real' left?" sneered Judas.

"And all of our party cursed you; but since you say that you were not the traitor, I think you ought to be tried."

Judas did not want to hear him out; but turned right about, and hurried down the street in the wake of the retreating crowd. He soon, however, slackened his pace, mindful of the fact that a crowd always travels slowly, and that a single pedestrian will inevitably overtake it.

When Pilate led Jesus out from his palace, and set Him before the people, Judas, crushed against a column by the heavy backs of the soldiers, furiously turning his head about to see something between two shining helmets, suddenly felt clearly that the worst was over. He saw Jesus in the sunshine, high above the heads of the crowd, bloodstained, pale with a crown of thorns, the sharp spikes of which pressed into His forehead.

He stood on the edge of an elevation, visible from His head to His small, sunburnt feet, and waited so calmly, was so serene in His immaculate purity, that only a blind man, who perceived not the very sun, could fail to see, only a madman would not understand. And the people held their peace—it was so still, that Judas heard the breathing of the soldier in front of him, and how, at each breath, a strap creaked somewhere about his body.

"Yes, it will soon be over! They will understand immediately," thought Judas, and suddenly something strange, like the dazzling joy of falling from a giddy height into a blue sparkling abyss, arrested his heart-beats.

Contemptuously drawing his lips down to his rounded well-shaven chin, Pilate flung to the crowd the dry, curt words—as one throws bones to a pack of hungry hounds—thinking to cheat their longing for fresh blood and living, palpitating flesh:

"You have brought this Man before me as a corrupter of the people, and behold I have examined Him before you, and I find this Man guiltless of that of which you accuse Him. . . ."

Judas closed his eyes. He was waiting.

All the people began to shout, to sob, to howl with a thousand voices of wild beasts and men:

"Put Him to death! Crucify Him! Crucify Him!" And as though in self-mockery, as though wishing in one moment to plumb the very depths of all possible degradation, madness and shame, the crowd cries out, sobs, and demands with a thousand voices of wild beasts and men:

"Release unto us Barabbas! But crucify Him! Crucify Him!"

But the Roman had evidently not yet said his last word. Over his proud, shaven countenance there passed convulsions of disgust and anger. He understood! He has understood all along! He speaks quietly to his attendants, but his voice is not heard in the roar of the crowd. What does he say? Is he ordering them to bring swords, and to smite those maniacs?

"Bring water."

"Water? What water? What for?"

Ah, lo! he washes his hands. Why does he wash his clean white hands all adorned with rings? He lifts them and cries angrily to the people, whom surprise holds in silence:

"I am innocent of the blood of this Just Person. See ye to it."

While the water is still dripping from his fingers on to the marble pavement, something soft prostrates itself at his feet, and sharp, burning lips kiss his hand, which he is powerless to withdraw, glue themselves to it like tentacles, almost bite and draw blood. He looks down in disgust and fear, and sees a great squirming body, a strangely twofold face, and two immense eyes so queerly diverse from one another that, as it were, not one being but a number of them clung to his hands and feet. He heard a broken, burning whisper:

"O wise and noble... wise and noble."

And with such a truly satanic joy did that wild face blaze, that, with a cry, Pilate kicked him away, and Judas fell backwards. And there he lay upon the stone flags like an overthrown demon, still stretching out his hand to the departing Pilate, and crying as one passionately enamoured:

"O wise, O wise and noble. . . ."

Then he gathered himself up with agility, and ran away followed by the laughter of the soldiery. Evidently there was yet hope. When they come to see the cross, and the nails, then they will understand, and then....What then? He catches sight of the panic-stricken Thomas in passing, and for some reason or other reassuringly nods to him; he overtakes Jesus being led to execution. The walking is difficult, small stones roll under the feet, and suddenly Judas feels that he is tired. He gives himself up wholly to the trouble of deciding where best to plant his feet, he looks dully around, and sees Mary Magdalene weeping, and a number of women weeping—hair dishevelled, eyes red, lips distorted—all the excessive grief of a tender woman's soul when submitted to outrage. Suddenly he revives, and seizing the moment, runs up to Jesus:

"I go with Thee," he hurriedly whispers.

The soldiers drive him away with blows of their whips, and squirming so as to avoid the blows, and showing his teeth at the soldiers, he explains hurriedly:

"I go with Thee. Thither. Thou understandest whither."

He wipes the blood from his face, shakes his fist at one of the soldiers, who turns round and smiles, and points him out to the others. Then he looks for Thomas, but neither he nor any of the disciples are in the crowd that accompanies Jesus. Again, he is conscious of fatigue, and drags one foot with difficulty after the other, as he attentively looks out for the sharp, white, scattered pebbles.

When the hammer was uplifted to nail Jesus' left hand to the tree, Judas closed his eyes, and for a whole age neither breathed, nor saw, nor lived, but only listened.

But lo! with a grating sound, iron strikes against iron, time after time, dull, short blows, and then the sharp nail penetrating the soft wood and separating its particles is distinctly heard.

One hand. It is not yet too late!

The other hand. It is not yet too late!

A foot, the other foot! Is all lost?

He irresolutely opens his eyes, and sees how the cross is raised, and rocks, and is set fast in the trench. He sees how the hands of Jesus are convulsed by the tension, how painfully His arms stretch, how the wounds grow wider, and how the exhausted abdomen disappears under the ribs. The arms stretch more and more, grow thinner and whiter, and become dislocated from the shoulders, and the wounds of the nails redden and lengthen gradually—lo! in a moment they will be torn away. No. It stopped. All stopped. Only the ribs move up and down with the short, deep breathing.

On the very crown of the hill the cross is raised, and on it is the crucified Jesus. The horror and the dreams of Judas are realised, he gets up from his knees on which, for some reason, he has knelt, and gazes around coldly.

Thus does a stern conqueror look, when he has already determined in his heart to surrender everything to destruction and death, and for the last time throws a glance over a rich foreign city, still alive with sound, but already phantom-like under the cold hand of death. And suddenly, as clearly as his terrible victory, Iscariot saw its ominous precariousness. What if they should suddenly understand? It is not yet too late! Jesus still lives. There He gazes with entreating, sorrowing eyes.

What can prevent the thin film which covers the eyes of mankind, so thin that it hardly seems to exist at all, what can prevent it from rending? What if they should understand? What if suddenly, in all their threatening mass of men, women and children, they should advance, silently, without a cry, and wipe out the soldiery, plunging them up to their ears in their own blood, should tear from the ground the accursed cross, and by the hands of all who remain alive should lift up the liberated Jesus above the summit of the hill! Hosanna! Hosanna!

Hosanna? No! Better that Judas should lie on the ground. Better that he should lie upon the ground, and gnashing his teeth like a dog, should watch and wait until all these should rise up.

But what has come to Time? Now it almost stands still, so that one would wish to push it with the hands, to kick it, beat it with a whip like a lazy ass. Now it rushes madly down some mountain, and catches its breath, and stretches out its hand in vain to stop itself. There weeps the mother of Jesus. Let them weep. What avail her tears now? nay, the tears of all the mothers in the world?

"What are tears?" asks Judas, and madly pushes unyielding Time, beats it with his fists, curses it like a slave. It belongs to someone else, and therefore is unamenable to discipline. Oh! if only it belonged to Judas! But it belongs to all these people who are weeping, laughing, chattering as in the market. It belongs to the sun; it belongs to the cross; to the heart of Jesus, which is dying so slowly.

What an abject heart has Judas! He lays his hand upon it, but it cries out: "Hosanna," so loud that all may hear. He presses it to the ground, but it cries, "Hosanna, Hosanna!" like a babbler who scatters holy mysteries broadcast through the street.

"Be still! Be still!"

Suddenly a loud broken lamentation, dull cries, the last hurried movements towards the cross. What is it? Have they understood at last?

No, Jesus is dying. But can this be? Yes, Jesus is dying. His pale hands are motionless, but short convulsions run over His face, and breast, and legs. But can this be? Yes, He is dying. His breathing becomes less frequent. It ceases. No, there is yet one sigh, Jesus is still upon the earth. But is there another? No, no, no. Jesus is dead.

It is finished. Hosanna! Hosanna!

His horror and his dreams are realised. Who will now snatch the victory from the hands of Iscariot?

It is finished. Let all people on earth stream to Golgotha, and shout with their million throats, "Hosanna! Hosanna!" And let a sea of blood and tears be poured out at its foot, and they will find only the shameful cross and a dead Jesus!

Calmly and coldly Iscariot surveys the dead, letting his gaze rest for a moment on that neck, which he had kissed only yesterday with a farewell kiss; and slowly goes away. Now all Time belongs to him, and he walks without hurry; now all the World belongs to him, and he steps firmly, like a ruler, like a king, like one who is infinitely and joyfully alone in the world. He observes the mother of Jesus, and says to her sternly:

"Thou weepest, mother? Weep, weep, and long will all the mothers upon earth weep with thee: until I come with Jesus and destroy death."

What does he mean? Is he mad, or is he mocking—this Traitor? He is serious, and his face is stern, and his eyes no longer dart about in mad haste. Lo! he stands still, and with cold attention views a new, diminished earth.

It has become small, and he feels the whole of it under his feet. He looks at the little mountains, quietly reddening under the last rays of the sun, and he feels the mountains under his feet.

He looks at the sky opening wide its azure mouth; he looks at the small round disc of the sun, which vainly strives to singe and dazzle, and he feels the sky and the sun under his feet. Infinitely and joyfully alone, he proudly feels the impotence of all forces which operate in the world, and has cast them all into the abyss.

He walks farther on, with quiet, masterful steps. And Time goes neither forward nor back: obediently it marches in step with him in all its invisible immensity.

It is the end.

CHAPTER 9

As an old cheat, coughing, smiling fawningly, bowing incessantly, Judas Iscariot the Traitor appeared before the Sanhedrin. It was the day after the murder of Jesus, about mid-day. There they were all, His judges and murderers: the aged Annas with his sons, exact and disgusting likenesses of their father, and his son-in-law Caiaphas, devoured by ambition, and all the other members of the Sanhedrin, whose names have been snatched from the memory of mankind—rich and distinguished Sadducees, proud in their power and knowledge of the Law.

In silence they received the Traitor, their haughty faces remaining motionless, as though no one had entered. And even the very least, and most insignificant among them, to whom the others paid no attention, lifted up his bird-like face and looked as though no one had entered.

Judas bowed and bowed and bowed, and they looked on in silence: as though it were not a human being that had entered, but only an unclean insect that had crept in, and which they had not observed. But Judas Iscariot was not the man to be perturbed: they kept silence, and he kept on bowing, and thought that if it was necessary to go on bowing till evening, he could do so.

At length Caiaphas inquired impatiently:

"What do you want?"

Judas bowed once more, and said in a loud voice—

"It is I, Judas Iscariot, who betrayed to you Jesus of Nazareth."

"Well, what of that? You have received your due. Go away!" ordered Annas; but Judas appeared unconscious of the command, and continued bowing. Glancing at him, Caiaphas asked Annas:

"How much did you give?"

"Thirty pieces of silver."

Caiaphas laughed, and even the grey-bearded Annas laughed, too, and over all their proud faces there crept a smile of enjoyment; and even the one with the bird-like face laughed. Judas, perceptibly blanching, hastily interrupted with the words:

"That's right! Certainly, it was very little; but is Judas discontented, does Judas call out that he has been robbed? He is satisfied. Has he not contributed to a holy cause—yes, a holy? Do not the most sage people now listen to Judas, and think: He is one of us, this Judas Iscariot; he is our brother, our friend, this Judas Iscariot, the Traitor! Does not Annas want to kneel down and kiss the hand of Judas? Only Judas will not allow it; he is a coward, he is afraid they will bite him."

Caiaphas said:

"Drive the dog out! What's he barking about?"

"Get along with you. We have no time to listen to your babbling," said Annas imperturbably.

Judas drew himself up and closed his eyes. The hypocrisy, which he had carried so lightly all his life, suddenly became an insupportable burden, and with one movement of his eyelashes he cast it from him. And when he looked at Annas again, his glance was simple, direct, and terrible in its naked truthfulness. But they paid no attention to this either.

"You want to be driven out with sticks!" cried Caiaphas.

Panting under the weight of the terrible words, which he was lifting higher and higher, in order to hurl them hence upon the heads of the judges, Judas hoarsely asked:

"But you know . . . you know. . . who He was. . . He, whom you condemned yesterday and crucified?"

"We know. Go away!"

With one word he would straightway rend that thin film which was spread over their eyes, and all the earth would stagger beneath the weight of the merciless truth! They had a soul, they should be deprived of it; they had a life, they should lose their life; they had light before their eyes, eternal darkness and horror should cover them. Hosanna! Hosanna!

And these words, these terrible words, were tearing his throat asunder—

"He was no deceiver. He was innocent and pure. Do you hear? Judas deceived you. He betrayed to you an innocent man."

He waits. He hears the aged, unconcerned voice of Annas, saying:

"And is that all you want to say?"

"You do not seem to have understood me," says Judas, with dignity, turning pale. "Judas deceived you. He was innocent. You have slain the innocent."

He of the bird-like face smiles; but Annas is indifferent, Annas

268

yawns. And Caiaphas yawns, too, and says wearily:

"What did they mean by talking to me about the intellect of Judas Iscariot? He is simply a fool, and a bore, too."

"What?" cries Judas, all suffused with dark madness. "But who are you, the clever ones! Judas deceived you—hear! It was not He that he betrayed—but you—you wiseacres, you, the powerful, you he betrayed to a shameful death, which will not end, throughout the ages. Thirty pieces of silver! Well, well. But that is the price of *your* blood—blood filthy as the dish-water which the women throw out of the gates of their houses. Oh! Annas, old, grey, stupid Annas, chock-full of the Law, why did you not give one silver piece, just one *obolus* more? At this price you will go down through the ages!"

"Be off!" cries Caiaphas, growing purple in the face. But Annas stops him with a motion of the hand, and asks Judas as unconcernedly as ever:

"Is that all?"

"Verily, if I were to go into the desert, and cry to the wild beasts: 'Wild beasts, have ye heard the price at which men valued their Jesus?'—what would the wild beasts do? They would creep out of the lairs, they would howl with anger, they would forget their fear of mankind, and would all come here to devour you! If I were to say to the sea: 'Sea, knowest thou the price at which men valued their Jesus?' If I were to say to the mountains: 'Mountains, know ye the price at which men valued their Jesus?' Then the sea and the mountains would leave their places, assigned to them for ages, and would come here and fall upon your heads!"

"Does Judas wish to become a prophet? He speaks so loud!" mockingly remarks he of the bird-like face, with an ingratiating glance at Caiaphas.

"Today I saw a pale sun. It was looking at the earth, and saying: 'Where is the Man?' Today I saw a scorpion. It was sitting upon a stone and laughingly said: 'Where is the Man?' I went near and looked into its eyes. And it laughed and said: 'Where is the Man? I do not see Him!' Where is the Man? I ask you, I do not see Him—or is Judas become blind, poor Judas Iscariot!"

And Iscariot begins to weep aloud.

He was, during those moments, like a man out of his mind, and Caiaphas turned away, making a contemptuous gesture with his hand. But Annas considered for a time, and then said:

"I perceive, Judas, that you really have received but little, and that disturbs you. Here is some more money; take it and give it to your children."

He threw something, which rang shrilly. The sound had not died away, before another, like it, strangely prolonged the clinking.

Judas had hastily flung the pieces of silver and the *oboles* into the faces of the high priest and of the judges, returning the price paid for Jesus. The pieces of money flew in a curved shower, falling on their faces, and on the table, and rolling about the floor.

Some of the judges closed their hands with the palms outwards; others leapt from their places, and shouted and scolded. Judas, trying to hit Annas, threw the last coin, after which his trembling hand had long been fumbling in his wallet, spat in anger, and went out.

"Well, well," he mumbled, as he passed swiftly through the streets, scaring the children. "It seems that thou didst weep, Judas? Was Caiaphas really right when he said that Judas Iscariot was a fool? He who weeps in the day of his great revenge is not worthy of it—know'st thou that, Judas? Let not thine eyes deceive thee; let not thine heart lie to thee; flood not the fire with tears, Judas Iscariot!"

The disciples were sitting in mournful silence, listening to what was going on without. There was still danger that the vengeance of Jesus' enemies might not confine itself to Him, and so they were all expecting a visit from the guard, and perhaps more executions. Near to John, to whom, as the beloved disciple, the death of Jesus was especially grievous, sat Mary Magdalene, and Matthew trying to comfort him in an undertone. Mary, whose face was swollen with weeping, softly stroked his luxurious curling hair with her hand, while Matthew said didactically, in the words of Solomon:

"'*The long suffering is better than a hero; and he that ruleth his own spirit than one who taketh a city.*'"

At this moment Judas knocked loudly at the door, and entered. All started up in terror, and at first were not sure who it was; but when they recognised the hated countenance, the red-haired, bulbous head, they uttered a simultaneous cry.

Peter raised both hands and shouted:

"Get out of here, Traitor! Get out, or I will kill you."

But the others looked more carefully at the face and eyes of the Traitor, and said nothing, merely whispering in terror:

"Leave him alone, leave him alone! He is possessed with a devil."

Judas waited until they had quite done, and then cried out in a loud voice:

"Hail, ye eyes of Judas Iscariot! Ye have just seen the cold-blooded murderers. Lo! Where is Jesus? I ask you, where is Jesus?"

There was something compelling in the hoarse voice of Judas, and Thomas replied obediently—

"You know yourself, Judas, that our Master was crucified yesterday."

"But how came you to permit it? Where was your love? Thou, Beloved Disciple, and thou, Rock, where were you all when they were crucifying your Friend on the tree?"

"What could we do, judge thou?" said Thomas, with a gesture of protest.

"Thou asketh that, Thomas? Very well!" and Judas threw his head back, and fell upon him angrily. "He who loves does not ask what can be done—he goes and does it—he weeps, he bites, he throttles the enemy, and breaks his bones! He, that is, who loves! If your son were drowning, would you go into the city and inquire of the passers-by: 'What must I do? My son is drowning!' No, you would rather throw yourself into the water and drown with him. One who loved would!"

Peter replied grimly to the violent speech of Judas:

"I drew a sword, but He Himself forbade."

"Forbade? And you obeyed!" jeered Judas. "Peter, Peter, how could you listen to Him? Does He know anything of men, and of fighting?"

"He who does not submit to Him goes to hell fire."

"Then why did you not go, Peter? Hell fire! What's that? Now, supposing you had gone—what good's your soul to you, if you dare not throw it into the fire, if you want to?"

"Silence!" cried John, rising. "He Himself willed this sacrifice. His sacrifice is beautiful!"

"Is a sacrifice ever beautiful, Beloved Disciple? Wherever there is a sacrifice, then there is an executioner, and there traitors! Sacrifice—that is suffering for one and disgrace for all the others! Traitors, traitors, what have ye done with the world? Now they look at it from above and below, and laugh and cry: 'Look at that world, upon it they crucified Jesus!' And they spit on it—as I do!"

Judas angrily spat on the ground.

"He took upon Him the sin of all mankind. His sacrifice is beautiful," John insisted.

"No! you have taken all sin upon yourselves. You, Beloved Disciple, will not a race of traitors take their beginning from you, a pusillanimous and lying breed? O blind men, what have ye done with the earth? You have done your best to destroy it, ye will soon be kissing the cross on which ye crucified Jesus! Yes, yes, Judas gives ye his word that ye will kiss the cross!"

"Judas, don't revile!" roared Peter, pushing. "How could we slay all His enemies? They are so many!"

"And thou, Peter!" exclaimed John in anger, "dost thou not perceive that he is possessed of Satan? Leave us, Tempter! Thou'rt full of lies. The Teacher forbade us to kill."

"But did He forbid you to die? Why are you alive, when He is dead? Why do your feet walk, why does your tongue talk trash, why do your eyes blink, when He is dead, motionless, speechless? How do your cheeks dare to be red, John, when His are pale? How can you dare to shout, Peter, when He is silent? What could you do? You ask Judas? And Judas answers you, the magnificent, bold Judas Iscariot replies: 'Die!' You ought to have fallen on the road, to have seized the soldiers by the sword, by the hands, and drowned them in a sea of your own blood—yes, die, die! Better had it been, that His Father should have cause to cry out with horror, when you all enter there!"

Judas ceased with raised head. Suddenly he noticed the remains of a meal upon the table. With strange surprise, curiously, as though for the first time in his life he looked on food, he examined it, and slowly asked:

"What is this? You have been eating? Perhaps you have also been sleeping?"

Peter, who had begun to feel Judas to be someone, who could command obedience, drooping his head, tersely replied: "I slept, I slept and ate!"

Thomas said, resolutely and firmly:

"This is all untrue, Judas. Just consider: if we had all died, who would have told the story of Jesus? Who would have conveyed His teaching to mankind if we had all died, Peter and John and I?"

"But what is the truth itself in the mouths of traitors? Does it not become a lie? Thomas, Thomas, dost thou not understand, that thou art now only a sentinel at the grave of dead Truth? The sentinel falls asleep, and the thief cometh and carries away the truth; say, where is the truth? Cursed be thou, Thomas! Fruitless, and a beggar shalt thou be throughout the ages, and all you with him, accursed ones!"

"Accursed be thou thyself, Satan!" cried John, and James and Matthew and all the other disciples repeated his cry; only Peter held his peace.

272

"I am going to Him," said Judas, stretching his powerful hand on high. "Who will follow Iscariot to Jesus?"

"I—I also go with thee," cried Peter, rising.

But John and the others stopped him in horror, saying:

"Madman! Thou hast forgotten, that he betrayed the Master into the hands of His enemies."

Peter began to lament bitterly, striking his breast with his fist:

"Whither, then, shall I go? O Lord! whither shall I go?"

★★★★★★★★★★★★★★★★

Judas had long ago, during his solitary walks, marked the place where he intended to make an end of himself after the death of Jesus.

It was upon a hill high above Jerusalem. There stood but one tree, bent and twisted by the wind, which had torn it on all sides, half withered. One of its broken, crooked branches stretched out towards Jerusalem, as though in blessing or in threat, and this one Judas had chosen on which to hang a noose.

But the walk to the tree was long and tedious, and Judas Iscariot was very weary. The small, sharp stones, scattered under his feet, seemed continually to drag him backwards, and the hill was high, stern, and malign, exposed to the wind. Judas was obliged to sit down several times to rest, and panted heavily, while behind him, through the clefts of the rock, the mountain breathed cold upon his back.

"Thou too art against me, accursed one!" said Judas contemptuously, as he breathed with difficulty, and swayed his heavy head, in which all the thoughts were now petrifying.

Then he raised it suddenly, and opening wide his now fixed eyes, angrily muttered:

"No, they were too bad for Judas. Thou hearest Jesus? Wilt Thou trust me now? I am coming to Thee. Meet me kindly, I am weary— very weary. Then Thou and I, embracing like brothers, shall return to earth. Shall we not?"

Again, he swayed his petrifying head, and again he opened his eyes, mumbling:

"But maybe Thou wilt be angry with Judas when he arrives? And Thou wilt not trust him? And wilt send him to hell? Well! What then! I will go to hell. And in Thy hell fire I will weld iron, and weld iron, and demolish Thy heaven. Dost approve? Then Thou wilt believe in me. Then Thou wilt come back with me to earth, wilt Thou not, Jesus?"

Eventually Judas reached the summit and the crooked tree, and

273

there the wind began to torment him. And when Judas rebuked it, it began to blow soft and low, and took leave and flew away.

"Right! But as for them, they are curs!" said Judas, making a slip-knot. And since the rope might fail him and break, he hung it over a precipice, so that if it broke, he would be sure to meet his death upon the stones. And before he shoved himself off the brink with his foot, and hanged himself, Judas Iscariot once more anxiously prepared Jesus for his coming:

"Yes, meet me kindly, Jesus. I am very weary."

He leapt. The rope strained, but held. His neck stretched, but his hands and feet were crossed, and hung down as though damp.

He died. Thus, in the course of two days, one after another, Jesus of Nazareth and Judas Iscariot, the Traitor, left the world.

All the night through, like some monstrous fruit, Judas swayed over Jerusalem, and the wind kept turning his face now to the city, and now to the desert—as though it wished to exhibit Judas to both city and desert. But in whichever direction his face, distorted by death, was turned, his red eyes suffused with blood, and now as like one another as two brothers, incessantly looked towards the sky. In the morning some sharp-sighted person perceived Judas hanging above the city, and cried out in horror.

People came and took him down, and knowing who he was, threw him into a deep ravine, into which they were in the habit of throwing dead horses and cats and other carrion.

The same evening all the believers knew of the terrible death of the Traitor, and the next day it was known to all Jerusalem. Stony Judaea knew of it and green Galilee; and from one sea to the other, distant as it was, the news flew of the death of the Traitor.

Neither faster nor slower, but with equal pace with Time itself, it went, and as there is no end to Time so will there be no end to the stories about the Traitor Judas and his terrible death.

And all—both good and bad—will equally anathematise his shameful memory; and among all peoples, past and present, will he remain alone in his cruel destiny—Judas Iscariot, the Traitor.

Laughter

1

At 6.30 I was certain that she would come, and I was desperately happy. My coat was fastened only by the top button, and fluttered in the cold wind; but I felt no cold. My head was proudly thrown back, and my student's cap was cocked on the back of my head; my eyes with respect to the men they met were expressive of patronage and boldness, with respect to the women of a seductive tenderness. Although she had been my only love for four whole days, I was so young, and my heart was so rich in love, that I could not remain perfectly indifferent to other women. My steps were quick, bold and free.

At 6.45 my coat was fastened by two buttons, and I looked only at the women, but no longer with a seductive tenderness, but rather with disgust. I only wanted one woman—the others might go to the devil; they only confused me, and with their seeming resemblance to Her gave to my movements an uncertain and jerky indecision.

At 6.55 I felt warm

At 6.58 I felt cold.

As it struck seven I was convinced that she would not come.

By 8.30 I presented the appearance of the most pitiful creature in the world. My coat was fastened with all its buttons, collar turned up, cap tilted over my nose, which was blue with cold; my hair was over my forehead, my moustache and eyelashes were whitening with rime, and my teeth gently chattered. From my shambling gait, and bowed back, I might have been taken for a fairly hale old man returning from a party at the alms-house.

And She was the cause of all this—She! "Oh, the Dev—! No, I won't. Perhaps she could not get away, or she is ill, or dead. She's dead!"—and I swore.

"Eugéniya Nikoláevna will be there tonight," one of my companions, a student, remarked to me, without the slightest *arrière pensée.* He could not know how that I had waited for her in the frost from seven to half-past eight.

"Indeed," I replied, as in deep thought, but within my soul there leapt out: "Oh, the Dev—!" "There" meant at the Polózovs' evening party. Now the Polózovs were people with whom I was not upon visiting terms. But this evening I would be there.

"You fellows!" I shouted cheerfully, "today is Christmas Day, when everybody enjoys himself. Let us do so too.?'

"But how?" one of them mournfully replied.

"And where?" continued another.

"We will dress up, and go round to all the evening parties," I decided.

And these insensate individuals actually became cheerful. They shouted, and leapt, and sang. They thanked me for my suggestion, and counted up the amount of "the ready" available. In the course of half an hour we had collected all the lonely, disconsolate students in town; and when we had recruited a cheerful dozen or so of leaping devils, we repaired to a hairdresser's—he was also a costumier—and let in there the cold, and youth, and laughter.

I wanted something sombre and handsome, with a shade of elegant sadness; so, I requested:

"Give me the dress of a Spanish *grandee.*"

Apparently, this *grandee* had been very tall, for I was altogether swallowed up in his dress, and felt there as absolutely alone as though I had been in a wide, empty hall. Getting out of this costume, I asked for something else.

"Would you like to be a clown? Motley with bells."

"A clown, indeed!" I exclaimed with contempt.

"Well, then, a bandit. Such a hat and dagger!"

Oh! dagger! Yes, that would suit my purpose. But unfortunately, the bandit whose clothes they gave me had scarcely grown to full stature. Most probably he had been a corrupt youth of eight years. His little hat would not cover the back of my head, and I had to be dragged out of his velvet breeks as out of a trap. A page's dress was no go: it was all spotted like the pard. The monk's cowl was all in holes.

"Look sharp; it's late," said my companions, who were already dressed, trying to hurry me up.

There was but one costume left—that of a distinguished China-man. "Give me the Chinaman's," said I with a wave of my hand. And they gave it me. It was the devil knows what! I am not speaking of the costume itself. I pass over in silence those idiotic flowered boots, which were too short for me, and reached only halfway to my knees; but in the remaining, by far the most essential part, stuck out like two incomprehensible adjuncts on either side of my feet. I say nothing of the pink rag which covered my head like a wig, and was tied by threads to my ears, so that they protruded and stood up like a bat's. But the mask!

It was, if one may use the expression, a face in the abstract. It had nose, eyes, and mouth all right enough, and all in the proper places; but there was nothing human about it. A human being could not look so placid—even in his coffin. It was expressive neither of sorrow, nor cheerfulness, nor surprise—it expressed absolutely nothing! It looked at you squarely, and placidly—and an uncontrollable laughter over-whelmed you. My companions rolled about on the sofas, sank impo-tently down on the chairs, and gesticulated.

"It will be the most original mask of the evening," they declared.

I was ready to weep; but no sooner did I glance in the mirror than I too was convulsed with laughter. Yes, it will be a most original mask!

"In no circumstances are we to take off our masks," said my com-panions on the way. "We will give, our word."

"Honour bright!"

3

Positively it was the most original mask. People followed me in crowds, turned me about, jostled me, pinched me. But when, harried, I turned on my persecutors in anger—uncontrollable laughter seized them. Wherever I went, a roaring cloud of laughter encompassed and pressed on me; it moved together with me, and I could not escape from this circle of mad mirth. Sometimes it seized even myself, and I shouted, sang, and danced till everything seemed to go round before me, as if I was drunk. But how remote everything was from me! And how solitary was I under that mask! At last they left me in peace. With anger and fear, with malice and tenderness intermingling, I looked at her.

"'Tis I."

Her long eyelashes were lifted slowly in surprise, and a whole sheaf of black rays flashed upon me, and a laugh, resonant, joyous, bright as the spring sunshine—a laugh answered me.

"Yes, it is I; I, I say," I insisted with a smile. "Why did you not come this evening?"

But she only laughed, laughed joyously.

"I suffered so much; I felt so hurt," said I, imploring an answer.

But she only laughed. The black sheen of her eyes was extinguished, and still more brightly her smile lit up. It was the sun indeed, but burning, pitiless, cruel.

"What's the matter with you?"

"Is it really you?" said she, restraining herself. "How comical you are!"

My shoulders were bowed, and my head hung down—such despair was there in my pose. And while she, with the expiring afterglow of the smile upon her face, looked at the happy young couples that hurried by us, I said: "It's not nice to laugh. Do you not feel that there is a living, suffering face behind my ridiculous mask—and can't you see that it was only for the opportunity it gave me of seeing you that I put it on? You gave me reason to hope for your love, and then so quickly, so cruelly deprived me of it. Why did you not come?"

With a protest on her tender, smiling lips, she turned sharply to me, and a cruel laugh utterly overwhelmed her. Choking, almost weeping, covering her face with a fragrant lace handkerchief, she brought out with difficulty: "Look at yourself in the mirror behind. Oh, how droll you are!"

Contracting my brows, clenching my teeth with pain, with a face grown cold, from which all the blood had fled, I looked at the mirror. There gazed out at me an idiotically placid, stolidly complacent, inhumanly immovable face. And I burst into an uncontrollable fit of laughter. And with the laughter not yet subsided, but already with the trembling of rising anger, with the madness of despair, I said—nay, almost shouted:

"You ought not to laugh!"

And when she was quiet again, I went on speaking in a whisper of my love. I had never spoken so well, for I had never loved so strongly. I spoke of the tortures of expectation, of the venomous tears of mad jealousy and grief, of my own soul which was all love. And I saw how her drooping eyelashes cast a thick dark shadow over her blanched cheeks. I saw how across their dull pallor the fire, bursting into flame, threw a red reflection, and how her whole pliant body involuntarily bent towards me.

She was dressed as the Goddess of Night, and was all mysterious, clad in a black, mist-like lace, which twinkled with stars of brilliants. She was beautiful as a forgotten dream of far-off childhood. As I spoke my eyes filled with tears, and my heart beat with gladness. And I perceived, I perceived at last, how a tender, piteous smile parted her lips, and her eyelashes were lifted all a-tremble. Slowly, timorously, but with infinite confidence, she turned her head towards me, and—

And such a shriek of laughter I never heard!

"No, no, I can't," she almost groaned, and throwing back her head, she burst into a resonant cascade of laughter.

Oh, if but for a moment I could have had a human face! I bit my lips, tears rolled over my heated face; but it—that idiotic mask, on which everything was in its right place, nose, eyes, and lips—looked with a complacency stolidly horrible in its absurdity. And when I went out, swaying on my flowered feet, it was long before I got out of reach of that ringing laugh. It was as though a silvery stream of water were falling from an immense height, and breaking in cheerful song upon the hard rock.

4

Scattered over the whole sleeping street and rousing the stillness of the night with our lusty, excited voices, we walked home. A companion said to me:

"You have had a colossal success. I never saw people laugh so— Halloa! what are you up to? Why are you tearing your mask? I say, you fellows, he's gone mad! Look, he's tearing his costume to pieces! By Jove! he's actually crying."

Lazarus

Leonid Andreyev

1

When Lazarus left the grave, where, for three days and three nights he had been under the enigmatical sway of death, and returned alive to his dwelling, for a long time no one noticed in him those sinister oddities, which, as time went on, made his very name a terror. Gladdened unspeakably by the sight of him who had been returned to life, those near to him caressed him unceasingly, and satiated their burning desire to serve him, in solicitude for his food and drink and garments.

And they dressed him gorgeously, in bright colours of hope and laughter, and when, like to a bridegroom in his bridal vestures, he sat again among them at the table, and again ate and drank, they wept, overwhelmed with tenderness. And they summoned the neighbours to look at him who had risen miraculously from the dead. These came and shared the serene joy of the hosts. Strangers from far-off towns and hamlets came and adored the miracle in tempestuous words. Like to a beehive was the house of Mary and Martha.

Whatever was found new in Lazarus' face and gestures was thought to be some trace of a grave illness and of the shocks recently experienced. Evidently, the destruction wrought by death on the corpse was only arrested by the miraculous power, but its effects were still apparent; and what death had succeeded in doing with Lazarus' face and body, was like an artist's unfinished sketch seen under thin glass. On Lazarus' temples, under his eyes, and in the hollows of his cheeks, lay a deep and cadaverous blueness; cadaverously blue also were his long fingers, and around his fingernails, grown long in the grave, the blue had become purple and dark.

On his lips the skin, swollen in the grave, had burst in places, and thin, reddish cracks were formed, shining as though covered with transparent mica. And he had grown stout. His body, puffed up in the grave, retained its monstrous size and showed those frightful swellings, in which one sensed the presence of the rank liquid of decomposition. But the heavy corpse-like odour which penetrated Lazarus' graveclothes and, it seemed, his very body, soon entirely disappeared, the blue spots on his face and hands grew paler, and the reddish cracks closed up, although they never disappeared altogether. That is how Lazarus looked when he appeared before people, in his second life, but his face looked natural to those who had seen him in the coffin.

In addition to the changes in his appearance, Lazarus' temper seemed to have undergone a transformation, but this circumstance startled no one and attracted no attention. Before his death Lazarus had always been cheerful and carefree, fond of laughter and a merry joke. It was because of this brightness and cheerfulness, with not a touch of malice and darkness, that the Master had grown so fond of him. But now Lazarus had grown grave and taciturn, he never jested, himself, nor responded with laughter to other people's jokes; and the words which he uttered, very infrequently, were the plainest, most ordinary, and necessary words, as deprived of depth and significance, as those sounds with which animals express pain and pleasure, thirst and hunger. They were the words that one can say all one's life, and yet they give no indication of what pains and gladdens the depths of the soul.

Thus, with the face of a corpse which for three days had been under the heavy sway of death, dark and taciturn, already appallingly transformed, but still unrecognised by anyone in his new self, he was sitting at the feasting table, among friends and relatives, and his gorgeous nuptial garments glittered with yellow gold and bloody scarlet. Broad waves of jubilation, now soft, now tempestuously sonorous surged around him; warm glances of love were reaching out for his face, still cold with the coldness of the grave; and a friend's warm palm caressed his blue, heavy hand. And music played the tympanum and the pipe, the cithara and the harp. It was as though bees hummed, grasshoppers chirped and birds warbled over the happy house of Mary and Martha.

2

One of the guests incautiously lifted the veil. By a thoughtless word he broke the serene charm and uncovered the truth in all its naked ugliness. Ere the thought formed itself in his mind, his lips uttered with a smile:

"Why dost thou not tell us what happened yonder?"

And all grew silent, startled by the question. It was as if it occurred to them only now that for three days Lazarus had been dead, and they looked at him, anxiously awaiting his answer. But Lazarus kept silence.

"Thou dost not wish to tell us,"—wondered the man, "is it so terrible yonder?"

And again his thought came after his words. Had it been otherwise, he would not have asked this question, which at that very moment oppressed his heart with its insufferable horror. Uneasiness seized all present, and with a feeling of heavy weariness they awaited Lazarus' words, but he was silent, sternly and coldly, and his eyes were lowered. And as if for the first time, they noticed the frightful blueness of his face and his repulsive obesity. On the table, as though forgotten by Lazarus, rested his bluish-purple wrist, and to this all eyes turned, as if it were from it that the awaited answer was to come. The musicians were still playing, but now the silence reached them too, and even as water extinguishes scattered embers, so were their merry tunes extinguished in the silence. The pipe grew silent; the voices of the sonorous tympanum and the murmuring harp died away; and as if the strings had burst, the cithara answered with a tremulous, broken note. Silence.

"Thou dost not wish to say?" repeated the guest, unable to check his chattering tongue. But the stillness remained unbroken, and the bluish-purple hand rested motionless. And then he stirred slightly and everyone felt relieved. He lifted up his eyes, and lo! straightway embracing everything in one heavy glance, fraught with weariness and horror, he looked at them—Lazarus who had arisen from the dead.

It was the third day since Lazarus had left the grave. Ever since then many had experienced the pernicious power of his eye, but neither those who were crushed by it forever, nor those who found the strength to resist in it the primordial sources of life—which is as mysterious as death—never could they explain the horror which lay motionless in the depth of his black pupils. Lazarus looked calmly and simply with no desire to conceal anything, but also with no intention to say anything; he looked coldly, as he who is infinitely indifferent to those alive.

Many carefree people came close to him without noticing him, and only later did they learn with astonishment and fear who that calm stout man was, that walked slowly by, almost touching them with his gorgeous and dazzling garments. The sun did not cease shining, when he was looking, nor did the fountain hush its murmur, and the sky overhead remained cloudless and blue. But the man under the spell of his enigmatical look heard no more the fountain and saw not the sky overhead. Sometimes, he wept bitterly, sometimes he tore his hair and in frenzy called for help; but more often it came to pass that apathetically and quietly he began to die, and so he languished many years, before everybody's very eyes, wasted away, colourless, flabby, dull, like a tree, silently drying up in a stony soil. And of those who gazed at him, the ones who wept madly, sometimes felt again the stir of life; the others never.

"So, thou dost not wish to tell us what thou hast seen yonder?" repeated the man. But now his voice was impassive and dull, and deadly grey weariness showed in Lazarus' eyes. And deadly grey weariness covered like dust all the faces, and with dull amazement the guests stared at each other and did not understand wherefore they had gathered here and sat at the rich table. The talk ceased. They thought it was time to go home, but could not overcome the flaccid lazy weariness which glued their muscles, and they kept on sitting there, yet apart and torn away from each other, like pale fires scattered over a dark field.

But the musicians were paid to play and again they took their instruments and again tunes full of studied mirth and studied sorrow began to flow and to rise. They unfolded the customary melody but the guests hearkened in dull amazement. Already they knew not wherefore is it necessary, and why is it well, that people should pluck strings, inflate their cheeks, blow in thin pipes, and produce a bizarre, many-voiced noise.

"What bad music," said someone.

The musicians took offense and left. Following them, the guests left one after another, for night was already come. And when placid darkness encircled them and they began to breathe with more ease, suddenly Lazarus' image loomed up before each one in formidable radiance: the blue face of a corpse, grave-clothes gorgeous and resplendent, a cold look, in the depths of which lay motionless an unknown horror. As though petrified, they were standing far apart, and darkness enveloped them, but in the darkness blazed brighter and brighter the supernatural vision of him who for three days had been under the enigmatical sway of death.

For three days had he been dead: thrice had the sun risen and set, but he had been dead; children had played, streams murmured over pebbles, the wayfarer had lifted up hot dust in the highroad—but he had been dead. And now he is again among them—touches them,— looks at them—looks at them! and through the black discs of his pupils, as through darkened glass, stares the unknowable Yonder.

3

No one was taking care of Lazarus, for no friends no relatives were left to him, and the great desert which encircled the holy city, came near the very threshold of his dwelling. And the desert entered his house, and stretched on his couch, like a wife and extinguished the fires. No one was taking care of Lazarus. One after the other, his sisters—Mary and Martha—forsook him. For a long while Martha was loath to abandon him, for she knew not who would feed him and pity him, she wept and prayed. But one night, when the wind was roaming in the desert and with a hissing sound the cypresses were bending over the roof, she dressed noiselessly and secretly left the house.

Lazarus probably heard the door slam; it banged against the side-post under the gusts of the desert wind, but he did not rise to go out and to look at her that was abandoning him. All the night long the cypresses hissed over his head and plaintively thumped the door, letting in the cold, greedy desert.

Like a leper he was shunned by everyone, and it was proposed to tie a bell to his neck, as is done with lepers, to warn people against sudden meetings. But someone remarked, growing frightfully pale, that it would be too horrible if by night the moaning of Lazarus' bell were suddenly heard under the windows—and so the project was abandoned.

And since he did not take care of himself, he would probably have starved to death, had not the neighbours brought him food in fear of something that they sensed but vaguely. The food was brought to him by children; they were not afraid of Lazarus, nor did they mock him with *naive* cruelty, as children are wont to do with the wretched and miserable. They were indifferent to him, and Lazarus answered them with the same coldness; he had no desire to caress the black little curls, and to look into their innocent shining eyes. Given to Time and to the Desert, his house was crumbling down, and long since had his famishing, lowing goats wandered away to the neighbouring pastures. And his bridal garments became threadbare. Ever since that happy day, when the musicians played, he had worn them unaware of the difference of the new and the worn. The bright colours grew dull and faded; vicious dogs and the sharp thorn of the Desert turned the tender fabric into rags.

By day, when the merciless sun slew all things alive, and even scorpions sought shelter under stones and writhed there in a mad desire to sting, he sat motionless under the sunrays, his blue face and the uncouth, bushy beard lifted up, bathing in the fiery flood.

When people still talked to him, he was once asked:

"Poor Lazarus, does it please thee to sit thus and to stare at the sun?"

And he had answered:

"Yes, it does."

So strong, it seemed, was the cold of his three days' grave, so deep the darkness, that there was no heat on earth to warm Lazarus, nor a splendour that could brighten the darkness of his eyes. That is what came to the mind of those who spoke to Lazarus, and with a sigh they left him.

And when the scarlet, flattened globe would lower, Lazarus would set out for the desert and walk straight toward the sun, as though striving to reach it. He always walked straight toward the sun and those who tried to follow him and to spy upon what he was doing at night in the desert, retained in their memory the black silhouette of a tall stout man against the red background of an enormous flattened disc. Night pursued them with her horrors, and so they did not learn of Lazarus' doings in the desert, but the vision of the black on red was forever branded on their brain. Just as a beast with a splinter in its eye furiously rubs its muzzle with its paws, so they too foolishly rubbed their eyes, but what Lazarus had given was indelible, and Death alone could efface it.

But there were people who lived far away, who never saw Lazarus and knew of him only by report. With daring curiosity, which is stronger than fear and feeds upon it, with hidden mockery, they would come to Lazarus who was sitting in the sun and enter into conversation with him. By this time Lazarus' appearance had changed for the better and was not so terrible. The first minute they snapped their fingers and thought of how stupid the inhabitants of the holy city were; but when the short talk was over and they started homeward, their looks were such that the inhabitants of the holy city recognized them at once and said:

"Look, there is one more fool on whom Lazarus has set his eye,"— and they shook their heads regretfully, and lifted up their arms.

There came brave, intrepid warriors, with tinkling weapons; happy youths came with laughter and song; busy tradesmen, jingling their money, ran in for a moment, and haughty priests leaned their crosiers against Lazarus' door, and they were all strangely changed, as they came back. The same terrible shadow swooped down upon their souls and gave a new appearance to the old familiar world.

Those who still had the desire to speak, expressed their feelings thus:

"All things tangible and visible grew hollow, light, and transparent—similar to lightsome shadows in the darkness of night;

"For, that great darkness, which holds the whole cosmos, was dispersed neither by the sun or by the moon and the stars, but like an immense black shroud enveloped the earth and, like a mother, embraced it;

"It penetrated all the bodies, iron and stone—and the particles of the bodies, having lost their ties, grew lonely; and it penetrated into the depth of the particles, and the particles of particles became lonely;

"For that great void, which encircles the cosmos, was not filled by things visible: neither by the sun, nor by the moon and the stars, but reigned unrestrained, penetrating everywhere, severing body from body, particle from particle;

"In the void hollow trees spread hollow roots threatening a fantastic fall; temples, palaces, and horses loomed up and they were hollow; and in the void men moved about restlessly but they were light and hollow like shadows;

"For, Time was no more, and the beginning of all things came near their end: the building was still being built, and builders were still hammering away, and its ruins were already seen and the void in its place; the man was still being born, but already funeral candles were burning at his head, and now they were extinguished, and there was the void in place of the man and of the funeral candles.

"And wrapped by void and darkness the man in despair trembled in the face of the Horror of the Infinite."

Thus, spake the men who had still a desire to speak. But surely, much more could have told those who wished not to speak, and died in silence.

4

At that time there lived in Rome a renowned sculptor. In clay, marble, and bronze he wrought bodies of gods and men, and such was their beauty, that people called them immortal. But he himself was discontented and asserted that there was something even more beautiful, that he could not embody either in marble or in bronze. "I have not yet gathered the glimmers of the moon, nor have I my fill of sunshine," he was wont to say, "and there is no soul in my marble, no life in my beautiful bronze." And when on moonlight nights he slowly walked along the road, crossing the black shadows of cypresses, his white tunic glittering in the moonshine, those who met him would laugh in a friendly way and say:

"Art thou going to gather moonshine, Aurelius? Why then didst thou not fetch baskets?"

And he would answer, laughing and pointing to his eyes:

"Here are the baskets wherein I gather the sheen of the moon and the glimmer of the sun."

And so it was: the moon glimmered in his eyes and the sun sparkled therein. But he could not translate them into marble and therein lay the serene tragedy of his life.

He was descended from an ancient patrician race, had a good wife and children, and suffered from no want.

When the obscure rumour about Lazarus reached him, he consulted his wife and friends and undertook the far journey to Judea to see him who had miraculously risen from the dead. He was somewhat weary in those days and he hoped that the road would sharpen his blunted senses. What was said of Lazarus did not frighten him: he had pondered much over Death, did not like it, but he disliked also those who confused it with life.

In this life—life and beauty;
beyond—Death, the enigmatical—

. . . . thought he, and there is no better thing for a man to do than to delight in life and in the beauty of all things living. He had even a vainglorious desire to convince Lazarus of the truth of his own view and restore his soul to life, as his body had been restored. This seemed so much easier because the rumours, shy and strange, did not render the whole truth about Lazarus and but vaguely warned against something frightful.

Lazarus had just risen from the stone in order to follow the sun which was setting in the desert, when a rich Roman attended by an armed slave, approached him and addressed him in a sonorous tone of voice:

"Lazarus!"

And Lazarus beheld a superb face, lit with glory, and arrayed in fine clothes, and precious stones sparkling in the sun. The red light lent to the Roman's face and head the appearance of gleaming bronze—that also Lazarus noticed. He resumed obediently his place and lowered his weary eyes.

"Yes, thou art ugly, my poor Lazarus,"—quietly said the Roman, playing with his golden chain; "thou art even horrible, my poor friend; and Death was not lazy that day when thou didst fall so heedlessly into his hands. But thou art stout, and, as the great Caesar used to say, fat people are not ill-tempered; to tell the truth, I don't understand why men fear thee. Permit me to spend the night in thy house; the hour is late, and I have no shelter."

Never had anyone asked Lazarus' hospitality.

"I have no bed," said he.

"I am somewhat of a soldier and I can sleep sitting," the Roman answered. "We shall build a fire."

"I have no fire."

"Then we shall have our talk in the darkness, like two friends. I think thou wilt find a bottle of wine."

"I have no wine."

The Roman laughed.

"Now I see why thou art so sombre and dislikest thy second life. No wine! Why, then we shall do without it: there are words that make the head go round better than the Falernian."

By a sign he dismissed the slave, and they remained all alone. And again, the sculptor started speaking, but it was as if, together with the setting sun, life had left his words; and they grew pale and hollow, as if they staggered on unsteady feet, as if they slipped and fell down, drunk with the heavy lees of weariness and despair. And black chasms grew up between the words—like far-off hints of the great void and the great darkness.

"Now I am thy guest, and thou wilt not be unkind to me, Lazarus!"—said he. "Hospitality is the duty even of those who for three days were dead. Three days, I was told, thou didst rest in the grave. There it must be cold . . . and that is whence comes thy ill habit of going without fire and wine. As to me, I like fire; it grows dark here so rapidly. . . . The lines of thy eyebrows and forehead are quite, quite interesting: they are like ruins of strange palaces, buried in ashes after an earthquake. But why dost thou wear such ugly and queer garments? I have seen bridegrooms in thy country, and they wear such clothes—

are they not funny—and terrible.... But art thou a bridegroom?"

The sun had already disappeared, a monstrous black shadow came running from the east—it was as if gigantic bare feet began rumbling on the sand, and the wind sent a cold wave along the backbone.

"In the darkness thou seemest still larger, Lazarus, as if thou hast grown stouter in these moments. Dost thou feed on darkness, Lazarus? I would fain have a little fire—at least a little fire, a little fire. I feel somewhat chilly, your nights are so barbarously cold.... Were it not so dark, I should say that thou wert looking at me, Lazarus. Yes, it seems to me, thou art looking. . . . Why, thou art looking at me, I feel it—but there thou art smiling."

Night came, and filled the air with heavy blackness.

"How well it will be, when the sun will rise tomorrow anew. . . . I am a great sculptor, thou knowest; that is how my friends call me. I create. Yes, that is the word . . . but I need daylight. I give life to the cold marble, I melt sonorous bronze in fire, in bright hot fire. . . . Why didst thou touch me with thy hand?"

"Come"—said Lazarus—"Thou art my guest."

And they went to the house. And a long night enveloped the earth.

The slave, seeing that his master did not come, went to seek him, when the sun was already high in the sky. And he beheld his master side by side with Lazarus: in profound silence were they sitting right under the dazzling and scorching sunrays and looking upward. The slave began to weep and cried out:

"My master, what has befallen thee, master?"

The very same day the sculptor left for Rome. On the way Aurelius was pensive and taciturn, staring attentively at everything—the men, the ship, the sea, as though trying to retain something. On the high sea a storm burst upon them, and all through it Aurelius stayed on the deck and eagerly scanned the seas looming near and sinking with a thud.

At home his friends were frightened at the change which had taken place in Aurelius, but he calmed them, saying meaningly:

"I have found it."

And without changing the dusty clothes he wore on his journey, he fell to work, and the marble obediently resounded under his sonorous hammer. Long and eagerly worked he, admitting no one, until one morning he announced that the work was ready and ordered his friends to be summoned, severe critics and connoisseurs of art. And to meet them he put on bright and gorgeous garments, that glittered with yellow gold—and—scarlet *byssus*.

"Here is my work," said he thoughtfully.

His friends glanced and a shadow of profound sorrow covered their faces. It was something monstrous, deprived of all the lines and shapes familiar to the eye, but not without a hint at some new, strange image.

On a thin, crooked twig, or rather on an ugly likeness of a twig rested askew a blind, ugly, shapeless, outspread mass of something utterly and inconceivably distorted, a mad leap of wild and bizarre fragments, all feebly and vainly striving to part from one another. And, as if by chance, beneath one of the wildly-rent salients a butterfly was chiselled with divine skill, all airy loveliness, delicacy, and beauty, with transparent wings, which seemed to tremble with an impotent desire to take flight.

"Wherefore this wonderful butterfly, Aurelius?" said somebody falteringly.

"I know not"—was the sculptor's answer.

But it was necessary to tell the truth, and one of his friends who loved him best said firmly:

"This is ugly, my poor friend. It must be destroyed. Give me the hammer."

And with two strokes he broke the monstrous man into pieces, leaving only the infinitely delicate butterfly untouched.

From that time on Aurelius created nothing. With profound indifference he looked at marble and bronze, and on his former divine works, where everlasting beauty rested. With the purpose of arousing his former fervent passion for work and, awakening his deadened soul, his friends took him to see other artists' beautiful works—but he remained indifferent as before, and the smile did not warm up his tightened lips. And only after listening to lengthy talks about beauty, he would retort wearily and indolently:

"But all this is a lie."

And by the day, when the sun was shining, he went into his magnificent, skilfully built garden and having found a place without shadow, he exposed his bare head to the glare and heat. Red and white butterflies fluttered around; from the crooked lips of a drunken satyr, water streamed down with a splash into a marble cistern, but he sat motionless and silent—like a pallid reflection of him who, in the far-off distance, at the very gates of the stony desert, sat under the fiery sun.

And now it came to pass that the great, deified Augustus himself summoned Lazarus. The imperial messengers dressed him gorgeously, in solemn nuptial clothes, as if Time had legalized them, and he was to remain until his very death the bridegroom of an unknown bride. It was as though an old, rotting coffin had been gilt and furnished with new, gay tassels. And men, all in trim and bright attire, rode after him, as if in bridal procession indeed, and those foremost trumpeted loudly, bidding people to clear the way for the emperor's messengers. But Lazarus' way was deserted: his native land cursed the hateful name of him who had miraculously risen from the dead, and people scattered at the very news of his appalling approach. The solitary voice of the brass trumpets sounded in the motionless air, and the wilderness alone responded with its languid echo.

Then Lazarus went by sea. And his was the most magnificently arrayed and the most mournful ship that ever mirrored itself in the azure waves of the Mediterranean Sea. Many were the travellers aboard, but like a tomb was the ship, all silence and stillness, and the despairing water sobbed at the steep, proudly curved prow. All alone sat Lazarus exposing his head to the blaze of the sun, silently listening to the murmur and splash of the wavelets, and afar seamen and messengers were sitting, a vague group of weary shadows. Had the thunder burst and the wind attacked the red sails, the ships would probably have perished, for none of those aboard had either the will or the strength to struggle for life. With a supreme effort some mariners would reach the board and eagerly scan the blue, transparent deep, hoping to see a *naiad's* pink shoulder flash in the hollow of an azure wave, or a drunken gay centaur dash along and in frenzy splash the wave with his hoof. But the sea was like a wilderness, and the deep was dumb and deserted.

With utter indifference did Lazarus set his feet on the street of the eternal city. As though all her wealth, all the magnificence of her palaces built by giants, all the resplendence, beauty, and music of her refined life were but the echo of the wind in the wilderness, the reflection of the desert quicksand. Chariots were dashing, and along the streets were moving crowds of strong, fair, proud builders of the eternal city and haughty participants in her life; a song sounded; fountains and women laughed a pearly laughter; drunken philosophers harangued, and the sober listened to them with a smile; hoofs struck the stone pavements. And surrounded by cheerful noise, a stout, heavy man was moving, a cold spot of silence and despair, and on his way, he sowed disgust, anger, and vague, gnawing weariness. Who dares to be sad in Rome, wondered indignantly the citizens, and frowned. In two days, the entire city already knew all about him who had miraculously risen from the dead, and shunned him shyly.

But some daring people there were, who wanted to test their strength, and Lazarus obeyed their imprudent summons. Kept busy by state affairs, the emperor constantly delayed the reception, and seven days did he who had risen from the dead go about visiting others.

And Lazarus came to a cheerful Epicurean, and the host met him with laughter on his lips:

"Drink, Lazarus, drink!"—shouted he. "Would not Augustus laugh to see thee drunk!"

And half-naked drunken women laughed, and rose petals fell on Lazarus' blue hands. But then the Epicurean looked into Lazarus' eyes, and his gaiety ended forever. Drunkard remained he for the rest of his life; never did he drink, yet forever was he drunk. But instead of the gay reverie which wine brings with it, frightful dreams began to haunt him, the sole food of his stricken spirit. Day and night he lived in the poisonous vapours of his nightmares, and death itself was not more frightful than her raving, monstrous forerunners.

And Lazarus came to a youth and his beloved, who loved each other and were most beautiful in their passions. Proudly and strongly embracing his love, the youth said with serene regret:

"Look at us, Lazarus, and share our joy. Is there anything stronger than love?"

And Lazarus looked. And for the rest of their life, they kept on loving each other, but their passion grew gloomy and joyless, like those funeral cypresses whose roots feed on the decay of the graves and whose black summits in a still evening hour seek in vain to reach the sky. Thrown by the unknown forces of life into each other's embraces, they mingled tears with kisses, voluptuous pleasures with pain, and they felt themselves doubly slaves, obedient slaves to life, and patient servants of the silent Nothingness. Ever united, ever severed, they blazed like sparks and like sparks lost themselves in the boundless Dark.

And Lazarus came to a haughty sage, and the sage said to him:

"I know all the horrors thou canst reveal to me. Is there anything thou canst frighten me with?"

But before long the sage felt that the knowledge of horror was far from being the horror itself, and that the vision of Death, was not

Death. And he felt that wisdom and folly are equal before the face of Infinity, for Infinity knows them not. And it vanished, the dividing-line between knowledge and ignorance, truth and falsehood, top and bottom, and the shapeless thought hung suspended in the void. Then the sage clutched his grey head and cried out frantically:

"I cannot think! I cannot think!"

Thus, under the indifferent glance for him, who miraculously had risen from the dead, perished everything that asserts life, its significance and joys. And it was suggested that it was dangerous to let him see the emperor, that it was better to kill him and, having buried him secretly, to tell the emperor that he had disappeared no one knew whither. Already swords were being whetted and youths devoted to the public welfare prepared for the murder, when Augustus ordered Lazarus to be brought before him next morning, thus destroying the cruel plans.

If there was no way of getting rid of Lazarus, at least it was possible to soften the terrible impression his face produced. With this in view, skilful painters, barbers, and artists were summoned, and all night long they were busy over Lazarus' head. They cropped his beard, curled it, and gave it a tidy, agreeable appearance. By means of paints they concealed the corpse-like blueness of his hands and face. Repulsive were the wrinkles of suffering that furrowed his old face, and they were puttied, painted, and smoothed; then, over the smooth background, wrinkles of good-tempered laughter and pleasant, carefree mirth were skilfully painted with fine brushes.

Lazarus submitted indifferently to everything that was done to him. Soon he was turned into a becomingly stout, venerable old man, into a quiet and kind grandfather of numerous offspring. It seemed that the smile, with which only a while ago he was spinning funny yarns, was still lingering on his lips, and that in the corner of his eye serene tenderness was hiding, the companion of old age. But people did not dare change his nuptial garments, and they could not change his eyes, two dark and frightful glasses through which looked at men, the unknowable Yonder.

6

Lazarus was not moved by the magnificence of the imperial palace. It was as though he saw no difference between the crumbling house, closely pressed by the desert, and the stone palace, solid and fair, and indifferently he passed into it. And the hard marble of the floors under his feet grew similar to the quicksand of the desert, and the multitude of richly dressed and haughty men became like void air under his glance. No one looked into his face, as Lazarus passed by, fearing to fall under the appalling influence of his eyes; but when the sound of his heavy footsteps had sufficiently died down, the courtiers raised their heads and with fearful curiosity examined the figure of a stout, tall, slightly bent old man, who was slowly penetrating into the very heart of the imperial palace.

Were Death itself passing, it would be faced with no greater fear: for until then the dead alone knew Death, and those alive knew Life only—and there was no bridge between them. But this extraordinary man, although alive, knew Death, and enigmatical, appalling, was his cursed knowledge. "Woe," people thought, "he will take the life of our great, deified Augustus," and they sent curses after Lazarus, who meanwhile kept on advancing into the interior of the palace.

Already did the emperor know who Lazarus was, and prepared to meet him. But the monarch was a brave man, and felt his own tremendous, unconquerable power, and in his fatal duel with him who had miraculously risen from the dead he wanted not to invoke human help. And so, he met Lazarus face to face:

"Lift not thine eyes upon me, Lazarus," he ordered. "I heard thy face is like that of Medusa and turns into stone whomsoever thou lookest at. Now, I wish to see thee and to have a talk with thee, before I turn into stone,"—added he in a tone of kingly jesting, not devoid of fear.

Coming close to him, he carefully examined Lazarus' face and his strange festal garments. And although he had a keen eye, he was deceived by his appearance.

"So, Thou dost not appear terrible, my venerable old man. But the worse for us, if horror assumes such a respectable and pleasant air. Now let us have a talk."

Augustus sat, and questioning Lazarus with his eye as much as with words, started the conversation:

"Why didst thou not greet me as thou enteredst?"

Lazarus answered indifferent:

"I knew not it was necessary."

"Art thou a Christian?"

"No."

Augustus approvingly shook his head.

"That is good. I do not like Christians. They shake the tree of life

295

before it is covered with fruit, and disperse its odorous bloom to the winds. But who art thou?"

With a visible effort Lazarus answered:

"I was dead."

"I had heard that. But who art thou now?"

Lazarus was silent, but at last repeated in a tone of weary apathy:

"I was dead."

"Listen to me, stranger," said the emperor, distinctly and severely giving utterance to the thought that had come to him at the beginning, "my realm is the realm of Life, my people are of the living, not of the dead. Thou art here one too many. I know not who thou art and what thou sawest there; but, if thou liest, I hate thy lies, and if thou tellst the truth, I hate thy truth. In my bosom I feel the throb of life; I feel strength in my arm, and my proud thoughts, like eagles, pierce the space. And yonder in the shelter of my rule, under the protection of laws created by me, people live and toil and rejoice. Dost thou hear the battle-cry, the challenge men throw into the face of the future?"

Augustus, as in prayer, stretched forth his arms and exclaimed solemnly:

"Be blessed, O great and divine Life!"

Lazarus was silent, and with growing sternness the emperor went on:

"Thou art not wanted here, miserable remnant, snatched from under Death's teeth, thou inspirest weariness and disgust with life; like a caterpillar in the fields, thou gloatest on the rich ear of joy and belchest out the drivel of despair and sorrow. Thy truth is like a rusty sword in the hands of a nightly murderer—and as a murderer thou shalt be executed. But before that, let me look into thine eyes. Perchance, only cowards are afraid of them, but in the brave, they awake the thirst for strife and victory; then thou shalt be rewarded, not executed. . . . Now, look at me, Lazarus."

At first it appeared to the deified Augustus that a friend was looking at him—so soft, so tenderly fascinating was Lazarus' glance. It promised not horror, but sweet rest and the Infinite seemed to him a tender mistress, a compassionate sister, a mother. But stronger and stronger grew its embraces, and already the mouth, greedy of hissing kisses, interfered with the monarch's breathing, and already to the surface of the soft tissues of the body came the iron of the bones and tightened its merciless circle—and unknown fangs, blunt and cold, touched his heart and sank into it with slow indolence.

"It pains," said the deified Augustus, growing pale. "But look at me, Lazarus, look."

It was as though some heavy gates, ever closed, were slowly moving apart, and through the growing interstice the appalling horror of the Infinite poured in slowly and steadily. Like two shadows there entered the shoreless void and the unfathomable darkness; they extinguished the sun, ravished the earth from under the feet, and the roof from over the head. No more did the frozen heart ache.

"Look, look, Lazarus," ordered Augustus tottering.

Time stood still, and the beginning of each thing grew frightfully near to its end. Augustus' throne just erected, crumbled down, and the void was already in the place of the throne and of Augustus. Noiselessly did Rome crumble down, and a new city stood on its site and it too was swallowed by the void. Like fantastic giants, cities, states, and countries fell down and vanished in the void darkness—and with uttermost indifference did the insatiable black womb of the Infinite swallow them.

"Halt!"—ordered the emperor.

In his voice sounded already a note of indifference, his hands dropped in languor, and in the vain struggle with the onrushing darkness his fiery eyes now blazed up, and now went out.

"My life thou hast taken from me, Lazarus,"—said he in a spiritless, feeble voice.

And these words of hopelessness saved him. He remembered his people, whose shield he was destined to be, and keen salutary pain pierced his deadened heart. "They are doomed to death," he thought wearily. "Serene shadows in the darkness of the Infinite," thought he, and horror grew upon him. "Frail vessels with living seething blood with a heart that knows sorrow and also great joy," said he in his heart, and tenderness pervaded it.

Thus, pondering and oscillating between the poles of Life and Death, he slowly came back to life, to find in its suffering and in its joys a shield against the darkness of the void and the horror of the Infinite.

"No, thou hast not murdered me, Lazarus," said he firmly, "but I will take thy life. Be gone."

That evening the deified Augustus partook of his meats and drinks with particular joy. Now and then his lifted hand remained suspended in the air, and a dull glimmer replaced the bright sheen of his fiery eye. It was the cold wave of Horror that surged at his feet. Defeated, but not undone, ever awaiting its hour, that Horror stood at the emperor's bedside, like a black shadow all through his life; it swayed his nights, but yielded the days to the sorrows and joys of life.

The following day, the hangman with a hot iron burned out Lazarus' eyes. Then he was sent home. The deified Augustus dared not kill him.

★★★★★★★★★

Lazarus returned to the desert, and the wilderness met him with hissing gusts of wind and the heat of the blazing sun. Again, he was sitting on a stone, his rough, bushy beard lifted up; and the two black holes in place of his eyes looked at the sky with an expression of dull terror. Afar-off the holy city stirred noisily and restlessly, but around him everything was deserted and dumb. No one approached the place where lived he who had miraculously risen from the dead, and long since his neighbours had forsaken their houses. Driven by the hot iron into the depth of his skull, his cursed knowledge hid there in an ambush. As though leaping out from an ambush it plunged its thousand invisible eyes into the man—and no one dared look at Lazarus.

And in the evening, when the sun, reddening and growing wider, would come nearer and nearer the western horizon, the blind Lazarus would slowly follow it. He would stumble against stones and fall, stout and weak as he was; would rise heavily to his feet and walk on again; and on the red screen of the sunset his black body and outspread hands would form a monstrous likeness of a cross.

And it came to pass that once he went out and did not come back. Thus, seemingly ended the second life of him who for three days had been under the enigmatical sway of death, and rose miraculously from the dead.

Life is Wonderful for the Resurrected

Have you ever happened to take a walk in a graveyard?

These enclosed, quiet corners, overgrown with succulent greenery, so small and so greedy, have a peculiar and eerie poetry of their own.

Day by day the newly dead are brought into them, and already the whole of the living, huge, noisy city is carried there, and already a new city is born and awaits its turn—and they stand, just as small, quiet, and greedy.

They have a peculiar air in them, a peculiar silence, and the murmur of trees is different there—elegiac, thoughtful, soft. It is as if these white birches cannot forget all those teary eyes that sought the sky between their greening branches, and it is as if it is not the wind but deep sighs that continue to sway the air and the fresh foliage.

Quietly, thoughtfully, you too wander across the graveyard. Your ear perceives soft echoes of deep moans and tears, and your eyes come to rest on rich gravestones, on humble wooden crosses, and on mute, nameless graves, which cover those who were mute all their lives, invisible and unknown. And you read the inscriptions on the gravestones, and all these people that disappeared from the world arise in your imagination. You see them young, laughing, loving; you see them vigorous, talkative, believing boldly in the immortality of life.

But, these people, they have died.

★★★★★★★★★★★★★★★★★★

But, do you really need to leave the house in order to visit a graveyard? Is it not enough for the night's gloom to envelop you and extinguish the sounds of the day?

How many gravestones, rich and lavish! How many mute, nameless graves!

But, do you really need the night to visit a graveyard? Is the day not enough—that restless, noisy day, with enough evils of its own?

Take a look into your own soul, and, whether it be day or night, there you will find a graveyard. Small, greedy, it has consumed so much. And you will hear a soft, sad whisper—a reflection of those old heavy wails, when the dead one who was lowered into a grave was very dear to you, whom you had no time to fall out of love with, nor forget; and you will see gravestones, and inscriptions, half washed away by tears, and quiet, mute little graves—small, sinister little bumps under which lies hidden that which was once alive, even though you did not know its life nor notice its death. But maybe it was the very best thing in your soul. . . .

But, why am I speaking: take a look. Do you not already look into your graveyard every day, however many days there are in the long, arduous year? Maybe it was only yesterday that you have recalled the departed dear to you and have wept over them; maybe it was only yesterday that you have laid someone to rest, someone who had experienced a long and arduous illness and who was forgotten even in life.

Here, under the heavy marble, surrounded by dense iron rails, rests the love of people, and her sister, the faith in them. How beautiful and marvellously good they were, these sisters! With what bright flame burned their eyes, what wonderful power did their white hands possess!

With what tenderness did these white hands bring cold drinks to parched, thirsty lips and nourished the hungry; with what loving care did they touch the ulcers of the sick and healed them.

And they died, these sisters, they died from the cold, so the gravestone says. They could not stand the freezing wind that enveloped their lives.

And here, further on, we have a rickety cross marking the place where a talent has been buried in the earth. Oh, how vigorous, loud, and cheerful he was; he took on everything, he wanted to do everything, and he was certain that he would conquer the world.

And he died—in some imperceptible and quiet way. He went into employment one day, disappearing there for a long time, and returned broken and sad. For a long time, he wept, for a long time he yearned to say something—and, without having said it, he died.

Here is a long row of little bumps. Who lies there?

Ah, yes. These are children. Little, frisky, playful hopes. There were so many of them, and they filled one's soul with bustle and cheer—but, one after another, they died.

There were so many of them, and they made one's soul so cheerful! The graveyard is quiet and the birches are rustling their leaves mournfully.

★★★★★★★★★★★★★★★★★

Let the dead rise! Open yourselves you gloomy graves, fall apart you heavy tombstones, and step aside you iron rails!

If only for one day, if only for a moment, set free those whom you are suffocating with your weight and darkness!

You think they are dead? Oh no, they are alive. They were silent, but they are alive.

Alive!

Let them see the radiance of the cloudless blue sky, let them breathe in the pure spring air, let them drink their fill of warmth and love.

Come to me, my sleeping talent. Why are you rubbing your eyes in that amusing manner—are you blinded by the sun? It shines so brightly, doesn't it? You're laughing? Ah, laugh, laugh—people have so little laughter. I too will be laughing with you. Look, there's a swallow flying—let's fly after it! The grave has made you heavy? And what is that strange horror I see in your eyes—as if a reflection of the grave's darkness? No, no, there's no need. Don't cry. I'm telling you, don't cry!

After all, life is so wonderful for the resurrected!

And you, my little hopes! Your faces are so funny and cute. Amusing chubby tot, who are you? I do not remember you. And what is making you laugh? Or has the very grave failed to frighten you? Quiet down, my children, quiet down. Why are you picking on her—see how small, pale, and weak she is? Live in peace—and don't spin me. Don't you know that I too was in the grave, and now my head is spinning from the sun, from the air, and from joy.

Ah, how wonderful life is for the resurrected!

You came too, you majestic, wonderful sisters. Let me kiss your delicate white hands. What is that I see? You brought bread? The gloom of the grave has not terrified you, and there, under that heavy mass, you were thinking about bread for the hungry? Let me kiss your feet. I know where they will walk now, your light, quick feet, and I know that flowers will spring from the ground upon which they tread—marvellous, fragrant flowers. You are calling me with you? Let's go.

This way, my resurrected talent—what, have the little floating clouds lulled you into reverie? This way, my little, frisky hopes.

Wait! . . . .

I hear music. Oh, chubby tot, don't shout like that! Where are these marvellous sounds coming from? Soft, harmonious, wildly-cheerful and sad. They speak of immortal life. . . .

. . . .No, don't be afraid. It will pass now. After all, it is from joy that I weep.

Ah, how wonderful life is for the resurrected!

The Lie

"You lie! I know you lie!"

"What are you shouting for? Is it necessary that everyone should hear us?"

And here again she lied, for I had not shouted, but spoken in the quietest voice, holding her hand and speaking quite gently while that venomous word "lie" hissed like a little serpent. (A hissing word is terser and more expressive than the periphrasis "a terminological inexactitude.")

"I love you," she continued, "and you ought to believe me. Does not this convince you?"

And she kissed me. But when I was about to take hold of her hand and press it—she was already gone. She left the semi-dark corridor, and I followed her once more to the place where a gay party was just coming to an end. How did I know where it was? She had told me that I might go there, and I went there and watched the dancing all the night through. No one came near me, or spoke to me, I was a stranger to all, and sat in the corner near the band. Pointed straight at me was the mouth of a great brass instrument, through which some-one hidden in the depths of it kept bellowing, and every minute or so would give a rude *staccato* laugh: "Ho! ho! ho!" From time-to-time a scented white cloud would come close to me. It was she.

I knew not how she managed to caress me without being ob-served, but for one short little second her shoulder would press mine, and for one short little second, I would lower my eyes and see a white neck in the opening of a white dress. And when I raised my eyes, I saw a profile as white, severe, and truthful as that of a pensive angel on the tomb of the long-forgotten dead. And I saw her eyes. They were large, greedy of the light, beautiful, and calm. From their blue-white setting the pupils shone black, and the more I looked at them the blacker they seemed, and the more unfathomable their depths. Maybe I looked at them for so short a time that my heart failed to make the slightest impression, but certainly never did I understand so profoundly and terribly the meaning of Infinity, nor ever realised it with such force.

I felt in fear and pain that my very life was passing out in a slender ray into her eyes, until I became a stranger to myself—desolated, speechless, almost dead. Then she would leave me, taking my life with her, and dance again with a certain tall, haughty, but handsome partner of hers. I studied his every characteristic—the shape of his shoes, and width of his rather high shoulders, the rhythmic sway of one of his locks, which separated itself from the rest, while with his indifferent, unseeing glance he, as it were, crushed me against the wall, and I felt myself as flat and lifeless to look at as the wall itself.

When they began to extinguish the lights, I went up to her and said:

"It is time to go. I will accompany you."

But she expressed surprise.

"But certainly, I am going with him," and she pointed to the tall, handsome man, who was not looking at us. She led me out into an empty room and kissed me.

"You lie," I said very softly.

"We shall meet again tomorrow. You must come," was her answer.

When I drove home, the green frosty dawn was looking out from behind the high roofs. In the whole street there were only we two, the sledge-driver and I. He sat with bent head and wrapped-up face, and I sat behind him wrapped up to the very eyes. The sledge-driver had his thoughts, and I had mine, and there behind the thick walls thousands of people were sleeping. and they had their own dreams and thoughts. I thought of her, and of how she lied. I thought of death, and it seemed to me that those dimly-lightened walls had already looked upon my death, and that was why they were so cold and upright. I know not what the thoughts of the sledge-driver may have been, neither do I know of what those hidden by the walls were dreaming. But then, neither did they know my thoughts and reveries.

And so, we drove on through the long and straight streets, and the dawn rose from behind the roofs, and all around was motionless and white. A cold, scented cloud came close to me, and straight into my ear someone unseen laughed:

"Ho! Ho! Ho!"

She had lied. She did not come, and I waited for her in vain. The grey, uniform, frozen, semidarkness descended from the lightless sky, and I was not conscious of when the twilight passed into evening, and when the evening passed into night—to me it was all one long night. I kept walking backwards and forwards with the same even, measured steps of hope deferred. I did not come close up to the tall house, where my beloved dwelt, nor to its glazed door which shone yellow at the end of the iron covered-way, but I walked on the opposite side of the street with the same measured strides—backwards and forwards, backwards and forwards. In going forward, I did not take my eye off the glazed door, and when I turned back, I stopped frequently and turned my head round, and then the snow pricked my face with its sharp needles.

And so long were those sharp, cold needles that they penetrated to my very heart, and pierced it with grief and anger at my useless I waiting. The cold wind blew uninterruptedly from the bright north to the dark south, and whistled playfully on the icy roofs, and rebounding cut my face with sharp little snowflakes, and softly tapped the glasses of the empty lanterns, in which the lonely yellow flame, shivering with cold, bent to the draught. And I felt sorry for the lonely flame which lived only by night, and I thought to myself, when I go away all life will end in this street, and only the snowflakes will fly through the empty space; but still the yellow flame will continue to shiver and bend in loneliness and cold.

I waited for her, but she came not. And it seemed to me that the lonely flame and I were like one another, only that my lamp was not empty, for in that void, which I kept measuring with my strides, there did sometimes appear people. They grew up unheard behind my back, big and dark, they passed me, and like ghosts suddenly disappeared round the corner of the white building. Then again, they would come out from round the corner, come up along-side of me and then gradually melt away in the great distance, obscured by the silently falling snow. Muffled up, formless, silent, they were so like to one another And to myself that it seemed as if scores of people were walking backwards and forwards and waiting, as I was, shivering and silent, and were thinking their own enigmatic sad thoughts.

I waited for her, but she came not. I know not why I did not cry out and weep for pain. I know not why I laughed and was glad, and crooked my fingers like claws, as though I held in them that little venomous thing which kept hissing like a snake: a lie! It wriggled in my hands, and bit my heart, and my head reeled with its poison. Everything was a lie! The boundary line between the future and present, present and past, vanished. The boundary line between the time when I did not yet exist, and the time when I began to be, vanished, and I thought that I must have always been alive, or else never have lived at all.

And always, before I lived and when I began to live, she had ruled over me, and I felt it strange that she should have a name, and a body, and that her existence should have a beginning and an end. She had no name, she was always the one that lies, that makes eternally to wait, and never comes. And I knew not why, but I laughed, and the sharp needles pierced my heart, and right in my ear someone unseen laughed:

"Ho! ho! ho!"

Opening my eyes I looked at the lighted windows of the lofty house, and they quietly said to me in their blue and red language:

"Thou art deceived by her. At this very moment whilst thou art wandering, waiting, and suffering, she all bright, lovely, and treacherous, is there, and listening to the whispers of that tall, handsome man, who despises thee. If thou wert to break in there and kill her, thou wouldst be doing a good deed, for that wouldst slay a lie."

I gripped the knife, I held in my hand, tighter, and answered laughingly: "Yes, I will kill her."

But the windows gazed at me mournfully, and added sadly: "Thou wilt never kill her. Never! because the weapon thou boldest in thy hand is as much a lie as are her kisses."

The silent shadows of my fellow-watchers had disappeared long ago, and I was left alone in the cold void, I—and the lonely tongues of fire shivering with cold and despair. The clock in the neighbouring church-tower began to strike, and its dismal metallic sound trembled and wept, flying away into the void, and being lost in the maze of silently whirling snowflakes. I began to count the strokes, and went into a fit of laughter. The clock struck 15! The belfry was old, and so, too, was the clock, and although it indicated the right time, it struck spasmodically, sometimes so often that the grey, ancient bell-ringer had to clamber up and stop the convulsive strokes of the hammer with his hand. For whom did those senilely tremulous, melancholy sounds, which were embraced and throttled by the frosty darkness, tell a lie? So pitiable and inept was that useless lie.

With the last lying sounds of the clock the glazed door slammed, and a tall man made his way down the steps.

I saw only his back, but I recognised it as I had seen it only last evening, proud and contemptuous. I recognised his walk, and it was lighter and more confident than in the evening: thus had I often left that door. He walked, as those do, whom the lying lips of a woman have just kissed.

3

I threatened and entreated, grinding my teeth:

"Tell me the truth!"

But with a face cold as snow, while from beneath her brows, lifted in surprise, her dark, inscrutable eyes shone passionless and mysterious as ever, she assured me:

"But I am not lying to you."

She knew that I could not prove her lie, and that all my heavy massive structure of torturing thought would crumble at one word from her, even one lying word. I waited for it—and it came forth from her lips, sparkling on the surface with the colours of truth, but dark in its innermost depths:

"I love thee! Am not I all thine?"

We were far from the town, and the snow-clad plain looked in at the dark windows. Upon it was darkness, and around it was darkness, gross, motionless, silent, but the plain shone with its own latent coruscation, like the face of a corpse in the dark. In the over-heated room only one candle was burning, and on its reddening flame there appeared the white reflection of the deathlike; plain.

"However sad the truth may be, I want to know it. Maybe I shall die when I know it, but death rather than ignorance, of the truth. In your kisses and embraces I feel a lie. In your eyes I see it. Tell me the truth and I will leave you for ever," said I.

But she was silent. Her coldly searching look penetrated my inmost depths, and drawing out my soul, regarded it with strange curiosity.

And I cried: "Answer, or I will kill you!"

"Yes, do!" she quietly replied; "sometimes life is so wearisome. But the truth is not to be extracted by threat."

And then I knelt to her. Clasping her hand I wept, and prayed for pity and the truth.

"Poor fellow!" said she, putting her hand on my head, "poor fellow!"

"Pity me," I prayed, "I want so much to know the truth."

And as I looked at her pure forehead, I thought that truth must be there behind that slender barrier. And I madly wished to smash the skull to get at the truth. There, too, behind a white bosom beat a heart, and I madly wished to tear her bosom with my nails, to see but for once an unveiled human heart. And the pointed, motionless flame of the expiring candle burnt yellow—and the walls grew dark and seemed farther apart—and it felt so sad, so lonely, so eery.

"Poor fellow!" she said. "Poor fellow!"

And the yellow flame of the candle shivered spasmodically, burnt low, and became blue. Then it went out—and darkness enveloped us. I could not see her face, nor her eyes, for her arms embraced my head—and I no longer felt the lie. Closing my eyes, I neither thought nor lived, but only absorbed the touch of her hands, and it seemed to me true. And in the darkness, she whispered in a strangely fearsome voice:

"Put your arms round me—I'm afraid."

Again, there was silence, and again the gentle whisper fraught with fear:

"You desire the truth—but do I know it myself? And oh! don't I wish I did? Take care of me; oh! I'm so frightened!"

I opened my eyes. The paling darkness of the room fled in fear from the lofty windows, and gathering near the walls hid itself in the corners. But through the windows there silently looked in a something huge, deadly-white. It seemed as though someone's dead eyes were searching for us, and enveloping us in their icy gaze. Presently we pressed close together, while she whispered:

"Oh! I am so frightened!"

4

I killed her. I killed her, and when she lay a flat, lifeless heap by the window, beyond which shone the dead-white plain, I put my foot on her corpse, and burst into a fit of laughter. It was not the laugh of a madman; oh, no! I laughed because my bosom heaved lightly and evenly, and within it all was cheerful, peaceful, and void, and because from my heart had fallen the worm which had been gnawing it. And bending down I looked into her dead eyes. Great, greedy of the light, they remained open, and were like the eyes of a wax doll—so round and dull were they, as though covered with mica. I was able to touch them with my fingers, open and shut them, and I was not afraid, because in those black, inscrutable pupils there lived no longer that demon of lying and doubt, which so long, so greedily, had sucked my blood.

When they arrested me I laughed. And this seemed terrible and wild to those who seized me. Some of them turned away from me in disgust, and went aside; others advanced threateningly straight towards me, with condemnation on their lips, but when my bright, cheerful glance met their eyes, their faces blanched, and their feet became rooted to the ground.

"Mad!" they said, and it seemed to me that they found comfort in the word, because it helped to solve the enigma of how I could love and yet kill the beloved—and laugh. One of them only, a man of full habit and sanguine temperament, called me by another name, which I felt as a blow, and which extinguished the light in my eyes.

"Poor man!" said he in compassion, although devoid of anger—for he was stout and cheerful. "Poor fellow!"

"Don't!" cried I. "Don't call me that!"

I know not why I threw myself upon him. Indeed, I had no desire to kill him, or even to touch him; but all these cowed people who looked on me as a madman and a villain, were all the more frightened, and cried out so that it seemed to me again quite ludicrous.

When they were leading me out of the room, where the corpse lay, I repeated loudly and persistently, looking at the stout, cheerful man:

"I am happy, happy!"

And that was the truth.

5

Once, when I was a child, I saw in a menagerie a panther, which struck my imagination, and for long held my thoughts captive. It was not like the other wild beasts, which dozed without thought, or angrily gazed at the visitors. It walked from corner to corner, in one and the same line, with mathematical precision, each time turning on exactly the same spot, each time grazing with its tawny side one and the same metal bar of the cage. Its sharp, ravenous head was bent down, and its eyes looked straight before it, never once turning aside. For whole days a noisily chattering crowd trooped before its cage, but it kept up its tramp, and never once turned an eye on the spectators.

A few of the crowd laughed, but the majority looked seriously, even sadly, at that living picture of heavy, hopeless brooding, and went away with a sigh. And as they retired, they cast once more round at her a doubting, inquiring glance and sighed—as though there was some-

309

thing in common between their own lot, free as they were, and that of the unhappy, eager wild beast. And when later on I was grown up, and people, or books, spoke to me of eternity, I called to mind the panther, and it seemed to me that I knew eternity and its pains.

Such a panther did I become in my stone-cage. I walked and thought. I walked in one line right across my cage from corner to corner, and along one short line travelled my thoughts, so heavy that it seemed that my shoulders carried not a head, but a whole world. But it consisted of but one word, but what an immense, what a torturing what an ominous word it was.

"Lie": that was the word.

Once more it crept forth hissing from all the corners, and twined itself about my soul; but it had ceased to be a little snake, it had developed into a great, glittering, fierce serpent. It bit me, and stifled me in its iron coils, and when I began to cry out with pain, as though my whole bosom were swarming with reptiles, I could only utter that abominable, hissing, serpent-like sound: "Lie!"

And as I walked, and thought, the grey, level asphalt of the floor changed before my eyes into a grey, transparent abyss. My feet ceased to feel the touch of the floor, and I seemed to be soaring at a limitless height above the fog and mist. And when my bosom gave forth its hissing groan, thence—from below—from under that rarifying, but still impenetrable shroud, there slowly issued a terrible echo. So slow and dull was it, as though it were passing through a thousand years. And every now and then, as the fog lifted, the sound became less loud, and I understood that there—below—it was still whistling like a wind, that tears down the trees, while it reached my ears in a short, ominous whisper:

"Lie!"

This mean whisper worked me up into a rage, and I stamped on the floor and cried:

"There is no lie! I killed the lie."

Then I purposely turned aside, for I knew what it would reply. And it did reply slowly from the depths of the bottomless abyss:

"Lie!"

The fact is, as you perceive, that I had made a grievous mistake. I had killed the woman, but made the lie immortal. Kill not a woman till you have, by prayer, by fire, and torture, torn from her soul the truth!

So thought I, and continued my endless tramp from corner to

310

corner of the cell.

6

Dark and terrible is the place to which she had carried the truth, and the lie—and I am going thither. At the very throne of Satan, I shall overtake her, and falling on my knees will weep; and cry:

"Tell me the truth!"

But God! This is also a lie. There, there is darkness, there is the void of ages and of infinity, and there she is not—she is nowhere. But the lie remains, it is immortal. I feel it in every atom of the air, and when I breathe, it enters my bosom with a hissing, and then rends it—yes, rends!

Oh! what madness it is—to be man and to seek the truth! What pain!

Help! Help!

LEONAUR

ALSO FROM LEONAUR
AVAILABLE IN SOFTCOVER OR HARDCOVER WITH DUST JACKET

MR MUKERJI'S GHOSTS *by S. Mukerji*—Supernatural tales from the British Raj period by India's Ghost story collector.

KIPLINGS GHOSTS *by Rudyard Kipling*—Twelve stories of Ghosts, Hauntings, Curses, Werewolves & Magic.

THE COLLECTED SUPERNATURAL AND WEIRD FICTION OF WASHINGTON IRVING: VOLUME 1 *by Washington Irving*—Including one novel 'A History of New York', and nine short stories of the Strange and Unusual.

THE COLLECTED SUPERNATURAL AND WEIRD FICTION OF WASHINGTON IRVING: VOLUME 2 *by Washington Irving*—Including three novelettes 'The Legend of the Sleepy Hollow', 'Dolph Heyliger', 'The Adventure of the Black Fisherman' and thirty-two short stories of the Strange and Unusual.

THE COLLECTED SUPERNATURAL AND WEIRD FICTION OF JOHN KENDRICK BANGS: VOLUME 1 *by John Kendrick Bangs*—Including one novel 'Toppleton's Client or A Spirit in Exile', and ten short stories of the Strange and Unusual.

THE COLLECTED SUPERNATURAL AND WEIRD FICTION OF JOHN KENDRICK BANGS: VOLUME 2 *by John Kendrick Bangs*—Including four novellas 'A House-Boat on the Styx', 'The Pursuit of the House-Boat', 'The Enchanted Typewriter' and 'Mr. Munchausen' of the Strange and Unusual.

THE COLLECTED SUPERNATURAL AND WEIRD FICTION OF JOHN KENDRICK BANGS: VOLUME 3 *by John Kendrick Bangs*—Including twor novellas 'Olympian Nights', 'Roger Camerden: A Strange Story', and ten short stories of the Strange and Unusual.

THE COLLECTED SUPERNATURAL AND WEIRD FICTION OF MARY SHELLEY: VOLUME 1 *by Mary Shelley*—Including one novel 'Frankenstein or the Modern Prometheus', and fourteen short stories of the Strange and Unusual.

THE COLLECTED SUPERNATURAL AND WEIRD FICTION OF MARY SHELLEY: VOLUME 2 *by Mary Shelley*—Including one novel 'The Last Man', and three short stories of the Strange and Unusual.

THE COLLECTED SUPERNATURAL AND WEIRD FICTION OF AMELIA B. EDWARDS *by Amelia B. Edwards*—Contains two novelettes 'Monsieur Maurice', and 'The Discovery of the Treasure Isles', one ballad 'A Legend of Boisguilbert' and seventeen short stories to cill the blood.

LEONAUR

ALSO FROM LEONAUR
AVAILABLE IN SOFTCOVER OR HARDCOVER WITH DUST JACKET

THE COMPLETE FOUR JUST MEN: VOLUME 2 *by Edgar Wallace*—*The Law of the Four Just Men & The Three Just Men*—disillusioned with a world where the wicked and the abusers of power perpetually go unpunished, the Just Men set about to rectify matters according to their own standards, and retribution is dispensed on swift and deadly wings.

THE COMPLETE RAFFLES: 1 *by E. W. Hornung*—*The Amateur Cracksman & The Black Mask*—By turns urbane gentleman about town and accomplished cricketer, life is just too ordinary for Raffles and that sets him on a series of adventures that have long been treasured as a real antidote to the 'white knights' who are the usual heroes of the crime fiction of this period.

THE COMPLETE RAFFLES: 2 *by E. W. Hornung*—*A Thief in the Night & Mr Justice Raffles*—By turns urbane gentleman about town and accomplished cricketer, life is just too ordinary for Raffles and that sets him on a series of adventures that have long been treasured as a real antidote to the 'white knights' who are the usual heroes of the crime fiction of this period.

THE COLLECTED SUPERNATURAL AND WEIRD FICTION OF WILKIE COLLINS: VOLUME 1 *by Wilkie Collins*—Contains one novel 'The Haunted Hotel', one novella 'Mad Monkton', three novelettes 'Mr Percy and the Prophet', 'The Biter Bit' and 'The Dead Alive' and eight short stories to chill the blood.

THE COLLECTED SUPERNATURAL AND WEIRD FICTION OF WILKIE COLLINS: VOLUME 2 *by Wilkie Collins*—Contains one novel 'The Two Destinies', three novellas 'The Frozen deep', 'Sister Rose' and 'The Yellow Mask' and two short stories to chill the blood.

THE COLLECTED SUPERNATURAL AND WEIRD FICTION OF WILKIE COLLINS: VOLUME 3 *by Wilkie Collins*—Contains one novel 'Dead Secret,' two novelettes 'Mrs Zant and the Ghost' and 'The Nun's Story of Gabriel's Marriage' and five short stories to chill the blood.

FUNNY BONES *selected by Dorothy Scarborough*—An Anthology of Humorous Ghost Stories.

MONTEZUMA'S CASTLE AND OTHER WEIRD TALES *by Charles B. Cory*—Cory has written a superb collection of eighteen ghostly and weird stories to chill and thrill the avid enthusiast of supernatural fiction.

SUPERNATURAL BUCHAN *by John Buchan*—Stories of Ancient Spirits, Uncanny Places & Strange Creatures.

LEONAUR

ALSO FROM LEONAUR
AVAILABLE IN SOFTCOVER OR HARDCOVER WITH DUST JACKET

THE COLLECTED SCIENCE FICTION AND FANTASY OF STANLEY G. WEINBAUM 1—INTERPLANETARY ODYSSEYS *by Stanley G. Weinbaum*—Classic Tales of Interplanetary Adventure Including: A Martian Odyssey, its Sequel Valley of Dreams, the Complete 'Ham' Hammond Stories and Others.

THE COLLECTED SCIENCE FICTION AND FANTASY OF STANLEY G. WEINBAUM 2—OTHER EARTHS *by Stanley G. Weinbaum*—Classic Futuristic Tales Including: *Dawn of Flame* & its Sequel The Black Flame, plus The Revolution of 1960 & Others.

THE COLLECTED SCIENCE FICTION AND FANTASY OF STANLEY G. WEINBAUM 3—STRANGE GENIUS *by Stanley G. Weinbaum*—Classic Tales of the Human Mind at Work Including the Complete Novel The New Adam, the 'van Manderpootz' Stories and Others.

THE COLLECTED SCIENCE FICTION AND FANTASY OF STANLEY G. WEINBAUM 4—THE BLACK HEART *by Stanley G. Weinbaum*—Classic Strange Tales Including: the Complete Novel The Dark Other, Plus Proteus Island and Others.

THE COLLECTED SCIENCE FICTION & FANTASY OF JACK LONDON 1—BEFORE ADAM & OTHER STORIES *by Jack London*—included in this Volume Before Adam The Scarlet Plague A Relic of the Pliocene When the World Was Young The Red One Planchette A Thousand Deaths Goliah A Curious Fragment The Rejuvenation of Major Rathbone.

THE COLLECTED SCIENCE FICTION & FANTASY OF JACK LONDON 2—THE IRON HEEL & OTHER STORIES *by Jack London*—included in this Volume The Iron Heel The Enemy of All the World The Shadow and the Flash The Strength of the Strong The Unparalleled Invasion The Dream of Debs.

THE COLLECTED SCIENCE FICTION & FANTASY OF JACK LONDON 3—THE STAR ROVER & OTHER STORIES *by Jack London*—included in this Volume The Star Rover The Minions of Midas The Eternity of Forms The Man With the Gash.

THE CRETAN TEAT *by Brian Aldiss*—The Cretan Teat is a wry and comic novel that interweaves its own fiction with an inner fiction about the discovery of a Byzantine painting of the Mother of the Blessed Virgin Mary suckling the infant Jesus and a fake ikon that becomes an instrument of Nemesis.